Sheena's Dreams

Marilyn Mayo Anderson

URBAN CHRISTIAN

www.urbanchristianonline.net

Urban Books, LLC
78 East Industry Court
Deer Park, NY 11729

ISBN 13: 978-1-60162-813-8
ISBN 10: 1-60162-813-7

First Mass Market Printing December 2011
First Trade Paperback Printing January 2009
Printed in the United States of America

10 9 8 7 6 5 4 3 2 1

*This is a work of fiction. Any references or similarities
to actual events, real people, living, or dead, or to real
locales are intended to give the novel a sense of reality.
Any similarity in other names, characters, places, and
incidents is entirely coincidental.*

Distributed by Kensington Publishing Corp.
Submit Wholesale Orders to:
Kensington Publishing Corp.
C/O Penguin Group (USA) Inc.
Attention: Order Processing
405 Murray Hill Parkway
East Rutherford, NJ 07073-2316
Phone: 1-800-526-0275
Fax: 1-800-227-9604

Sheena's Dreams

This book is dedicated to my Lord and Saviour, Jesus Christ, the one and only wise God.

Acknowledgments

First, giving honor to my Lord and Savior Jesus Christ. I can do *nothing* without you, Jesus, and I can accomplish anything *with* you. Thank you, Lord, for loving me and giving me the grace to write this novel, so that it will minister your Word and love to every reader.

I thank my mother, Mable Parker Mayo, for always being there for me, ready to fight my battles if necessary. You are a Steel Magnolia. I appreciate your love and support. Hugs and kisses from your baby girl.

To my sons: Deron and Kenneth: *"Ye are blessed of the Lord which made heaven and earth"*—Psalm 115:15

Deron: You've encouraged me when I was doubtful, and made me laugh with your great sense of humor. You always listen patiently to my dreams and constantly remind me that, *"I can do all things through Christ, which strengtheneth me."*—Philippians 4:13

Kenneth: Thanks for your encouraging words, your wisdom, and knowledge. You've blessed me with your thoughtfulness and insight on life. Thank you for reminding me what the scripture says in Ecclesiastes 3:1—"*To every thing there is a season, and a time to every purpose under the heaven.*"

Kiereny, my beautiful granddaughter: You are the daughter that I never had. It's been a pleasure to watch you grow into a bright, intelligent, teenager. This novel, *Sheena's Dreams,* was so titled because of your suggestion. Thank you for listening to the Spirit of the Lord.

Adrian, my handsome grandson: I'm grateful that you are in my life.

Yvonne Mayo Wilkins: If given the power to choose whom I would want for a sister, I would still pick you, hands down. I am blessed to have you in my life. Thank you for supporting me, for always speaking encouraging words, not only to me, but also to any one you encounter. Proverbs 31:26—"*She openeth her mouth with wisdom; and in her tongue is the law of kindness.*"

To my five brothers: Alvin, Marvin, Wayne, Kendall, and Terry Mayo: I'm blessed to have brothers like you guys. You are not only my brothers, but also my friends.

Alvin: My oldest brother, you are strong and determined—a soldier.

Marvin: You have great compassion for your loved ones—provider/caretaker

Wayne: You are a man of few words, but you have a good heart—businessman

Kendall: You inspire others to think beyond the box—entrepreneur

Terry: You are smart, full of wisdom, and have a great sense of humor—joy

To my nieces, Devona Alexander, Tamara Armston, Velvet Mayo, Tyshea Gupton, Resa Knight: It's a blessing to be the aunt of kind, graceful, beautiful, young ladies such as yourselves.

To my nephews, Travis Alexander, Stephen Wilkins, and Tevin Mayo, I'm proud to be the aunt of respectful, strong, handsome, gentlemen like you guys.

To my huge extended family of aunts, uncles, and cousins: I love you all. Thanks for the support and prayers.

To my friend, Nancy Blount: Thank you for keeping me lifted up in prayer.

To Mary Jenkins-Williams, Clara Parker-Brinson, Grace Armstrong-Cobb, and Linda Barnes, my friends of over thirty-five years: Thank you guys for praying for me, listening to me talk about my dreams and encouraging me to pursue them over the years. Good friends last a lifetime.

I want to thank Carl Weber and the Urban Books publishing family for giving me the opportunity to become a part of a family of many talented authors. To my editor, Joylynn Jossel: You are insightful, sharp, talented, and thoughtful. It was a pleasure to work with you. Thank you for your kindness, understanding and patience with me. I've learned so much about writing etiquette through you. I appreciate your frankness that was communicated in a gracious manner. Be blessed.

If I have neglected to mention *anyone*, please accept my apologies, and know that it was not intentional.

To each reader: It is my sincere prayer that you will be blessed. "*Beloved, I wish above all things that thou mayest prosper and be in health, even as thy soul prospereth.*"—3rd John 1:2

Chapter 1

"Oh, no! Oh, God!" The .38-caliber gun felt like a hard cold slab of ice as it slid out of her hand and onto the dining room's plush carpet. She stood a few feet behind him in a trance as she watched him fall to the kitchen floor face down with such an arduous thud, that the sound seemed to resonate in her ears. Her strength left her as she fell on her knees and crawled to his limp body.

The blood spilled from his back onto the kitchen floor, and in her effort to reach him, she'd gotten the sticky fluid all over her hands and knees.

"Oh, my God! I can't believe I killed him!" she screamed in agony as she stared at the bright red substance on her hands and watched in horror as it oozed from his body. Her mind went into instant replay, displaying the moments of intense frustration she'd felt just moments before she shot him.

The woman had nervously fumbled in her purse as tears streamed down her face. She retrieved the gun she had recently purchased, and as he turned to walk out of the room, laughing maliciously, she frantically pointed the gun at him and fired. It happened as quickly as a blink.

"Honey, I didn't mean to do this to you," she sobbed. "I just wanted to stop you from hurting me. Help, please. Somebody help me!"

Sheena bolted up in the bed as she heard herself screaming. It was 3:31 A.M. She looked over at her husband, Jason, as he sat up abruptly in bed and turned over to look at her.

"Sheena, baby, are you okay?" Jason inquired. This had been the third time in less than a month that Sheena had woken up screaming. "What nightmare did you have this time?"

Sheena refused to share the dreams with him before, but this time, she felt led to do so, believing that after the third time, the dream might have a significant message.

"I had the same dream as before, Jason. It was about you. You were lying on the floor dead in a pool of blood, bleeding from a gunshot wound in your back."

"Oh? What happened? Who would want to kill *me*," he joked. "And who'd shoot me in the *back* of all things?" He tried to humor Sheena as he held her in his arms. "Did you see who killed me?"

"*I* did it, at least the woman looked like me." Sheena replied as she shivered while pulling the covers up over her. "It was horrible, Jason. You kept provoking me, and I became so angry that I shot you in the back when you walked away from me."

Jason roared with laughter. "Sheena, baby, you know that you couldn't hurt a fly." He kissed her on the cheek as he held her in his arms. "Try to go back to sleep, baby. You'll be all right; it was just another bad dream."

There was a soft knock on the door. "Momma, may we come in?" Joseph asked. "We heard you screaming."

The children entered the room before Sheena or Jason could answer.

"Are you okay?" Jeremiah inquired. They ran, jumped on the bed and hugged Sheena while they looked suspiciously at Jason.

"I'm fine, babies," Sheena assured them as she hugged and kissed Joseph, Jeremiah, and Jessica. "I just had another terrible dream and I woke up screaming from it. I'm going to be okay."

"Are you s—sure, Momma?" Joseph, the older son asked, his voice cracking from being upset. He peered at his father with skeptical eyes.

"I'm sure, honey. Go back to bed now, it will be time to get up and go to school soon and you guys need to get your proper rest."

Jason smiled at his two sons and daughter. "Your momma's fine, guys. She just had another bad dream. I'm not going to let anything happen to her; you guys can go back to bed now."

He hugged the boys after he gave them a soft thump on their heads. Eight-year-old Joseph and Jeremiah, identical twins, walked slowly back to their room, glancing back at Sheena for reassurance.

"It's okay guys, I'm fine," she said.

Five-year-old Jessica was curled up in her mother's arms. Jason walked around to Sheena's side of the bed and picked Jessica up and kissed her. "Come on, baby girl, it's time for you to go back to bed. Momma's gonna be all right."

Jessica wrapped her arms around Jason's neck as he carried her off to bed. "Daddy, don't let Momma have any more bad dreams, okay?"

"I won't, sweetheart," he told her as he rubbed her back while walking out of the room.

After tucking Jessica in bed, Jason walked across the hall to check on the boys. They were sitting up in their beds talking, but immediately clammed up when he entered the room.

"What's up, guys? You're supposed to be sleeping, not talking." Jason walked to Jeremiah's bed and tucked him in and then to Joseph's bed to tuck him in.

Joseph, who was the more outgoing of the twins, looked intently at his father. "Daddy, can I ask you something?"

"Sure, son, you know you can ask me anything."

Joseph glanced at Jeremiah and cleared his throat. "Daddy, did you . . . hit Mommy? Is that why she was screaming?"

Jason was astounded by his son's question. He sat down on the bed beside him. "J," Jason called Joseph by his nickname, "I want you to listen to me, and listen good. I would never *ever* hit your mother. She means too much to me. Besides, it's not right for a man to hurt a woman. That's something that you don't *ever* have to worry about; okay, son?" He walked back to Jeremiah's bed and assured him of the same thing. He looked across the room at Joseph. "What made you ask something like that, J?"

"After we went to bed, we heard you talking real loud at Momma like you were mad. We woke up when we heard Momma screaming, so we thought you had hit her."

"Son, I'm sorry you guys heard that. All parents argue sometimes, but I would never do anything that mean to your mother." Jason looked at Jeremiah. "Okay, JJ?"

Jason came home from work later and later each night. He became angry with Sheena when she questioned him about his whereabouts. After Jason lied about working late, Sheena informed him that she'd called his office several times, and he didn't answer. Jason got angry and accused her of nagging him so much that he purposely ignored her phone calls, so he could finish his work.

JJ, nickname for Jeremiah, looked at his father and nodded his head, indicating that he understood. Joseph, on the other hand, just looked at Jason with a blank stare on his face, one that Jason couldn't interpret.

"All right guys, lights out. Good-night, I'll see you in the morning, okay?" Joseph's question reminded Jason of himself when he was that age. Only, he didn't *suspect* that his father hit his mother; it was a fact.

On Jason's way back from their room, he sat on the chair in the hallway and hung his head down, remembering how helpless he felt when his mother tried to comfort him after his father had loudly cursed her out, and seconds later, he heard her scream from the hard licks. She often came into his room afterward with tears standing in her eyes as she rocked him back and forth in her arms, trivializing the incident by saying, "It's okay, baby. Daddy had a bad day, but he'll be all right in the morning."

Even now, Jason was still amazed at the way his mother pretended everything was fine. His father was now seventy-three years old, and had professed salvation, but a part of Jason still hated him for what he had done to his mother.

Having *lived* that nightmare had such an impact on Jason that he vowed to never lay a finger on a woman. He walked back in their bedroom where Sheena was sitting up waiting for him.

"Are the kids all right?" she asked him as he turned the lights out.

"I guess so. You'll never believe what J asked me." He shared the conversation with her.

"Humph, I'm not surprised he asked you that."

"Why? You know I would never hit you, Sheena."

"Think about it. The way you were raising that baritone voice of yours at me tonight, what else would they think? You need to learn how to speak to me in a decent manner, no matter what issues you have with me. And frankly, Jason, I'm not going to tolerate your behavior anymore. Your mother may have been a sucker for your father, but don't take my meekness for weakness. That dream I had may become a reality one of these days."

Jason looked at Sheena and smirked, replying sarcastically, "Sheena, I'm shaking in my boots. You don't have the nerve to shoot me or anybody else, with your *saved*, Holy Ghost filled self."

"I am saved, but being saved doesn't mean that I'm skittish. If you keep disrespecting me the way you do, you are going to find out just how courageous I am."

"I know you aren't scary, Sheena. I just thought I'd humor you to relieve you of the stress of the nightmares you've been having."

"Those nightmares *were* scary though. God forbid they come true."

"Do you want to talk about it?" He pulled her into his arms.

"I guess so. Are you sure you want to know?"

"Baby, you don't need to keep these dreams to yourself. Like you said, they may have some meaning behind them."

"I hope not, but in the past I've had dreams that came true. It's like the Lord is warning me about things in my future."

As she proceeded to tell him about her dreams, Jason looked at Sheena dubiously. Jason believed the church Sheena attended had turned into a cult. He was convinced they had brain washed her with scriptures they had misquoted from the Bible. "I don't think there's anything to the dreams. I think you are under a lot of stress by working, taking care of the children, and going to church. Why don't you consider quitting your job? You know I'll take care of you, and you don't have to be at that church every time the doors swing open."

Sheena was dismayed by Jason's lack of concern for her feelings. "I can't believe how callous your heart is sometimes. You should be just as concerned as I am about these dreams. After all, they could have a significant effect on *your* life."

"The only significance those dreams have is that they are a manifestation of the stress you're under from working with those children everyday."

"If I am under any stress, it comes from you and your erratic behavior. You must be out of your mind if you think I'm going to quit my job. And as far as church is concerned, I don't go enough, if you ask me. I need to start going to Bible Study on Wednesday nights. You need to start going to church, too, and give your life to Christ."

Nothing irritated Jason more than when Sheena admonished him about getting his life right with God. "I've confessed salvation and I'm just as saved as you are. You need to get a grip and pay more attention to your man; that's your problem."

"Right, blame me for your ill behavior. So you have confessed salvation? If that were true, you wouldn't get angry every time I mentioned church, or God, and especially scriptures from the Bible."

"I'm just as saved as you are, only I'm not judgmental."

"How am I judgmental?"

"For one thing, you criticize everything I do."

"How do I criticize you, Jason? I only try to encourage you every chance I get."

"You whine because I don't go to church. 'You need to read the Bible,'" he mocked. "'Why don't you pray sometimes, Jason?' Sometimes you sound like a broken record. You're a judgmental snob."

"Jason, I'm not a snob and you know it. I certainly don't judge you, I just want my husband to draw nigh to God, that's all."

"I am nigh to Him." Jason softened his tone a little. "I would love to get close to my wife too." He pulled her close to him and attempted to caress her but Sheena looked at him like he had the plague. When she didn't respond, he growled, "This is exactly what I'm talking about, you're always quoting scriptures, but you don't abide by them. Where's my due benevolence, Sheena?"

Frowning, Sheena said, "What are you talking about?"

"You need to familiarize yourself with 1 Corinthians 7:3. It states: 'Let the husband render unto the wife due benevolence; and likewise also the wife unto the husband.'"

Sheena stared at Jason incredulously. "It's strange how men seem to know that scripture, if they don't know anything else in the Bible."

Jason turned his back to her, pouting like an angry child, pulling the covers off of her and pretended to go to sleep.

Sheena sat in bed uncovered, glaring at Jason momentarily. She had an urge to snatch the covers back off of him and then kick him off the bed. Instead, she moved closer to the edge of the king sized bed and curled up in the fetal position.

If only you knew how often lately I have contemplated killing you, Sheena thought. You don't hit me, but the infidelity hurts just as bad. She instantly became convicted and prayed silently. Lord, forgive me for harboring evil thoughts about killing my husband. I am tired of him disrespecting me, though, Lord. She whispered, "Please show me what to do, Jesus. I can't take this anymore."

Chapter 2

Sheena helped the children get dressed for school. Although Jason had his faults, she felt blessed to have a husband that helped her transition into her day smoothly. Jason was the first one to get up every morning. He always made breakfast for everyone and by the time Sheena was showered and dressed, he had the children sitting at the table eating. He would go shower and get dressed for work while she supervised the children's preparation for school.

Sheena watched her husband as he reentered the kitchen. He was immaculately dressed, as usual. Jason had on a brown Armani suit with brown Alligator shoes, a white shirt and a necktie that coordinated with his suit perfectly. Her stomach fluttered as though it were filled with butterflies every time she saw him. But because he was as arrogant as he was handsome, she tried to hide her obvious attraction from him.

Jason was six-foot-five-inch tall, had smooth dark brown skin that was as flawless as a mirror, and the physique of an *Ebony* Fashion Fair male model. He worked out constantly to maintain that build, because in his career as a banker, he rarely did any physical work.

Sheena's career as a third grade teacher was very meaningful to her. Witnessing the excitement in her students' eyes after accomplishing the task of reading a difficult book or solving a math problem, was confirmation to her that she had chosen the right career for herself. Her students' parents often told her that they believed she was anointed by God to work with children. Sheena was grateful that someone appreciated her, because she felt Jason with his selfish disposition, sure didn't seem too.

Sheena knew that she wasn't a pretty woman. She didn't even consider herself to be attractive; just a "Plain Jane." She was five foot six, a*n average height,* not too tall, not too short. She had reddish light brown skin with freckles, and short hair that she always kept styled to perfection. She'd always wanted long hair, but that was something that eluded her, so she worked with what she had. She didn't have a nice figure, but she dressed well so that her clothes always looked tailor-made for her.

As she watched Jason interact with the children, Sheena wondered about the change in her husband's attitude toward her since they'd been married. She reminisced about their first meaningful colloquy. When they were dating, Jason always complimented her on her appearance. Now, he hardly noticed her, and when he did, he rarely ever had anything positive to say to her.

Sheena remembered how he admitted to have watched her for over six months before he approached her at the college they attended in North Carolina. He told her that he liked the way she carried herself, so ladylike, and that he knew she was going to be his wife one day.

At the time, Sheena had been dating her high school sweetheart and Jason had the reputation of being a player. So, she dismissed his advances toward her and interpreted his conversations as him using one of the trump cards he was famous for using around school to sustain his player image.

She ignored Jason for months, until receiving the news that her boyfriend of three years had been killed in a car accident. All of her fellow students and friends consoled her as best they could, but Sheena had gone into such a deep depression that she dropped out of school and had no intention of returning. She moved back in with her parents, who lived in Asheville, North Carolina, a city surrounded by the magnificent Blue Ridge Mountains.

Sheena became withdrawn to the point of living like a recluse. One evening, she sat in her bedroom and watched the resplendent sunset around the Blue Ridge Mountains. The mountains always inclined her to sing praises to God. However, she allowed depression to overtake her as she dwelled on the joy she and her deceased boyfriend shared.

Her trip down memory lane was interrupted when her mother knocked on her bedroom door. She informed Sheena that one of her friends from college had driven from North Carolina Central University in Durham, the school they attended, to see her.

"Whoever it is," Sheena had told her mom, "I don't want to be disturbed. I don't want to be bothered with any so-called fellow students!"

Her mother had scolded her. "Stop being rude and come downstairs and act like you've had some home training. The least you can do is come down and say hello to the young man."

Sheena was curious. The only male that she knew well enough to drive to Asheville to see her was Kevin. She'd talked to him on the phone that morning and he had told her that he was on his way home to D.C. for spring break. She went downstairs and was pleasantly surprised to see that it was Jason Grey.

Jason was such a humorous person, that he had her laughing constantly, something she hadn't done in months. He was definitely a smooth talker, because before she realized what was happening, he had cunningly convinced her to come back to school for the fall semester. Her parents were grateful to him for that. They had tried to convince her to go back to school for weeks, but to no avail. Jason kept in touch with Sheena from that day until she returned to school.

Eventually, they started dating, and slowly, the pain of losing her boyfriend subsided as she began to spend more and more time with Jason. Sheena was a Christian, so she convinced Jason to start going to church with her. He reluctantly agreed, but found that he enjoyed the church services more than he had anticipated.

In the long run, he gave his life to Christ; or rather he led Sheena to believe that he had given his life to Christ. His Christ-like imitations and charm convinced Sheena that he was the man for her. Jason was two years older, so he graduated two years before she did and attended graduate school at UNC Charlotte in Charlotte, North Carolina, where he obtained his masters degree by the time she had graduated from college.

They married the following August and went on a week's honeymoon to Jamaica three weeks before she started her first teaching position at the elementary school near their home in Charlotte. Jason purchased a four-bedroom, three and a half bath home in a prestigious, affluent neighborhood the spring before she graduated.

Jason has been a good provider from day one, she admitted as she looked around their elegantly furnished home. However, Jason's lack of affection toward Sheena made her feel depressed and lonely. She thought about the scripture in III John 1:2: "*Beloved, I wish above all things that thou mayest prosper and be in health, even as thy soul prospereth.*" She felt like Jason's behavior had stressed her out to the point it was affecting her health negatively.

She lost her train of thought when Jason cleared his throat as he stood in the doorway posing with that million-dollar smile. His handsome face was glowing, revealing the deep dimples she adored. Sheena knew he was waiting for her to give him her nod of approval for the way he was dressed. She had grown really tired of his predictable adolescent need for affirmation from her every morning, assuring him that he looked nice in his clothes.

Her mind flashed to his rude behavior toward her last night so she looked at him from head to toe and then turned away from him impetuously, responding with, "Oh, Jason, before I forget, your father called to remind you not to forget the board meeting this morning at eight o'clock."

She proceeded to clear the table of the dirty dishes without so much as giving him another glance. She could hear the disappointment in his voice because she neglected to show him the admiration he sought.

He walked up behind her and gave her a kiss on the cheek. "I haven't forgotten. That's why I'm leaving early."

Sheena didn't respond to the dry kiss. "You know how your father is. He wants to make sure you're on top of things."

He gently pushed his body into hers as she leaned over the sink. She still didn't react to him. Instead, she eased out of his embrace and studied the expression on his face. Jason showed no genuine affection toward Sheena. He touched her body mechanically. Sheena was tempted to ask him what happened to him, why had he become so distant lately.

Who am I kidding? She mused. I know what has happened to him; another woman has happened to him.

Chapter 3

Jason was agitated with his father for constantly calling him and reminding him of his responsibilities. "After twelve years of working with him he should know that I'm dependable," he snapped at Sheena as he walked toward the door.

"Don't take it out on me," Sheena countered. "I'm only the messenger."

Jason's jaw line hardened as he frowned at Sheena. He was too proud to apologize and irritated because she didn't go weak in the knees for him, as usual. He glared at her for a moment before he turned to walk out. "I don't have time for your sarcasm this morning, Sheena." He hugged Jessica, and he and the twins performed their ritualistic handshake before he opened the door to leave.

"Have a blessed day, honey," Sheena called to him.

Jason didn't so much as acknowledge her remark. After he entered the garage and stepped inside his S 500 Mercedes, a fleeting thought occurred to him about Sheena's recent dreams. Nonetheless, he quickly brushed that thought aside, cranked the sleek white machine and waved good-bye to the kids as they stood in the doorway. He rolled the window down and told Sheena that he would be late coming home that night. The icy look she gave him sent chills down his spine. He backed out of the garage and sped off to work. He looked in the mirror, admiring himself and smirked. "What's wrong with me? I know my sweet shy Sheena wouldn't hurt me for the world. That woman loves herself some Jason Grey!"

Jason secured his first position in the bank that his father owned in Charlotte. His father started him off as a loan officer, a position that he was over qualified for, but he accepted it because his father wanted him to learn the banking business thoroughly. He knew that one day, Jason and his other son, Jonathan, would take over the family owned business when he retired.

Jonathan, however, sought a career in the military after graduating college, so that left Jason with the responsibility of assuming the family business. Jacob, Jason's father, was old fashioned; although he had four daughters, he believed a man should pass his business down to his sons. Besides that, he didn't trust any of his sons-in-law to handle his finances.

Jason didn't resent taking over the family business; it wasn't a bad gig, but he had a difficult time bonding with his father. The bad memories of his father abusing his mother were still quite vivid in Jason's mind.

Jacob was a good provider for the family, but he would take the stress of launching a black-owned business in the sixties out on his family. If Jason obeyed one thing in the Bible since he was a child it was Ephesians 6:1–3: Children, obey your parents in the Lord: for this is right. Honour thy father and mother; which is the first commandment with promise; that it may be well with thee and thou mayest live *long on the earth.* Even though he was tempted, Jason didn't disrespect his father. His mother made sure of that.

Except for that one time.

But if that was disrespect, he believed his father deserved it. Jason never told his mother about the time when he jacked his father up beside the wall and threatened to kill him if he ever hit his mother again. He was sixteen at the time, but his muscles had developed quite a bit from lifting weights. His then six foot three frame was a force to deal with too. Jason's father never hit his mother again; at least, Jason didn't *think* he had. She wouldn't admit it anyway.

Jason's mind drifted back to when he was a preteen, when his mother constantly made him read those scriptures. One day, when he was about twelve, he asked his mother, "Why do you always stop me from reading at Ephesians 6:3? What about Ephesians 6:4?" He looked at the open Bible and read, "And you fathers, provoke not your children to wrath; but bring them up in the nurture and admonition of the Lord." Jason looked back at his mother. "Shouldn't you tell Daddy to read that?"

Flushed from embarrassment, she looked away from him and said, "I do, son, every chance I get. Maybe he will listen and learn one day. Your father is a good man, Jason, he doesn't mean any harm when he acts the way he does. Baby, you just be sure that you don't treat your wife the way he treats me."

"Momma, why don't you just leave him? He's so mean to you and he shouldn't hit you either. One day, I'm going to kill him if he don't stop."

"If he *doesn't* stop." His mother corrected his English before she answered the question. "He doesn't mean it, son, he's under a lot of pressure. I didn't want to let you six kids grow up without a father, that's why I've stayed with him. Children need their father. As long as he doesn't put his hands on you, he'll be fine. I'm sure he'll calm down once he gets his business going like he wants it. He provides so well for us."

Jason was proud that he never had the urge to hit his wife. He didn't realize what a negative psychological effect his dad had on him, though. Although he didn't physically abuse Sheena, he mentally abused her every chance he got.

He had to admit that Sheena was a Christian woman, because she did her part to obey God's Word as it read in Ephesians 5:22. She would often admonish him to read the Bible and to talk to their pastor so that he would do better, but Jason's pride often rose up.

"I don't *need* to talk to the pastor," he'd tell Sheena. "He's a man walking around in pants just like me. And another thing, I know the Bible as well as either of you. *You* are the one that needs to get saved and stop acting like a hypocrite."

He challenged her with his constant insults. Jason would prefer she stood up to him, because he didn't get much pleasure from patronizing her, but it was just something she allowed him to do. "As long as she takes it, I'm going to dish it out."

Chapter 4

Sheena gathered the kids and drove off to school. It was a blessing to have them all go to the school where she taught. Jessica was in kindergarten, so Sheena was relieved of the stress of having to pick her up from her mother-in-law's home every afternoon like she used to. Jason had insisted that his mother keep his baby girl because he didn't want her in daycare. Mrs. Grey was a retired pre-school teacher, so she taught Jessica the basics at home. Jason would take her to his mother's house in the mornings and Sheena would pick her up after school.

Mrs. Grey, as Sheena still called her after ten years of being married to her son, was an over bearing mother-in-law, forever prying into her and Jason's business. She never failed to let Sheena know how lucky she was to have such a good husband. *If only she knew.*

Sheena's thoughts were interrupted when Joseph said, "Momma, where are you going? You just passed the school."

"Oh, Lord! Sorry kids. I'll go to the next light and turn around." Joseph and Jeremiah looked at each other. Sheena whirled around and drove back to the school parking lot. She had to get herself together; Jason's philandering was beginning to affect her more than she realized.

After turning the car around and driving back to the school, Sheena walked Jessica to her classroom and then walked down the hall to her own room. Jeremiah and Joseph had proudly informed her the year before that they were big boys now and didn't need to be escorted to their class by their mother. She smiled slightly at the thought of it.

Sheena was relieved to be in her classroom where she could forget about her problems, at least for a few hours. A few minutes later, the children where arriving.

"Good morning, Mrs. Grey," they said as they came in one by one.

"Good morning, children." Sheena stood in the doorway and patted each child on the back.

The hours passed quickly, and before Sheena could catch her breath, she and her children were back in the car for the ten-minute drive home.

As Joseph, Jeremiah, and Jessica did their homework, Sheena prepared dinner for her family. She fed the children, checked their homework, helped them get their baths, and tucked them away in bed for the night.

"Where's Daddy?" Jessica asked.

"He had to work late, honey. He'll be in to say good-night when he gets home, okay?" She closed the children's bedroom doors, cleaned the kitchen, took a shower, put on a nice outfit, and waited for Jason to come home. All kinds of negative thoughts entered her head concerning his whereabouts. Just as she was about to dial his office, he walked in the door.

Sheena looked at the clock. It was nine-thirty. She was about to lash out at him, but decided to adhere to James 3:13 instead.

"How's it going, baby?" Jason asked coyly.

She decided to answer him according to Proverbs 15:1, which said: *A soft answer turneth away wrath; but grievous words stir up anger.* Sheena scanned his face. "I'm blessed. How are you?"

"I'm okay, a little tired." The phone rang. She attempted to answer it, but Jason indicated he would get it. "You really look nice tonight, baby. Is there a special occasion?"

"No, there's no special occasion. We just have to talk tonight, rather, I'm going to do the talking and you are going to listen for a change." Sheena stared at him with hard eyes. He looked like the cat that ate the canary. "Aren't you going to get that?"

He picked up the phone. "Hi, Momma." He listened intently to what she said. "I'll be right there."

Sheena couldn't compose herself any longer. "What do you mean, you'll be right there? You just walked in the house. Jason, you need to get your priorities straight. *If* that was indeed your momma."

"Sheena, you need to get a grip. Who else would call here and I would tell them I'd be right there? She said she had been calling constantly for the last hour. Didn't you hear the phone ring?"

"No, because I was in the bathtub for about forty-five minutes, trying to relax by listening to my CeCe Winans CD. I heard it ring ten minutes ago, but when I saw your mother's number, I assumed she was calling to have her nightly chat with you. It didn't occur to me to check voicemail for messages. So, I got dressed, picked up a book to read, and waited for you to get home. Where have you been all evening anyway?"

"I told you this morning that I would be working late."

"There's not that much working in the world. It's nine-thirty. What do I look like to you? A fool or a stupid fool?"

"Look, Sheena, I don't have time to discuss this with you right now. Momma called to let us know that Daddy is in the hospital. He's had a stroke, but the doctors are running more tests now to see how severe it is. I'm leaving for the hospital. I'll call you and let you know how he's doing." He rushed out the door, leaving Sheena standing in the middle of the floor.

"Oh, my God," Sheena whispered. She walked back to Jason's recliner, the chair she usually sat in when she yearned for his attention. "Please God, let Daddy Grey be all right."

Chapter 5

"Whew!" Jason exhaled loudly as he sat in his car. "I have got to be careful." As he drove off, he thought about the evil look in Sheena's eyes as she questioned him. Sheena had accepted Jason's working late as being a credible reason for coming home late so often. But after three months of the same lie, Jason realized she had figured out by now that he was having an affair.

The second he pulled up into the hospital's parking lot, his cell phone rang. "Ruby, I don't have time to talk to you right now."

"Baby, I just wanted to let you know that you left your wallet. It must have fallen out of your pocket in your rush to get undressed. My goodness," she purred, "the way you acted tonight, Sheena must not be taking care of business at all." She laughed provocatively as she teased him. "By the way, baby, I took some money out of your wallet. I need some extra money in addition to what you gave me this month to buy our daughter some more shoes."

"I'll pick it up on my way from the hospital, some time tonight." Jason grieved as he thought about having fathered a child by Ruby.

"The hospital? What are you doing there?"

"My father had a stroke. Momma called me a few minutes ago. I'm on my way in now to see how he's doing."

"I'm so sorry, Jason. I'm sure that he'll be fine. The important thing is that they got him to the hospital early. He'll have a better chance of recuperating fully."

"Thanks for the words of encouragement. I'm in the hospital now, so I have to turn my phone off. I'll talk to you later."

"Do you want me to meet you at the hospital?"

"What? You know you can't meet me here, Ruby. What has gotten into you lately?"

"Well, now is as good a time as ever for your family to learn about Cassandra."

"Get real, Ruby. You know this is neither the time nor the place. Besides, this is no way for my wife to learn that I have a child by my former girlfriend."

"You mean your present and future woman, don't you?"

"I have to go. I'll see you when I pick up my wallet. It'll probably be late though, depending on how Dad's doing."

"The later, the better, baby." Ruby moaned seductively in the phone, "I'll be ready for you."

Jason didn't bother to reply, he clicked the END button.

As soon as he walked in the emergency room, Jason's mother rushed over to him. "Jason, I'm so worried about your father. They are running more tests on him now. The doctors said that it was a good thing that I called the ambulance, because they were able to stabilize him right away."

"What happened, Momma?"

"We were eating dinner when he just slumped over on the table. He had been complaining about his head hurting all afternoon. Of course, you know how worked up he gets when he worries about his business. I told him to let you handle the problem, but you know how much of a control freak your daddy is." Jason nodded in agreement. "Anyway, the next thing I knew, he was slumped on the table, so I called 911. When the paramedics arrived, they said that he had had a stroke." Catherine mumbled quietly, "Lord Jesus, cover my husband under your blood."

"I'm sure he'll be fine, Momma." Jason gently put his hand under his mother's elbow and ushered her toward the green plaid sofa across from the nurses' station. "Have a seat right here, Momma, while I consult with the doctor."

The doctor ushered Jason to a corner. "His condition is very critical right now," the doctor informed him, "but we are doing all that we can to get him stable. The good news is your mother had him brought here early, so his chances for survival are exceptional. I'll keep you posted." The doctor excused himself and went back into the examination room.

After an hour, the doctor came back out and consulted with the family. He had admitted Jacob to a room and let the two of them know that it would be a valiant attempt for Jacob to survive the stroke, but with a strong will to live and a lot of therapy, he could make a full recovery.

Sheena made arrangements for her neighbor's teenage daughter to stay with the children while they slept. She prayed for her father-in-law all the way to the hospital. When she arrived in the E.R. she witnessed Jason and his mother having an intense conversation, but she could not hear what they were saying.

"Jason," his mother was scolding him, "I know you were with that ole, no good Ruby, weren't you? I told you about that hussy when you were dating her in college. She wasn't any good then, and she's not any good now. You are going to mess around and let that sorry woman make you lose your wife and everything else."

"Momma, I'm not going to lose Sheena, that woman loves me to death."

"If she finds out you have been running around with your ex-girlfriend, she might *just* love you to death, boy, but it won't be the kind of love you expect. That girl will hurt you, Jason. She might be quiet, but don't take her quietness for granted. Women like Sheena will take a lot, but when they are fed up, they will hurt you and hurt you badly."

"Momma, believe me, Sheena's not going to hurt me, and she's certainly not going to leave me. She's grateful that I chose to marry her anyway. I've got Sheena in my back pocket."

"Okay, back pocket. Don't lose your family for some pretty heifer that you *know* ain't no good. Beauty isn't everything. Even though your wife is plain looking, and has some curious ways, she's a good wife to you. That whorish Ruby isn't worth losing your marriage over."

Jason's jaw line hardened. "Come on now, Momma, you don't know what you're saying. You're being judgmental about Ruby. It's more to it than that."

"What? I know you aren't talking about cheap, hot, sex. Tramps like her come a dime a dozen."

Jason sighed. "No, it's not that, our relationship is more serious than that."

"Oh, so now you are in a *serious* relationship with her?"

"Momma, I can't go into details about us right now. I have something to tell you, but now is not the time. I'll tell you when things are more situated with Daddy."

"What is it? I knew something was wrong when you came over yesterday. Did that—" Catherine paused when she saw Sheena walking toward them. "Hi, baby, thank you for coming here at this late hour."

"Of course I'd be here for my husband and his family, Mrs. Grey. Where else would I be?"

Sarcastic as always . . . and Jason can't understand why we don't get along? Catherine mused. Despite being irritated with Sheena, Catherine explained Jacob's prognosis to her as calmly as she could.

Sheena tried hard to listen carefully, but she was more focused on Jason's behavior. She watched him keenly. She didn't get the gist of what they were talking about, but she picked up on Jason's sneaky expression. She noticed Catherine squinting her eyes at Jason. She knew his mother was privy to the information too, whatever, or whoever it was.

Jason went to Sheena and hugged her. He was trying to gauge from her reaction to him how much she had heard. He decided to pick up his wallet tomorrow from Ruby's house. Sheena held on to him tightly. There was no way he could get away from Sheena's grip tonight.

Chapter 6

"The doctor suggested that we go home and get some rest and come back tomorrow," Jason informed Sheena. "Momma insisted on staying with him because he's in stable, but still critical condition."

"I understand that perfectly, honey. I would do the same thing for you." Sheena studied her husband's face. To her, he looked antsy. She was convinced it didn't have anything to do with his father's condition.

Jason kissed Sheena on the forehead. "I know you would, Sheena. You're a good wife."

"Oh? You noticed? By your reactions to me lately, I didn't think you noticed or cared."

"Baby, you know I care about you. I've just been preoccupied with work lately."

"You've been preoccupied with *something* lately."

"What's that supposed to mean?"

"Figure it out, Jason. We should leave. I left the children with Kim. Although she's seventeen, I don't feel comfortable leaving my children with her. She *is* a hormone raging teenaged, boy-crazy, girl. I'll see you at home."

Jason hesitated. "I'll be there in a few minutes."

"What are you talking about? Aren't you going to follow me?"

"I noticed we were out of eggs this morning. I'll stop by Wal-Mart on my way home to pick some up."

Sheena knew Jason was lying. She walked up to him and stared in his eyes. Her instincts told her that he was making an excuse to stay behind so he could contact the woman he'd been seeing. She glanced at her watch. "It's late, I'll ride with you." Her voice was shrewd. "I don't want to drive home by myself at this late hour. You can bring me back here in the morning to pick my car up."

"What? Uh . . . okay, baby." He frowned.

"What's wrong? That's not a problem, is it?"

Jason couldn't think of a lie to tell Sheena as to why she couldn't ride with him, so he had no alternative but to agree with her. "No, that's fine; no problem at all." Jason cut his eyes at Sheena as they walked toward the elevator. She seemed to read his mind sometimes. He wondered if she *was* psychic or something. He ushered Sheena to his car. "You ready?"

"I sure am, Big Daddy." Sheena winked and smiled at him victoriously.

Jason opened the passenger door for Sheena, and then walked around to the driver's side and got in the car. He frowned slightly. He remembered he'd left his wallet at Ruby's house. Sheena gave him a puzzling look. He smiled at her and reached over her to unlock the glove compartment.

Sheena knew that Jason didn't have his wallet when he opened the glove compartment to retrieve money. She knew that is where he kept some petty cash in case of emergencies. "Where's your wallet?"

"I left it on the dresser this morning when I rushed out to go to work," he lied.

After arriving home, Sheena paid the baby-sitter and sent her home. She put the eggs they purchased, in the refrigerator. "Jason?" she said as she pulled another full carton of eggs out for him to see.

"Yeah, baby?" he said as he walked toward the stairs.

"We already had a full carton of eggs," she said accusingly. "You couldn't have overlooked this."

"Humph," was all Jason could think of to say. "I'm going to bed, Sheena, I'm beat. Good-night."

Sheena followed him upstairs. She walked to the dresser. "I don't see your wallet, Jason. You didn't leave it here. You must have left it somewhere else."

Jason didn't answer. He stepped in the bathroom and took a long shower, hoping she'd be asleep when he finished. She wasn't. Sheena was sitting up in the bed with her legs crossed Indian style, reading a book.

Man! I thought she'd be sleep by now. He slipped into bed with her and kissed her passionately and attempted to make love to her. He noticed that she was not responding to him. "What's wrong, baby? Are you tired?"

"No, I'm not tired." She pushed him off of her. She sat up in bed and faced him, frowning. "Yes, as a matter of fact, I *am* tired."

"Make your mind up," Jason scoffed, clearly frustrated. "Either you're tired or you're not."

"Do you think that I'm so dense that I don't know what's going on with you?"

"What *now*? You have been torn out of the frame ever since this morning. What is your problem this time?"

"*You* are my problem. You really think that I'm clueless, don't you?"

"Clueless about what?" Jason continued to caress Sheena, touching her vulnerable spots, hoping that he would distract her. He was unpleasantly surprised when Sheena punched him in the face. "Sheena, what is wrong with you?"

"You know what is wrong with me," she hissed as she pushed him off of her and sprang up in bed with her fists clenched.

Jason rubbed his face. Her mean right hook stunned him. "Sheena, I don't know *what* you are talking about. What's gotten into you lately? Are you crazy? You're acting like a rattlesnake or something. You've never been *violent* before."

"There's a first time for everything, Jason. I need to slap the taste out of you!"

"Baby, I don't know what has happened to you; maybe you are under too much stress working with all those children." He pulled her to him and tried to hold her.

Sheena tried to punch him again. He pinned her to the bed. "You need to calm down, Sheena. What's wrong with you?"

"Get *off* of me! Let me up before I start screaming."

Jason immediately let her go, shaking his head. "You've lost it. You better get some psychiatric help or something, woman."

"*I* haven't lost it. *You* have. You have been patronizing me for the last three months now. I have had enough of your insolent, pompous, commandeer attitude. You have the audacity to be running around with some slut and then come home after you've been with her and treat *me* like I'm a peon that should be *honored* to be in your royal presence!"

"What are you talking about? You're getting more paranoid by the day. You need to quit that job, because those children are driving you nutty. I work sixteen hours a day—"

She held her palm to his face. "You *need* to stop lying. At least be a man of integrity and own up to your mess. If there's one thing that I hate, it's a liar."

"Sheena, you need to relax. It's all in your mind." Jason pretended to be offended. "You know that I don't have time to cheat on you. It seems like the longer we've been married, the more jealous you get. This crap is getting old."

"If I am jealous, it's because you have given me good reasons to be. Having to tolerate your disloyalty to me, now *that's* what's getting old."

"You need to stop this foolishness. Now, I'm going to try to get some rest. I have to get up early and check on Daddy before I go to work. I assure you, baby, nothing's going on in my life but work, you, and our children."

"And I *assure* you, if, or when I catch you and that harlot, I'm going to kill both of you. Take me for a joke if you want to, Jason. I can *show* you better than I can tell you."

Jason watched Sheena in amazement as she rubbed her fist in his face. He tried to hold her in his arms to calm her down. He had never seen her that angry before. She was usually mild mannered and calm, even when he knew he had mistreated her. Her eyes sparkled like fire as she twisted out of his hold. "Sheena, I—"

Sheena interrupted him. "Jason, don't keep insulting me with your lies."

He hung his head, pretending to be remorseful. "Baby . . ."

Her face softened. "You need to get saved. I have been praying for you constantly, but *you* need to repent and get yourself together."

"Saved?" I *am* saved."

"Have you confessed Romans 10:9? *That if thou shall confess with thy mouth the Lord Jesus, and shalt believe in thine heart that God raised him from the dead, thou shalt be saved.*"

"No, I haven't, but I'm just as saved as you are. How did this turn into a Bible study anyway? I'm trying to get you to do your wifely duties."

"I don't mind doing my duties, as you call it, but as long as you are running around with that slut, you can forget about touching me. Like I said, you need to open the Bible and read those scriptures and repent for your sins."

Jason knew his wife was right, but he wanted to justify his perfidiousness by turning the tables on her. "I *know* what those scriptures say. But you need to take a good long look in the mirror."

Sheena raised her eyebrows. "*Me?* What are you talking about?"

"You act like Miss High and Mighty." He raised his right hand up in the air, waving it. "Praise the Lord, thank you, Jesus, I don't *ever* do anything wrong angel floating on a cloud just arrived from heaven. And not five minutes ago you were sitting in the bed with your fist rubbed in my face, threatening to *kill* me and somebody else, that doesn't even exist. You better get *yourself* together and get saved."

Jason was a mastermind at making Sheena feel guilty about *his* misconduct. He smirked inwardly, feeling victorious about having accomplished his mission when he saw the sorrowful look on her face.

"I was wrong to say I'll kill you and her, Jason. I repent for that, but I have been a good wife to you all these years and you don't even appreciate me." Her mood changed again. "But just know this, I have taken all the trash I'm going to take from you, so if you feel that you can't change and get your act together, expect to receive some divorce papers served to you real soon." Sheena's eyes riveted Jason's to the point that it made him uneasy. She turned her back to him and moved to the edge of the bed.

The telephone rang. Sheena sprang up. "I *know* she's not calling *my* house." Her eyes pierced Jason's. "Well, answer it!"

Jason answered the phone confidently. He knew it wasn't Ruby. Although he shared a lot of personal information with Ruby, he was not naïve enough to give her his home phone number. He would soon learn that he underestimated Ruby.

"Hello," he answered. "Oh, hi, Cathy." Sheena relaxed as Jason continued speaking. "Of course you and Reana can come and stay with us while you're here for Daddy. I'm sure she won't mind." He nodded at Sheena for a sign of agreement. Sheena glared at him and turned her back on him. "It will be fine, Cathy. We'll see you when you get here tomorrow." Jason hung up the phone.

"Your sister and niece can come, Jason," Sheena talked to him with her back still turned to him, "but don't think for a moment that anything has changed. And don't even think you are going to pawn them off on me like you usually do, so you can be free to roam the streets like a dog in heat. The ultimatum is still the same. Either get it together, or we're finished."

Jason didn't say a word. He smirked at her, lay on his back, and folded his hands behind his head. Although Sheena was angry, he was confident she was bluffing about ending the marriage, because he could tell she wanted him, even now.

To his surprise, Sheena slid out of bed, grabbed her pillow and walked out of the bedroom.

Chapter 7

Jason turned over. He staggered into the bathroom to take a shower. While he was in the bathroom, the children had come into the bedroom. When he came out, Jessica was jumping up and down on the mahogany high-posted king sized bed as though it was a trampoline. The twins were sprawled across the beige and burgundy damask chaise, looking at cartoons on the forty-two-inch Plasma TV that was placed over the fireplace.

"Hi, Daddy," Jessica said as she ran across the bed and jumped in his arms. "Momma slept with me last night," Jessica announced excitedly. "And she told me that Aunt Cathy and Reana are coming here today. I'm so happy!"

"Yes, they are, sweetheart. Your mother is going to spank your behind for jumping on the bed like that, you know," Jason replied.

"Don't tell on me Daddy, okay?" Jessica hugged Jason, squeezing him tightly around the neck. "It's so much fun jumping on the bed."

Jason kissed Jessica on the cheek. He marveled at the way Jessica always tried to manipulate him into letting her have her way. She was definitely Daddy's little girl.

"Okay, sweetheart," he agreed as he winked at her. "We'll keep it our little secret."

"I'm just so happy that they are coming over. Now I can share my room with Reana the way J and JJ share their room."

"That's my girl." Jason put Jessica down and turned to the boys. "Hey, guys, what's up?" Joseph and Jeremiah ran up to him and wrestled him down to the bed. "Man, you guys are getting stronger every day." He pretended that he couldn't get up.

"Yep," Joseph declared as he formed his arm to make a muscle. "Look, Daddy, we work out three times a week, just like you do."

Jason felt Joseph's muscle. "Man, that's a hard muscle. Let me see yours, Jeremiah."

"Daddy, my muscle is almost as big as yours." Jeremiah looked at Jason admirably. "When I grow up, I'm going to be just like you, Daddy."

Jason felt a twinge of guilt and hung his head down when Jeremiah said that. "Thanks, son, but when you grow up, I want you and Joseph to be better men than me, okay?"

"Daddy," Joseph inquired, "are you still taking us to see the Charlotte Bobcats play Miami Heat this weekend?"

"Yeah, J, I haven't forgotten. We have seats in the V.I.P. box too."

"What's that?"

"Son, those are the best seats in the house!"

"Wow! We are going to have fun, aren't we, Dad?"

"I plan on us having a good time with just us men. You, Jeremiah, and me."

"Cool!"

"What about you, JJ? Are you excited?"

"Yep! I can hardly wait." Jeremiah slapped his dad's hand in a high five.

"I don't want to go *anyway*," Jessica said, as she tried to walk in her mother's high-heeled shoes. "Momma said Aunt Cathy, Reana, me and her are going shopping to buy new clothes."

Joseph teased Jessica. "Yeah, y'all will be doing girly stuff. Who wants to do girly, girly stuff anyway?"

"I know, right," Jeremiah conceded.

"*We* do!" Jessica answered antagonistically.

"Okay, guys, that's enough." Jason warned them. "Let's go see what your mother is up to."

The children ran downstairs and Sheena urged them to sit down and eat breakfast.

"I decided to cook for my babies this morning she told them. I hope that you guys enjoy these *eggs* that your daddy went out and bought especially for us." She shot Jason a look that he could have sworn were arrows of hatred. "Jason, I cooked these just the way you like them; here, sit down and eat."

"Hey, baby. How are you feeling this morning?" Jason hoped she was in a better mood. He kissed her on the mouth softly.

"I'm blessed. How about you? Here, honey; sit down and eat."

Jason cringed inwardly at the evil smile on Sheena's face and the coldness in her eyes.

Sheena pulled the seat out for him to sit down. "Come on, honey, your eggs are getting cold."

"This is a surprise, baby. You've never volunteered to cook breakfast before."

"Just like you, I'm full of surprises."

"I see you are." Jason looked at Sheena inquisitively.

"Honey, what's wrong?" Sheena inquired, her eyes glistening like fire. "You're not eating. You act like the food has poison in it or something."

Jason raised his eyebrows skeptically. When he was in college, his friend, Robert's girlfriend had poisoned Robert's food after she'd found him with someone else. During his hospital stay, Robert's advice to Jason was to never eat a woman's cooking after he's made her angry. In college, Jason laughed, and didn't take him seriously. This morning, he had second thoughts.

"I'm sorry, baby, I'm just not hungry. I will take some juice though. I need to go see how Daddy's doing this morning."

"Oh, okay, honey." She smirked at him as she poured the juice. "I'm not working today. I called in for a substitute. I'm going to get things situated before Cathy and Reana arrive."

"All right. I'd better get going. I have to leave for work right after I check on Daddy."

"Wait a minute, Jason."

"What?"

"I left my car at the hospital, remember?"

Jason was in such a hurry to get out of the house that he had forgotten. He was on a mission also; he had to swing by Ruby's house to pick up his wallet. "Humph. I forgot all about that. I'll drive my old truck and you can take my car to the hospital to get yours."

"Hellooo? Put your thinking cap on, Jason. How am I going to drive *two* cars?"

"Oh, yeah. Humph. How are the kids going to get to school this morning?"

"I arranged for Silvia to pick them up on her carpool this morning."

Jason looked perplexed and scratched his head.

"Forget about it, Jason. I'll make arrangements to pick my car up."

"How?"

"I'll call a cab."

"Good thinking, baby. Okay, I gotta run. I'll call you and let you know how Daddy's doing."

"Great. I'll see you tonight. No later than *six*, right?" Sheena squinted her eyes at her husband.

"Yeah, baby, I'll see what I can do."

"You can do it, honey. I'll see you at *six*," she repeated emphatically.

"I planned to go to the hospital after I left work, Sheena. Don't be indecorous now."

"I'm not being ridiculous. I'll see you at six and then we can all ride to the hospital together. Bye, honey." She blew him a kiss and smirked.

"Humph," was all Jason said. Sheena watched him as his jaw line hardened. "Evil, that's just pure evil," Jason mumbled to himself as he exited the house.

He unlocked the door to his car and sat back on the tan leather seats. He turned on his cell phone and looked at the display screen. Seven missed calls. He checked the messages. All calls were from Ruby. "I have got to do something about this situation. But how in the world am I going to tell Sheena about Cassandra?"

The phone rang. It was Ruby.

Chapter 8

Sheena helped the children get dressed for school. Shortly afterward, Silvia was outside blowing her car horn to pick them up and take them. Sheena finished applying her makeup and then picked up the phone to call her mother.

"Hi, Momma. I just wanted to let you know that Daddy Jacob had a stroke last night." "Oh, my God!" Lois gasped. "I'm sorry to hear that, baby. Is he going to be all right?"

"I think so. The doctors have given him a good prognosis. I . . . well . . . I guess I'd better go. I have to prepare for Jason's sister and her daughter. They are going to stay with us while they're here."

"Is everything all right, Sheena? You sound distant and hollow."

"Yeah, I guess so."

"You guess so?"

She paused. "No, Momma, it's not. Jason's involved with some woman. It's tearing me to pieces, I want to kill him, Momma."

"I'm sorry to hear that, Sheena." Lois exhaled loudly into the phone. "Well, you know that you can't kill him. Your first move should be prayer, to ask God to give you directions on how to handle this situation. Remember Proverbs 3:5–6. It says, 'Trust in the Lord with all thine heart; and lean not unto thine own understanding. In all thy ways acknowledge him, and he shall direct thy paths.' I know you are hurting like nobody's business, but you have to be wise and not do anything rash."

"I just want him to hurt like he's hurt me."

"Baby, you need to get your Bible out so we can read right now and then pray. The Bible tells us that vengeance is God's."

"I have been praying for so long, Momma." Sheena sighed wearily. "I'm tired. I don't know what I'm going to do."

"You keep on praying, baby. The effectual fervent prayer of a righteous man availeth much."

"I know Momma, but—"

"Don't start doubting God's Word now. You sound like you need a vacation from Jason for a couple of days. Maybe you should pack up the kids and come home for the weekend."

"This weekend wouldn't be a good time. I want to stay around to see how his father is progressing. Besides, his sister will be here. Plus, Jason promised the twins that he would take them to see the Charlotte Bobcats play this weekend. They are so excited about spending the day with their daddy."

"I bet so."

"I think they enjoy being with Jason more than they do the actual game."

"I'm sure they do. Boys love being with their daddy, it doesn't matter what they're doing."

"You're right, Momma. That's why I don't want to leave this weekend."

"I understand. Maybe next weekend, then. You need to take some time away from him so you can get away and pray and think about what you are going to do. You don't sound so good to me. Would you like for your father and me to come down to see you, instead?" Lois fumed inwardly. She could hardly wait to give Jason a piece of her mind. He had hurt her child, and for that, he was gonna pay!

"No, Momma, I'll be fine. I don't really have anywhere for you all to sleep because Cathy will be here."

"If necessary, we can stay at a hotel. I want to be there for you if you need me."

"I know, Momma. Thanks anyway, but I'll be all right. Besides, I know why you *really* want to come, so you can read Jason the riot act." Sheena laughed.

"You do know your momma, don't you, baby? I bet when I finish with him, he'll straighten up and fly right!"

"I know, right. Jason always said you were the meanest woman he's ever encountered. I'm going to try to take your spiritual advice first, before I do anything drastic."

"You're right, baby. I shouldn't be speaking peace one minute and war the next, but I'm not gonna stand for him abusing you. You have to keep me in prayer, too, 'cause I still have issues with my temper, especially when it comes to someone mistreating my baby girl."

"I will, Momma. I understand how you feel. The way I've been feeling lately, I'm beginning to think that I inherited your temperament after all."

"Let's hope not, I shiver when I think about how hot tempered I was before I gave my life over to Christ."

"I'm glad I was too young to remember, but Daddy told me about a couple of episodes he experienced with you."

"Don't remind me, child. I thank God your daddy is a praying man."

"Amen. Anyway, Momma, I have a busy day, but I'll keep you posted; okay? I do need to get away for a while, so, I believe I will come up there next weekend. If Cathy is still here then, Jason can entertain her, she's *his* sister anyway."

"That's right."

"On second thought, I probably shouldn't leave him home. It will just give him all the free time that he wants to be with that woman."

"You don't need to worry about him and his womanizing now. You need to take care of yourself first. Don't let that man stress you out now; stress can kill you."

"You're right, Momma. I'll call you and let you know for sure about next weekend on Monday; okay?"

"Okay, baby. Take care of yourself. Stay in the Word, now. I love you."

"I love you too, Momma. Give Daddy my love. Bye."

Sheena went down the hall to check the guest suite. Everything was spotless. "Maybe I should dust a little anyway," she said aloud. After she finished tidying up, she picked up the phone to call a cab.

As the cab driver pulled up to the hospital parking lot, she directed him to her car. Cathy had called Sheena on her cell phone that morning, inquiring if Sheena would pick her and her daughter up at the airport. Sheena cranked the luxury vehicle, a GMC Denali, and adjusted the tan leather seat. She enjoyed driving the Denali Jason had purchased for her a month ago. The only downside was that she believed he bought her the vehicle because of his guilty conscience for being unfaithful to her.

Sheena pulled out onto the interstate and peered down at the driver in the Honda Accord that swerved into her lane to make an unsafe turn onto the off ramp. "Lord have mercy, there are some crazy drivers out here! That woman needs to either take driver's lessons or stay off the road."

As the driver sped by her, Sheena looked at the license plate, a habit she picked up as a child while traveling with her parents. It was a Florida plate with the name "RubyKiss." *No wonder, an out-of-state driver. She's probably lost or something.*

Sheena glanced briefly at the passenger because the man was gesturing at the woman in animated motions. Sheena figured the crazy driver had probably scared him half to death. That's when Sheena noticed that the man resembled Jason. Suddenly, as she drove down the highway, her mind began churning with negative thoughts of her husband's whereabouts. She considered calling him to see where he was; or better yet, driving by the bank to see if his car was parked outside.

"No," she said, shaking her head. "I'm not going to let Jason control my thoughts with his mind-controlling spirit all the time." She refocused her attention on driving, shaking off the thought of Jason being stupid enough as to be riding right beside her with his other woman.

Chapter 9

Ruby was still shaken up from the near-missed accident minutes earlier. She pulled over into the hotel's parking lot. "Are you crazy, Jason? You almost made me crash into that SUV! What's wrong with you, wanting me to make that sharp turn at the last minute?"

"Whew! Sorry, baby. That was close." Jason whistled loudly.

"It sure was a close call, you maniac. You almost made me run into that car!" she repeated, her hands shaking. "I've told you about waiting until the last minute to show me where to turn."

"Ruby, that was Sheena, she thinks that I'm at work. I didn't want to take any chances of her seeing me in the car with you. I saw her glance over here at us; I hope she didn't see me well enough to identify me."

"If I had known that was Sheena, I would have laid on the horn so she *could* see you. That would have made my day! It's about time for her to know about Cassandra *and* me."

"I'll get around to telling her, Ruby. I can't just spring some news like that on my wife like it's no big deal."

"If you don't hurry up and tell her, I'm gonna to do it myself. I'm tired of playing around with you! My daughter—correction, *our* daughter—deserves to live well just like Sheena and her kids."

Jason noticed that people walked by the car staring at them because of the racket Ruby was making. His head begin to ache. "Let's go, people are beginning to stare."

"I don't give a flip who stares! I'm too nervous to drive right now anyway; look at how I'm shaking!" Ruby held her hands out for Jason to see them trembling.

After Jason had enlightened her about Sheena, she was more angered by the fact that Jason tried to protect himself from being seen by Sheena than she was shaken from the car incident.

"You are shaking, aren't you?" he teased her. "I thought you had nerves of steel and here you are trembling like a leaf on a tree."

"So you think it's funny, huh?"

"I was just kidding, baby. Get out and let me drive so you can calm down, okay?" After Jason started driving, he waited until he thought she had calmed down before he started talking. "Ruby, just let me make sure Daddy's all right first. I promise you I'll sit Sheena down and tell her everything."

Ruby screamed, "I'll give you two weeks! Whether your father is well or not, your family is going to know about Cassandra!"

"For the love of peace, Ruby, I said that I would tell her, and I will. Give it a rest for five minutes, will you?" Jason was grateful that Ruby didn't have his home address. He knew how vicious she could be when she wanted something. It was not beneath Ruby to knock on his front door, and happily tell Sheena about Cassandra.

She put two fingers in his face. "You got two weeks, Jason. You hear me? *Two* weeks!"

Jason stared at her for a moment and then he shook his head. "You are one evil woman."

Ruby turned her face to the passenger window so he wouldn't see her conniving grin as she thought, *You ain't seen nothing yet.*

Chapter 10

After Jason drove Ruby back to her home, and after their escapade, Jason showered and went back to work. Ruby had taken the entire day off work. She busied herself on the computer, keying in the information she found from Jason's wallet.

"Well, now, Miss Ruby," she congratulated herself, "you have hit the jackpot." She looked at his bank account thoroughly. She got an adrenaline rush, in anticipation of what she was going to do. She proceeded to transfer money from his account into hers, all the while, voicing her thoughts. "I'll just take a few hundred dollars for now. He's quite a success financially. Hmmm, and this is only one of his accounts. I made a mistake by letting Jason go years ago, but I'm gonna make up for it now."

Ruby was a transfer student from Bethune Cookman College in Florida. She met Jason shortly after she'd arrived at North Carolina Central. One of Jason's sisters was an administrator there. Ruby did work-study under her guidance. Jason's sister liked Ruby so well that she introduced her to Jason. From the beginning, Ruby and Jason were drawn together like two magnets. They were inseparable. After several months of dating, they became known as the golden couple on campus.

Ruby was impressed with Jason because she thought he was 'fine as wine.' In addition, he was highly intelligent and an athlete. Unfortunately for her, he was arrogant, spoiled, conceited and selfish.

Ruby was not academically gifted; she was a "C" student at best. Her appearance, however, was very appealing. She possessed the kind of beauty that renowned modeling agencies sought after and the type of figure that most girls desired. In spite of her drop dead gorgeous looks, Ruby's unscrupulous character left a lot to be desired.

Despite their differences, the couple continued to date, having nothing in common but an overwhelmingly strong physical desire for each other. A meaningful conversation between the two of them was nonexistent. The relationship could have been described as a combination of lust and contempt.

Jason always had a wandering eye. He could not get enough of pretty women. Other women on campus competed viciously with Ruby for Jason to the extent that Ruby constantly caught him in compromising positions with them. Whenever she even suspected him of talking to anyone, she would cause a scene no matter where they were. She became so obsessed with him that she flunked out of school and spent all of her time stalking him.

The only way that he eluded her was during summer break, when he moved back home with his parents. She couldn't stalk him there because she did not know his parents' address. Jason never took Ruby home to meet his parents because he told her he knew that his parents would not approve of her. She still remembered word for word what she told Jason when he said that to her. "I don't give a hot flame whether they like me or not!"

He told her, "That's exactly what I mean. You have no character and your mannerism and lack of respect for elders is a disgrace. You have the beauty of an African queen, but you behave as though wolves raised you."

In reality, Ruby felt as though wolves *had* raised her. Her family didn't come close to emulating The Huxtables. Most times, she felt like

an unwanted foster child. Life was a party to her
parents. They consumed alcohol, smoked, and
hosted card games almost every afternoon after
returning home from work.

For as long as Ruby could remember, she had
to survive the best way she could. Her parents
provided the shelter, food, and clothes, but it
was up to her to take care of herself.

Once, they even told her, "You had better learn
how to care for yourself, or you will be lost in this
world because we are not always going to be here
for you."

"What a joke." Ruby laughed halfheartedly at
the recollection of it. Since when had they *ever*
been there for her? She'd had to practically raise
herself. Ruby grew up determined that she would
be nothing like her parents. Neither of them graduated high school, so she was determined to finish
high school and then go to college.

Jason was one of the most decent people she
had known in years, so she wasn't inclined to let
him get away. But in her strong drive to conquer
his heart, she had almost caused him to spurn
her. Her obsession with him was relentless.

After Jason disappeared during summer vacation, Ruby assessed her behavior, miraculously
sobered up, sought counseling and painstakingly
relinquished her feelings of obsession toward

him. When he returned to school for the fall, they reunited for a brief period. Although she knew she vexed his spirit sometimes, Ruby was shrewd enough to know Jason also coveted her affection. She fulfilled his unquenchable thirst for attention. They resumed the twisted relationship that existed between them briefly, but Jason's logic and superficial pride concluded the relationship to be unhealthy. Ruby's counseling helped her considerably to distinguish between love and obsession, so they agreed that it would be best for them to go their separate ways.

Ruby moved back home to Florida and discovered a month later that she was pregnant. She was so distraught that she considered having an abortion, but sought counseling again and, after a few sessions, decided to have the baby. She also decided not to tell Jason. It was clear that he didn't love her and she did not want to raise her baby in a discontented relationship the way she had been raised.

Twelve years later, Ruby saw Jason on the cover of the prestigious financial magazine, *Black Enterprise*, with his wife and three children, and she saw the opportunity to make a better life for her daughter and herself. Therefore, she devised a plan to move to Charlotte, North Carolina. She had no problem obtaining a position with a dental office because she had years of experience. Finally, she found an apartment in a decent part of town and set up shop.

Ruby had been in town for two months and during that time, she researched Jason thoroughly. She frequented places where she knew he would be until she "just happened" to cross paths with him one day. Jason was glad to see her after all those years and was impressed that Ruby had kept herself up so well. They began to meet for lunch on a regular basis. Ruby knew exactly how to seduce Jason, and to her surprise, she had him back in her bed much sooner than she had anticipated.

When she informed him about Cassandra, he was in utter shock. He couldn't deny the child as being his from the time line that she quoted to him. When he asked to see her, Ruby told him that she had left the child with her parents who, by the way, were "saved" now. Once she got settled, she would send for their daughter. When he asked to see a picture of her, he commented that she didn't resemble him at all because her pictures revealed her to be the spitting image of Ruby.

Ruby planned to break up Jason's marriage so she would have her rightful place in his life. She thought that it would be an easy task, because she knew Jason had always been a sucker for a pretty face and a shapely figure. She was appeased in the fact that if Sheena looked like her picture on the cover of *Black Enterprise*, she was no competition for her.

"I can't believe Jason married that Plain Jane. She's only a fraction away from being ugly," Ruby laughed as she admired herself in the mirror.

She sat back down at the computer and finished the transaction. The account she tampered with happened to be the one Jason had set up for Sheena. Although it was in his name, he had opened it the first year they were married, for Sheena's household funds and for spending money, or anything she might need. Sheena handled statements from the State Employees Credit Union solely.

"Well, I have finished my mission for today," Ruby said proudly. "Now, for tomorrow . . ."

Chapter 11

Jason worked until one o'clock and then took a lunch break to go see how his father was doing. His mother met him at the door.

"Come on in, son." Catherine's face glowed and her voice was cheerful. "He seems to have improved slightly since you left this morning."

"That's wonderful news, Momma. I'm glad ole Pops is pulling through."

"You really do love your father, don't you, son?"

"Momma, you know I love Dad; I just find it difficult to deal with him sometimes. *You* of all people should be able to relate to that."

"You're right. He's a hard rock, but he is my husband for better or for worse."

Jason's countenance hardened. "I don't know how you did it all these years, Momma, but you stood by his side."

"You'll understand one day, son. Your wife sticks by you, even though you mistreat her."

"I don't want to talk about Sheena right now. I'm too exhausted."

"If you stayed home like you are supposed to, you wouldn't be so exhausted. Can't no man handle more than one woman at a time, especially if he is taking care of business right. One of those women is gonna be disappointed and disgusted with your performance.

Jason's small squinty dark eyes blared open. "Momma! I'm surprised at you, talking like that."

"Don't be surprised at nothing I say, Jason. I might be old, but I know what I'm talking about. I have been married for a long time. I'm not just your Momma; I'm a woman too. Jacob missed the ball a lot."

Jason threw both hands up. "Okay, Momma. You're about to reveal too much information."

"You're right, son. Anyway, you shouldn't be out here running around on your wife with all of these ole diseases and stuff going on nowadays."

"Here we go," Jason exhaled wearily.

Catherine ignored his remark. "You know it's the truth; you better be careful." She paused. "Son, what were you going to tell me before Sheena came in last night?"

Jason had to recall their conversation. "I know you think that I'm just involved with some ole street woman, don't you?"

"You mentioned her to me once or twice; that Ruby . . . whatever her last name is."

"Dickens. Ruby Dickens."

"I don't care what her last name is; the first one either. All I know is that you need to stop cheating on Sheena. She's not my idea of the kind of woman you should've married, but she did give you three beautiful children. Don't lose everything you have for that trifling woman."

"Momma, she's not trifling. I wish that you wouldn't say things like that about her."

"Oh, you're defending her now?"

Agitated with his mother's question, Jason answered her crossly. "No, Momma, it's not about defense."

"You sounded defensive to me. If memory serves me correctly, you came running home twelve years ago, seeking refuge from that . . . what was it you called her? Oh yeah, that "possessive lunatic?"

Jason started laughing. "You got me, Momma. But Ruby's changed now. She's not like that anymore."

"I see she's still got your nose wide open. That girl is still the same, probably worse. She's just wiser, more cunning and she's learned how to be discreet."

"Momma, you don't know what you're talking about. Ruby is a different person."

"Oh, really? How is it that she ended up in Charlotte? Does she have any relatives here? She is from Florida, right?"

"Yes, she's from Florida. She's familiar with North Carolina, remember we went to school together at Central."

"If I recall correctly, Durham and Charlotte are not next door to each other. It's not like they're only ten or fifteen miles apart. So, again, how did she end up in *Charlotte* of all places, all the way from Florida?"

"I guess her job transferred her, Momma. I didn't ask her, and it never occurred to me to do a background check on how she ended up here."

"Maybe you should have done a background check on her. Women like her can't be trusted a bit farther than you can throw 'em."

"You can be a vicious little thing when you put your mind to it, can't you, Momma?" Jason said, sarcastically.

"No, I'm not vicious. You just need to use your head, that's all. The one that's on your shoulders, that is."

"Momma! You just come out and say anything nowadays, don't you?"

"Talking in riddles to you hasn't made an impact, so I have to be frank with you, son."

"She probably did come to Charlotte for me, but she has her reasons."

"I'm sure she does. Think about it, Jason, you were featured in *Black Enterprise* as one of the most successful young businessmen in America this year. When did that article run?"

"Eight months ago, in the February issue."

"And it was about six months ago, wasn't it, that you told me you'd bumped into your old girl-friend, right?" Jason nodded. Catherine smirked. "And you all have been involved for how long?"

"A little over three months now. Why?"

"The timing doesn't strike you as strange?"

"No, Momma, it doesn't."

Catherine looked at Jason incredulously. "I know you are not going to sit here with your intelligence and tell me that you think that her coming here is a coincidence."

"When I bumped into her in the restaurant downtown, I thought it was a coincidence; but now I know it was fate."

"Fate? Jason, do you know how you sound? That Jezebel calculated everything. I can almost promise you that she saw you and your family in that magazine and came up with a plan to scheme her way back into your life."

Jason massaged his temples. "Momma, it's possible that she did find her way back to me through the magazine. The reason why I said it was fate was because she *needed* to find me."

"Why? What reason did she *need* to find you? To break up your family so she could take Sheena's place in your life?"

"No, she needed to find me because we have a child together, Momma."

Catherine was flabbergasted. "Since when? Have you been seeing her through the years?"

"No. I saw her for the first time almost four months ago after she moved back to Florida."

"Well, how did you get her pregnant? The last time I checked, it took nine months to have a baby. Something is not adding up; you met up with her on some of your business trips to Florida, didn't you?" Frowning at him she asked, "Or *were* they business trips?"

"When I went to Florida, it was strictly business. I thought about her a few times, but I didn't try to contact her. She got pregnant back in college when she moved back home. She chose not to tell me about it though."

"So this child is about eleven or twelve years old? I thought you were speaking of a recently born child."

"She's eleven." Jason stood up and walked over to his father's bed. "I thought I saw Daddy move."

Catherine walked to the bed and rubbed her husband's hand. "Jacob, squeeze my hand if you can hear me." She felt a slight pressure from Jacob's hand. "Jason, get the nurse. Maybe they can do something to wake him up."

Upon getting the call, the nurse came in and checked on Jacob. "He's still unconscious, Mrs. Grey, but it's a good sign that he tried to squeeze your hand. His vitals are good. He's stable, but it may take some time for him to regain consciousness. Sometimes being unconscious is a good thing."

"Why?" Catherine asked, irritated at the nurse. "How can that be a good thing?"

"Because the body is healing itself, ma'am. God has equipped our bodies with the ability to heal ourselves.

"So keep praising God for your husband's healing and encourage him to praise God too. It's believed that people in comas can hear you even if they don't respond to you."

Catherine rubbed the nurse on her back. "God bless you, baby. I'm going to pray that the Lord blesses you with the desires of your heart. It's encouraging to see a compassionate nurse."

"He'll be fine, Mrs. Grey." The nurse adjusted Jacob's bed and left the room.

Catherine was elated. "That's good news, isn't it, Jason? Prayer changes things, son."

Jason was uncomfortable talking about prayer and anything associated with "religion," as he called it. "Whatever you say, Momma."

"Son, you used to love going to church when you were little. I know you strayed for a while, but after you met Sheena, you started going to church again and reading the Bible. What happened?"

After becoming an adult, Jason was never sincere about church. He did what was necessary to conquer Sheena's love. "Momma, can we not talk about church right now?"

Catherine squinted her eyes at him. "You need to get back in the Word, son."

"Yeah, right." Jason exhaled loudly. "Getting back to the subject at hand, we were talking about Ruby."

"Ah, yes, Miss Ruby and your alleged child."

"She's my child, Momma."

"How do you *know* this? Have you seen her? Did you get a DNA test done? I would be skeptical if I were you."

"You are not me. Besides, I trust Ruby to tell the truth. She was a piece of work back then, but she was an honest piece of work. I know Ruby; she wouldn't lie about something like that."

"Have you seen the child, Jason? Where is she? I would like to see her for myself. If she is a Grey, I'll see it in her."

"No, I haven't seen her. I've seen photos of her; she looks like Ruby spit her out. She doesn't resemble me at all, but that doesn't mean anything."

"Uh-huh. Maybe, maybe not, time and tests will tell."

"Ruby wants to bring the girl up as soon as I tell everybody about her. She doesn't want to tell her about me until she knows that I'm ready to be a father to her."

"How convenient," Catherine said thoughtfully. "Well, if the child is yours, you know that I will open my arms to her. On the other hand, you have a dilemma on your hands. How are you going to drop this news in Sheena's lap? Lord, have mercy, son; you might jeopardize everything you have. This is going to be a tough trial for Sheena. Having an affair is one thing, but bringing an outside child home is a burden that even your *sweet, shy, Sheena*, as you call her, might not want to bear."

"I know, but I have to tell her. There's no way to avoid it."

"Jason, if you had treated your wife differently, more respectful, and tried to be faithful to her, it's possible that she would be willing to accept the child eventually. After all, the child *was* born before you met her. Only God knows."

"According to Ruby, she was conceived shortly after I started seeing Sheena. Ruby didn't know it, but by the time I came back for the fall semester, I was already talking to Sheena. You remember the spring break when I went to the mountains to find Sheena after her boyfriend died?"

"Oh, yeah. I remember you telling me about that." Catherine smiled. "I distinctly remember you saying, 'Momma, I think I've met the girl that I'm going to marry one day.'"

"Yes, that's what I said. Sheena was a refreshing change from Ruby and all those other wild girls that I ran around with. She was a classy lady. And still is."

"Well, I pray that your classy lady can endure the news you are about to shock her with."

"So do I," Jason said, wistfully rubbing his hands together. "So do I."

"You need to seek the Lord for directions before you talk to her."

"Yep, I guess you might be right, Momma."

"I know I'm right. Anyway, had you adhered to Proverbs 5:18, nineteen things might not be so bad for you now." She opened her Bible that lay on Jacob's bed. "Listen, son. It says, *Let thy fountain be blessed; and rejoice with the wife of thy youth. Let her be as the loving hind and pleasant roe; let her breasts satisfy thee at all times; and be thou ravished always with her love.* You should read the whole chapter, it's a blessing."

Jason became irritated with Catherine for quoting scriptures to him. "I don't need to hear another sermon from you, Momma. I get enough sermons from my wife."

"It would be nice if you respected her enough to listen to her."

"Yes *ma'am*," he said sarcastically. "You are right as rain. When did you become so fond of Sheena anyway?"

"I've always liked Sheena. Even though she acted a little dizzy at times, she is a good wife to you. Your wife is the kind of wife spoken of in the Bible—a virtuous woman."

"Humph." Jason sighed.

"You are blessed enough to have a wife like that, but you have taken that girl for granted."

Jason felt offended by Catherine's statement. "I have been a good provider for Sheena and my children. She doesn't want for anything. My wife doesn't even have to work. She knows that I will provide for her and do my best to make sure that she has every thing she needs and wants." He stood up suddenly to leave. "I have to get back to work, Momma. I'll be back tonight to check on Daddy."

"Jason, I'm sorry if I hurt your feelings, but sometimes, the truth hurts. Sure, you provide well for your wife and the children. But you're neglecting to give her what she needs the most."

"And what's that?"

"Love, respect, faithfulness, your time. Most of all, read Ephesians 5:25, which states, *Husbands, love your wives, even as Christ also loved the church, and gave himself for it . . .*"

Jason threw his hands up in defeat. "Are you and Sheena in cahoots or something? That's her favorite scripture."

Catherine smiled sweetly at her son. "Have you read it?"

"Not lately. Sheena gets so self-righteous when she speaks about those scriptures, that I *don't* read them just to annoy her."

"That pride is going to come back to bite you one day. Sheena is your wife, she's not the enemy. She doesn't have an evil bone in her body. She's never hurt you."

"I know, I know, give it a rest, Momma. I heard you loud and clear." Exhaling loudly, he added, "I've been away from work too long; I should get going. I'll see you tonight. Oh, by the way, Cathy is going to come stay with us until Dad gets better." He kissed his mother on the cheek. "See you soon."

"All right, son. I'm going home to freshen up and rest for a while. I believe your father will be okay until I get back."

"He'll be fine, Momma, you need to go home and take a nap, you do look tired. I gotta go. See you tonight." As soon as Jason was outside the hospital, he checked the messages on his cell phone. There were three from Ruby. He deleted them without listening to them.

One message was from Sheena. He pressed the button to listen.

"Hi, honey. I picked Cathy up from the airport and we are home now. We are about to start cooking dinner, so I expect to see you tonight at about *six*." Jason noticed that she emphasized *six* again. "Love ya."

I guess I'd better show up on time tonight, because Sheena doesn't sound like she's in the mood for foolishness.

Chapter 12

Sheena and Cathy prepared dinner together while the children did their homework. Six-year-old, Reana played with Jessica's dolls while she waited for Jessica to finish her homework.

"Sheena, every time I visit, I have to walk all over the house to see what you've decorated differently." Cathy looked around the den. "I just love your taste in furniture; it's so elegant. And the way you accessorize is so artful. It's as though you are telling a story from all the different cultures."

"Thank you, Cathy. I enjoy making our home comfortable for us, it's truly a blessing. Your home is lovely too, by the way."

"Yeah, it's small, but it's sufficient for Reana and me."

"It must be exciting to live in California. Every time we come to visit you, you show us a fun time."

"It's okay. San Diego is just like anywhere else a person might stay. After a while, it becomes mediocre. It's awfully lonesome out there since my husband, Frank, and I separated three months ago."

"I can imagine. How are you handling things by yourself?"

"Do you mean financially?"

"I was referring to emotionally, but are you doing all right financially?"

"I'm doing okay. As for emotionally, I have good days and bad days, but I know that I'm better off without him. He takes good care of Reana and he comes by to give me money and to see if I need anything."

"That's good. He must be genuinely concerned about you."

"I guess. I suspect that he wants us to get back together though."

"Are you considering that?"

"At times. It would be good for Reana because she misses her father terribly. But as for us, he needs to seek help for his control issues. I had no idea that he would turn out to be a control freak like Daddy is."

"I understand. Jason has issues with your father over how he treated your mother all those years."

"I know. I think Daddy got worse after we all left. Jason is the baby of the family, so he was left there alone with them for ten years. Momma thought that she was through having children; but she was surprised when she became pregnant with Jason ten years after Jonathan was born. Being there alone with them made him permeate Daddy's unruly behavior."

Sheena nodded. "He and Jason work together, but there's always an uncomfortable tension between them."

"If you'd grown up with Daddy, you'd understand why. He loved us, but he didn't bend his rules for anything. Whatever he said stood. No ifs, ands or buts. He was a very good provider, but he didn't know how to relate to us."

"Jason is his father's son," Sheena admitted candidly.

"He is a good provider, but he doesn't know how to relate to us. Well, correction ...to *me*. He loves those children to no end."

"He loves you, too, Sheena. He's so proud of you." Cathy's smile brightened. "He's always talking about what a good wife and mother you are."

"That's news to me. He rarely has anything good *to* say to me."

"If he doesn't, it's because of his pride. Jason always was too arrogant for his own good. Momma spoiled him rotten. But I know he loves those children because he dotes over them, unlike Daddy did us. That man ruled with an iron fist. Poor Momma tried effortlessly to convince him to be more lenient with us, but if she got too assertive with him, he would smack her."

"He would hit her in front of you guys?"

"Oh, no, never. He would always escort her into their bedroom. He would raise his voice at her and then we would hear the smack."

"That's terrible. What would your mother do?"

"Nothing but come back out of the room with a sour smile on her face, acting like nothing happened. I suppose she didn't think that we were smart enough to know what was going on."

"I couldn't imagine my dad hitting my momma."

"We lived through it, that's probably why Jason is so insensitive to you. It's not right, but thank God that he doesn't hit you, girl."

"No, *he* should thank God that he doesn't hit me, because if he did, I would kill his butt. That's one thing that my daddy taught me; not to let any man hit or beat me."

"I agree with you, girl. Even though Frank was controlling, he wasn't dumb enough to try that. After I saw the junk Momma took off of Daddy, I vowed never to live my life like that. That's why I put his domineering rear end out." Sheena laughed as Cathy demonstrated Frank's behavior in an animated manner.

"I hear you." Sheena's expression saddened after she stopped laughing. "Your brother doesn't hit me, but he's mentally abusive and he's involved with someone else. I don't know who she is, but he's been seeing her for a few months now."

Cathy gasped. "Are you sure, Sheena?"

"I'm positive." Tears fell from Sheena's eyes. "He's hardly ever home, and when he is, his thoughts are preoccupied with her. I can be sitting or lying beside him, but I can tell he's not here with me emotionally. When I try to get his attention, he just insults me. It hurts, Cathy, and I am going to file for a divorce if he doesn't break it off with her."

Cathy hugged Sheena. "I'm so sorry. I had no idea. If I did, I would fuss him out and straighten his sorry butt out. Jason knows better than this; I'm disappointed in him."

"His brain might know better, but evidently, his libido has taken control."

"I'll talk to him as soon as I can get him alone." Cathy pretended to flex her muscles. "He respects his big sister. I don't pamper him like Momma and my sisters do. I bet when I finish with him, he'll get his act together."

"Don't feel obligated to talk to him, Cathy. He *is* your brother, and blood is thicker than water."

"Yes, he is my brother, but he's not right, and I don't like the fact that he is abusing you this way. You have been an outstanding wife to him and he needs to wake up and smell the coffee."

Sheena wiped her tears away with the back of her hands. "Cathy, I didn't want to involve you in our business, but I just feel so overwhelmed."

"I understand, girl. But I detected that something was wrong anyway."

"How? I tried to be myself."

"Yes you did. But the Lord has blessed me with the spirit of discernment. I could sense your pain when you picked me up from the airport."

"Was it that obvious? I guess I've always been transparent, haven't I?"

Cathy smiled. "No, you have always been so . . . what's the word . . .?"

"Air headed?"

"No silly." Cathy laughed as she patted Sheena on the arm. "Lighthearted. Bubbly."

Sheena was grateful to Cathy for her benevolence. "You are a good sister-in-law, Cathy. Thank you for the kind words."

"There's no need to thank me. You are a special person. One of God's peculiar people that He speaks about in . . . where is that scripture?" She reached for her purse. "Girl, you know I keep my Bible nearby," she laughed. Cathy took a moment to search her Bible's concordance. "Oh, yeah, Deuteronomy 14:2." She flipped a few pages and said, "Here it is: *For thou art a holy people unto the Lord thy God, and the Lord hath chosen thee to be a peculiar people unto himself, above all the nations that are upon the earth.* If Jason knows what's good for him, he'll recognize that."

"I don't think that Jason cares one way or the other."

"I'm sure that he does, but somebody has caught his attention momentarily. He'll come to his senses. Just read Psalm 91 and Psalm 121; they always comfort me. God is always with you, baby."

The children came into the kitchen. Sheena collected herself and forced a bright smile for them.

"Is it time to eat yet?" Jessica asked.

"Yes it is, sweetheart." Cathy said cheerfully. "You guys go and wash your hands and then we can eat."

"Where's Daddy, Momma?" Joseph inquired. "I thought he said he was going to be home by six."

Sheena looked at the clock on the wall. It was six-forty-seven. *I should have known he wouldn't*

show up; he's probably with that woman again.
"He was supposed to be here, J. I guess he got
tied up again." Frowning, she looked at the clock
again, and then at the door.

Cathy watched Sheena as she flung the dish-
towel on the kitchen counter. "Maybe he's on his
way, Sheena," she reasoned.

"I doubt it. Cathy, will you feed the children? I
have a headache, I am going to take some medicine and lie down for a while."

Cathy noticed that Sheena was on the verge
of tears again. "I'll be glad to, Sheena. Get some
rest; I'm sure you'll feel better when you get up."

Sheena headed for upstairs just as Jason
opened the front door.

"Hey, baby. Sorry I'm a little late, traffic on
I-85 was terrible, as usual," Jason stated. Sheena
didn't answer him or acknowledge his presence;
she just kept walking. He gently pulled her back
and turned her body so that she faced him. He
saw tears running down her face. "Come on,
baby, I'll walk you up."

Chapter 13

Jason had called Ruby on his way home from work, to cancel their evening together. He explained to her that Sheena insisted he get home by six. He let Ruby know that they had to be more careful because Sheena had begun getting too suspicious. Jason also let her know that his sister had come to town and would be staying at their house. So he wasn't going to be rude to her and not show up on her first night there.

Ruby couldn't have cared less about Sheena's demands, and she told him that his sister would still be at his house when he got home. Standing firm, Jason told her that his family took precedence over her. That infuriated Ruby and she threatened to drive over to his house, if he didn't come over to see her.

Ruby was so angry she wanted to scream. She needed to blow off some steam, so she called her co-worker's house. Brittany answered on the first ring.

"Hey, Brittany," Ruby said before blowing a heavy breath into the phone.

Brittney asked, "What's wrong with you, girl?"

"That stupid joker actually had the nerve to call me at the last minute and tell me that he's not coming over! He's got some nerve canceling on me after I cooked all of this food for his trifling behind!" Ruby was acrimonious. "I've got a good mind to take this food over to his house, ring the doorbell and dump it on that swollen fat head of his!" She stumped around in the kitchen, slamming the food into plastic containers.

"Believe me, Ruby, I know how you feel. I've been stood up so many times by my friend that it's not even funny. Sometimes, I wonder if he's even worth wasting my time over." Brittany was seeing a prominent married man in Charlotte also. She and Ruby had that in common, but both were smart enough not to reveal their lover's identity. Brittany listened patiently while Ruby vented.

"I had a fun night planned for us, too. I went out and bought all of these adult toys and this edible lingerie that he loves. He's going to pay me for this stuff. Unlike him, I don't have money to burn!" Ruby placed the food containers into the refrigerator. She paced around in her apartment holding the cordless phone to her ear.

"I know what you mean, Ruby. I'm trying to get all the money I can get from my friend. I've got to get it while I can. I don't blame you, I would make him pay me back too."

"I guess he thinks he's Mr. Big Stuff. He must have forgotten who he's playing with. If he thinks he's going to slide in here like a snake and slither out whenever he wants to, he'd better think again."

Brittany's phone beeped. She asked Ruby to hold for a second. It was her married friend. When she clicked back over to Ruby, she said, "Ruby, it's him." She chuckled. "I know you're upset, but will it be okay if I called you back as soon as we finish talking?"

"No, girl, don't do that. Go on and talk to your man. I'll be fine; I just need to get out of here. I can't sit around here twiddling my fingers thinking about him all night. Thanks for listening, girl. I'll see you Monday, okay?" Ruby placed the cordless phone back in its cradle. She went into the bedroom, darting her eyes evilly at the décor she had worked so hard on all evening, getting ready for Jason.

He's still just as selfish and thoughtless as he was when I was dating him, she thought. She walked into the bathroom and snatched her make-up case out of its designated place. Ruby was a neat freak, almost to the point of being obsessive-compulsive. "Look at this crap! I hate for things to be unorganized!"

Ruby looked into the mirror as she began to reapply her make-up. Seeing her distorted reflection stunned her. "I have got to get a grip; I look like a rabid dog or something. I'm standing here talking to myself like a crazy woman." She took three deep breaths to try to calm down. It worked. She felt like she needed some fresh air. She decided to get dressed and go downtown and check out the new club that Brittany had told her about.

Ruby pulled out her slinkiest black dress, slipped it on, put on her black four-inch stilettos and pranced around in front of the mirror. "Now that's what I'm talking about!" She was very pleased with the way she looked.

Ruby was a mixture of three nationalities. Her mother was Seminole Indian of the Micanopy Tribe, and her father was Cuban and black. Although she was proud of all of her heritages, she preferred to be considered as just being black. It irritated her when people asked her what race she was or what she was mixed with.

Ruby's mind was churning. "I don't have to sit around here and wait on Jason's slow married behind. I'm going out and have some fun for a change." Besides, she concluded, as long as she had Cassandra to dangle over his head, he would be around anyway.

The phone rang and Ruby was sure it was Jason. She let the answering machine take the message, hoping he'd get irritated with her for not answering.

"Hi Ruby, I hadn't heard from you in a while and I wanted to know if you were doing all right," her mother said. "Baby, I hope you aren't still trying to break Jason and his wife up. You can do better than that as pretty as you are, okay? You don't have to stoop to the level of dating a married man. I know that he is your child's father and I'm sure he'll take care of his responsibilities, but what you're doing is wrong."

"I know she's not going to preach to me on the answering machine." Ruby picked up the handset. "Hi, Momma; I'm here."

"Oh, I didn't think you were there."

"I was about to walk out the door." Frowning, Ruby sighed loudly. She laid her small black purse on the oak sofa table.

"Where are you going?"

"I'm going *out,* Momma."

"Not with that married man, I hope."

"Momma, I'm a grown woman. If it is any of your business, no, I'm not going out with Jason."

"That's a relief. Where *are* you going then?"

"Momma! Why are you so nosy?"

"As long as I'm keeping your daughter I have a right to be nosy. And speaking of Cassandra, when are you coming down here to get this child?"

"Soon, maybe in another month or so. Jason's father had a stroke, so he hasn't told the family yet. I told him that I would give him two weeks. If he hasn't told them by then, I'm going to do it if I have to go to his house and call that plum face wife of his out in the street and tell her."

"Ruby, don't you do that. That girl hasn't done anything to you. Don't go over there starting no trouble now."

"She needs to know. They all do. My child has the right to live well just like those brats of hers."

"Girl, I'm warning you, don't try to break up that home. I thought you claimed you cared so much about Jason. Those are *his* brats too, you know."

"I do care for Jason, I love him, I've always loved him. That's why that skimpy wife of his is getting out of our lives. Cassandra and I are going to be living in that big, nice, brick house and driving an expensive SUV, too, because he's gonna buy me one. I already know what kind I want."

"Ruby, it sounds like you *love* the material things that Jason can give you. I don't believe you love him all that much."

"Momma, I know how I feel." Ruby was determined that her daughter wasn't going to grow up in a tiny two-bedroom trailer, set up in a rundown trailer park all of her life like she did. "As for his kids, I didn't mean to call them brats. I guess I'll have to put up with them when they visit."

"Ruby, baby, you are living in a dream world. You are going to have to do more than put up with them."

"*Whatever*. I'm not going to be taking care of them all the time."

"Do you actually think that he is going to put his wife and children out the door for you? And what about Cassandra?"

"What *about* her? She'll be happy as a lark staying with Jason and me. As for his other children, I'm sure he'll provide well for them."

"And his wife. Has he told you that he is going to leave her for you?"

"No, but it'll only be a matter of time. Once she finds out about his affair with me, his not-so-ex-girlfriend who just happens to have his daughter, *she* will leave *him*."

"Don't be too sure about that. Once she learns all the details, it's possible she may seek refuge in Jesus and eventually find the strength and courage to forgive him. She may even be strong enough to accept Cassandra into their lives."

"I doubt it. She's too high and mighty to let her Christian friends see her stoop low enough to accept her husband's love child."

"How do you know this?"

"I know because Jason talks about her all the time. He gets so frustrated with her and her religious beliefs."

"So he *says*. He must not be too frustrated, 'cause he's still there with her. He's just saying what he has to so he can keep coming over to yo' place and jumping in yo' bed."

"Momma, thanks for the pep talk but I gotta go. Tell my baby that I love her and I'll see her soon. Where is she anyway?"

"I let her spend the night with her best friend. They are having a sleep over."

"Do you know the girl's parents? Momma, don't let my daughter stay with any ole Sally, Jane or Keisha."

"Ruby, I'm not stupid. You know I ain't gonna let my grandbaby stay with people that I don't know. The little girl's grandparents are good friends of ours. They are just as protective of their grandbaby as we are of ours."

"Okay, Momma, I'm depending on you to take care of my baby, now."

"I understand that, Ruby. I may not have been a good Momma to you, but I'm doing the best that I know how to do to make it up to you through your daughter."

"I know you are, Momma. Sometimes I still have nightmares about the way you and Daddy left me all alone while you were out partying."

"I understand, baby. I hope you find it in your heart to forgive your Daddy and me one day."

"I have, Momma. If I hadn't, I wouldn't let you and Daddy keep my little girl."

"Thank you, Ruby. That means so much to us. Anyway, I don't want you to be that type of woman that pastor was teaching on last Sunday."

"What type of woman?"

"The *other* Proverbs woman. The Bible says: *And, behold, there met him a woman with the attire of an harlot, and subtil of heart.* That was his subject for the day. You'll probably need to read the whole chapter from the first verse so you can get a good understanding."

"Okay, Momma, I'll read it before I go out, but I have to go now. I'll talk to you later."

"Wait a minute, Ruby, one more thing."

Ruby became irritated. *This is just one more of her schemes to keep me on the phone.* "Momma, no. I'll call you Sunday."

"I wanted to tell you—"

"Bye, Momma. I love you." She hung up just as her mother was about to say something.

Ruby took the time to read the scriptures her mother told her about. "Is she kidding me? That's not me, and Jason sure isn't naïve by any means." Ruby got in her car and headed for downtown. She blasted her favorite old school CD by Earth, Wind, and Fire. She was about to pass the exit on Interstate 77 that led to the suburb where Jason lived.

At that point, she decided to ride by his house, just for the heck of it. She had written down his address from his driver's license. Shortly, thereafter, she got directions through MapQuest to his house. Ruby followed the directions one evening when she was riding around Charlotte, learning her way around the city. She pulled up to the street and parked one house down from his. Within seconds of parking, she saw Jason and Sheena coming out of the house.

"Well, well, isn't that special." Ruby watched Jason walk with his arm around Sheena's waist. When he opened the car door for his wife, Ruby had the urge to ram her car into the back of the Denali. The thought vanished when three children and another woman with a little girl walked to the vehicle and got in it. "Next time baby, next time. I'll fix your two timing butt."

Chapter 14

As Jason sped down the interstate toward the hospital, his mind was preoccupied with thoughts of Ruby. He had spotted a white Honda, the same kind of car Ruby drove, parked on the street near his house. When he called her a few hours earlier, to cancel their date, Ruby had threatened to come to his house. Experience had taught him that she was capable of doing just that. The thought of her actually following through with her threat unnerved him.

Jason reached for Sheena's hand and noticed that she gently eased her hand out of his. He glanced at her. "Are you okay, baby?"

"I'm fine. Are *you* doing all right? You seem preoccupied."

"Oh, yeah. I'm doing fine. I was just thinking about the conversation we had upstairs, about the problems with our relationship," he lied.

Sheena peeped in the back seats, hoping that Cathy and the children weren't listening. Joseph and Jeremiah had her full attention while Jessica and Reana were in the third row seat playing "Miss Mary Mack."

"I hope that you are seriously considering the magnitude of it and what it means for our marriage."

"I heard you, Sheena, and I'm going to do better. I don't understand why you were so upset because I wasn't home exactly at six o'clock."

"Your not being there directly at six wasn't what upset me."

"What was wrong then?"

"I explained that to you when we talked. You said you heard me."

"I did hear you," Jason said. " I just don't understand why you have been so moody lately."

"Maybe that's the problem, Jason. You *heard* me, but you didn't *listen* to me."

Jason shook his head in defeat. "I don't understand you anymore. I do everything that I know to please you, but you are still complaining."

"No, you don't do *everything* to please me. You are dropping the ball on one important thing. And you know what that is."

Jason looked at Sheena in disbelief. "I'm not the one who dropped the ball." He turned the radio up a little louder. "Is that too loud for you guys back there?"

"No, Daddy, that's the way we like it," replied Jeremiah."

"It's fine," stated Cathy. She could sense that Jason and Sheena were having an intense conversation and wanted to block out anyone else from hearing it.

"Sheena, every time I've tried to touch you in the last two weeks, you have rejected me. You freeze up like an icicle. What more am I supposed to do?"

"Jason, think. If I have to keep repeating myself, that confirms that you really don't care one bit about the way I feel."

Jason exhaled deeply. "Sheena, I'm at my wit's end. What do you *want* from me?"

"A faithful husband for starters," she whispered. Sheena glanced in the backseat again. It had grown quiet. "Now is not the time to discuss this, Jason. You don't realize how deep your voice gets when you get upset."

Jason peered in the backseat through the rear view mirror and released a deep-throated grunt. Pulling into the hospital parking lot, he said, "All right, guys, this is it." He helped everybody out of the SUV. "You kids will probably have to wait in the lobby. I'm depending on you guys to be good while we visit Grandpa, okay?"

"I'll be in charge, Daddy," replied Joseph. "Since I'm the oldest, they have to listen to me, right?"

"You aren't our boss," Jeremiah retorted.

"And you sure can't tell me what to do," Jessica announced with her little hands on her hips. Reana stood quietly by her mother's side and didn't say anything.

Jason smiled at his children. "Okay, okay, that's enough bickering. J, you can be in charge only if you manage everything well. Don't try to bully your brother, sister, and cousin. You got me?"

Joseph liked being in charge. "Got you, Dad."

Sheena intervened. "Someone will be looking out for you guys, too, so be on your best behavior."

Cathy, Sheena and Jason took the elevator upstairs and walked down the long corridor to I.C.U. Jason put his arm around Sheena's waist and noticed how she tensed.

Catherine met them at the door. She hugged Cathy tightly. "Hi, baby. It's good to see you. How's my baby girl doing?"

"I'm fine, Momma. The question is, how is Daddy?"

"Your daddy's doing much better," Catherine beamed. "The doctor said his vitals are good, and if he keeps improving they'll transfer him from I.C.U. to a regular room."

"That's good, Momma. Has there been any sign of him coming out of the coma?"

"Jason saw him move his hand slightly yesterday. He hasn't moved today, that I'm aware of anyway. But I talk to him constantly and I believe that he's aware of my presence. It'll only be a matter of time." She turned to Jason. "That pretty little nurse that was here yesterday when you were here has been taking good care of my Jacob. She's just as sweet as she can be. She must be one of God's special angels." Catherine hugged Jason and rubbed him on his back.

"What pretty little nurse?" Sheena asked Catherine while her eyes switched to Jason, checking his reaction.

Jason's jaw line hardened. They both ignored Sheena's inquiry. "She's just doing her job, Momma. I'm glad to hear that Daddy's improving though."

Catherine walked over to Sheena and hugged her. As usual, Sheena grew rigid. Catherine noticed the deep circles under Sheena's eyes. "How are you doing tonight, baby?"

"I'm doing well, Mrs. Grey," Sheena replied as she pulled away from Catherine.

"You look a little tired and peaked to me. Have you been getting enough rest? Is my son treating you okay?" Catherine shot Jason a suspicious look.

"He's . . . your son, Mrs. Grey. I'm sure he's kept you posted," Sheena replied sarcastically.

Catherine's eyes darted from Sheena to Jason. Jason looked away from her. Sheena could tell by their body language that Catherine knew what was going on. She was convinced that Catherine did not mind that Jason had a mistress. Catherine didn't try to hide the fact that she was not very fond of Sheena and that she tolerated her only because of the children.

Catherine laughed sheepishly. "Sheena, Jason is a good man. I hope you know that. He wouldn't do anything to hurt you."

"So you've told me." Sheena walked past Catherine and stood beside Jacob's bed. "He looks a lot better than he did last night." She rubbed Jacob's arm gently. "You are going to be fine, Daddy Grey. Many prayers have gone up for you. I want you to keep the faith and pray too, okay?" Sheena felt everyone's eyes on her back; she felt isolated. *I've got to get out of here.* "Jason, I am going down to check on the children. I'll be back shortly."

Jason scratched his head. He didn't know how to respond; it seemed as though he irritated her, no matter what he did. "All right, baby, I'll just sit here and talk to Momma and Cathy until you get back." They waited until Sheena was well out of earshot before either of them spoke.

"Jason," Cathy spoke up first. "What in the world is going on with you?"

Jason exchanged glances with his mother. "What are you talking about, sis?"

"Don't play innocent with me, Jay. Sheena told me about your little girl toy."

"She did what?"

"Yes. Sheena told me that you were messing around with some woman. She said you come home late every night and that she knows that work is certainly not the reason why."

Jason looked at Cathy defensively. "Sheena doesn't know what she's talking about. She's always been a jealous woman. Lately, she's been paranoid with jealousy. You saw how she reacted when Momma mentioned Daddy's nurse."

"She's not paranoid, Jason."

"Cathy, you have just become *hard* since Frank left you."

"First of all, Frank didn't leave me, I put his controlling butt out. And second, don't try to flip the script. We're talking about you."

Jason dropped his head shamefully. He'd never been able to deceive Cathy before, so he wasn't about to try to now. "I am seeing someone, Cathy, but it's not what you think. I'm not running around with some floozy."

"Who is she then, some beauty queen that works in the bank?"

"No, she's someone that I used to date a long time ago."

"That's even worse, Jay. Does Sheena know her?"

"She knows her indirectly."

"What does that mean?"

"Sheena knew of our relationship when we were in college."

Cathy thought back for a moment. "Oh. no, Jay. I know you aren't hung up with her again."

"Don't forget to tell her the rest, Jason," Catherine said, shaking her head.

"Momma, you know about this?" Cathy said to her mother.

"Your brother told me about it two days ago."

"Momma, I bet that's why Sheena is so distant to you. I'm sure she has put two and two together. The way you are always rubbing it in that 'Jay is a good man,' she probably thinks that you are cloaking for him."

"I wouldn't do anything like that. All I try to do is assure Sheena that Jason loves her, because like Jason said, she *is* a tad bit jealous."

"Everybody knows that you spoiled Jason rotten, Momma. He is self-centered and, and . . . highfalutin too."

Jason interrupted Cathy. "Hey! Girl you need to watch your mouth. Why are you and Momma talking about me in the third person anyway?"

Cathy gave him the "talk to the hand" sign.

Jason lamented. "All y'all women are some vicious hyenas when it serves your purpose, aren't you?"

Both women ignored him.

Cathy turned her back to Jason and faced Catherine. "Sheena can see how you pamper him. All she hears from you is, 'Jason this, and Jason that.' It wouldn't hurt for you to consider her feelings sometimes. Why don't you try being nicer to her, Momma?"

Catherine sighed. "I try to be nice to her, but it's not easy. You saw how sarcastic she was to me."

"I guess she *was* sarcastic to you. You shouldn't have made that remark about how tired she looked," Cathy told her mother.

"Cathy, that girl has been distant to me since the first time I met her. She's not distant like that toward Jacob. She acts like she loves him to pieces."

"Momma, are you jealous of Sheena and Daddy?"

"Honey, please!"

Jason interrupted their conversation again. "You two need to stop. This is ridiculous. Why can't the two of you get along? I don't think that I've ever been in the room with you two for longer than ten minutes before you were arguing."

Catherine and Cathy looked at Jason intently. "We weren't arguing," they said simultaneously.

"We are just having a mother-daughter chat," Catherine declared.

Jason scowled. "You could have fooled me."

"Anyway," Cathy spoke up, "we were talking about *you,* not Momma and me. Don't try to change the subject." Cathy folded her hands on her stomach and looked Jason directly in his eyes. "Now, what is the *rest* that you are supposed to tell me?"

"Now, Cathy, don't blow a gasket when I tell you this." Jason took a deep breath. "Ruby and I have a daughter together."

"You have a *what* together?"

"A daughter."

"Momma, is Jay joking?"

"No," Catherine said wearily.

"How long have you known about this, Momma?"

"Two nights ago when he informed me about his reunion with Ms. Ruby Dickens."

Cathy flopped down in a chair. "Jay, how long have you known about this daughter?"

"About three months now. Ruby sprang it on me a month after we started seeing each other. I was just as shocked as you are. I had no idea I had fathered another child."

"How old is this child?"

"Eleven. Ruby said she found out she was pregnant shortly after she moved back to Florida."

"Does Sheena know?" Cathy shook her head in disbelief while answering her own question. "Of course she doesn't know."

Jason shook his head too. "No, and I have to figure out a way to tell her soon. Ruby has already threatened to tell her; she's given me two weeks."

Cathy gasped. "Lord have mercy, Jay. I hope that Sheena can take it. She's already hurt by your infidelity.

"The best thing for you to do is sit her down and talk to her. First of all, you need to stop disrespecting her with your lies and admit that you are cheating on her, and if she's still calm enough to listen to you, pray that God will guide you on how to break the news to her."

Jason looked at Cathy as though she was an alien. "*Pray?*"

"Yes, pray. If you ever needed to pray, now is the time."

Catherine agreed. "That's what I've been trying to tell him." She gave Cathy and Jason a quick nod toward the door.

Sheena walked into the room and looked from Cathy, to Catherine to Jason. Her eyes rested on Jason. "What's going on?"

"Oh, nothing much," Jason replied. "We were just talking about old times." It was a partial truth.

The nurse came in and informed them that visiting hours were over.

"I'll be staying here again tonight," Catherine reminded Jason. "Your sisters, Aretha, Shirley, and Terri, will be driving in together some time tonight. They are going to be staying at the house. They know where the key is, so they'll let themselves in."

"Is Jonathan coming home, Momma?" Cathy asked.

"Yes, he is, but he couldn't get a flight out of Germany until tomorrow, so he won't get here until sometime Sunday afternoon."

"Oh, good. It'll be a family reunion. It's not a good reason to get together, but it will be when Daddy wakes up."

"Okay, guys, I'll see you all tomorrow," Catherine sighed. "I'll keep you informed if anything changes." The three of them looked at Catherine strangely. "I mean in the event your Daddy wakes up during the night."

"All right, Momma," Jason said as he kissed her on the cheek. He put his arm around Sheena's waist as they walked down the corridor. Again, he noticed her stiffen.

They gathered the children, stopped by a fast food restaurant, ordered to-go meals for the children, and headed home.

"It sure is quiet in this car," Jason joked. The children had half-eaten their meals and fallen asleep. Cathy pretended to be sleep too. He reached for Sheena's hand. She eased her hand into her pocket and stared straight down the road.

It's going to be a cold night, Jason thought as he made his way home.

Chapter 15

By the time they arrived home from the hospital, it was nine-forty-five. Sheena went upstairs and helped the children get ready for bed. Jason and Cathy were downstairs. They had ordered a pizza for their dinner. While they set the table with paper plates and cups, they quietly discussed Jason's outside child.

"Jay, how in the world are you going to handle this news? I can tell that Sheena has already reached her breaking point with you."

"How do you know this? Has she told you something that I don't know about?"

"No; no more than the fact that she knows you are having an affair with someone. I can tell by the way she reacts to you. It doesn't take a rocket scientist to figure out that she's on the edge."

"I know. She acts as though she can't stand for me to touch her. I don't want to lose my wife, but I've got to find a way to break this news to her gently."

"There *is* no gentle way. Just be honest with her and pray that she doesn't go off on you."

"Now that you mention 'going off,' she's had several dreams of killing me."

"Oh?" Cathy eyebrows shot up.

"She's awakened screaming on several occasions from the nightmare. She said that she had shot me in the back and I was lying on the floor dead in a pool of blood."

"That's awful, Jay. Sometimes our dreams can be warnings. I certainly hope that hers was just a nightmare."

"I'm sure that's all it was." Jason laughed. "Can you imagine mousy Sheena shooting me in the back?"

"When you've hurt a person bad enough, you can't predict what they might do. Sometimes quiet people can hurt you the worst because they keep their feelings bottled up inside. You know the old cliché about still waters running deep."

"Yeah, that might be true, but I don't believe Sheena could do something like that."

"With the news you have to spring on her, it could be the catalyst to the dream. Just stay prayed up, and from now on, be more respectful to her."

"You don't think that I respect my wife?"

"You put on a good show out in public. But I have noticed how you demean her when you're at home. Try not to be condescending to her when you speak to her. I heard you guys' conversation on the way to the hospital. She has a valid point."

"What were you doing eavesdropping?"

"No. As loud as you were talking, I didn't have to eavesdrop. Besides, I have my own problems; I don't need to listen to yours. The point is, the way you relate to your wife during the day is integral to how she responds to you in bed. In other words, making love begins long before you get in bed at night."

"All women think alike, don't they? Sheena complains all the time that I disrespect her constantly, but I'm nice to her when we go to bed. What's a man suppose to do to get his wife to give him some loving?"

Cathy held up her fingers to demonstrate her point. "Stop cheating for one. Number two, stop lying to her. Number three, respect her, and four, give her some quality time."

"The reason that I'm cheating is because she's not taking care of business."

"That's a bunch of bologna and you know it! Why is it when men cheat, they try to blame their wives for their weakness? You cheat because you *want* to. I bet you didn't have any complaints about Sheena until you ran into that hot tail Ruby again, did you?"

Jason shrugged his shoulder. "Sheena is all right, but she just doesn't have it like Ruby's got it."

"Well, I guess your libido is going to make your decision for you."

"What decision?"

"Jay, Sheena is thinking about divorcing you. Are you willing to let her go for that sleazy Ruby? You know as well as I do that all Ruby wants is money and a chance to live Sheena's life."

"I have already told Ruby over and over that I'm not going to leave my wife for her. She just wants to be with me and let her daughter, *our* daughter get to know me."

"Jay, you are a highly intelligent man, but you are not using the common sense God gave you. How long do you think that she is going to be willing to be the other woman?"

"Ruby will have to accept my position for what it is. She knows that I am a married man. I love Sheena too much to give her up just for a good roll in the hay."

"So you do love Sheena?"

"Of course, I do. What did you think? I've always loved her and I always will."

Cathy threw her hands up in the air. "Maybe I'm just slow or confused, but brother, you are going to have to enlighten me. Here you are with a wonderful wife who loves you with all her heart. She seemingly does everything that she knows how to do to please you and is a good mother to your children. She's independent; she knows that she could stay at home and depend on you for finances, but she doesn't because she desires to be your helpmeet. She's a virtuous wife to you, Jay. What more do you want?"

"I don't want anything more. I can't explain it so that it will make sense to you. I didn't intend to get involved with Ruby again, it was just something that happened."

"Nothing just happens. Your involvement with her was orchestrated. She probably planned it out carefully and you fell for it just like a sheep going to slaughter."

"Momma thinks the same way you do. She thinks the way Ruby suddenly showed up in town was too much of a coincidence. The more that I think about it, the more I'm convinced that Momma might be right."

"Whatever the case may be, the fact is, she didn't put a gun to your head and force you to go to bed with her. That was on *you*. You are just as guilty as she is for getting involved with her. No, you are guiltier, because you knew you had a wife and three kids at home. You *wanted* to be with her. You just thought you could have your cake and eat it too."

Jason sat at the table and rubbed his eyebrows. "I can't argue with you. You are right as rain. Before we got together, I thought about my marriage for a minute, but it's always been hard for me to resist Ruby. I guess she's just got what it takes to turn me on."

Cathy threw her hand up. "Yeah, yeah, whatever; I guess she does. She's even got a daughter by you so she can hang on to you. Don't think for one minute that she won't use that little girl for her trump card to keep you either."

"Yes, I've given that some thought too. I want to be a father to my daughter, but I don't want to be blackmailed by Ruby to stay with her so I can see my daughter."

"It looks like you have to do some praying, brother. How long did you think that you could keep up this charade?"

"What charade?"

"Don't get dense on me now. I'm talking about the charade of juggling two women at one time. Do you think Sheena is going to keep putting up with your infidelity?"

The telephone rang. Jason picked up the receiver to answer it. He heard Sheena say hello three times. The only reply on the other end was a click. Jason hung the phone up. *I hope that wasn't Ruby.* "No, I *know* she's not gonna put up with it," he told his sister, shaking off the feeling that Ruby was getting bolder. "I tried to end it with Ruby weeks ago. I was hoping that Sheena never found out."

"Well, it's too late for those hopes."

Jason took a deep breath. "Anyway, one night as I was walking out, I thought for the last time, she shocked me with the news about Cassandra."

"What did I say earlier? She played that trump card."

"I guess so."

"As far as Sheena goes, she already knows that there is somebody else. I'm sure she has known from the beginning. Men think that they can hide things from their wives, but they can't, especially if she is a praying woman. The Lord takes care of His children. And Sheena has a strong anointing of discernment."

Jason stood up so briskly that the chair he was sitting in fell over. "I get tired of you all talking about religion so much. That's what wrong with y'all. Your minds are on that Bible when they should be on what's going on in the world."

"You had better get your mind on the Bible and stop being so arrogant, Jay. You need to humble yourself and pray and go back to the Word of God, because you are going to need God to help you get through this situation."

Jason held up his hands in contempt. "Okay, Cathy; are you finished preaching now?"

"I'm not preaching. I'm just trying to get you to see the light. God loves you Jay, but He doesn't love what you are doing. I wish you would give your life back to Christ. Your life will be so much better, and you will have peace of mind and joy too."

"I have joy, and peace *too,* Cathy."

"You are fooling yourself. If you keep slipping around with that money hungry Ruby, she is going to make you more miserable than you were the first time you were with her. Handle your business, and get things right with God, then He'll make a way to fix things with your wife and miraculously work a way out for your daughter to be a part of you all's lives without you being physically involved with Ruby."

Jason had forgotten how exasperating Cathy could be when it came to her "religion." He felt the urge to get away and get some fresh air. He stood up to leave. "Cathy, all this talk about religion has made me lose my appetite."

"I'm not talking about *religion* Jay. I'm talking about you seeking a *personal relationship* with God."

"Look Cathy . . ." Jason couldn't think of a good response to his sister's persistent persuasion to convert him. "I'm going to go out for a while. When Sheena comes down, tell her that I said I'll be back shortly."

Cathy watched Jason as he walked toward the door. "Jay."

"What *now*?"

"Tell Sheena yourself."

Sheena had come down the back stairs entry to the kitchen. "Tell me what?" She walked up to Jason and put her hands on her hips.

"I was about to go out for a while, so I asked Cathy to let you know."

"Go out where? It's ten-thirty at night. Where are you going, Jason?"

"Just *out*, Sheena."

"Oh no, no, *no!* You aren't going anywhere, Jason Grey! I'm sick and tired of you walking out on me to be with that hussy. When the phone rang, I guess that was your signal to leave, wasn't it? Well, she is going to be disappointed tonight, because you aren't going anywhere."

"What are you talking about? What signal? I swear!" Jason threw his hands up in the air. "Your jealousy is driving you more paranoid by the minute. You need to stop this craziness."

Cathy looked at Jason and shook her head. "Jay, don't talk to your wife like that. It's so disrespectful."

"Cathy, I don't want to be rude in front of you, but Sheena is going off the deep end with this jealousy thing. I can't even go to the store without her accusing me of going out to meet someone."

Sheena challenged him. "So where were you going? Oh, let me guess, we are out of *eggs* again."

Highly frustrated, Jason blew a deep breath in Sheena's face. Usually Sheena would back away from him when he did this, but this time she stood her ground.

"I'm out of this." Cathy sat back down to eat her meal. "All I can say, Jason, is get yourself together. Don't ruin a good thing."

Jason headed for the door. Sheena followed him. Cathy proceeded to eat her pizza, but dropped it back on the plate when she heard Jason shout, "Sheena! What's wrong with you?"

"You try to walk out that door and I'll show you better than I can tell you." To Cathy's surprise, Sheena had the tip of a butcher's knife pointed at Jason's neck.

Chapter 16

The men in the club swarmed around Ruby like bees. Several women watched her like a hawk, afraid that she would take their men away from them.

Excusing herself from the men at the bar, Ruby said, "I'll be back shortly, guys. I need to freshen up." She sashayed into the powder room, touched up her makeup and then relaxed in the elegantly decorated ladies' room for a few minutes. A couple of the women followed her inside and sat near her, pretending that they were reapplying their makeup. But Ruby knew that they were keeping tabs on her to make sure that she did not leave with their men. This was comical to Ruby.

She opened her cell phone and dialed Jason's house. Jason had refused to give the number to her; he told her that he wasn't going to disrespect his wife that way. That didn't stop her from getting it anyway. Ruby always considered herself to be clever. She smiled inwardly, remembering how she got the number. After they had made love one night and Jason had fallen asleep, Ruby scanned through the contacts on his cell phone until she found the listing for his home. Then she entered and saved the number on her cell phone.

Jason's home phone rang twice as Ruby sat with her cell nestled close to her ear, still aware of the nosy women who'd followed her into the restroom to "powder their noses." On the third ring, Sheena answered, saying hello three times. Ruby was tempted to ask for Jason, just to hear his wife's reaction, but decided against that. Instead, she pressed the END button on her phone.

She wouldn't stir the water today because she'd promised Jason that she would give him two weeks to tell Sheena about Cassandra. But if he failed to follow through, she planned to drive up to the house and introduce herself to Sheena in person.

Ruby stood up and smirked at the other women. She intentionally sang the lyrics to the song, "Love the One You're With," just loud enough for the other women to hear her as she walked back into the club.

Chapter 17

Cathy eased from her chair and stood a safe distance in front of Sheena. Jason stood perfectly still with the look of utter disbelief on his face.

"Sheena, honey, please put the knife down," Cathy pleaded. "I know that you are hurting, but please don't do this. Sheena, please . . ."

Sheena had a blank look on her face as though she was in a trance. Seconds later, she lowered the knife and laid it on the counter. "Jesus!" She focused on Jason. "Look what I've let you reduce me too. Lord, God, help me!"

Jason backed away from Sheena like a baby who had touched a hot flame. Meanwhile, Cathy led Sheena to the kitchen table to sit down. "It's going to be all right, honey. Just sit here and calm down. Take some deep breaths and exhale slowly." They sat at the table silently for many minutes.

Easing out of the door, Jason sat in his car in the garage, shocked by his wife's unusual behavior. After a brief silence, Jason heard laughter coming from the kitchen. He was perplexed that one minute, Sheena was about to cut his throat and the next minute, she was laughing hysterically. As curious as he was, he refused to go back inside to see what was going on. He reclined his car seat all the way down and tried to relax.

After Sheena stopped laughing, she apologized to Cathy. "I am so sorry that you witnessed that, Cathy. Please forgive me."

"I'm not sorry. What if I hadn't been here? Oh, I hate to think what could have happened."

"I guess it is a blessing that you were here, girl. If you hadn't been, I could have killed your brother. That would have been tragic for everybody. Think about the children, Cathy. Oh, Lord, have mercy!" Sheena's laughter was gone and her hands trembled.

"Maybe you should go lie down."

"I'm okay. I haven't gone off the deep end yet. It's just that when the phone rang and I could hear her breathing on the other end, it just made me so angry."

"Yeah, I can imagine."

"What really made me angry was when I came downstairs and he was about to leave. I'm sure he was going to meet her because I heard him when he picked up the extension." Sheena inhaled deeply. "I just lost it. I have never done anything that stupid and reckless before."

"You are under a tremendous amount of pressure, Sheena."

"You're right, I am. I need to get away from him." Tears streamed down her cheeks. "I think that I will go and visit my mother this weekend. I told her that I would wait until next weekend to come because I wanted to be around to see how your father was doing. But I need to go now. I'm packing my luggage and the children's and driving up there tomorrow morning."

"I think that's a good idea."

"If it wasn't so late, I'd leave right now." Sheena smiled through her tears. "It was rich to see the fear in his face though. That's what he gets for calling me a dizzy broad all the time."

"That's cruel."

"That's your brother."

"That scene was scary. I think you shook him up pretty good."

"You *think*?"

They both laughed, but the laughter was cut short.

"Seriously, though, Sheena, I think it would benefit you to get away for a weekend."

"I know that it would. In fact, my sanity dictates that I get away."

At that moment, Jason entered the house and both women looked at each other. He peered at them but didn't utter a word to either of them. He walked upstairs, taking the steps two at a time.

Cathy whispered. "I thought he'd left."

"So did I. I guess I need to go up and apologize to him."

"No, don't apologize right now. Give him time to absorb this and let him clear his mind."

"Yes, I suppose you're right."

"I'm still hungry," Cathy joked. "You think you can let me eat my pizza this time without flinging a knife out?"

Sheena smiled. "I'll try and contain myself."

Cathy reheated the pizza. "I'm putting two slices in here for you, okay?"

"I'm not really hungry."

"You should try to eat something. You are already stressed out, starving yourself will only make you more prone to the stress." Sheena didn't reply. When Cathy turned around to look at her, she had tears in her eyes. "Stop that now. You are going to make me cry." She handed Sheena a napkin to wipe her eyes. Cathy tried to make the atmosphere lighter. "Here are your two *thin* slices of pizza. I've got three huge slices, I need to eat so I won't be so skinny." They both laughed because at five-foot-five and 175 pounds, Cathy was hardly skinny.

Sheena managed to force the first slice of pizza down. "I can't eat anymore. I think that it's time for me to go to bed and relax my mind. I'll see you in the morning."

"Okay, honey. I'll clean the kitchen up and then I'm going to bed too." Cathy sighed. "It's been a long day."

Sheena threw her leftovers away. "Cathy, I apologize again for my behavior. You have barely been in town for twelve hours, and I've acted like some crazed drama queen, instead of making you comfortable in our home."

Cathy shook her head. "Don't stress out about it, Sheena. This too, will pass." She hugged Sheena. "Now, get some rest."

"Good-night. Thanks for being so understanding. God bless you."

"God bless you too." Cathy silently prayed for Sheena and Jason as she cleaned the kitchen.

When Sheena entered the bedroom, she found Jason sprawled across the bed, pretending to look at TV.

"Jason," she called his name softly.

He didn't reply, but he stared at her.

"I'm sorry. I don't know what came over me."

He continued to stare at her as though she was a science experiment gone badly.

"Jay?"

Although it was his nickname, he preferred Sheena to call him by his full name. She always enunciated his name and other words perfectly; that was one of the things about her that he admired. "Sheena, I don't want to talk about it right now. We'll talk in the morning."

Sheena headed for the bathroom without saying anything else.

Jason noticed the tears rolling down her face. "Sheena."

She stopped in her tracks but didn't turn around to face him. "Yes, Jason?" she whispered through tears.

"For whatever it's worth. I'm sorry too. I'm sorry I have hurt you so badly."

Sheena nodded her head and walked into the bathroom. She took a long shower. When she came out, Jason was lying perfectly still and was making a light snoring sound. She got in bed, peeked over at him and whispered good-night.

Jason was only pretending to be asleep. He didn't reply. *It's going to be hard to turn my back and go to sleep on her after tonight.*

Chapter 18

At 4:05 A.M., Sheena awoke from a fitful sleep. After an hour of lying there just listening to Jason's snoring, she arose and crept into the huge walk-in closet and began packing her clothes. She eased in the bathroom, took a quick wash up, and then dressed in a sweat suit, not bothering to apply her makeup as she slipped out of the bedroom. Jason didn't even stir.

Sheena walked quietly down the hallway and peeped in on Jessica, Jeremiah, and Joseph. They were sleeping peacefully. She knocked quietly on Cathy's bedroom door.

Cathy sat up impetuously. Reana was curled up next to her.

"Who is it?"

"It's me, Cathy," Sheena whispered. "May I come in?"

"Sure, come on in." She gave Sheena a puzzled look. "What's wrong? Are you okay? Did you and Jay have an argument or something?" "No, not at all. Jason is sleeping like a log. I couldn't sleep though." She hesitated. "Cathy, may I ask a huge favor of you?"

"Of course. I'll help if I can."

"I can't stay here another minute. I've already packed a bag for my trip. Will it be too much of an imposition for you to stay here and keep the children while I'm gone?"

"No, of course not, but I thought you had planned to take them with you."

"I had; but I don't think my mind is in any condition to deal with them properly. I just need a day or two to myself."

"Sheena, you know I'll be glad to keep them. Are you going off to be alone? I thought you were going to visit your parents for the weekend."

"I am. My parents will give me as much space as I need. When I'm ready to talk, Momma will be there to listen. Daddy will be pacing around outside tinkering with his old truck, but he'll be there if I need him."

"Oh. I feel better knowing that you won't be alone. Are you leaving *now*?"

"Yes, I want to get an early start before Interstate 40 gets too crowded. Lord willing, I'll be there by seven-thirty."

"Have you already called your parents?"

"No, I'll call them on my way."

"What did Jason have to say about you leaving?"

"I haven't told him. We only spoke a few words to each other last night. He was sleeping so soundly, I didn't have the heart to wake him up."

"He always was a sound sleeper."

"Yeah, but I think he's still jumpy from last night. He looked at me like I had two heads when I went in the room."

"He probably is jumpy, but I'm sure he considered the fact that he provoked this incident too."

"Maybe. In any case, I should get going. I'll call to let you all know that I arrived safely. Kiss the kids for me and tell them that I love them and I'll be back Sunday afternoon."

"Sure. What do you want me to tell Jason?"

Sheena hesitated. "Just tell him that I went to visit my parents. I'd better go now. Make yourself at home and if you need anything, please feel free to call me. My parents' number is in the address book in the kitchen drawer. And you have my cell number. Bye now."

"Bye, Sheena." Cathy got out of bed and hugged her. "Take care of yourself. Be blessed."

"You too." Sheena walked quietly back down the hallway. Through the slightly open door,

she could see that Jason was still sleeping. She
tiptoed downstairs and went out the front exit;
this time, unlocking the car door with the key
because she didn't want to chance the horn beep-
ing. She cranked up the quiet, smooth running
engine and drove away.

Chapter 19

Sheena pulled into her parents' driveway at 7:35 A.M. She sat in the SUV for about five minutes, basking in the warm fall sunrays. The crisp fresh mountain air always seemed to calm her spirit. She took a deep breath and relaxed her head against the seat. The song, "I Will Lift Up Mine Eyes, Psalm 121," playing on the CD, was pertinent.

Sheena scanned the mountains that seemed to blaze with beauty in the morning sun. Suddenly, she felt the urge to praise God. "Oh, Lord, I love you. I praise your holy name. Hallelujah; you are an awesome God." She closed her eyes and sang along with the song. A sweet peace had overcome her, a peace she hadn't experienced in a long time.

"Lord, I want to thank you. I praise you for your mercy that's new every morning. How excellent is thy name in all the earth! Thank you for this peace, this joy that I feel. Only you can love me like you do, Jesus."

When she opened her eyes, she saw her mother standing in the doorway, smiling. Sheena checked to make sure she had engaged the parking brake, grabbed her purse and walked to the door. "Hi, Momma. I didn't realize you were standing in the door. How long have you been there?"

Her mother hugged her tightly. "Long enough to see you in the car giving God His praise. He is worthy to be praised, isn't He, baby?"

"Amen. I feel so relaxed. It seems as though these mountains, this awesome beauty that only God could have created, encourages me to praise Him."

"One glance at this grand view tends to have that effect." Lois looked up at the mountains admiringly. "I suppose we take 'em for granted because we live here, but once you take the time to enjoy this breathtaking canvas, you realize God *is* the *I am*."

Sheena agreed. "He is all that I need. I may *want* certain things, but God is all that I *need*."

"Glory to God in the highest." Lois surveyed Sheena. "I cooked a hearty breakfast for you, baby. I want you to sit down and eat every bite."

"I'm not hungry, Momma." Sheena stopped short as Lois opened the screen door for her.

"Wait a minute, Momma. I forgot to get my luggage."

"Don't worry about your suitcase right now. We can get it later." Lois nudged her gently inside. "Why aren't you hungry? Did you stop to get breakfast on your way here?"

"No. I don't have much of an appetite. I would like some coffee though, decaffeinated if you have it."

"Nonsense. You need to eat a good meal. You know I keep decaffeinated for you because Gerald and I don't drink that stuff." Lois looked Sheena up and down, inspecting her in the way only an overprotective mother would after her child comes into the house screaming from the pain of a fall. "Sheena, you have lost quite a bit of weight since I saw you last summer. Please sit down and enjoy this breakfast."

"Really, I'm not hungry."

"When did you eat last?"

Sheena shrugged. "Last night, I think. I ate a slice of pizza."

"Girl, if you don't sit your little butt down and eat, I'm going to spank your behind. I got up as soon as you called. I showered, tidied up your room and then I started breakfast so everything would be ready for you when you arrived."

"I didn't mean for you to go to any trouble for

me. I just wanted to come up here and relax for a couple of days."

"I haven't gone through any trouble. I wanted to cook for my daughter. Don't be selfish and disappoint your old momma now. You know how I am when I get disappointed," Lois smiled.

Sheena didn't want to disappoint her mother, although she knew that Lois was using psychology on her to get her to eat. "Okay, I guess I can stand to eat something. I noticed that my pants were a little baggy on me."

"I would say more than a *little* baggy. Those sweat pants are about to lap on you." Lois pulled the elastic band on Sheena's sweat pants and then let it slip from her fingers, causing a popping sound. Sheena laughed lightly. Lois walked into the hallway, and into the dining room. "Come on in the dining room, honey. Remember how we used to have breakfast in here every Saturday morning?"

"I do. I miss those days sometimes. I didn't realize until now how much I miss having someone to take care of me."

"Well, you're here now and nothing pleasures me more than taking care of my baby."

"Thanks, Momma. You are such a sweet person."

"So are you, Sheena. You're one of a kind."

"Where's Daddy?"

"Where else? He's out there in his barn, playing with his toys."

"Toys?"

"Yeah, baby. Between his lawnmower, that old truck, or his tools . . . he's forever tinkering on something."

Sheena sighed. "Well, at least you know where he is." She rubbed her temples.

"Oh, I'm not complaining. I just wish that he would tinker on me more."

Sheena looked at her mother in disbelief. "Momma!"

"Don't Momma me, girl. I haven't conked out yet." Lois and Sheena laughed together.

"You are still funny, Momma. I haven't laughed like that in a while."

"You know what the Word says in Proverbs 17:22, baby girl. *A merry heart doeth good like a medicine; but a broken spirit drieth the bones.*"

Sheena's countenance changed. "I can vouch for that."

"That's going to change, little girl. You are going to be healed from all that pain in Jesus' name. It may take a little time, but God is able to heal all of your wounds. I consulted the concordance in the Bible and I found lots of scriptures for you to read while you're here. You are going to feel much better when you leave too."

Sheena smiled again. "Momma, you're still calling me little girl after all these years."

"I know you're a grown woman, grown folk as they say, but you are still my little girl. Now, let's eat; our food is getting cold."

"Aren't you going to call Daddy to eat with us?"

"He'll come in at eight o'clock. He is so predictable, you can set your watch by him."

"At least he's dependable."

"Yep. That's what I love about him. He's always been dependable."

"That's sweet, Momma."

"What is?"

"To hear you speak so well of Daddy after all of these years."

"He deserves it. He has been there for me through thick and thin."

"I wish that I could say the same for Jason. He's a great provider and he loves our children to death, but he hasn't treated me so well."

"It's not over yet, Sheena. I have a feeling that he is going to learn how to really appreciate you and love you before it's over."

"I doubt it."

"You have to exercise faith, baby. Things aren't always as simple as they appear."

"Oh? You sound like you know something that I don't."

"No, I don't. I'm speaking from my experiences with life."

"You and Daddy haven't had any serious problems in your marriage have you? You always seemed comfortable with each other to me."

"We are now, but things were terrible with us for a while. If it wasn't for Gerald seeking the Lord and asking for direction, we wouldn't be together today."

"That's surprising. I always thought you were the one with the relationship with God."

"No, baby girl. I was the wild one. I thank Jesus every day for my husband. He convinced me to seek a relationship with the Lord."

"Oh? What a surprise."

"You shouldn't be surprised. Gerald has always been the peaceful, quiet one; you know that. I was a force to be reckoned with until I gave my life over to Christ."

"That must have been before my time, huh?"

"Not really. By the time you came along, I had changed some, but I still used to give your daddy a fit. I think he spent a lot of nights praying for me."

Sheena smiled. "Momma, when you get angry, you do tend to get a little outrageous sometimes."

Sheena sat down at the country styled oak table and both women prepared their plates.

"I do; but your Daddy puts up with me somehow. I suppose that's why he's always outside tinkering in that barn."

"He's happy though, isn't he?" Sheena put a fork of homemade hash browns into her mouth; she swallowed, and chewed a piece of thick sliced country bacon, followed by scrambled eggs, and homemade blueberry muffins. "Boy, this food is *so* good!"

"Thank you, baby, I'm glad you're enjoying it. You need to eat some more." Lois spooned more hash browns and put two more pieces of bacon on Sheena's plate before answering her daughter's earlier question. "Oh, yeah. I make sure he's happy every chance I get." Lois stood up to clear the dishes. I treat him right, if you know what I mean." Lois shook her abundant hips playfully.

Sheena doubled over with laughter. "You are something else."

"Let me stop acting silly. I shouldn't even be discussing our private life with you anyway. Look at you over there blushing. You're red as a beet."

"I'm fine, Momma. It's good to know that somebody has a good marriage."

"You can too, baby. God is able to do anything. He saved my marriage and He can do the same thing for you, if that's what you desire."

"As if your marriage was ever in any real trouble."

"Sheena, when and if the time is right, I may share some things with you. But right now, we are not going to keep talking about such things."

Sheena stared at the floor.

"Cheer up little girl. I'm going to put some praise music on and we are gonna go sit in the living room and enjoy our morning."

"Whatever you say, Momma." Sheena sighed.

"If you want to, later on we can go to the mall. I need some new shoes and you know how much fun it is to go shoe shopping."

"That sounds great. I could use some new shoes for the winter season."

"Good, we'll go whenever you're ready."

"Momma, do you mind if I go outside and lie on the hammock? I want to relax and enjoy this cool mountain breeze."

"Baby, you do whatever makes you happy. Stay out there as long as you like." Lois looked at the clock on the wall when she heard Gerald walk in the house through the kitchen door. "Right on time," she grinned. "Are you ready to eat, Gerald?"

Gerald was a man of few words. "Yeah, babe." He walked over to Sheena and pecked her on her cheek. "Hey, pumpkin; I'm glad to see you."

"Hi, Daddy. I'm glad to see you too. You have been working hard this morning, haven't you?"

"Not really." He patted her on her arm, his form of communication for "I love you." Gerald disappeared across the hall, into the half bath to wash his hands. When he returned to the dining room, he sat while Lois prepared his plate.

Sheena stood up and put her dirty dishes on the counter near the sink. "Momma, I'll wash the dishes."

Lois shook her head in protest. "I got this. Go on outside and lay in the hammock, baby. Relax yourself."

"Are you sure you don't want me to wash them?"

Lois looked sternly at Sheena and pointed toward the back door. Sheena pecked her on the cheek and walked outside to the hammock in the backyard. She eased into the hammock, closed her eyes and listened to the wind whispering softly through the trees. It was as though God was lulling her into a sweet peaceful sleep.

Chapter 20

Jason rolled over and glanced at the clock. "It's eight-twenty-three? I can't believe I slept this late." He usually woke up at six-thirty on Saturday mornings to mow the grass. Once he finished mowing, he would take a shower, and usually go out and order breakfast for the family. After they ate, he would take Sheena's vehicle to get it detailed and then repeat the process with his own car.

Jason's eyes roamed the room. He didn't see Sheena. She usually slept late on Saturday mornings, at least until nine. He got out of bed and walked toward the bathroom, assuming she was in there. The door was wide open. There were no signs of her having taken a shower, so he figured she must have slept in Jessica's room again. Jason shaved, took his shower and got dressed. He put on his favorite pair of comfortable jeans and a black crew neck sweater that showed off his abundant muscles and chiseled stomach. Then he put on some Nike sneakers.

Jason sprinted down the steps. He looked for the keys, but they weren't in the usual place. "Sheena, where are you? I'm about to take your truck to have it detailed.

What did you do with the keys?" When he didn't get a reply, he walked through the living room, crossed the foyer and entered the kitchen and den. Thinking that she was outside on the deck, or outside in the back yard, digging in her flower garden, Jason checked outside, but she was nowhere in sight. He sprinted back upstairs and checked the children's rooms.

"Humph, that's odd." He went back downstairs and scoped the garage. When he opened the garage door, he remembered that he'd left her truck in the driveway the night before. He opened the front door, but the truck was not there. Jason figured she must have gone to the grocery store because sometimes she would leave early in the morning to beat the crowds. He decided to go have his car detailed first. He'd take care of hers later.

He hadn't driven out of his neighborhood before his cell phone rang. He looked at the window. "Why am I not surprised?" He flipped the phone open. "Yes, Ruby?"

"Don't answer me like that. I saw you and that ole crone getting in her car last night."

"Ruby, you need to watch your mouth about the way you talk about my wife. So that *was* you sitting outside my house last night."

"Darn straight. I told you not to play with me. The next time I'm coming up to the door and ringing the doorbell. And since when do you care about what I say about that frog?"

"It's too early in the morning to hear this crap. What do you want?"

"What do I *want*? You must be out of your freaking mind. What do you *think* I want?"

"Let me guess; some money."

"That too. You need to get your fine butt over here. I missed you last night."

"Yeah, right. What did you do last night after you staked my house out?"

"Not that it's any of your business, but I went to that new club downtown last night."

"Oh?" Jason frowned.

"Yep. I had a good time too. Danced my butt off. I met a lot of handsome men too." Ruby was trying to make Jason jealous. "I brought one home but he wasn't as good as you are in bed."

It worked. "Ruby, I know you aren't that sorry, are you?"

"Two can play that game, baby. If you can stay home and be with your wife, I can go out and get me a man too. What's good for the goose is good for the gander." Ruby knew how to get under Jason's skin.

"If I come over there and find somebody over there, I'm going to jack you and him both up."

"He's gone now, Jason. You know I just get what I want, then I ditch 'em." She laughed evilly through the phone and waited for his reaction.

"Ruby, I'm through with your trifling tail. I don't need a woman that I can't trust."

"And I don't need a part-time man. I need somebody who can be on the job whenever I need him to be."

Infuriated, Jason clicked the END button.

Ruby was lying on her couch, satisfied that she had made Jason jealous. She thought Jason knew her better than to believe that she would stoop low enough to bring some strange man home with her. She had no intentions of catching a fatal disease. Nor did she want to chance getting hacked up by some maniac.

She went into her tiny kitchen to make breakfast. There was a loud knock on the door, plus the person kept ringing the doorbell. "Who *is* it?" she asked, irritated by the constant ringing. She flung the door open. "What a surprise," she cooed. "What brings you by so early this morning?"

"Don't play with me, Ruby." Jason pushed past her and stormed to the bedroom.

Ruby followed him. "What is your malfunction? Didn't your momma give you any home training?"

"Evidently, yours didn't give you any." Satisfied that there weren't any signs of another man having been there, he gently pushed Ruby up against the wall.

Ruby responded eagerly. "She didn't. Let me show you just how little training I have."

After they finished their intimate rendezvous, Jason went into the bathroom to take a shower. She joined him.

"Jason, you know you need to go ahead and leave Sheena. She can't make you happy like I do."

"I can't do that, Ruby. I'm not going to leave my wife. I've told you that over and over."

Ruby quickly fired up. "You sorry dog! You came storming in here like a jealous crazy man, scared that I had been with somebody else, had your way with me and now you are going to tell me that you are not leaving that bony tail wife of yours?"

"You knew I was married before we started sleeping together, Ruby. I made it clear to you then, that we couldn't have a public relationship because of my wife. You said you were okay with that." Jason scanned Ruby's naked body.

In Ruby's eyes, Jason appeared to look down at her like she was a hooker. Ruby sailed on Jason like a panther. She beat him with her fist as hard as she could. "Oh, you *will* leave her, you sorry dog. Or she's gonna leave you, one; I'm going to make sure of that!"

Jason pushed Ruby off of him and stepped out of the shower. "Ruby, I don't hit women, but if you put your hands on me one more time, I'm not going to be responsible for my actions."

Ruby's fury increased. She followed him, walking through the house, dripping wet. "Get out of my house, Jason. Get out of my life too." She shoved him, causing him to stumble. Crying hysterically she said, "I'm too through with you. Get out!"

Jason gathered his things, and got dressed. "Ruby, I'm sorry. I shouldn't have let this situation get this far. Please forgive me. I realize now how much I've hurt you."

"Oh, but not as much as I'm going to hurt you."

"I'm sorry. I didn't realize how much you cared. I don't know how to say this . . ."

Ruby glared at Jason like an animal. "Just say it, Jason."

"We don't need to see each other anymore. It's obvious we're not good for one another."

"You might be right. Because if I keep seeing you and you keep playing with my feelings like this, I'm going to *kill* you; plain and simple."

Jason rubbed his head. "I didn't mean for this to happen, Ruby. We just . . . you know how we are. What about Cassandra?"

"What *about* her?"

"I would like to meet her and try to be a father to her."

"You're kidding, right? I don't want her to know your sorry behind."

"So, if we can't be together, then I can't see my daughter?"

Ruby scowled and her words were bitter. "That about sums it up."

"You know you're wrong."

"You know *you're* wrong for playing with my feelings."

Jason shook his head. "You're right. I'm sorry I did this to you." Jason's ego kicked in. "But you have some responsibility in this situation too, Ruby."

Ruby attempted to slap him, but he caught her hand. "Get out, you *pompous* snob!"

"Maybe when things cool down we can sit down like adults and discuss Cassandra and when I'm going to see her. I'm going to take care of my responsibilities to her, whether you want me to or not."

"Get out! I *hate* you, Jason." She picked up one of her expensive African figurines and threw it at him.

Jason barely ducked out of the way as the statue whirled by him and crashed into the wall. At that point, Jason knew it was time to go. He left without saying anything else.

Ruby screamed at him as he closed the door. "You haven't seen the last of me, Jason Grey!"

She grabbed a robe and wrapped it around herself and then walked in her spare bedroom and turned the computer on. She opened the file to his financial institution. "You doggone right you gonna take care of your responsibilities."

Ruby transferred several thousand dollars from the account to her account. The account she tampered with this time was Jason and Sheena's joint checking account. She figured she had better get all the money she could from his account. She knew he'd receive a statement any day, and once he detected the missing money, he would trace it to her.

Jason drove back home with his mind racing. When he walked back into the house, everyone was sitting at the kitchen table eating breakfast, except Sheena. It was then that he realized that her vehicle was still not in the driveway or the garage.

All the children ran up to him and hugged him. He greeted them all halfheartedly. "Where's your mother?"

Cathy answered for them. "She's gone to visit her parents. She should be back by late Sunday afternoon."

Jason was flabbergasted. "She didn't mention anything to me about going to visit her parents."

"Maybe she thought you were too busy to listen."

Jason glared at Cathy. "Cathy, don't start." Jason's forehead wrinkled. He exhaled loudly. "When did she leave?"

"She left around five something this morning. She asked me to take care of the children, so that's what I'm doing." Cathy stood up to take her plate to the sink. She gasped when she saw the left side of Jason's face. "What happened to your face? There's a dark bruise on it."

Jason ignored her remark. "I need to talk to my wife," he mumbled. He pulled his cell phone out and used the speed dial function to call Sheena's number. It rang, but went to voice mail. He dialed her parents' number and walked into the living room for privacy.

When Lois answered the phone, she refused to let him talk to Sheena. Jason hung up and went upstairs to shower again, just in case, to make sure he smelled fresh. He then changed clothes so he could drive to Sheena's parents' house.

As soon as he stepped back into the bedroom, the phone rang. *It's probably Sheena,* he thought to himself.

"Hi, Jason, I have good news!" It was his mother. "Your father woke up this morning. He's asking to see all of you guys. Your sisters are already on the way over here. You, Sheena, and Cathy need to get over here too."

"Is he doing all right, Momma?" Jason asked, cautiously.

"He's doing fine. I'll see you when you get here, son."

"I may not stay but a few minutes, Momma."

"Why?"

"Because I have to drive to Asheville to see Sheena."

"What in the world are you talking about?"

"Sheena's not here, Momma. She left early this morning to visit her parents. I just found out that she left and I need to talk to her pronto."

"Is her momma or father sick or something?"

"No Momma, she just went up there to visit them."

"That was sudden, wasn't it? She didn't say anything about it last night."

"I guess she just made up her mind to go this morning."

"And she didn't discuss it with you?"

"No. I was sleep when she left."

"That wife of yours does some strange things."

"Momma, don't talk about my wife like that."

"Oh, I get it. You must have done something to upset her and that's why she left you."

"Momma, Sheena didn't leave me; she just wanted to visit her parents."

"Uh-huh. You aren't fooling me, Jay. Where were you that you are just finding out that your wife is gone?"

"I'll see you in a few minutes, Momma."

"You don't have to answer. I told you that that hot potato was going to destroy your marriage, didn't I?"

"Later, Momma." Jason walked into the closet and packed an overnight bag. He had forgotten that he had promised to take the twins to the basketball game on Sunday. He took a deep breath. "I don't know how I could have been so stupid!"

Chapter 21

Sheena woke up feeling refreshed. She had dreamed that she and Jason were living together happily and peacefully. He had given his life to Christ, and moreover, he was working in the church as an usher.

As dreams can sometimes be confusing, Sheena didn't understand one part of it. There was a beautiful little girl that was in the house visiting them. The little girl was introverted and quite reserved when Sheena attempted to relate to her. Ironically, children tended to be drawn to Sheena; but this child seemed annoyed by her presence.

"Lord, I don't understand what that dream represents," Sheena whispered as she stretched on the hammock, "but my life is in your hands." She looked up at the mountains and took a deep breath and exhaled slowly. And then she prayed. "Lord, I thank you. You are so good to me. Bless my parents for being there for me, Jesus. Give them the desires of their hearts and please continue to let them live in good health."

Sheena lay on the hammock relaxing for a few minutes before she decided to get up and go inside. She looked at her watch. Two hours had passed. She had been more stressed out than she realized. She hadn't taken a nap outside since she was a little girl. She walked into the kitchen. "Momma, where are you?"

"I'm in the living room, baby."

Sheena joined her. "Momma, what on earth are you doing?"

"I'm looking at these old photos of you. You were such a pretty little girl."

"Only a mother could say that. You know as well as I do that I've never been pretty. Not even attractive for that matter."

"You were always pretty to me, and to your Daddy too. I'm disappointed to know that you are still self-conscious about the way you look."

"Momma, don't patronize me. I look in the mirror every day. I didn't inherit any of your mother's Cherokee Indian blood, the hair, or the looks. I don't even resemble you or Grandma. Sure, I may have a pleasant disposition, but you can't honestly sit here and tell me that you think I'm pretty."

"You *are* pretty. Girl, you may not be the most beautiful woman in the world, but you are beautiful to me. You are my daughter, so that makes you pretty to me."

"Like I said, no one can say that but my mother. Besides, you've always said that looks aren't everything, so I've learned to accept who I am."

"You look like your father; and I don't know a man handsomer than he."

"That's because you love him like you love me. I'm grateful for your love, too, Momma. I don't know what I would have done without you when I was growing up."

"I don't know what I would have done without you, little girl."

Sheena's phone rang. She took it out her purse and looked at the display. "It's Jason, Momma."

Lois watched Sheena as she paced the floor. "Are you gonna answer it?"

"No. I don't want to talk to him right now. I'll call him back later, maybe." Sheena checked her phone for missed calls. "I see where he's called several times."

"Well, I may as well tell you. He called here and I told him you were resting. He kept insisting that it was urgent he talks to you. I asked him had his father gotten any worse. He said he was stable but his condition is still serious."

"Thank God he hasn't taken a turn for the worse. I've been praying for him often."

Lois nodded. "Anyway, you know me; I asked him what was so urgent that he couldn't wait until you finished your nap?"

"What did he say?"

Lois mocked the way Jason talked in an articulate proper tone. "He said, 'It's imperative that I talk to my wife right away.'" Sheena smiled. "And then he asked me if I could please wake you up. I asked him if the children were all right."

"Were they?"

"He said they were fine and that his sister was taking care of them. So, I asked him again what was so urgent that it couldn't wait until you woke up."

"What was his reply?"

"He said, 'Mrs. Andrews, I just need to talk to my wife. Can you *please* put her on the phone?' I could tell that he was highly upset with me for questioning him the way I did, but I didn't give a flip. He's the reason that you are stressed out the way you are."

"If I know you, Momma, you gave him the third degree."

"You got that right. *You* might act like a kitten with him, but he's dealing with a lioness when he's talking to me."

"Momma, did he disrespect you?"

"Disrespect *me*? No, I'm sure he wanted to curse me out, but one thing I can give him credit for is that Jason has always been very respectful toward your father and me."

"That's good to know."

"Sheena, I'm not trying to tell you what to do, but you need to stop letting that man talk to you any ole way. You know I warned you about that when you first got married."

Sheena drooped down on the couch. "I remember," she lamented.

"It's all good and fine to try to be soft spoken and humble, but when he starts disrespecting you, you need to get him straight!"

"I have. Lately he's been very offensive, but he pushed me over the edge last night. I surprised myself at my reaction."

"What happened last night?"

Sheena filled her mother in on the occurrences from the night before.

"Sheena Ann Andrews, you have your mother's temper after all, don't you?"

"I suppose I did inherit some of your tenacity."

"Who knew? All this time, I thought you were a little kitten. You are a roaring tigress when you're pushed against a wall."

"I guess I am. Jason pushed my last tolerant nerve when he started walking out the door to meet that skank."

"I know he did. I thank God that Cathy was there to talk you down, though. I certainly don't want to be going to jail to see my child, or have to comfort my grandchildren after their mother killed their father."

"I don't want that to happen either. Now you can understand why I couldn't wait until next weekend to come here. I was on the brink of insanity."

"You don't have to explain it to me. I'm just glad the Lord looked out for you, and I'm glad you had sense enough to get away from the situation before it built into something else."

"Amen." Sheena opened her phone and listened to Jason's messages. "He really sounds desperate, Momma. Do you think that I should call him?"

"Don't lay that burden on me, baby. I'll do anything that I can to help you relax so you can heal and recover, but telling you how to run your business is not a part of the deal."

Sheena closed the phone. "I'll call him back later. Are you ready to go to the mall?"

"As soon as I freshen up." Lois stood and walked toward the stairs. "Give me ten minutes."

"Okay. But take your time, Momma." Sheena went to her truck and got her luggage. She went upstairs to her room, freshened up and changed into a neater outfit. When she got back downstairs, Lois was sitting on the couch waiting for her. "I'm ready when you are, Momma."

"Okay, let me go out here to see if your daddy wants us to bring him something back."

"I'm going to the car."

Lois nodded.

Sheena made her way to the truck where she sat and waited for her mother to join her. As soon as she settled in comfortably, her phone rang. It was Jason.

Chapter 22

During the time that Sheena and her mother sat on the couch talking, Jason, Cathy, and the children were on their way to the hospital to see Jacob. Jason had put his overnight bag into the car, anticipating leaving the hospital and driving to Asheville.

"Jason," Cathy spoke, "I really don't think you should go running up there behind Sheena. Give her a day or so to relax."

"I appreciate your advice, but I really need to talk to her." "What's so important that it can't wait until she returns tomorrow night?" "Cathy, I'm not being nasty to you, but this is really none of your business."

"It was some of my business last night." Cathy lowered her voice. "Jay, if I hadn't been there, Sheena might have slit your throat," she whispered.

Jason peered in the rear view mirror at the children. "Don't bring that up in the car, Cathy.

I don't want them to know what happened last night."

Cathy looked in the backseat. Joseph and Jeremiah were engrossed with the game on their Nintendo DS. Jessica and Reana were busy dressing up their dolls. "They didn't hear me, Jay." Cathy turned the radio up a little. "You still don't get it, do you?"

"Get what?"

"Your wife was at the breaking point last night. Heck, she had broken through the point and fallen down the mountain."

"I *know* this, Cathy. Why do you think that I'm trying to communicate with her?"

"You should have done that a long time ago."

"I don't need your judgmental criticism right now. I realize that I have made a mess with my wife. Why do you think that I'm trying to contact her?"

"Well, it's good to know that you have thought about your actions, but if you had seen how distraught Sheena was this morning, you'd respect her enough to give her a little space."

"Why did you let her leave in that condition, then?"

"She wasn't a basket case, Jason. She was coherent, and had considered carefully what she needed to do."

Jason looked away from the road momentarily and asked Cathy, "What she needed to do?"

"Yes."

"What was that?"

"In her words, she said that she needed to get away from you." Cathy noticed Jason's countenance sadden.

"Humph."

"Give her the time she needs; she'll be back tomorrow."

"You don't understand, Cathy, I don't need to keep procrastinating from having this conversation with Sheena."

"Why? Has that she-devil been threatening you or something?"

"Yes, she has; and that she-devil doesn't give idle threats either."

"How could you be so—?"

"Cathy, please. I could use a little compassion right now, not another one of your tongue lashings."

Cathy laughed. "You do look pitiful right now."

Jason's face hardened. "Thanks a lot, big sis."

"I was just trying to cheer you up a little, bro. It's going to be all right; I have been praying for you all constantly."

Jason didn't respond to her statement.

"Jay, did she put that bruise on your face?"

"Who?"

"You know who I'm referring to."

He didn't answer Cathy.

"Well, did she?"

"Yeah, Cat, she did. You satisfied now?"

"No, I'm not satisfied. Don't get smart with me; that's your problem. It's *you* walking around with that ugly bruise on your face, not *me*."

Jason ignored Cathy's remark. He navigated up the driveway leading to the hospital's main entrance. "We're here, guys. Aunt Cathy is going to walk you in, okay? I'll be up shortly." He looked at Cathy, hoping that she wouldn't disagree.

Cathy got out and opened the back door to the car. "You guys go stand over there by the door," she told the children, "I'll be right behind you." Joseph and Jeremiah exchanged looks. Jason could tell that they knew something wasn't right.

"Jay, I know you want to see your wife to try to straighten this situation out, but do you think it's wise to go up there with that bruise on your face?"

Jason rubbed his face where the bruise was. "I hadn't thought about that. I was so focused on seeing Sheena and talking to her."

Cathy pointed at his bruise. "How were you going to explain that to her?"

"You know, that hadn't even occurred to me; you have a good point. Sheena is not so oblivious that she can't figure out what happened."

"She's not oblivious at all. You don't give your wife enough credit. Just because she's let you get away with your infidelity thus far, and has tolerated your insults and disrespect, doesn't mean that she is living in the clouds."

"That's true. I do agree with you, I believe last night was the straw that broke the camel's back."

"So are you still going up there with that face?"

"On second thought, I shouldn't go. I would hate to have to try to explain this to her. And heaven forbid explain it to her mother. That woman has a wicked temper. I'll just keep calling Sheena until she answers."

"If she does answer, Jay, don't bombard her with a lot of talking. Just let her know that you're concerned about her and tell her that you love her."

Jason smiled and hugged his sister. "Thanks, Cathy. Your heart is not completely stony, is it?"

Cathy laughed. "Oh, you got jokes, huh?"

"Yep, I still got jokes."

"Very funny. Ha, ha. There's still a little flesh left in my heart that Frank didn't take."

Jason's countenance was lighter. "I'll be up in a minute, sis; I want to try her one more time before I come upstairs. I'll feel better if I can hear her voice."

Cathy gave him the thumbs up sign and joined the children waiting at the entrance.

Jason drove off to find a space in the hospital's parking lot. Once he parked, he touched the speed dial for Sheena's number.

Chapter 23

"Hello?" "Hey, baby. I finally reached you," Jason said in a mellifluous tone. "Why didn't you let me know that you were leaving this morning?"

"What?" The sound of Jason's voice annoyed Sheena. "What do you want, Jason?"

Jason looked at his phone as though he could see Sheena. *Man, it's worse than I thought.* He tried to sound cheerful. "I want to speak with my wife. That's not a crime, is it? Did your mother tell you that I called?"

"She did."

"Why didn't you return my calls?"

"I was occupied."

"Too occupied to return your husband's calls?"

"What do you want? What's the emergency?"

"Sheena, I really need to talk to you."

"About *what*?"

"About . . ." He remembered what Cathy had told him. "Baby, I just wanted to let you know that I love you."

Sheena didn't respond.

"Did you hear me? I also wanted to let you know that I was really worried when I woke up this morning and you were gone."

"Why?"

"Why? I was worried because you're my wife and it's so unlike you to do something that spontaneous. I was concerned about you, especially after last night."

"If that's what it took to find out that you are concerned about me, I should have done it months ago."

"I didn't mean it like that. Of course I care about you. You mean the world to me."

"Sure, I mean the world to you, Jason," Sheena replied sarcastically. "Me and your girlfriend too."

"Sheena, I'm calling you to ask you to forgive me. It's over between us."

"You finally decided to be a man of integrity and admit that you *are* fooling around, huh? It's about time you respected me enough to stop lying to me."

"I shouldn't have cheated on you or lied to you. I deserve everything you do to me."

"You do, Jason." Sheena breathed hard in the phone. "I have to go now. I have things to do. I'll see you when I see you."

"You're coming home tomorrow, aren't you? We can talk then, and hopefully we can straighten this situation out. Maybe things can get back to normal again."

"Ha!" Sheena barked into the phone. *"We* don't have a situation to straighten out. This is *your* mud, not mine. I haven't done anything wrong that needs straightening out. And as far as being *normal* again, things will *never* be normal again."

"You're right, Sheena. I hope you can forgive me at least long enough to hear me out." Sheena was silent. "Oh! I forgot to tell you that Daddy came out of his coma; we're on our way up to see him now."

Sheena's voice warmed up momentarily. "That's wonderful news! Praise the Lord."

Jason felt the warmth in Sheena's voice. "I'm relieved too. I was worried about him for a while there."

"God is good."

Jason laughed nervously. "Yeah, He is."

Sheena's heart suddenly hardened toward Jason. She knew Jason only agreed with her to pacify her. He usually got arrogant when she praised God. "I have to go now, Jason," she said coldly. "I have things to do."

"I'll see you tomorrow night, right? I love you."
The only response he received from Sheena was a
click of the phone.

Chapter 24

Lois opened the truck door and witnessed Sheena crying. "What's wrong?" "He called me again, so I decided to answer. Momma, he finally admitted that he had been seeing someone." Lois got into the truck with Sheena. "You already *knew* that." "I did. But to actually hear him admit it, it just hurt more than I thought it would." "You wanted him to stop lying to you and admit he was cheating, didn't you?"

"Yes, I did, but . . ." Sheena wiped the tears from her eyes, "I am so angry with him for betraying me like this." "I know, baby, but he finally swallowed that pride and told you the truth."

"It still doesn't hurt any less."

Lois didn't say anything. She wanted Sheena to feel comfortable talking to her without her constantly interrupting. She rubbed her daughter's shoulder gently. "What made me so angry is that he had the audacity to ask me for forgiveness in the same breath. He actually said the words, 'I love you,' as though that would make the pain go away. I suppose she dumped his butt, now he's trying to rebound to me so he won't be by himself."

Lois listened patiently to her daughter while she talked and cried.

"He had the nerve to tell me that I meant the world to him. I told him that I'm sure I did, that I'm sure his girlfriend did too." Sheena's face became distorted. "I *hate* him. I should have killed his butt when I had the chance."

Lois felt the need to intervene. "Now, Sheena, I know you're hurting, but don't forget who you are, baby."

Sheena stared at Lois in disbelief. "What are you talking about, Momma? Who I am is a woman who loved her husband and was nothing but good to him, but he chose to go out in the street and lay up with some trifling piece of trash! Who I am is a woman who's been played for a fool!"

"Sheena, you have every right to be angry, but don't let bitterness take control."

"I'm not bitter. I just *hate* him; that's how I feel."

"You're bitter too. I'm not judging you, but you are bitter." She picked up Sheena's Bible from the backseat and flipped through the pages. "Here honey, read this."

Sheena read Ephesians 4:31 and 32. "Let all bitterness, and wrath and anger, and clamour, and evil speaking, be put away from you, with all malice; And be ye kind one to another, tender-hearted; forgiving one another, even as God for Christ's sake hath forgiven you." She dropped her head and began to cry. "How am I supposed to forgive him, Momma?"

"It's hard, but do it the same way God forgives you for your sins. Here. Here's a good example in Psalm 25:18 which says: Look upon mine affliction and my pain; and forgive all my sins."

Sheena read the whole chapter silently, but didn't say anything.

"Now read this baby." Lois flipped through more pages.

Sheena's eyes scanned Psalm 86:5, then she said, "I'm trying to understand. I just need a little time. It's hard."

"I understand. You aren't going through anything that I haven't experienced."

"Daddy was unfaithful to you too?"

"No. Not to my knowledge. I can't stake my life on that, because he is a man, but as far as I know, he's been a faithful husband."

"Well, Momma, you couldn't possibly understand exactly how I feel."

"No, I can't understand *exactly* how you feel. Jesus is the only one who knows that, but I know how tormenting adultery can be."

"I don't mean to be disrespectful to you, but I doubt if you do. You have to have experienced it, Momma."

"I have experienced it, baby girl."

Sheena gave her mother an exasperating look.

"Remember this morning, I told you I may share something with you when the time was right?"

"Yes, I remember."

"Well, now seems like the right time. I know how betrayal feels because I was the cheater, not the one being cheated on."

Sheena didn't want to believe her ears. She looked away from Lois. "Momma, how could you have done that to Daddy?"

"Stupidity. I allowed myself to get involved in a relationship with another married man. I'm not going to go into the details." Lois spoke in a sassy tone. "You don't need to know all of my business."

Sheena didn't respond. She knew how sharp her mother's tongue was. "Daddy forgave you?"

"I'm still here, aren't I? It took him some months, but eventually, he forgave me."

"You two stayed in the same house after that?"

"No, he took you and moved in his own apartment. When I discovered where he lived, I stopped by his house every other day to ask for his forgiveness."

"You let Daddy *take* me?"

"I really didn't have a choice, Sheena. I didn't have the financial means to take care of you."

"Who took care of me besides Daddy? I can't imagine him taking care of a baby by himself."

"Your great aunt, Sadie. She would come over to baby-sit you while your daddy worked. He took care of you after his work day was over."

"How old was I?"

"About two; no, you were three years old."

"You know, I vaguely remember some older lady being in my life a long time ago. Until now, I couldn't place those memories, or why I had them."

"Those were memories of Aunt Sadie. She passed away six months after she kept you. Her health was bad and she didn't really have the strength to keep you, but she did it to help Gerald out."

"So, after you kept going to him, he caved in and forgave you?"

"Not right away. I was so persistent that I would go by his house every other morning before he went to work with the excuse that I wanted to see you. Finally, he told me that I had given up the right to call you my daughter when I started dog hunting, and that if I didn't stop bothering him, he would have a restraining order taken out on me." Lois sighed. "Nothing hurt more than when he told me that I wasn't fit to be your mother."

"Oh, Lord. Daddy was almost too through with you, wasn't he?"

"He was hurting, baby."

"What happened then?"

"I realized that he was serious, so I gave him the space that he needed. One day, he dropped you off by the house and told me his aunt couldn't keep you any longer while he worked. He then announced that he had been offered a job out of town and that he had accepted it and would be leaving soon."

"Did he leave?"

"No, I asked him not to leave because of what I did to him. I did my best to convince him that I wouldn't bother him, so he stayed in town. Later, after he saw I was sincere, we worked out visitation arrangements for you. Eventually, he got to the place where he could stomach my presence for longer than an hour. He was already saved, so weeks later, I asked him if I could start going to church with him. Of course, he was wary of my motives. His grandmother invited us to come to her house after church for dinner every Sunday. After we ate, she would pray for us."

"Daddy is a good man." Sheena laughed between tears.

Lois frowned and gave her a questionable look.

"I had to laugh at myself," Sheena explained. "It's ironic how much I sounded like Mrs. Grey when she's reminding me that Jason is a good man."

"He's a good man in general, but you don't have to put up with his mistreatment and cheating ways. Just because she allowed Jacob to disrespect her, is no excuse for her or Jason to expect you to knuckle under to him."

"I agree, Momma. When she starts praising him, I tune her out because I don't want to dishonor her by speaking what's on my mind. She'd be crushed if I did."

"That's right, but if she gets too carried away, you need to let her know where you stand. Some mothers-in-law mean well, but they can be overprotective of their sons, even when they know they're wrong."

Sheena nodded in agreement. "Anyway, I'm glad you and Daddy worked it out."

"You're not as happy as I am. If he hadn't forgiven me, you would have grown up in a different life."

"I know." Sheena stared up at the mountains. She was silent for a few moments. "Momma?"

"Yes, baby?"

"I want to forgive Jason, but I don't know if I have it in me to forgive him. I know I won't be able to ever trust him again and marriage without trust is worthless."

"Just seek God for directions. He'll show you the way."

"I don't think I can forgive him, it hurts too bad."

"All things take time. Just live one day at a time."

"Are you telling me that I shouldn't leave Jason?"

"I'm not going to make that decision for you. That's between you, him and Jesus."

Noticing them sitting in the vehicle so long without moving, Gerald became concerned and went out to meet them. Tapping on the window, he asked, "Lois, is everything all right?" He looked at Sheena with such compassion that she got out of the SUV and hugged him.

"I'm okay, Daddy." Sheena dried her eyes on his shirt the way she used to when she was a little girl. "I was just venting while Momma sat here patiently and listened to me."

Gerald cast his eyes on Lois.

"She's fine, honey," Lois assured him. "She just needed to get some things off of her chest."

Gerald responded to Lois with raised eyebrows.

"I'm sure, Gerald. She's going to be all right." Gerald held his eyes on Lois and bowed his head as if to say, "Okay."

Lois laughed her usual hearty laugh when she looked at Sheena. "Sheena, baby, go back inside and freshen up again so we can go to the mall for real this time." Sheena looked into the mirror on the truck. She managed a weak smile.

"Oh, God, I need to do something, don't I? I sure can't go anywhere looking like Elvira."

Gerald and Lois exchanged glances and smiled at each other. It hadn't dawned on Sheena, until now, that they had shared those same loving glances for years. They didn't exchange words audibly; one look said it all. She watched her father walk back to the barn. She noticed her mother's eyes following him as he walked. They were full of love. She thought that it must be nice to have a love like theirs, and in spite of what things looked like, she wondered if she and Jason could ever share that same kind of love.

Chapter 25

Jason held the phone in his hand and looked at it for a few seconds. He couldn't believe that Sheena had hung up on him. Turning the phone off, he slid it in his pocket. When he entered the lobby of the hospital, he was so preoccupied with thoughts of Sheena that he didn't see Jessica run up to him. He almost walked over her. She wrapped her arms around his legs.

"Daddy, I miss Momma. Is she coming home tomorrow?"

"I hope so, baby girl. I miss her too." He picked up Jessica and kissed her on the cheek. "I have to go see Grandpa now, okay?"

"Okay, Daddy, but Joseph and Jeremiah are being mean."

"How are they being mean?"

"They were saying that Momma left us and that it's your fault because you make Momma cry all the time."

Jason's heart felt like it skipped a beat. He felt awful that his children had witnessed their mother crying because of his actions. "Your mother hasn't left us, sweetheart. She's gone to visit your grandparents. When did they see your Momma crying?"

"Last night . . . when y'all were going upstairs. Joseph said she cries a lot."

Jason felt like a heel. "I'm sorry you guys saw her crying, she was upset about something. I talked to her and she was feeling better by the time we went to the hospital last night."

"So, why did you holler at her when we were in the car?"

Jason was startled by Jessica's questions. He hadn't realized that the children had heard their conversation the night before, or at least the *tone* of it. "Baby girl, sometimes parents may raise their voices at each other. That doesn't mean they're leaving each other."

"Momma didn't take us with her though," Jessica whined. "Joseph said you made her mad and that's why she left without us."

Jason made a mental note to talk to Joseph. He hadn't recognized, until now, how sensitive Joseph was and how alert he was to his surroundings. Jason understood now the strange look that Joseph gave him sometimes. It was the same look he had given his father when he was young. Joseph was protective of his mother, just like he had been. "Jessica, listen to me . . . Sheena has not left us. She just needed to see her parents and she wasn't prepared to take you guys this time. I assure you, she's coming back tomorrow night, okay?" *I hope she does.*

"You promise?"

"I promise." Jason sat Jessica down in one of the lounge chairs. He walked over to the twins to reassure them as well. "J, JJ, your mother is not mad at me," he lied. "She did not leave you guys; she wanted to see her parents and she knew you would be in good hands with Aunt Cathy.

She will be back tomorrow night, probably with lots of stuff for you guys. "

Joseph looked doubtful at Jason, but he nodded his head in acceptance. Jeremiah imitated Joseph's gesture. Jason knew he had to talk to Joseph as soon as possible because he didn't want his son to grow up to resent him, the way he had resented Jacob at times.

The boys walked away from Jason and joined Jessica and Reana who sat quietly, playing with her dolls.

"Hey guys," Jason said, following close behind. They looked up at him. "Where's your aunt?"

"She's already upstairs," Jeremiah informed his father. "Ms. Erma is watching us."

Jason looked toward where Jeremiah pointed. "Oh, okay. I'm going on up to see Grandpa, too. When we come back down, we'll go out and get some lunch, okay?"

Joseph and Jeremiah smiled. They both loved to eat out. Jeremiah asked, "May we go to get some pizza?"

"You all had pizza last night, didn't you?"

"No, we ate burgers and fries last night. Remember, Daddy?" Joseph reminded him. "We ate in the truck on our way home."

"Oh, yeah, yeah, that's right. I guess I'm getting old, aren't I, Joseph?" He recalled that he had ordered it, but it was *Cathy* who was eating pizza the night before.

"You're kinda old, but not old-old like Grandma and Grandpa," Joseph joked.

Jason laughed and gave Joseph a high five. On his way to the elevator, Jason stopped to speak to Ms. Erma, his neighbor, who sat at the information desk as a volunteer. She had told Cathy to go on upstairs to see her father, and she'd keep an eye on the children. Jason thanked her, and then he took the elevator upstairs to see his father. En route, he began to consider what his philandering had done to his family. He realized that getting involved with Ruby had not only affected his relationship with Sheena; it had had an adverse effect on his children too, especially Joseph.

Jason found himself praying. "Lord, forgive me for what I've done to my wife and children. I know it's been a long time since you've heard from me, but if you can find it in your heart to have mercy on me, I'll do my best to make it up to Sheena and my children. I know I can't bargain with you, God, but if it's not asking too much, please give my wife the grace to forgive me. I know that I don't deserve her, but I love her and need her, Lord. More importantly, I need you, Jesus." His prayers were interrupted when the elevator door opened. He exited the elevator and walked toward his father's room.

Catherine greeted him at the door. "Jason, isn't it a miracle? I told you prayer changes things."

This time, Jason didn't recoil when his mother mentioned prayer. "It seems so, Momma." He smiled as he noticed his father's weak wave. "How's it going, Daddy? It's good to see you woke, man." Jacob tried to reach out for him, so Jason bent down and hugged him. "You look much better, Daddy. How are you feeling?"

Jacob tried to utter something. His eyes kept roaming the room.

Jason looked at his mother in defeat. "What's he trying to say, Momma? I can't understand him."

"I'm not sure, but I think that he wants to know where Sheena is."

"Oh," Jason said, facing Jacob. "Sheena is at her parents' house for the weekend. She'll be back tomorrow."

Jacob tried to speak again. He had a concerned look in his eyes. "Where . . ." It was the only utterance he could force before his words became inaudible. It was just too difficult for him to speak.

"Daddy, don't try to talk so much right now, okay? You have to give yourself time to recuperate." Jason rubbed his father on the head. "I called Sheena and let her know you had awakened." Jason sounded as though he was trying to reassure himself. "She'll be in to see you tomorrow night, if she gets home early enough."

His sisters entered the room. They noisily greeted and hugged him. Cathy was sitting in a chair in the corner of the room, studying Jason's expression. Jason noticed the worried look on her face, so he tried to look and sound cheerful.

"I see you all still have the loudest mouths in Charlotte," he joked with his sisters. "What's up, girls?"

"We're doing well," Shirley, the oldest, answered for them all while the others nodded their heads in agreement.

"Where's Sheena?" Aretha asked.

"She's in Asheville visiting her parents," Jason told them.

"I'm surprised she's not with you, standing on your heels," Terri remarked as she smirked at Shirley and Aretha. "You are married to one jealous woman."

"Don't even start your mess, Terri," Cathy warned her. "Now is not the time."

Jason shook his head at Terri. "You've never liked Sheena, have you?"

"Since you asked, no, I really don't care for her, Jay. She's always been too possessive over you. We can't even have a conversation with you without her hovering like a buzzard." Aretha and Shirley nodded their sentiments.

"Maybe if you all stopped talking about my old girlfriends in front of her, she wouldn't be so insecure."

Terri fired back at Jason. "She knew you had women before you met her. She was lucky to get you, Jay, considering how . . . *challenged* she is in the looks department to put it nicely."

Jason's eyes bored through Terri's. "Terri, I've been in the room with you all of three minutes and you have managed to put you foot in your mouth already."

"Jay, I don't mean any harm, but you know you could have married somebody that looked a little better than that." Terri saw the anger on Jason's face and immediately regretted her statement. She looked at Catherine for support. "Momma said the same thing too." Catherine didn't say anything; she dropped her head and pretended to adjust Jacob's hospital gown.

"Is that right?" Jason countered. "I didn't marry Sheena for her looks; I married her because I loved her. Terri, I don't want to ever hear you speaking negative about my wife again, you hear me?" He looked at Shirley, Aretha and his mother. "That goes for the rest of you too!" Jason's voice carried an edge of harshness.

None of them replied. They dropped their heads in shame and walked up to the bed to chat with Jacob. Cathy smiled and gave Jason a thumbs up for rebuking his sisters and mother concerning Sheena.

Jacob lay on the bed in silence, looking from one person to another as though he wanted to tell them to stop.

The nurse came in the room. "Visiting hour is over. You all will have to leave now." She checked

Jacob's vital signs. "He's doing okay, but our monitors show a noticeable increase in his heart rate since you all came in. He does not need to be overexerted. You all can come back to see him again tonight, but just for a short while. And please check the drama at the door before you come in."

Everyone left except Catherine. She insisted on staying. "I'll be here until you guys get back tonight. If he's still improving, I'll leave to go home tonight with you all."

"Okay, Momma," Cathy replied. "We'll see you tonight."

Aretha, Terri, and Shirley walked ahead of Cathy and Jason. They held the elevator door for them. All of his sisters, except Cathy, were engrossed in a conversation concerning their father. Cathy remained quiet and watched Jason as he stood in the elevator facing the doors with his head hung down. When the door opened, his sisters rushed over to see the children. They engaged in a playful conversation with them.

Cathy linked her arm into Jason's. "Jay, are you okay? Did you get in touch with Sheena?"

"Yeah, I'm okay. I reached her, but judging from her response to me, she doesn't want to hear what I've got to say. I've finally pushed her over the edge, Cat. I don't think she's in a forgiving state of mind. I don't know why I expected anything different from her, considering what I've done to her."

"Give her time, Jason. Did you do what I told you to do?"

"Oh, yeah. She didn't respond; she just hung up on me."

"She'll come around." Cathy sighed. "These things take time and patience; a lot of patience. She's been patient with you all of these months, now it's your time to return the favor."

"You're right. You know, Cathy, I didn't realize until today what a wonderful virtuous wife I have. The ironic thing is, now it may be too late to show my appreciation to her."

"It's never too late for anything, Jay."

"If you had heard the distance in her voice, you might not be so sure. If I didn't know any better, I'd say she hates me."

"She doesn't hate you. She's probably tormented with hurt from your betrayal. Sheena has too much love inside her to hate anybody."

"I'm not just anybody. I'm her two-timing husband; I committed the *ultimate* betrayal against her. Some things a person can feel. I didn't believe her when she said she was going to file for a divorce. I even smirked at her when she said it, but now, I wouldn't be surprised to receive some separation papers from her."

"No, Jay, I don't think it'll come to that. Sheena wouldn't do something that rash."

"It won't be rash, Cathy. She's told me several times that she dreamed about killing me. Maybe last night her dreams became a reality to her."

"She was out of character last night, that's for sure. That's all the more reason that you should pray for your wife. After all, she's spent a tremendous amount of time praying for you." Cathy braced herself, waiting for Jason to resist her advice about prayer.

He surprised her when he said, "I have, Cathy. I prayed for her—for us in the elevator on my way up to the room. Now let's just hope God heard me."

Chapter 26

Sheena and Lois shopped all afternoon. Sheena was usually reserved about the way she spent money. Today, she felt as though she was purging herself of pent up emotions. She bought four pairs of shoes for herself, two tailored suits, four pairs of slacks with matching sweaters and two dresses. She went shopping for the twins, buying them several outfits, and five outfits for Jessica. She had an urge, out of habit, to buy something for Jason, but didn't. *He's the reason I'm up here shopping like a mad woman anyway.*

"Sheena, let's take a break baby. I'm not as young as I used to be and my legs are starting to ache. I need to sit down," Lois moaned.

"Oh, I'm sorry, Momma. I was so focused on shopping, I forgot all about your legs." "Once I sit down, I'll be fine. I'm glad to see you enjoying yourself though."

"I've heard people say that shopping is therapeutic, they could have a valid point. I haven't felt this great in a long time."

"I've heard that also. And I've heard people say that it's just a temporary relief from the problem that is bothering them."

Lois and Sheena walked a few feet toward some benches and sat down.

"Whatever. It's a good feeling," Sheena laughed while she gathered her bags. She had already made several trips to the SUV with packages she had purchased. "Momma, I'd better take these bags to the truck. I guess I'm finished shopping now. When I come back, I'll buy us dinner at the Jamaican restaurant." She studied her mother's expression. "Is that all right with you?"

"That's fine with me, baby, but I don't want you to spend all your money. You have already bought three pairs of shoes for me. I could have paid for my own shoes. Now you want to buy me dinner."

"The least I could do was to buy you some shoes. You have done so much for me today, listening patiently while I cried myself into a stupor."

"You are going to be fine, baby. All you need is some time to relax and enjoy yourself."

"I do feel relaxed. Maybe I should have done this more often. I'm enjoying spending Jason's money."

"Are you trying to get revenge on him by spending his money?"

"Now that you mentioned it, I probably am. I'm usually very cautious about the way we spend money, but I don't care about his money anymore. He probably was giving that hussy a portion of our savings anyway."

"You were doing fine until you mentioned Jason and that woman. Now look at you. Your whole demeanor has changed."

Sheena exhaled deeply. "You're right. I'm not going to mention them again. I'm going to focus on enjoying my time with you and Daddy. I don't get to see you guys that often. So, I'm going to make the best of our time together."

"That's what I'm talking about. You go ahead and put the bags in the car. I'll sit right here and wait until you get back."

Sheena walked to the car, put the packages in it, and locked the door. As she walked back to the mall entrance, her phone rang. She looked at the caller ID, and reluctantly answered it. "What do you want, Jason? I told you that I'm busy."

"Jessica wanted to speak with you, Sheena. Are you doing all right?"

"I'm doing fine," Sheena said harshly, "now that I got away from *you*. Put her on the phone." Sheena talked to Jessica and the twins and assured them that she would be home the next evening before they went to bed. She heard Jason tell them to let him speak to her before they hung up. When he said, "How's it going, baby?" she hung up.

After she and her mother were seated in the restaurant, Sheena mentioned the phone call to Lois. "I can't stand to hear the sound of his voice. He knows that I don't want to be bothered with him right now. That's why I left."

Lois listened to her daughter without saying anything.

"If he had been a faithful husband like he should have been, I wouldn't have had a reason to leave. Now he's using the children to try to lure me back home."

"I'm sure they miss you, Sheena. It's natural for them to want to speak to you, especially after you left them so suddenly. They probably feel like you abandoned them."

"I've been gone less than twenty-four hours. How could they possibly feel like that?"

"You've been there for them every possible moment. Unlike with Jason, they are not accustomed to you not being there."

"I guess you're right." The waitress came to take their orders. When she left, Sheena resumed the conversation. "Momma, I've been thinking."

"About what?"

"...m going to go back home, submit the re-
...red resignation for my job, file for a divorce,
pack the children up and move back up here."

Lois was astounded. "Sheena, you've been up
here for less than twenty-four hours as you said,
so how could you have possibly made a decision
like that in such a short time?"

"I've been thinking about it all day. I miss
home and I want my children to grow up here in
the serene mountain atmosphere."

"You came up here to relax and clear your
mind, remember. You weren't supposed to make
a madbrained decision like that."

"I've given it a lot of thought, Momma."

"That's the problem."

"What's the problem?"

"You have been *thinking*, and not praying.
You need to seek God for directions before you
make a final decision so suddenly."

Sheena stared at Lois.

"Don't stare at me like that, girl. You know
what you are supposed to do. When we get home
you are going to pick that Bible up and talk to
Jesus the way you know how to do. He might
not give you an answer right away, but you know
what else you have to do."

"What's that?"

"Find you a prayer closet. Your bedroom, just the way you left it before you got married. I suggest you use it."

Sheena gave her mother a weak smile. "Momma, you have never minced words, have you?"

"No, I haven't. Tough love is what you need right now and tough love is what I'm gonna give you."

They returned home after a long day of shopping. Gerald met them at the door. "You guys stayed a long time. I don't know how y'all women can shop all day." He shook his head and went upstairs.

Lois followed him. "Gerald, are you hungry? We brought you dinner from the mall." Sheena didn't hear his reply; they disappeared into their room and did not come back out.

Sheena went in her room and closed the door. She prayed for what seemed like hours. She fell asleep across the bed with her clothes on. When she awoke the next morning, her parents were already dressed for church.

"Good morning, Momma; Daddy." She admired them as they exchanged seductive looks at each other. "Momma, I think I know what I have to do now. I had a good talk with Jesus last night."

"Good. Prayer helps, baby. We're on our way to church, don't you want to join us?"

"I had planned to go with you guys, but since you're already dressed, I don't want to make you late, so I'll meet you guys there."

"All right, we'll see you there."

After her parents left, Sheena showered and dressed for church. She answered a strong urge to call her children to see how they were doing. The phone rang several times before Joseph picked it up.

"Hi, J. Where is everybody? Are you guys doing okay?" Sheena asked.

"We're doing okay, Momma."

Sheena could sense the tension in his voice. "What's wrong, Joseph?"

Joseph hesitated before he spoke. "Aunt Cathy cooked breakfast for us, but it didn't taste too good." Sheena smiled. Cathy never was a great cook, she mused. "Are you coming home today?"

"Yes, I'll be home late this evening, probably in time to tuck you guys in for bed, okay?"

"Okay, Momma. We miss you."

"I miss you guys too. Where is your father?"

"I don't know. Some wild lady came over here this morning, she was ringing the doorbell like a crazy person, when Daddy answered the door, she was standing there screaming at him."

"What?" Sheena voice was elevated and her forehead creased. "Where were you guys?"

"We were in our room getting dressed for church. Daddy was going to take us to church this morning."

"Oh, he was?" Sheena shook her head in disbelief. She knew Jason only went to church when he wanted to redeem himself with her.

"Yes. He said it was about time that he went back to church, and after we left church, he was going to take us to see the Charlotte Bobcats vs. Miami Heat game."

"That's great, J. I hope you all have fun." Sheena was curious about the visitor. "Do you know who that lady was, Joseph?"

"No, but she must have known Daddy, because she was cursing at him. He closed the door and went outside where she was, so we ran to your and Daddy's room so we could see; that's when we saw her kick Daddy."

"Oh, really? What happened then?"

"We heard Daddy tell her to leave or he was going to call the police."

"Did she leave?"

"Yes, after she slapped him and then she got in her car and left."

"I'm sorry you had to witness that, J."

"Momma, do you know her?"

"No, I don't think so, but I have an idea of who she is."

"She was mean. She kept calling you names."

"Joseph, look, I don't know what's going on, but I should be home in a couple of hours. I'll find out what's going on then. I know one thing, she better not bring her behind to my house again. I am not going to tolerate her acting crazy in front of my children."

"I have to go now, Momma. Aunt Cathy is waiting for me in the car. I ran back to answer the phone, because I was hoping that it was you."

"I'll be home soon, baby. You guys stay with your aunt until I get there. I love you. Bye."

"Bye, Momma. I love you too."

Sheena wrote her parents a note explaining why she had to leave, then she called Jason on his cell phone. He didn't answer so she left him a message. "Jason, I'm coming home to pack my things, pack the children up and get the heck out of your life so that you can have your precious girlfriend in peace. Joseph told me about this wild woman coming to *my* house, which I'm assuming is the slut that you've been running around with. I have taken a lot of junk off of you, Jason, but you have gone too far this time. When I find out who she is, I'm going to beat the living daylights out of her too."

"I'm filing for a divorce, so you can sell the house, or move your woman in it, I don't give a fat baby's behind what you do. I'm sick of you, I hate you and the sooner I get away from you, the better off I'll be! I should have left your philandering butt the minute that I became suspicious of your lies!" She clicked the phone off.

Fortunately, Sheena had left all of her bags in the car from the day before. She picked up her small suitcase, dumped her belongings in there and took off, headed straight for Charlotte.

Chapter 27

Ruby was furious. "How dare he call me and curse me out, accusing me of taking some of his freaking money!" Ruby knew that she was guilty, but she was angry because she expected the call from Jason to be one of an apology, with him begging her to take him back.

She drove recklessly down the highway. "He must have thought I was bluffing when I told him I was coming over there. He should know that I don't play!" Ruby was disappointed that Sheena didn't come to the door. She planned to get revenge on Jason by telling Sheena about Cassandra before he had the chance to tell her. Ruby drove home so fast, she barely remembered entering her front door. She headed straight for the bathroom to take a bath. "I need to wash his sorry self out of my life." While the water was running in the tub, she picked up the phone to call her mother. Her mother answered on the first ring.

"Thank God, you finally returned my calls," her mother stated.

"What's wrong, Momma?"

"I've been calling you all morning. Thurman found out where you were living somehow. He's on his way up there. I just wanted to warn you to be on the lookout for him."

"How in the world did that fool find me?"

"I don't know. You need to be on the lookout for him though, Ruby. You know how insanely jealous he is. He left here raging, talking about he knows where you are and he was going to go find you and drag you back here. He sounded like he was out of his mind. He said that he had a good mind to blow Jason's brains out. Ruby, he has been jealous of you and Jason ever since you married him. I told you not to marry him while you were pregnant with Jason's baby."

"At the time, he insisted that it didn't matter to him that I was carrying another man's child," Ruby reasoned.

"Men may say that, but sometimes they can't handle the reality of it after the child is born."

"I wish that I had taken your advice to just have my baby and let you and Daddy help me raise her. I just didn't want my child to be illegitimate."

"It might have made a difference if, over the years, you all had had a child together, but by

Cassandra being the only child you had, it just reminded him of you and Jason. I could understand if you were not able to have more children, but you deliberately wouldn't have a baby for him. That was not right, Ruby; you should have given him a child. He wants a son of his own so badly."

"There's no guarantee that we would have had a boy. I didn't want to mess my figure up having a bunch of children, trying to give him a son. And another thing, I'm not keeping him from having a son. If he wants to, he could have had a son with any of those young hoochie mamas he works with. According to him, they all want him. He should have taken advantage of the opportunity."

"You're still selfish to the bone, aren't you? I'm sure Thurman wanted a son with his wife, not any ole body he could get with. If he told you that those young girls wanted him, he was trying to make you jealous."

The bathtub had filled with water. Ruby turned the water off and walked into her bedroom. "I'm just looking out for number one. Isn't that what you and Daddy drilled into me when I was growing up?"

Ruby's mother ignored the remark she made. She knew how vicious Ruby could be when it benefited her.

"So he didn't sign the divorce papers I left for him?"

"No, he didn't sign the papers. He looked at 'em and tossed 'em back on the table. That man has one thing on his mind and that is bringing you back home. Just be careful, Ruby." She paused. "Here, your baby wants to speak to you."

Cassandra eagerly took the phone from her grandmother. "Hi, Mommy."

"Hi, sweetheart. How's my baby doing?"

"I'm doing good. I miss you though, Mommy. When are you going to send for me?"

"I was going to surprise you, baby. I made reservations last night for you, Pa-Pa, and Ma-Ma to fly up here next weekend."

"Oh, good. I've never flown on a plane before. That should be exciting. Am I going to stay up there with you, Mommy?"

"No, baby, not yet. I want to wait until the Christmas and New Year's holidays are over. Before school starts for the New Year, I am going to fly down there and have your school transcript sent to the school up here, then you can fly back with me and start going to your new school."

"That's great. I can hardly wait!"

"I can't wait either, sweetheart. I miss you so much."

"Ma-Ma, guess what?" Cassandra screamed over the phone. "Mommy is sending for us next weekend and I'm going to be moving up there with her after Christmas." She spoke back into the phone. "Mommy?"

"Yes, Cassandra?"

"Did you tell my daddy about me yet?"

Ruby was amazed at how mature her daughter was. "I did, baby, and he can't wait to meet you."

A year earlier, Cassandra had overheard Ruby and Thurman arguing late one night, and that's how she learned that Thurman wasn't her natural father. She stood in their bedroom doorway, crying after hearing the upsetting news. Ruby and Thurman apologized to her vehemently, but the damage had been done. They explained the situation as gently and honestly as they felt a ten-year-old girl could understand.

Cassandra was profoundly affected by the news, but Thurman did every thing in his power to convince Cassandra that he loved her, and as far as he was concerned, she *was* his daughter and that she always would be.

Thurman's relationship with Ruby, however, deteriorated rapidly. She became cold and insensitive to his needs, confirming his insecurities that she still carried a torch for Jason Grey. They constantly argued and sometimes fought to the point that Cassandra begged them to let her move in with her grandparents.

Shortly thereafter, Ruby's co-worker showed her the picture of Jason and his family on the cover of *Black Enterprise*. She had no idea that Ruby knew him, she was merely raving about the extremely handsome executive featured on the cover. She was impressed with his accomplishments, but couldn't understand why a man of his status had married such a common looking woman.

Ruby laughed at her co-worker's comment, but when she looked at the magazine, she was utterly shocked to see it was Jason. Being the shrewd woman that she was, she didn't divulge this information to her co-worker. Ruby bought her own copy of the magazine and proceeded to mastermind a plan to reunite with him.

"I can't wait for you to meet him either, sweetheart," Ruby said into the phone receiver to her daughter. "You are going to really like him."

"I already think that I like him, Mommy. He sounds really nice."

"That's sweet, baby. Hopefully, you and he will bond and grow to love each other one day."

"I hope so, but I still love Thurman. He still seems like my daddy too."

"He is, Cassandra . . . in every way that counts. He's been in your life ever since the day you were born."

Cassandra sighed deeply. "Yeah, I know, Mommy. Pa-Pa wants to speak to you." Cassandra gave the cordless phone to her grandfather.

"Hey there, what's going on? When were you planning on telling us about this trip to North Carolina?"

"That was the purpose of my call, Daddy. I went ahead and made reservations for you all last night. I assumed that it would be all right with you guys."

"I told you about that word *assume,* Ruby. You know what it spells."

"I know, Daddy, I just wanted to surprise you guys. Besides, it's been six months since I've seen you all and I was getting homesick for you."

"We miss you too. It's so quiet around here without you. We were used to you coming over here livening up the place."

Ruby teased her father. "Is that your way of telling me you love me, Daddy?"

"Uh-huh, I reckon it is. Where did you get enough money to buy us roundtrip tickets anyway?"

"I have my sources. Besides, that's not for you to worry about."

"I have an idea where you got it from. Ruby, I've told you about spending a man's money now. You already went through Thurman's money, what little he had, and you treated him like he was something nasty under the bottom of your shoe. Now you scamming Jason and he's a married man. Chile, you had better turn your life around and get saved. These men ain't gonna keep putting up with your foolishness."

Ruby was ruffled by her father's advice, but she grew up acknowledging his intolerance for her rebellious behavior, so she listened unobtrusively as he proceeded to quote scriptures from the Bible.

"Ruby, don't just sit on the phone like a bump on a log, go get your Bible."

Ruby clicked her tongue as she lay the phone down on the bed. She was irritated with her father for preaching to her every time she called. She was perturbed, but knew it would be in her best interest to obey him. "I got it, Daddy."

"Okay, you ready?"

"Uh-huh."

Her father instructed her to turn to various scriptures. "After I hang up, I want you to read the rest of Chapter two of Jeremiah, following up with Chapters three, four, and five." Ruby didn't respond. "You hear me?"

"Yes, Daddy. I heard you."

"I'm not judging you, baby cakes," he told Ruby, referencing to her nickname, "I want you to come back to the Lord because I love you and I don't want to see any harm come to you."

Ruby smiled. It was rare that her father told her he loved her. "I understand, Daddy."

"You are playing a dangerous game, and you are also hurting God with your backsliding ways, honey. I was so grateful to Jesus when you finally gave your life to Him. Since you left the Lord, you have changed back into your old ways. Whatever it is that you're looking for, God has it for you. Just ask for it, and according to His Word, He'll give it to you, because that's how much He loves you."

Ruby rolled her eyes up toward the ceiling. "I hear you, Daddy," she said unemotionally.

"Don't just be a hearer of the Word, be a doer of the Word, Ruby. I wish that I could undo the way that we raised you, but I've repented, and so has your momma; and God has forgiven us. He'll do the same thing for you. Your momma and I pray Jeremiah 14:7 every night before we go to bed. So don't think that I'm picking on you."

"I know you're not." Ruby changed the subject. "Daddy, are you all going to use the tickets I purchased to come up here?"

Randy hesitated before he answered. "I reckon we will, baby cakes. We do want to see you, and your baby *needs* to see you."

Ruby smiled, pleased that her father accepted the trip. "I sure could stand to see the sight of some faces that love me too."

"No doubt. When are we scheduled to come up there?"

"You'll have to get up early Friday morning. Daddy, you all are going to have to be at the airport no later than 4:30 A.M., *not* P.M.; so don't miss your flight. It's scheduled to leave at six. It would be better if y'all were there by four."

"Lord willing, we'll be there."

"Call me before you get on the plane so I'll know that you are about to leave, okay? I'll put some money in the mail today so you can buy a prepaid cell phone. That way, you won't have to use a pay phone when you get to the airport."

"I'll let Cassandra do that. I'm not too keen on all of that new fangled junk y'all use these days."

"All right, I'll be waiting for you guys at the airport. I love you, Daddy. Give Momma a kiss for me."

Ruby hung up the phone, walked into the kitchen and poured herself a glass of wine. She sauntered back into the bathroom, undressed, and slipped in the tub of warm soapy water. She commenced to read the scriptures her father instructed her to read. Who knows? With the way her life had gone lately, maybe something in the Bible could speak to her broken heart.

Chapter 28

Sheena arrived in Charlotte two and a half hours later. She couldn't speed the way she wanted to because the treacherous conditions of the mountains' steep decline prevented her from doing so. Logic prevailed over her emotions, because she wanted to arrive home in one piece. No one knew better than she how fatal careless driving in those exquisite, glorious mountains could be. That was how her former boyfriend died.

For a while after his death, Sheena was petrified to drive through the mountains, so her father would take her to school in Durham and after she got better acquainted with Jason, he would drive her home during holidays. Her thoughts jolted back to the present as she eased her Denali into the garage.

"He's not here," she mumbled. "Probably somewhere with that ole cow he's been running around with." Sheena was glad to be home. She remembered the message she'd left Jason on his cell phone before she left Charlotte. She had told him that she was leaving him.

She stepped out of the truck and immediately changed her mind. She decided to pack Jason's bags instead. She would have them waiting in the garage for him when he got home. Sheena opened the back door, looked around, and was pleased that everything was clean and in order the way she had left it. She expected the house to be in shambles when she returned.

She walked up to their bedroom, checked things out, stepped into the enormous walk-in closet and mechanically pulled three large suitcases out. She began to stuff Jason's clothes in them. Then, she walked back into the bedroom and opened his dresser drawers, grabbing an armful of underwear and socks, throwing them into the suitcase.

Sheena let the tears roll down her cheeks. "I didn't think that it would come to this, Lord, but there's nothing else for me to do now, but put him out."

There is one other thing you can do, she heard the still small voice within her say. *Pray.* Sheena ignored it and gathered the bags one by one, taking them downstairs and pulling them out to the garage.

When she looked at her watch, it was 3:30. She had worked so diligently packing Jason's bags that she was unaware of the time. She was exhausted from the drive home and the physical exertion of taking the heavy suitcases downstairs to the garage.

Sheena slowly climbed the stairs and sat on the top step. She folded her arms across her knees and lowered her head down. She got a whiff of her underarms and grimaced. Standing, she walked to their bedroom into the bathroom and took a shower. After showering, Sheena fell across the bed and was asleep in a matter of minutes.

The shrill sound of the telephone awakened her. Before she answered it, she noticed the message light blinking. "Hello?"

"Hey, Mommy!" Jessica squealed through the phone. "I'm happy you're home. I missed you. How long have you been home?"

"Since one-thirty, I think, Jessica." She looked at the time on the clock radio. It was 5:50. "Where are you guys? I hoped you would be here when I got home."

"Reana and I are at Grandma and Grandpa's house. Daddy took J, and JJ to that game he promised to take them to. Uncle Jonathan and his family are here too."

"Oh, really? That's nice, honey. Is your aunt Cathy there too?"

"No, she and my other aunts are gone to the hospital to see Grandpa. Uncle Jonathan and Aunt Mary are lying down. They kept going to sleep on the couch, so Daddy told them to go take a nap. They must be really tired, right, Momma?"

"Yes, I'm sure they are exhausted. Riding on a plane a long way causes you to get jet lag."

"What is that?"

"I'll explain that to you at a later time, honey. What else did you guys do today?"

"After that mean lady came over here and left, we went to church. Aunt Cathy took us in Daddy's car, and Daddy met us there. He drove his old truck. He loves that raggedy truck, doesn't he, Mommy? It's so loud too. But it's fun to ride in."

Sheena smiled as she listened to her daughter chatter. "So he went to church today, huh?"

"Yes, and he got in the line for prayer too. I've never seen Daddy do that before."

"Neither have I, baby, but that's nice."

"I have to go now. I want to go play dolls with Reana. Oh, Daddy said he is going to take us home when they get back from the game. Bye, Mommy." Jessica hung up before Sheena could say anything else.

Sheena checked the messages. The call was from Jonathan, letting Jason know they had arrived at the airport and would take a cab to their mother's house.

Sheena was still sitting on the bed when she heard the front door slam shut. She peeped over the top of the staircase into the foyer. It was Jason. She waited for the twins to come running up the stairs. It was quiet as a mouse downstairs and there wasn't a sign of the boys being anywhere in the house. Then it dawned on her; she had talked to Jessica less than five minutes ago and she said that Jason was coming to pick her and Reana up after the game was over. Sheena figured that he must have dropped the boys off and left.

Sheena watched Jason as he climbed the stairs two by two. She felt butterflies flittering in her stomach. Although she thought it was over between them, she still felt that warm sensation running through her body whenever she saw him.

"Sheena, are you upstairs, baby?" When he reached the top step, Sheena was standing there lording over him with her eyes gleaming with hatred.

She had a sudden urge to push him back down the stairs and struggled within, trying to control the love/hate passion she felt for Jason. She snapped at him like a turtle. "Where else would I be? This is my house. The question is, what are you doing here?"

"I listened to your message over and over, baby. I came home to try to talk you out of leaving."

Jason slowly walked toward Sheena. She was still glaring at him. He stepped back out of her space. "Sheena, baby, if you would just give me a chance to explain what happened—"

"If you call me baby one more time, I'm going to shove your long behind down those stairs!"

Jason held up his hands in a peaceful gesture. "I hear you, Sheena. I don't deserve to call you that."

"You got that right! And you can't explain anything to me. A picture might be worth a thousand words, but your girlfriend's actions today told the whole story. Where do you get off allowing her to come to my house? Are you crazy?"

"Sheena, you know better than that, I wouldn't allow her to come here. Ruby is so head strong that she bombarded her way over here."

"Ruby?" Sheena scrunched her face up at the sound of her name.

Jason nodded. "She was angry because I cursed her out about stealing money from my account."

"Stealing money from your account? How did she get access to your account?"

"I left my wallet at her place one night and she probably rambled through it and found my information."

"So that's where your wallet was that night, huh? I don't even want to hear any more of your sad lies, Jason. Just shut up!" Sheena had one hand on her hip and one pointed in his face.

Jason stood his ground, but he didn't say anything.

"Ruby . . . Ruby now why does that name sound so familiar?"

"You probably remember her from school."

Sheena massaged her temples as she tried to recall. "Oh, no! I know you aren't running around with that maniac that you were dating in school. I don't remember her that well, but I do remember the gossip about you guys. I thought she moved back to Florida years ago."

"She did, but she moved up here a few months ago." Jason had planned to reveal the details about who he had had the affair with to Sheena that night. Ruby's appearance and performance that morning made it more difficult for him to explain anything. He decided it would be best to wait until a later date to tell her about Cassandra.

"How did she get to Charlotte? We went to school in Durham. I thought you claimed that she never knew where your folks lived. Now she's practically living with you; another convenient lie."

"I didn't lie to you, Sheena. She didn't know where I lived."

"How did she find you then? Or have you been seeing her over the years?" Sheena didn't give Jason a chance to respond. "Oh, let me guess, you moved her up here, didn't you? Now I understand why you had so many trips to Florida. I suppose it wasn't feasible for you to keep flying to see her. Either that, or you couldn't get enough of her. How long have you been *keeping* your mistress, Jason?"

Jason dropped his head in disbelief at the way Sheena spewed accusations at him. He turned away from her to walk toward the bedroom. "Sheena, I hadn't heard from her until four months ago."

"Wait a minute." She pointed at his face. "What's this?" "How did you get that ugly bruise on your face?"

"I'm ashamed to say, but this is a gift from Ruby. She delivered it right in front of the neighbors." Jason knew he couldn't tell her the whole truth; that the bruise was a manifestation of

Ruby's temper while he was at her house the day before.

Appearances were very important to Sheena; she became more concerned about the neighbors than what happened to Jason. "You mean to tell me that you all were carrying on in the front yard to the point where the neighbors saw you?"

"*She* was carrying on like some wild animal. She got so loud that the neighbors came out of their houses to see what was going on."

"Lord, have mercy. I'm never going to live this down. I can see Ms. Erma running her mouth now. I hope my church member down the street didn't see you all. I won't be able to face them at church." Sheena followed him into the bedroom. "It wasn't enough that my children had to witness your mud, but now all the neighbors know. You know what, Jason? You deserve everything she does to you. As a matter of fact, you two deserve each other."

"No, Sheena, I don't want her, I want you—"

"It's a little too late to come to that conclusion now. How *did* you two meet up again then? You avoided explaining that lie to me."

"You didn't give me a chance to explain. You won't let me get a word in edgewise."

Sheena walked up to him and looked him eyeball to eyeball. "You have my undivided attention. Explain."

"She saw our picture on the cover of *Black Enterprise*. She investigated the information in the magazine. I guess. I bumped into her in a restaurant downtown."

Sheena was quiet for a moment. "You know, I am tempted to believe the part about the magazine. But I hope that you don't expect me to soak in the part about you and her *bumping* into each other. And now she lives here? Come on, Jason. Surely you don't think that I'm that gullible?"

"I know that you aren't gullible, but it's the truth, she moved up here to be with me. I wasn't aware of that at the time. I thought it was just a coincidence—us running into each other. But as time has passed, I know now that she orchestrated everything."

"And woe is you, right! You were just an innocent little boy caught in the web of the black widow spider." Sheena stared Jason down.

"Sheena, I'm not pretending to be innocent in this situation. I just made a huge mistake by getting involved with Ruby again. If I could take it back, I would. Believe me, I wish that I hadn't ever laid eyes on her. I have repented and asked God to forgive me of my sins; now I'm asking you to *please* forgive me. Sheena—"

"Stop right there. Don't patronize me by trying to con me with your hypocritical plea for forgiveness. I'm not God, Jason, I can't tell if you are sincere or not; but I know one thing, I can't just forgive you and forget about what you've done to me as easily as I flip this light switch on. You really hurt me. What hurt the most was the lying and the snide hateful remarks you made toward me. I did my best to be a good wife to you, and how did you repay me? By 'keeping' your old girlfriend set up like she was your wife or something. When I think about the many nights you came home late, lying about working when I *knew* you were with somebody, it makes me sick!"

Jason didn't interrupt her.

"And all the times you verbally abused me, disrespected me and laughed in my face. But you know what? I'm partly to blame, because if I hadn't allowed you to disrespect me, you wouldn't have done it. You are a piece of work, Jason, and I am an idiot for letting you fool me ten years ago. I should have known back then that you were a wolf in sheep's clothing." Sheena rushed past Jason and headed for the stairs.

Jason was right on her heels. He grabbed her arm and whirled her around. "Sheena, please don't leave. Let's try to get a grip and talk about this in a calmer manner. At least, hear me out."

Sheena looked at Jason's hand that was wrapped tightly around her arm. He had a wild look in his eyes. "W—What are you going to do, Jason? Try to *beat* me into staying with you?"

When he saw the look of fear in her eyes, he loosened his grip on her. "You know I wouldn't hit you, Sheena."

"I—I don't know any such thing," she said nervously. "After all, you are your father's son." Then, she remembered that her mother told her that if she was afraid of a man, don't let him know it; bluff him, then pick up the first thing she saw and crown him with it. Gathering some courage she said, "Just remember one thing, I'm *not* Catherine Grey. I will *kill* you if you ever lost your mind and hit me!"

Jason threw his hands up in the air and backed away from her. "I was just trying to prevent you from leaving; that's all. I just want a chance to talk to you."

"I'm through talking to you. I've heard enough lies from you to last me a lifetime." She continued to walk downstairs. He followed her into the den, where she sat in his favorite recliner and turned on the TV. Jason sat on the couch across from her.

"By the way," she said calmly, "I'm not going anywhere." She waited until he relaxed and got comfortable in his seat. He seemed to breathe a sigh of relief. "But you are." Jason sat up abruptly. "This is *my* house, there's no reason for me to leave. I'm not gonna hop away like some scared rabbit, because I haven't done anything wrong. The kids and I are quite comfortable here. I'm not going *anywhere*. I've worked too hard to make this a home for us." Sheena's eyes sparkled like fire. "Your gold digging girlfriend isn't sliding her skank behind in here; not in my house! Since you've become so fond of her, I want you out of here, not tomorrow, not next week, but tonight."

Jason was speechless.

"Don't be surprised, Jay," she taunted him, "I'm sure your woman will welcome you with open arms."

Jason looked intently at Sheena. "I'm not going to leave either. This is my house too. *I* pay the mortgage. *I* pay for the cars and all the other bills around here."

Sheena leaped out of her chair and stood over him. "You don't pay everything around here. I pay living expenses too, but that's irrelevant. The point is, you chose to go outside the marriage and play the harlot, and so since you want to play, now you're going to pay. You are going to continue to pay the mortgage, all of the utilities and for my car too! My little Toyota was fine with me, but since you insisted that I needed a new vehicle, you are going to continue to pay for it. I didn't need a new car. You wanted me to have a new car for *your* obnoxious image."

"Sheena, you know that Corolla was too small for you and the kids. You'd had that car since you graduated college."

She pushed his head back with her finger. "That's beside the point. I liked my car. I didn't ask you to go out and buy that big thing."

"So you don't enjoy the truck then?"

"Yes, I enjoy it . . . but don't try to change the subject. You are good at that. Whenever I try to get my point across, you try to flip the script, but not today, Jack! Oh, no, honey, the kids and I are going to continue living here because we shouldn't have to suffer or be uprooted because you chose to be with Ruby."

Jason had never seen Sheena this angry. "I haven't chosen to be with Ruby, Sheena. I want us—"

"*Us*," she stated matter-of-factly, "doesn't exist anymore."

He looked at Sheena and shook his head. Deciding that it was time to go pick up the kids, Jason stood. He reasoned that Sheena would change her mind if she saw how heartbroken they would be by his departure.

"Your clothes are already packed. You can pick them up in the garage." Sheena blew him a kiss. "Good-bye, and good riddance!"

Chapter 29

Sheena watched Jason as he walked through the kitchen and out the side door to the garage. She listened to the garage door open, then close a few seconds later. Sheena was disappointed that Jason had not been more resistant to being put out. She sat back in the recliner, emotionally drained from the episode she and Jason had shared. She fully reclined the chair.

Closing her eyes, Sheena wondered why she was surprised. She reasoned that he had been with Ruby for months now so he probably would have eventually left so he could be with her anyway. Tears rolled freely down Sheena's cheeks. "Ten good years of my life wasted, gone, poof, just like that." She felt a sudden rush of false hope invading her rational thought process.

She considered the fact that Jason said he wanted to work things out, and that he seemed sincere when he explained things to her. She wanted to believe he was telling her the truth.

After all, their picture was on the cover of *Black Enterprise*, so it's possible that Ruby planned the whole thing. Sheena sat up suddenly. She realized that she was making excuses for him. She knew that she had to face facts: Jason was with Ruby because he wanted to be. Even if Ruby had planned it, she didn't hold a knife to his throat. *Oh Lord, but I did.*

"Lord," she prayed, "he's caused me to experience pain that I didn't think was possible. I thought it hurt badly enough when Derek died, but there's no comparison. I knew I would never see Derek again, but I still have to associate with Jason because of the children. In a way, divorce can be more painful than death." Sheena stood up. "Jesus, please help me to be strong, because I can't allow depression to overtake me the way it did when Derek died. I have to consider the welfare of the children. I can't afford to feel sorry for myself."

She acknowledged the hunger pangs in her stomach. "When is the last time I ate something?" she wondered aloud. Realization slowly set in that she hadn't eaten since she left her mother's house that morning. Sheena knew she needed to call her parents because she was sure they wanted to know what was happening with her. She felt weak from hunger, so she decided to call them later that evening.

Sheena went upstairs to their bedroom to freshen up. She glanced around the room. "I might as well get used to being in this big room by myself." She stared down at the king sized bed. The thought of sleeping in that big bed alone wasn't something she looked forward to. She felt the tears welling up inside. "No," she scolded herself, "I'm not going to cry anymore; I'm tired and I don't want my eyes and face to be red and puffy when the children see me."

The doorbell rang. "Who in the world could this be?" Sheena was sure that it wasn't Jason, because he had a key.

She looked out of her bedroom window. "That's strange. I don't see a car outside." The doorbell chimed again; twice. Sheena hurried downstairs to answer the door. She opened it without looking through the door's peephole.

"Hi, Sheena, I hope that you don't mind me dropping by unannounced." Her neighbor stood in front of Sheena with a big smile on her face. "Well aren't you going to invite me in?"

"Ms. Erma, this is not a good time. Is there something that you need?" Sheena asked.

Erma pushed past Sheena into the foyer, her eyes darting from room to room. "No, I just wanted to check on you to make sure you were all right."

Sheena was normally polite to her neighbors, but Erma had a tendency to be uncommonly nosy. Using the term "an inquiring mind" was an understatement for her. Sheena looked at her from head to toe. "Ms. Erma, you know I'm not a rude person, but as I said before, this is not a good time."

"Are you sure you're okay? I saw the commotion going on over here this morning." She tilted her head to one side. "Who was that woman that attacked Jason? She *beat* the mess out of him. When she left, Jason went tearing down the street after her. I didn't see *you* come outside, so I was wondering if something happened to you. What's going on over here?"

Sheena was finished being polite. "You actually have the unmitigated gall to come to my house demanding to know what's going on? What goes on in this yard, in this house is my business, not yours, Ms. Erma. I'm aware of what went on this morning. I don't need the CIA reporting to me either. Now you need to leave before I throw you out."

Erma was astounded by Sheena's reaction to her, which was aggressive and uncouth. She was accustomed to Sheena's quiet unassuming demeanor.

"Well! I was just being a concerned neighbor. I have seen Jason come and go all day today, but I hadn't seen hide nor hair of you! I thought something might have happened to you, especially since you didn't show your face when that woman came over here acting like a fool. You don't have to worry about me looking out for you anymore." She turned around and walked to the door in a huff. "You sure are a better woman than I am, 'cause if it had been me, I would have beat the crap out of that hussy. I probably would have shot that loony tune!"

Sheena felt badly for speaking to Erma in such a harsh tone. She knew that despite Erma's pretense to be offended, she was deeply hurt. Although Erma was nosy, she seemed sincere in her concern for Sheena. Jason and the children were very fond of her too. Her parents had taught her to be respectful of her elders. Erma was seventy-eight years old.

Sheena called to her. Erma stopped at the door. "I'm sorry for speaking to you harshly, Ms. Erma, but you caught me off guard. This isn't a good time for me to have company. First of all, I wasn't here today, I was visiting my parents in Asheville. Joseph told me what happened when I called home. Secondly, I appreciate your being concerned about me." Sheena gave Erma a faint smile. "Thirdly, if I had been here, I would have done the same thing to her. If I knew where she lived, I would go to her house and kick her butt. But what's done is done. I can handle the problem from here."

Sheena held the door open for Erma. "I don't want to be rude, but I am rather busy. I have things to do, so if you'll excuse me . . ." She told her curtly, "Good-bye, Ms. Erma."

Erma stood in the doorway as though she was expecting an explanation from Sheena about what she was going to do.

"Have a good day." Sheena smiled at her and closed the door in her face.

She headed for the kitchen to make something to eat. A sandwich and some Chamomile tea was her snack of choice; then she retreated to the deck to try to relax and enjoy the fall breeze. The foliage had changed colors and turned to vivid reds, oranges, and yellows, but the beauty didn't compare to the scenery in the mountains. Sheena dozed off for a short while but was awakened by the sounds of the children in the house and was surprised to see it had turned dark outside.

"Momma, where are you?" Jessica called.

"I'm out here on the deck!" She looked at her watch. It was 7:30. "Humph, that was a refreshing cat nap."

Jessica and the twins joined her on the well-built deck that Jason had constructed for Sheena's last birthday. They hugged and kissed her and told her how much they missed her. The twins were anxious to tell her about their afternoon at the new stadium and the Charlotte Bobcats' game. They chattered on and on about the wonderful time they had with Jason. Sheena was pleased to hear that Jason had kept his promise to the boys.

"Where *is* your father?" she asked.

"He's outside in the garage. He was moving the suitcases out of the way so that he could park his car," Joseph informed her.

Sheena was surprised that he hadn't put the luggage in his car. "Moving them where Joseph?"

"I don't know," Joseph shrugged. "Out of the way, I guess. Who's are they anyway? Did you take that many suitcases with you when you went to Grandma's?"

"No, I didn't. They belong to your father."

"Why does he have suitcases in the garage? Is he going on another business trip?"

Before she could answer, Jason walked out onto the deck and sat on the lower level. "No, J, I'm not going on a business trip," he told his son.

"Where are you going then?" Jessica asked.

Jeremiah was curious also. "Yeah, Daddy; where *are* you going?"

Sheena was about to answer for him when the doorbell chimed. Jason went inside to answer the door and opened it for his brother, Jonathan, and his sister-in-law, Mary. They followed him through the house, into the kitchen.

"Sheena, where are you girl?" Mary asked.

"I'm out here on the deck." Sheena replied dryly. She gathered her paper plate and napkins, then tossed them in the trash can as the company joined her on the deck.

"We wanted to come over to see you," Mary chattered in a high-toned voice. "I expected to see you at Momma Catherine's house when Jason dropped off Jessica today. Jason told us that you were visiting your parents and that you would be back tonight. After we rested up, I told Jonathan that before I did anything else I wanted to see Sheena. You know, it's strange seeing Jason without you. You two are like peanut butter and jelly." Mary hugged Sheena and sat down, talking excitedly to her as though they were best friends.

Sheena cut her eyes at Jason. She heard her sister-in-law ask her, "Have you been to see Daddy Grey, Sheena?"

"Not since Friday night, but Jason told me that he has improved greatly. I'm glad to know that he has come out of that coma." She watched Jason and Jonathan as they walked into the kitchen, wondering if and how much he had clued his brother in on their business.

"We had planned to go see him tonight, but Momma Catherine called and told us that he was a little tired and that the nurse suggested that we wait until tomorrow."

The mention of Catherine's name irritated Sheena. "Yes, Mrs. Grey is sticking by her man, isn't she? I suppose she thinks we should all be like her."

"Momma does love her husband, girl. She can be a little overbearing when it comes to Jonathan too. I'm just glad that we don't live close by. Seeing her once a year is sufficient for me." Mary laughed.

"I thought you two were really close."

"We are, close enough." She laughed again. "How are you and she getting along these days?"

"About the same. She never lets me forget how lucky I am to be married to her son."

"Girl, according to him, *he's* the lucky one. Jason talked about you constantly today. I can tell that he loves you very much."

Sheena looked at Mary suspiciously. "Humph. You think so?"

"I know so. He's expressed often how blessed he feels to have you as his wife. He speaks so highly of you, girl."

Sheena suspected that Jason asked Mary to persuade her not to end the marriage. She figured the expression on Mary's face would reveal if she knew anything. She wanted to confirm her suspicions. "It's getting cool out here, don't you think? Let's go inside." Sheena waited until they were seated comfortably at the kitchen table before she spoke again. She poured some tea for Mary and herself. "I'm surprised at this news, Mary. I thought he might have been bragging about his new woman."

Mary's face blushed red of embarrassment. "Sheena, I don't know what you're talking about. Jason's only talked about you. He hasn't mentioned anybody else to us . . . at least not to me."

"I'm sure your husband knows all about it."

"If he does, he hasn't said anything to me."

"You know what they say, the wife is always the last to know."

Mary frowned. "Are you sure, Sheena?"

"As sure as I am that his girlfriend came over and beat his sorry rear end in front of his children this morning!" Jason and Jonathan entered the room in time to hear Sheena blurt out the news to Mary.

"I'm sorry, Sheena, I had no idea." Mary stood up. "Jonathan, did you know about this?"

"No, I had no idea either." He looked at Jason. "What's going on, man?"

Jason shoved his hands in his pockets. His voice was sad when he admitted, "That's part of the news I had to share with you, but there's more."

"More?" Jonathan questioned him, frowning. "What more could there possibly be? Jason, you have a good wife and great kids, man, what's going on with you?"

"It's a long story, Jonathan; one that I am not proud of." Jason could feel Sheena's eyes shooting darts in his back. The phone rang.

"This is probably his woman calling now." Sheena rushed over to answer it. "Hello?" It was her mother. Sheena turned briefly to her sister-in-law. "Mary, would you please excuse me? I need to take this call upstairs."

Mary was still clearly taken aback by the news; she didn't say a word. She indicated to Sheena that she understood with a bow of her head.

Sheena covered the phone mouthpiece with her hand and directed her statement to Jason. "Your little plot to bring your brother over here so you can front to him and Mary isn't going to work. I still want you out of here."

Chapter 30

By the time Sheena was finished with her phone call and came back downstairs, Jonathan and Mary had left. She entered the kitchen where Jason and the children were. They were eating the Japanese food that her in-laws had brought over. She admired the apparent closeness shared among them. She stood there silently watching them for a moment until Jeremiah noticed her. "Hey, Momma. I made a plate for you." "Oh, Jeremiah, that was so nice of you, but I'm not hungry, sweetheart."

"You need to eat something, Momma," Jeremiah urged her. "Daddy said that you probably haven't eaten all day."

Sheena looked at Jason and rolled her eyes at him. "How would you know what I've been doing all day? You've been busy getting beat up by Wonder Woman."

"Sheena," Jason pleaded with his eyes, "let's not do this in front of the children. We were trying to have a family dinner. Would you please join us?"

"Why should I be inconspicuous? *She* sure wasn't."

Joseph shifted in his seat. "Are you guys going to get a divorce?"

Sheena and Jason stared at each other. "Jason, why don't you answer your son. Since your guest had the nerve to come over here showing her butt this morning, you do the honors."

Jason faced Joseph. "J, I'm sorry you guys had to see that this morning. JJ, Jessica, I apologize for what happened."

Joseph walked around the table and stood in front of Jason. "Who was that mean lady, Daddy? And why was she kicking and hitting you like that?"

Jason took a deep breath and exhaled slowly. "She . . . I thought she was a friend of mine, J." Sheena cleared her throat loudly. Jason prayed silently. *Lord, please help me with this; I didn't want to hurt my family like this.* "I can't really explain it to you guys, but I made a huge mistake by talking to her and spending time with her."

"Humph!" Sheena said in a high-pitched voice.

Joseph watched his mother's expression. "She was your *girlfriend*?" he asked his father accusingly. Sheena looked at Joseph in amazement and then back at Jason, waiting for him to answer.

"Don't be silly," Jessica intervened, "Daddy doesn't have a girlfriend. He has a *wife* and that's Mommy."

Jason dropped his head shamefully, and then looked back up at Sheena who had a smirk on her face. "No, Joseph, she was not my girlfriend; she was someone that I used to know a long time ago."

"But Daddy, if you knew her from a long time ago, why was she so mad at you? And why did she start fighting you?"

"It's a long story, J. I am going to sit down with you soon and try my best to explain it to you so you will understand, but I think that everybody is so tired right now that it won't make sense. So, for now, let's have our dinner and then get ready for bed. You guys have school tomorrow and your mother and I have to go to work."

"You didn't answer my question though, Daddy," Joseph persisted.

Frowning from frustration and his son's direct questions, his voice deepened when he said, "Which question, Joseph?"

Sheena looked directly at Jason and cleared her throat. "You need to watch your tone, Jason. There's no need to get upset with Joseph. He has every right to question you when you allow something like this to happen at our home."

"I'm sorry, son," Jason said apologetically. He put his hand on Joseph's shoulder gently. "I didn't mean to raise my voice at you. What were you saying?"

"A—Are you and Momma getting a d—divorce?" he stammered.

Jason looked at Sheena. She didn't budge. "I don't want a divorce from your mother, J, but I have done some things to hurt her really badly. I may have to leave for a while though, if she can't find it in her heart to forgive me."

Jessica ran over to Sheena. "Mommy, please don't make Daddy leave. Please forgive him so he can stay. I don't want my daddy to leave!" She started crying.

Sheena looked at Jason while she held Jessica in her arms. "Thanks a lot, Jason. You were smart enough to shift the blame for *your* wrongdoing on me again." She refocused her attention on Jessica. "Stop crying, baby. I'll see what I can do to make life better for all of us."

"Does this mean that you and Daddy are gonna stay together?" Jeremiah inquired.

"I don't know what I'm going to do, JJ, but I do know that I love you guys with all my heart and I don't want you all to worry about such grown up stuff, okay?"

"We both love you guys," Jason intervened. "I love your mother with all my heart too. God will show us a way to work things out."

Sheena glared at Jason. *I can't believe he actually brought God into this conversation. He's really working it.* "Guys, let's eat our meal and prepare for bed, okay? We'll talk about this later. Come on, sit down and eat, it's getting late."

After the children had eaten, Sheena sent them upstairs to get ready for bed. She did the dishes while Jason sat at the kitchen table watching her. He attempted to have a conversation with her, but she gave him the silent treatment.

"Sheena, we need to talk." She didn't acknowledge him. "Sheena, did you hear me?" She continued to do the dishes, ignoring him.

Normally, Jason would irritate her until she broke the silence, but under the circumstances, he knew he needed to be more sensitive to her feelings. After she finished, she went upstairs to check on the children and to tuck them in bed.

Meanwhile, Jason was in the library, talking on the phone to Cathy. He left the door open so he saw Sheena when she came back downstairs fifteen minutes later. She went into the den, turned the TV on and pretended to look at it. Jason followed her into the room.

"Sheena, we really need to talk in depth before you make a rash decision like this. I do love you. I'm sorry for the way I've treated you these last few months, and if you can be patient with me, I *will* make it up to you. I don't want a divorce; I want to make a better life with you—"

Sheena slammed her hand on the chair arm. "Jason, you're giving me a headache!" She stood up. "I'm going upstairs to my bedroom and get ready for bed.

"I'm tired too, I'll join you."

"Note that I said *my* bedroom."

He gently pulled Sheena to him. The disgusted look she gave him said it all. She tried to wiggle out of his arms.

"Let me go, Jason. Your touch makes my skin crawl. Every time you touch me, all I can see is you touching *her*."

Jason let her go. "I'm sorry, Sheena; I wish that I could fix things as though nothing happened. If you will give me another chance, I'll make every thing up to you."

"But you can't fix it. It's too late now. You even involved the children in your mess. I can't believe you pulled that maneuver in the kitchen in front of the kids either."

"What maneuver?"

"Bringing God in the conversation. You walk around here acting like an atheist, but when it suits your fancy, you turn Christian all of a sudden.

"I've never acted like an atheist and you know it. Just because I don't weave God into every sentence I speak doesn't mean I don't know Him."

"Whatever, you've always been manipulative, haven't you? But you have pulled your last contrivance on me. I'm going to talk to a lawyer tomorrow. I can't forgive you, I don't have the strength to keep trying."

"I—"

"If you want to stay, stay, if you want to leave, leave. I'm sure Ruby will welcome you in her home. I'm through trying to convince you to stay here with me when it's obvious you want to be with her."

"I don't want to be with her. Here is where I want to be." In his frustration, Jason attempted to hug her.

"Don't . . . put your hands on me. At any rate, whether you leave or stay, this isn't going to be a real life *War of the Roses*. She walked upstairs, closed the bedroom door and locked it, leaving Jason standing at the bottom of the stairs, bewildered.

Chapter 31

The next morning, Sheena was surprised to awaken to the smell of breakfast cooking. After she showered and dressed, she walked into the kitchen and observed Jason bustling around in the kitchen making a plate for the children like he normally did.

Cathy and Reana were sitting around the kitchen island with the children. When Jason noticed Sheena standing in the doorway, an invigorating smile showed on his face.

"Good morning, sleepyhead, I made your favorite breakfast," Jason said in a smooth tone.

Sheena uttered an unemotional, "Good morning," to him. She felt her stomach flutter like butterflies were in it. Sheena stared at Jason momentarily. She loved the way his muscles flexed in his tight fitting muscle shirt. The baggy jeans he wore accentuated the lower part of his sculptured body. She cleared her throat and focused on Cathy. "Good morning, Cathy. When did you and Reana get here?"

"Good morning, girl. We got here about eleven fifteen last night. It was so crowded at Momma's house, that I asked her if I could drive her car over here to spend the night with you all. I talked to Jason last night and he said it would be okay to come over."

Jessica stopped eating and ran up to Sheena for a hug. Sheena picked her up and kissed her. "How's my baby this morning?"

"I'm good, Momma, especially after Daddy came in and woke me up for school. I'm glad you didn't make him leave."

Sheena ignored Jessica's remark. "Go finish your breakfast, honey." She kissed the boys and Reana on their cheeks, then sat at the table and continued to talk to Cathy, ignoring Jason's stare. "You know you're welcome anytime, Cathy. Besides, you left all of your things here anyway, didn't you?"

"I did, but I thought about staying and spending some time with my sisters. But girl, they talk so loud and so much that I needed a break! Those Grey girls know they can run their mouths," she laughed.

"They sure can," Sheena agreed, smiling. "How did you get to be so quiet? You don't seem to fit in with them." She addressed the children. "If you guys are finished eating, you need to scurry upstairs and get dressed for school." She turned her attention back to her sister-inlaw. "I'm sorry, Cathy."

"Somebody had to be the quiet one. I guess I don't fit in with them because they were so much older than me. By the time I was born, they were already eight, nine and ten. Momma had us in spurts. Momma had Shirley, Aretha, and Terri within a span of three and half years. Eight years later she had me and one year later she had Jonathan. Everybody thought she was through, but ten years later, Jason pops up. Girl, Catherine and Jacob were doing their *thang*, I tell you." She used her fingers as quotation marks to emphasize the word.

"They sure were. Nobody can accuse them of not being active." Sheena glanced over at Jason, who was sitting quietly by, listening at their conversation.

"Aren't you going to eat your breakfast?" he asked Sheena.

"No," she answered curtly. "I'm not hungry." Sheena walked over to the refrigerator and poured herself some juice. In her peripheral vision, she could see Jason checking her out.

"You look nice today, Sheena, that's a new outfit, isn't it?" Jason asked her.

"It is. I bought it with your money Saturday," she said as she stared at him. In spite of the warm feeling she felt inside when she looked at him, Sheena had to act tough with Jason. "I bought these stilettos too; do you like them?" She placed one of her feet on the bottom rail of the barstool.

"Yeah, they're sexy. I like the new look." Jason smiled as he scanned her body.

"Well, get used to it. I bought several more *expensive* things with your money. I'm not going to be frugal with the money anymore. I may as well spend it before you give it all to Ruby. By the way, I wanted to check the balance on our joint spending account, because I used the debit card. But I couldn't do anything, because the account has been closed." Sheena sipped her juice, then sauntered over to Jason and stood in his face. "Why?"

Cathy cleared her throat. Sheena ignored the fact that she was there. Not wanting to be in the midst of their conversation, Cathy left the room, taking Reana with her.

"What happened to the money, Jason?"

Jason didn't respond to her. He could tell she was ready for a fight. He shook his head and started eating his breakfast.

"Don't ignore me! What happened to the money?" Sheena demanded.

Jason stopped eating and looked up at her. "I told you what happened to it yesterday."

"There was twenty two thousand dollars in that account. Did she take all of it?" Jason shook his head. "Well, how much did she take?"

Jason looked straight ahead, past Sheena. His jaw line hardened. "Seven thousand dollars."

"She embezzled seven thousand dollars from our account and you're sitting there acting like it's no big deal!"

"I discovered yesterday morning that the funds were missing. I traced it to her. So, I closed the account. I'll get the money back, Sheena."

"You doggone right, you're going get it back. If it's not back in my *personal* bank account by tomorrow at this time, I'm pressing charges on her butt!"

"Sheena, that won't be necessary."

"What? You're joking right?"

"I said I'd get it back. It may take a while, but it will be replaced in *your* account." Jason shook his head at Sheena.

"There's no need to shake your head at me. You should have kept your butt home and she wouldn't have had access to your private information. She's not going to get away with stealing my hard earned money. I want it all back; every red cent."

Sheena tore open her statement from the State Employees Credit Union and scanned it. She glared at Jason. "Did you withdraw six hundred dollars from my account last month?"

Jason frowned. "No. You know I don't touch your household account."

"That witch had access to my personal account too? How could you have been so careless; you're in the banking industry! Did she have that much power over you?" Sheena walked around the table and stood in front of Jason. "Why did you do it Jason, *why*?"

"It was something that just—"

"Don't you dare let that simple lie come out of your mouth! Nothing in life just happens."

"What can I say? I made a foolish mistake."

"It wasn't a mistake. You kept seeing her over and over again. If I hadn't confronted you with it, you'd still be seeing her."

"I know you won't believe it, but I tried to break it off with her several times."

"You didn't try hard enough. What did she do, put a gun to your head?"

"In a sense, she did."

"Oh, so now you're going to patronize me?"

"No, not at all. It's more complicated than you think."

"Complicated? How can it be complicated? Either you wanted to be with her or you didn't."

"It isn't that simple."

"It *is* that simple. You should have gotten rid of the hussy. You just didn't want to because you loved being with her. What did she do, bewitch you? Are you in love with her?"

Jason considered telling Sheena about Cassandra, but decided now was not the time. "No, I'm not in love with her. I've never loved Ruby, it's always been the same for us."

"And what's that?"

"A physical thing."

"You know what? You're making me really angry telling your shiftless lies."

Jason stared into Sheena's eyes. "I'm not lying."

"So, how many more women have you been with?" Sheena held Jason's stare.

"I've never cheated on you before."

Sheena face became distorted. "Do you really expect me to believe that?"

"It's the truth."

"You wouldn't know how to tell the truth if your life depended on it."

"I don't know what to say to convince you, Sheena, but I'm being honest with you. There's been no one else in my life besides you."

"You mean besides *Ruby* and me, don't you?"

"You know what I mean."

"I don't know anything anymore. You've lied to me and disappointed me more times than I care to think about."

"Well, I'm not lying to you now and I regret that I've disappointed you the way I have."

"I regret that I was so blind to your conniving antics. Deep down inside, I knew you weren't saved when I agreed to marry you."

"Why did you marry me then?"

Sheena wanted Jason to feel the pain that she was experiencing at the moment. "Because I was still mourning over Derek and I thought marrying you would be the solution to my problem." It worked. She observed the painful expression on his face as he walked away from her.

"Well, I guess we learn something new everyday don't we?" he mumbled.

"Don't act so surprised, Jason. From what I overheard at your mom's house the first time you introduced me to your family, I was just a rebound to you."

"What are you talking about?" Jason turned back around to face her. His face was full of confusion.

"You remember when you came back into the house and I was suddenly ready to go?"

"Yes, I remember. You said you had a terrible headache."

"I didn't have a headache; I overheard your mother and sisters laughing and talking about me."

"Are you sure they were talking about you?"

"I'm positive. They were saying that I was about the homeliest girl they had seen you with and the only explanation for you marrying me was because you must not be over Ruby. 'She's definitely a rebound,' they said, laughing."

"Who said that?"

"Terri and Aretha were the most vocal. Shirley and your mother laughed, but your mother did make the comment that you'd better think twice before you had some children with me."

"I'm sorry you heard that. Why didn't you come to me about it?"

"Why? Crying to you wouldn't have made a difference. That was their opinion. You don't sound surprised; they must have had the conversation with you too."

"They made some remarks about you, but I put them in their place and let them know that I wasn't marrying you to be my trophy wife. I wanted to marry you because I loved you."

"Considering the fact you got involved with your old girlfriend proves their point though."

"What does my involvement with Ruby have to do with proving their point?"

"The fact that you went running back to her proves that you weren't over her. I was . . . *am* just a rebound to you."

"You know you aren't a rebound. If you were, I wouldn't have stayed married to you. When people rebound, they're just with that person for convenience."

"Right. You conveniently stayed with me until she came back into your life."

"Sheena, that can't make sense, even to you."

"What do you mean even to me? Am I supposed to be gullible now too?"

"No, you know . . . where is all this coming from? You know you aren't now or never have been a rebound to me."

"I don't know that. But I do know that you are sleeping with your old girlfriend again, so evidently they knew what they were talking about."

"I can't apologize to you enough for my mistakes, but I am sorry. It's over between us and I would like nothing more than to try to make it up to you."

"How do you propose to do that?"

"The only way I know how to, one day at a time until I regain your faith and trust in me."

"I don't see how you expect me to get over the fact that you rebounded to me after you and Ruby broke up. There was a time when I thought you loved me, but now your family's words keep echoing in my head."

Jason became weary with her accusation. "For the last time, Sheena, I married you because I loved you."

"You keep saying *loved* me. So is that a part of the past too?"

"No, I still love you, but this conversation about rebounding is meaningless, and you know it."

"Not to me. I've doubted your love for me sometimes; now I know why."

"You doubted my love because you have always been insecure concerning any woman that you thought looked at me for longer than five seconds."

"You know why I'm insecure, don't you?"

"No, I don't know why, because I've never given you a reason to mistrust me."

"You have now."

"You're right, Sheena. I can't undo the past. All I can do is ask you to forgive me and work toward making up for my mistake."

"I wish I could forgive you, Jason, but I can't."

Jason held his head down, tapping it with the tips of his fingers. "Well, I guess there's nothing more to say then."

Sheena countenance saddened because she saw the way Jason retreated suddenly. "I guess not." She thought he would have fought harder for their marriage.

"Besides, I was just a rebound for you too, so I guess we're even. You aren't the only one hurt. It doesn't pleasure me any to know that I was just a rebound to you. Now I understand why you've been so distant at times."

Sheena immediately felt convicted. "Jason, I didn't mean that. I was in so much pain that I wanted to hurt you like you hurt me. Derek's the only person from my past that I knew would bother you."

"Well, whether you meant it or not, I'll never know. So you see, no matter how much I try to convince you that you're not a rebound, I can't do it. It's up to you to believe me or not."

Sheena considered his statement. "I didn't mean that, Jason, really. I'm sorry for saying that."

Jason shrugged. "Humph."

"I still don't understand why you got involved with her again though. What was it about her? Why did you get back with her after all these years? I need to know. Why would you jeopardize our marriage like this?" Sheena walked up to Jason and looked him directly in his eyes. "What is it about her that you couldn't resist? Why, Jason? I just want to know *why*?"

Jason knew that Sheena was wired up, and when she got like that, she didn't relent until she was satisfied that she'd gotten the answer she wanted.

"We've always had this . . . I don't know, uncontrollable passion between us, I guess. I really don't feel comfortable talking to my wife about another woman." Jason watched Sheena in amazement, as her face grew red with anger.

"Don't worry, you won't have a wife *to* talk to after today. You can have her and you all can be as passionate as you want to be and act like two dogs in heat for all I care! I'm going downtown and hire a lawyer."

"Sheena, wait." Jason pleaded.

"Wait for what?" Sheena hissed.

"What about the kids?"

"I'm not going in to work today. I've already arranged for a substitute. *You* take the children to school today!" And on that note, Sheena left the room.

Chapter 32

After Sheena stormed out of the room, Jason went to his makeshift bedroom, the library, to finish getting dressed. He sat down on the couch, and surprising himself, began to pray. "Lord, I praise you. I thank you for your mercy. I humbly ask you to touch my wife's heart so she'll have the ability to forgive me. Please restore my marriage and give me the wisdom to know how to become a better husband to her.

"Lord, I know it's possible that Cassandra may be the final straw in her decision to divorce me, but I will be less than a man to have a daughter in the world and not take care of her. I need your direction on how to tell her about my daughter and grant me with a miracle so she will accept Cassandra. Jesus, thank you in advance for working the situation out for all of us."

There was a knock on the door.

"Daddy we're ready for school," Joseph announced. "Momma left to go somewhere and she said for you to take us to school."

"I'll be right out, J." Jason tied his tie and joined the children. He looked at his watch. It was 7:55. Jason was usually at work by now. "You guys got everything, don't you? I won't have time to turn around and come back for anything."

Jeremiah checked his and Jessica's book bag. Joseph checked his. "We have everything Daddy."

Cathy was standing in the foyer. "I can take them to school for you if you're running late."

"Thanks, Cathy, but I'll do it. I can take the time to drive my kids to school. Who's going to say anything about me being late," he joked. "I'm the head honcho."

Jason headed for the garage. The children followed him, and they got in the car. The ten minute ride to school was filled with Jessica's chatter. She monopolized Jason's attention. Jeremiah and Joseph talked to each other quietly. Jason parked the car and walked Jessica to her class. His intention was to walk the twins to class too, but they politely informed him that they were too old to have their father walk them to their classroom. They each gave him a high five and said good-bye.

Jeremiah turned around and asked him, "We'll see you at home tonight won't we, Daddy?"

Jason was surprised at his question. He realized they must have still been feeling insecure about last night's conversation. "I'll be there JJ, as soon as I leave work. See you, son. Have a good day."

Jason hopped back into his car and headed for work, saying a silent prayer of thanks for restoration of his family. He remembered how he often heard Sheena teach the children the Word in Luke 11:10: *For every one that asketh receiveth; and he that seeketh findeth; and to him that knocketh it shall be opened.* His cell phone rang. "Maybe this is Sheena." He answered without looking at the caller ID "Hello?" he answered.

"Hi," the caller announced.

It wasn't Sheena.

Chapter 33

"What do you want now, Ruby? Didn't you cause enough trouble when you showed up at my house yesterday?" "I called to apologize for that. I really lost control when you called me and cursed me out about your money."

"You *stole* my money, seven thousand dollars. I need to press charges on your rogue butt. If you needed some money for Cassandra, all you had to do was ask. Instead, you had the nerve to start cursing like a sailor when I asked you about it."

"You shouldn't have approached me like that; I don't take kindly to people talking to me like I'm less than human."

"I don't take kindly to people stealing from me."

"Look, Jason, I called to apologize for stealing your money and for coming over to your house yesterday."

"What were you thinking? I knew you were capable of doing some crazy stuff, but to steal from me and then come over to my house and fight me in front of my children and neighbors, I don't understand you. I thought I knew you, Ruby, but I guess I don't know you at all."

"I said that I'm sorry, I just wanted to hurt you like you hurt me. I truly apologize."

"And that's suppose to make everything all right?"

"No, of course not, but do you think you can find it in your heart to forgive me?"

"*Forgive* you? Just like that. My children witnessed you attacking their father, how do you think that made them feel?"

"I regret doing that. I said I'm sorry."

"So is that it?"

"What about your wife, what did she have to say?"

"That's the reason you came over isn't it? Hoping that Sheena would see you. You told me not to take your threats idly, and I guess you proved your point. As far as Sheena is concerned, she wasn't home. She was visiting her parents."

"Oh," Ruby said flatly.

"You can be proud of yourself though, Joseph told her everything. Mission accomplished. I had not planned on leaving her, but your scheme to make her leave me worked. She's on her way downtown now to see a lawyer." Ruby was quiet. "Aren't you proud of yourself? You broke up my home, just like you said you would."

"I'm not proud of what I did, Jason. But, I didn't do this alone and you know it."

"*Touché.*"

"I just wanted to be with you."

"You're still as selfish as ever."

"I *know* you aren't calling *me* selfish. You kept coming back for more. I didn't force myself on you."

"You're right. I made a mistake by getting back with you and now I'm going to lose my family for it, but I guess I got what I deserved."

"What are you going to do now?"

"We're not going to be together if that's what you're hoping for."

"Actually, I don't want us to be together either."

"What kind of sick game are you playing? You did everything in your power to get me to leave home, and when I wouldn't, you devised a plan so my wife would leave me. Well, you won, she's filing for the divorce; now you can go and break up someone else's home. That's how the game is played isn't it?"

"I have to admit, when I came to Charlotte, I had every intention of breaking you and your wife up. But I understand how wrong and sinful I've been, so now I know what I need to do."

"And what is that?"

"Ask you for forgiveness and get out of your life."

Jason looked at the phone. "I don't believe that you are sincere, Ruby. You've played these games too many times."

"I know I have, but after I drove home yesterday, I took a good long look in the mirror and I didn't like what I saw."

"Really?"

"Really. I called my parents and I had a long talk with my father. He strongly suggested that I pick up the Bible and read some scriptures that he thought pertained to me, so I did. I meditated on those scriptures for hours, and after that, I prayed and asked God to forgive me. I believe that He has, and now I'm asking you to forgive me too."

Jason exhaled loudly. "I don't know what to say." His forehead wrinkled.

"Say that you forgive me," Ruby said sweetly.

"Okay. I forgive you, and in addition to your apology, I want my money back. Since you were wise enough to embezzle it out of my account, be smart enough to put it back, because Sheena has already detected the missing funds. She asked me what happened to it this morning. She watches our money like a hawk."

"I can't."

"What do you mean you can't? I know you couldn't have possibly spent seven thousand dollars in two days."

"I haven't spent it all, but I purchased something important for Cassandra."

"Like what?"

"Things that she'll need when she comes to live with me, like a bedroom suite for her room. It's going to be delivered in a few days. I ordered it from the furniture store Saturday."

"Let me get this straight. You transferred the money from my account Saturday morning and by Saturday night you bought some furniture?"

"Yep. I went shopping that evening to buy her new clothes, and when I passed by the furniture store, I walked in and saw a bedroom ensemble that was on sale for $2,500.00, so I bought it."

"Unbelievable. I've never seen anything like it. You need to seek therapy on money matters, because you definitely need help in that arena."

"I just need money; that's all. I wasn't born with a silver spoon in my mouth like you were."

"You're kidding right? I'm not wealthy by any means. I had to work hard for every penny I've made. My old man saw to that."

"You may not be rich, but you sure aren't suffering for anything."

"Forget it, Ruby; I hope you enjoyed that money because, as of yesterday morning, you won't have the opportunity to embezzle anymore from me."

"So, I take it that I'm forgiven?"

"I won't press any charges on you, but Sheena might. She's already threatened to do just that."

"You're not gonna let her do that, are you?"

"I can't control what she does. I tried to talk her out of it, but she was highly upset about that money."

Well, I hope she doesn't press charges on me. Even though I was wrong, I don't want to go to jail. I was just trying to do something special for my daughter."

"By embezzling? I hope you have taught her better morals than that."

"I have. To be honest, I wanted to get revenge on you for breaking up with me. I never considered the consequences of my actions."

"I know you did it out of spite. I can't judge you though, because I'm partly to blame for using you too."

"So, do you forgive me?"

"Sure, why not? Now what?"

"We go our separate ways. It won't be easy for me; but I know what I need to do."

"What's that?"

"Rededicate my life back to Christ and trust that He'll direct my path."

"I forgive you, Ruby. I need to rededicate my life back to Christ too. Can you forgive me for hurting you? I know I led you on too. I shouldn't have played with your heart or your feelings. If anyone is to blame for this mess, it's me, because I knew I had a wife and kids and I knew what my intentions were toward you."

"Your intentions were to have your cake and eat it too, right?"

"Right. I've always cared for you, Ruby. If circumstances were different, maybe we could have made a relationship work between us, but there's always been too much passion between us, and not enough peace. We were always bad for each other. I'm sorry I hurt you; you are a special woman, but we just don't have what it takes to be a couple . . . ."

"You don't have to keep trying to explain things to me. I knew what I was getting into when I came up here. I was so disappointed in my husband—"

"What? Your *husband*?"

"I should have told you, Jason . . . I'm married. I've been married to Thurman Porter for eleven years now."

Jason parked his car in his parking space at the bank. "You're *married*?"

"Yep. I know this is shocking news, but we've been separated for months now. I filed for a divorce, but he hasn't signed the papers yet."

Jason couldn't believe what he was hearing.

"Are you still with me, Jason?"

"Yes, I'm still here. *Married*; I just find it hard to believe."

"It's true. I'm sorry I withheld that information from you. I was hoping that my divorce would be finalized before I told you."

"And what was your specific plan then?"

"I had hoped to get a second chance with you."

"So you were hoping that Sheena and I would break up so you and I could be together?"

"I wanted that at first, but the more time I spent with you, I could sense that you really did love your wife, and that I was just a familiar extracurricular activity to you."

"You are blowing my mind. I should have never gotten involved with you again, Ruby. I had no idea you were so deceptive," Jason said angrily.

"It wasn't my intention to deceive you. I felt trapped in a boring marriage, and when I saw you on the cover of *Black Enterprise* magazine, I started reminiscing about our time together. I thought maybe we could try again."

Jason took a deep breath and exhaled slowly, trying to calm down. "How would that be possible when I had a family . . . and so did you?"

"I don't know, I just wanted out of my marriage and I saw you as the solution. Knowing that you were Cassandra's father was the main reason I wanted to be with you."

"Am I Cassandra's father? You said that you have been married for eleven years now. Is he the child's father or am I?"

"Without a doubt, you are. Thurman married me when I was pregnant. He and I grew up together. We've known each other since we were six years old. When I turned twelve, I used to hang out at his parents' house when my parents left me home alone. We dated in high school briefly, but nothing ever came of it. After I moved back to Florida, I saw him at the hospital, where he works. He suggested we go out on a date. I was already pregnant, but he said that didn't matter. We talked for months, and when I was seven months pregnant, we got married."

"He married you while you were carrying another man's child?"

"He sure did. Momma warned me not to marry him while I was pregnant, but he insisted that it didn't matter to him, because he had always loved me. I believed him and didn't want my baby to be illegitimate. I've always cared for him too, so that's why I married him. I thought in time, I'd grow to love him, but . . ." Her voice trailed off.

Jason cleared his throat. "We need to finish this conversation at another time, because I need to get into the office, but I want to hear everything."

"Okay, I want to tell you everything too. Maybe then you'll understand my situation better."

"How has he treated Cassandra over the years?"

"He loves her like she's his own daughter. He's never mistreated her."

"I still can't believe you had my daughter all these years and never let me know."

"We thought it best if she considered Thurman to be her father. He's been there for her ever since the day she was born. He was in the delivery room with me when she came out. He loved her the minute he saw her."

"Now that I know she's my daughter, I want to be responsible for her. I want to be a part of her life too."

"You'll get a chance to meet her this weekend. She and my parents are flying here Saturday morning. I spent a portion of the money purchasing tickets for them to fly here. She knows about you and is anxious to meet you."

"I'm anxious to meet her too, but I thought you said she didn't know about me?"

"I'm sorry. I lied about that too. I didn't want to risk ruining our relationship by telling you everything too soon."

"That's what I meant earlier, a relationship based on dishonesty will never work. That's a lesson I've learned recently."

"I understand that now. I've withstood some hard knocks in life, but I think I have finally seen the light."

"We need to meet somewhere so we can talk in depth before I see her, Ruby. I need to know all the details, so I will know what to expect."

"I'll tell you everything. Can we meet at my place Thursday morning?"

"I . . . don't think so. Thursday is Thanksgiving Day, you know. My family and I are getting together for dinner and for a welcome home party for my dad. He's being released from the hospital Wednesday."

"What about Wednesday during lunch hour?"

"No, that's not a good time. I have a meeting scheduled at that time. I can meet you Wednesday afternoon at . . . ." he pulled out and looked at his pocket agenda . . . "two. We can meet at the restaurant on Sugar Creek Road."

"Our usual meeting place?"

"Yes, but it won't be business as usual. That's gotta end."

"I know. I need to get my life back straight with God. Maybe by some miracle, Thurman and I can work things out."

"Are you sure you want that? There's no need to continue to stay in a marriage that's not working. In spite of everything, you're a good person, Ruby. You deserve to be loved too."

"Thanks. I've tried to be a good person. I've screwed my life up grasping for the wrong star, but deep down inside, I've known I had my star all along."

"You sound like you care for Thurman more than you knew."

"I do. After reading the Word and praying last night, I've come to realize that I had my appointed husband all along, similar to Boaz, spoken of in the Bible in the Book of Ruth."

"That's great, Ruby. Now I don't feel like I've used you. I guess we used each other for our own selfish reasons. I know this might sound weird, but we need to pray for each other that God will work a miracle out for us in our marriages."

"That doesn't sound too weird. We do need to pray for each other; after all, we have a daughter together. We need to ask God to give us wisdom about how to deal with that too."

"God is a miracle worker, Ruby."

"I know He is, but what made you say that?"

"Because when I heard your voice on the phone, I knew it was going to be the same ole same ole. But look at what has happened. God has touched your heart to repentance and mine too."

"Amen. I'd better let you go. I'll see you Wednesday at two. Be blessed."

Jason was in awe. "You be blessed too." He sat in the car for a few minutes thinking about their amazing conversation. "Jesus, if you can work a miracle out like that, I know you can show me how to save my marriage." He entered his office with an optimistic outlook for the first time in months.

Chapter 34

Sheena sat in the lawyer's office with mixed emotions. On one hand, coming here to file for a separation felt right, on the other, she regretted having to end her marriage to a man she still obviously loved. Her lawyer tried to convince her to give it some thought before filing, but she felt compelled to set the gears in motion for a divorce.

"If I don't do it now," she told the lawyer, "I probably won't file, so it's now or never."

"That statement is a good indication that you should wait, Mrs. Grey," the lawyer replied. "You seem confused and angry too . . ."

"Of course, I'm angry. Wouldn't any woman be?"

"Yes, of course. I'm not implying that you don't have the right to be angry. I'm simply advising you to give it more thought. Take a week, or at least until after the Thanksgiving holidays before you make a decision."

"I'm sure my decision will be the same then as it is now."

"Are you positive you want to file a petition today? After all, this is just a consultation."

Sheena stared at her blankly like a deer lost in the headlights of a car. "I . . . think so. I probably should go ahead and proceed with this."

"Mrs. Grey, please take my advice and think about it a few more days. I can set you up an appointment to come in to see me next . . . let me see," she checked her appointment book, "Wednesday. If you want to proceed with filing the papers, I'll be glad to work with you."

"If that is your advice, I suppose I can accept it for now. But if I come in next week feeling the same way, I expect you to start the paperwork, or I will find another lawyer."

"Great. If nothing has changed by your appointment next week, I'll be happy to start the procedure. In the meantime, you should try to relax over the holidays so you'll be able to make rational decisions and not angry ones." She walked around her desk and extended her hand to Sheena. "Don't look so sad, Mrs. Grey. Be encouraged." She handed Sheena her business card.

Tears rolled down Sheena's cheeks. "Thank you."

"Be strong, Mrs. Grey." She hugged Sheena. "It's ironic that I am a divorce lawyer, because I always counsel my clients against divorce, if that's at all possible. But if it is not, I work diligently to ensure my clients that they will be represented well."

"You were highly recommended; that's why I chose you. Thank you for your time and if I feel the same way, I'll see you next Wednesday. In any case, please have a great holiday."

"You do the same. Good-bye."

Sheena drove away from the lawyer's office feeling relieved. However, as she drove along the interstate, she began to have second thoughts about letting the lawyer talk her out of filing. She reasoned that she must be a good lawyer, because some lawyers would have urged her to start the proceedings immediately, so they could start calculating the money they would make. Sheena concluded that the lawyer seemed genuinely concerned about her state of mind.

Sheena was approaching Jason's bank. "I should surprise him by stopping by his office." She decided to do just that. She parked her SUV beside his Mercedes, and went into his office. Jason's secretary was about to buzz him to let him know she was there, until Sheena advised, "Don't buzz him, I want to surprise him."

Sheena tiptoed into his office and was surprised at what she saw.

He was kneeling in front of the couch praying. She heard him praying for restoration of their marriage and thanking God for ending the relationship he had with Ruby. She cleared her throat to interrupt him.

Obviously taken aback by her unexpected appearance, Jason stood up abruptly and sat on the couch. "Sheena, what a surprise. What brings you by?"

"I was in the neighborhood."

Jason smiled at the old cliché. "I'm glad you stopped by. I was just praying for us."

"I see. When did you become a praying man?"

"Since I realized the mistakes that I have made with you. I've repented of everything, Sheena. You may find this hard to believe, but I am sorry for hurting you."

"I'm sure you are sorry for getting caught."

"No, I'm sorry for hurting you and my children. Hindsight is always twenty-twenty, if I knew then what I know now, I would be a better man."

"You're right, if I knew ten years ago what I know now, I would be a better woman, because I wouldn't be married to your unfaithful behind."

Jason dropped his head, sorrowfully. "I wish that I could take your pain away." He pulled her close to him.

"Don't put your hands on me; it gives me the creeps." She backed away from him. "Speaking of creeps, I heard you praying for your girl."

"I was thanking God that our relationship is finally over."

"And when did the two of you confirm that. It's not over unless she agrees, you know? In other words, she'll still harass you and especially me."

"We talked this morning."

Sheena frowned. "You mean to tell me you saw her this morning? You are a no good, lying, snake!"

"Sheena, hear me out. I didn't *see* her this morning. She called me on my cell phone."

Sheena sneered at him. "Oh, so that makes it okay, right?"

"No. She called me to apologize for her actions yesterday."

"She should have apologized with her crazy self. She needs to apologize to the children, and to me too."

"You're right. The point is, she agreed that we should stop seeing each other."

"So she suddenly had an epiphany?"

"Yes, the best kind. She's opened her heart to Jesus."

"Humph! I suppose you think that I'm just going to forgive and forget and life can go on as usual, huh?"

"No, I don't expect you to forgive and forget as though nothing happened. Just don't give up on us, Sheena. I need you in my life. I love you."

Sheena's body language stiffened. "You know I went to see a lawyer, Jason."

"I know. What happened? Did you file for a separation?"

Sheena frowned and rubbed her arm. "No; I wanted to, but she advised me against filing."

"Great. You won't regret it, Sheena. I'll do everything in my power to repair our marriage."

"Don't get too happy, Jason. She asked me to postpone my decision until after Thanksgiving. I have an appointment with her on next Wednesday. By then, I'll have made my decision. Right now, my mind is in favor of a divorce."

"Sheena . . ."Jason hesitated. Sheena stared at him expectantly. "Would it matter if I told you Ruby was married?"

Sheena pondered his question for a moment. "Not really." She stormed out of the office, leaving Jason standing in his tracks, flabbergasted.

Chapter 35

The next two days passed uneventfully for the Grey household. They resumed their daily activities as usual, with the exception of Jason still sleeping in the library.

Once Jason got to work Wednesday morning, one of his clients called to schedule an emergency meeting with him. After that, the rest of his day was booked; he barely had time to take fifteen minutes for lunch. Jason called Ruby and cancelled their meeting until the Friday after Thanksgiving. Ruby agreed because an unexpected change had occurred in her life also.

Sheena reluctantly agreed to ride with Jason to visit his father at home that Wednesday night. Upon their arrival, the family catered to Sheena in an attempt to make her comfortable. Jason had informed everyone about their circumstances, so his mother and siblings were on their best behavior. In spite of their differences, they respected Sheena and didn't want Jason and her to get divorced.

Sheena spent most of her time encouraging Jacob to strive to achieve the goals that the physical therapist had set for him so that he could recover fully.

Cathy and her sisters were preparing the menu for Thanksgiving Day. Jason and Jonathan watched a football game on television. Mary had taken the children out to a restaurant. Catherine waited patiently for Sheena and Jacob to finish their conversation. After Jacob had fallen asleep, Catherine told Sheena that she wanted to speak to her alone. They withdrew to the formal living room.

"I wanted to get you alone to let you know how much I appreciate you being a good wife to my son," Catherine stated.

Sheena didn't respond.

"I know we've had our differences in the past, but I am proud to have you as my daughter-in-law."

Sheena squinted her eyes at Catherine. "When did you discover this, Mrs. Grey?"

"I've always been proud of you, Sheena. I just want to make amends with you and apologize for anything that I may have done or said to hurt you over the years."

"Did Jason ask you to speak to me? I'm sure that you are aware that I am considering filing for a divorce. I'm positive that you know all about him seeing his ex-girlfriend again."

"Yes, I knew about it, but believe me, I did not approve of it. I did the best I could to discourage Jason from seeing her. I knew she was nothing but trouble. I told him she wasn't worth him risking his marriage for."

"Humph!"

"I can understand if you don't believe me. I love Jason, but he knows that I don't uphold him in his wrong. I've talked to him, read him scriptures from the Bible, and prayed for him too."

"Oh, really?"

"Yes, really. He finally realized what he had gotten himself into and I believe he tried to break it off with her several times, but she is not the type of woman to take no for an answer."

"And how do you know this?"

"Because my son told me so."

"And what your son says is gold, right?"

"No . . ." Catherine took a deep breath. "Sheena, I know that he's telling the truth because he has called me and asked me to pray for him. He is truly sorry for what he has done. You know how he rejected the Word of God whenever we even mentioned the Bible, but I believe he has repented and asked God to forgive him; he is really sorry for hurting you and the children the way he has."

Sheena stood in front of Catherine and clapped her hands softly. "Bravo. You have made a terrific speech for your precious son. What's next? My son is a *good* man, pep talk? I should be so lucky to have him talk?"

Catherine was angered by Sheena's sarcastic remarks. Her face flushed, but she maintained her composure. "Sheena, I'm sorry if I hurt you with those remarks, but that was my way of assuring you that Jason loved you."

"Did he tell you that he loved me so much that his woman came to my house and beat the crap out of him in front of his children?"

"He told me how she acted. I'm not surprised given her past history."

"What history?"

"She used to fight him all the time. That's why he broke up with her. She didn't have any etiquette. No control whatsoever. He had to leave school during his summer vacation to get rid of her. He was impressed with you when he met you. After talking to you, he called me and told me, 'Momma, I have met the woman that I want to marry one day. She's a real lady, unlike that wildcat Ruby.'"

"I might be compelled to believe you except for the fact that he became involved with that *wildcat* again after all of these years."

"He made a terrible mistake, Sheena. I can imagine how she enticed him again. She is a very beautiful woman; and she is the type to do whatever it takes to get what she wants."

"You can't blame it all on her. She didn't force him to be with her."

"No, she didn't. He played his part in this too. I'm ashamed to admit it, but Jason always was attracted to a pretty woman with a shapely figure. His priority was in the wrong place when it came to that."

"No it wasn't. He married me didn't he? I'm neither pretty nor shapely. You were surprised when he brought me home, remember?"

Catherine's face looked clueless. "What are you talking about?"

"You really don't remember?" Catherine shook her head indicating that she didn't. "Let me refresh your memory; and I quote, 'Jason, that girl is homely. I know you can do better than that. You had better think about what your children are going to look like if you have some with her. Of all the pretty girls you've dated, *this* is who you're going to marry?' " Sheena put her hands on her hips. "That's what you said, Mrs. Grey, word for word."

Catherine was embarrassed. "I can't deny it. I did say that. I didn't realize you heard me. I'm sorry I ever said anything that cruel about you."

"Well, you said it. And over the years, you've reinforced your belief by your actions."

"How? I am proud that Jason married you. I couldn't ask for a better daughter-in-law."

"You're always gloating about how the children look just like Jason. I can almost hear the relief in your voice that they don't look like me."

"That's not true, Sheena. All of the kids have your reddish brown complexion with those freckles; they just have Jason's features. And Jessica has hair just like your mother's side of the family. If I said that you were homely, I'm sorry."

"You said it, no doubt about that."

"If truth be told, I think you are a pretty woman. You are such a humble person that it makes you pretty. A person's persona has a lot to do with the way they look."

"It doesn't matter. I am who God made me."

"Yes you are. He made a wonderful human being when He made you, too. I love you, Sheena, and I hope that you can forgive me for running my mouth in the past. I'll make up for it in the future, if you let me." Catherine hugged Sheena. This time Sheena didn't pull away. She hugged her back.

Jason and Jonathan walked in the room in time to witness the event. "Look at my two favorite girls," Jason replied. "God has worked another miracle right before my eyes.

Chapter 36

Thurman had shown up on Ruby's doorstep the same day that she and Jason had agreed to stop seeing each other. She was shocked to see him waiting on the front stoop of her apartment when she got home from work. They argued for hours, until Ruby gave up and called a truce. They agreed to be civil toward each other long enough to go out to dinner together.

To her surprise, they had a pleasant dinner, and when they returned to her home, they resumed their conversation like rational adults. Ruby suggested that they read those same scriptures from the Bible that her dad had given her to read. Before the night was over, they both had rededicated their lives back to Christ.

Ruby admitted to Thurman that she did love him, but was in denial until recently. She was honest enough with him to tell him the whole truth about the fantasy she had for years of being with Jason, but knew that it was just that, a fantasy.

He said that he needed time to know if he could forgive her and he would make a decision on whether they should get a divorce or not. They prayed together and agreed that Thurman should stay, at least through the Thanksgiving weekend.

Jason and Ruby met the Friday after Thanksgiving Day at the designated place. They postponed meeting that Wednesday, because in addition to Jason's hectic schedule, Ruby's family had arrived that Wednesday morning. They decided to drive to North Carolina instead of flying so that they could have Thanksgiving Dinner together.

Ruby sat smiling across the table from Jason, her dark eyes gleaming. "You look happy Ruby," Jason said as he smiled at her.

"I am happy. For the first time in years, I'm truly happy, Jason. I thank God for forgiveness and for my husband. I do love him. I feel like a hypocrite saying that to you, but I really do love Thurman."

"I can see it in your face. I hope that you two will be able to work things out."

"I believe we are going to, but it's going to take lots of time and patience though."

"That's great." Jason had a far-away look in his eyes.

"What's wrong? How are things going for you and Sheena?"

"About the same. I think she's still going to file for a divorce. She is very distant with me. She barely speaks to me anymore."

"I'm sorry, Jason. I know this may sound silly, but do you think it would help if I talked to her? I'll explain the situation to her and apologize to her. It might make a difference if she knows that I'm already married."

Jason smiled, his dimples deepened. "She already knows that you're married. I told her the same day you told me, it didn't make a difference. Ruby, you are probably the last person she wants to listen to."

"You're probably right," she said thoughtfully." Ruby changed the subject. "We need to make some arrangements so that you can see Cassandra before we leave."

"We? Are you leaving too?"

"Yes. It's for the best. Cassandra needs me and she really doesn't want to move away from her grandparents. Besides, Thurman and I can't work things out if I'm living here and he's in Florida."

"I guess you're right. When are you leaving?"

"I'll be moving a week from today."

"I would say that I hate to see you go, but we both know it's for the best. I'll pray for you, and please pray for me."

"I will Jason, and I believe that God is going to make a way for y'all's marriage to be restored too."

"Thanks." He pinched her on her cheek lightly. "You are full of surprises aren't you?"

"I am, aren't I?" Ruby laughed. "No one could have told me six months ago that I would be sitting here saying *those* words."

Jason laughed. "Yeah, life is funny."

Ruby reached across the table and put Jason's hand in hers. A slight frown creased Jason's forehead. "Jason, I know that Cassandra is yours, but I don't want you to have any doubts."

"I believe you, Ruby."

"That's good to know, but the first thing Sheena is going to want to know is, do you have proof." She let his hand go. "So, I think we should make an appointment to have a DNA test done before we go back to Florida."

Jason meditated on Ruby's suggestion for a moment. He nodded his head. "You're right, she will want to see some proof."

Ruby nodded. "If it were me, I would want some proof too. I'll call and set up an appointment when I get back home."

"Great. Just let me know and I'll be there. I've decided to wait until after Sheena returns from visiting her parents for the weekend before I tell her about Cassandra. Sheena will have the information she needs to make her decision by Wednesday. I hate to hurt her with more secrets, but she has to know. If she divorces me because of this, I can't say a word."

"I should have never told you about her."

"If you hadn't told me and I found out about her years later, I would have never forgiven you. You should have told me when you found out you were pregnant."

"Yes, I should have, but back then, I was so distraught that I didn't know what to do. But, that's water under the bridge now. I'm relieved that you know though. Everything will work out for all of us, I'm sure." Ruby reached over and placed her hand over Jason's hand.

"I'm glad you're sure, because I'm not."

"Jason!" A high pitch voice screeched from behind him. Jason recognized the voice.

No. This can't be happening! he thought. Jason looked around to see Sheena glaring at him.

She had gone to visit a friend before she left town to visit her parents. By sheer coincidence, her path took her by the restaurant where she saw Jason's car parked, and coincidently, she noticed the license plates "Ruby Kiss" on the white Honda parked right beside his car. When she pulled up beside his car, she saw Jason having lunch with a lady outside on the deck.

"What is going on here?" Sheena angrily demanded to know.

Jason was shocked. "Sheena . . . I—"

"I *nothing!*" She looked to the woman sitting across from Jason. "So this must be Ruby." She looked Ruby over, noticing how pretty and petite she was. She watched Ruby enviously as a long lock of curly black hair floated down in her face and onto her shoulder. "You liar. I knew you were still seeing her." She walked around to Ruby's side of the table and stood over her, pointing in her face. "You are a trifling excuse for a female. I am going to beat the crap out of you for coming to my house acting like an idiot in front of *my* kids!"

She balled up her fist and drew back to hit Ruby. Ruby stood up. In her haste to stand up, the contents of Ruby's purse spilled. Sheena thought she saw a gun in her purse. Jason jumped up to hold Sheena back. Sheena struggled to get out of Jason's hold on her. Without taking her eyes off of Sheena, Ruby reached for her purse. All of a sudden, several shots rang out. Jason grabbed Sheena to protect her, covering her with his body.

"Get down, lady!" someone yelled at Ruby.

"Oh, my God!" she screamed.

Chapter 37

After the commotion, Ruby opened her eyes to assess the damage. She focused on Sheena when she heard her screaming, "Help, please somebody help! My husband's been shot!"

Initially, Sheena thought she had gotten shot when she felt the warm sticky fluid oozing down her blouse. Ruby stared at Jason's bleeding body. He had been shot in the back and he was bleeding profusely.

Sheena had a flashback to the dream she'd had three months ago. *Oh my God, that dream was a warning about Jason getting shot, only I didn't do it.* "Somebody please call an ambulance!" Sheena held Jason in her arms, as he lay limp on her lap, seemingly not breathing. She stared at the blood on her hands, momentarily in a trance. "Jason, please don't d—die!" She sobbed pitifully, "Lord, Jesus . . . have mercy."

A policeman rushed over to where they were. He bent over and touched Jason's neck for a pulse. Sheena's body trembled. She anxiously waited for him to say something.

"I think he's going to be fine, Miss. He's got a pulse; it's weak, but he's breathing. The ambulance has already been dispatched."

"Oh, my God, what happened?" Ruby questioned the policeman in a confused state. She stooped over to pick up the contents from her purse. She placed the silver compact, which Sheena had mistaken for the end of a gun back in her purse.

"Some smart guy decided he wanted to rob the place. One of the customers sitting in the back of the restaurant noticed him and called 911 on their cell phone. When he realized we had slipped in through the back door, he decided to make a run for it and have a shoot out."

Ruby ached to comfort Jason, but knew it wasn't her place, so she stood by silently and prayed. When the ambulance arrived, Sheena jumped in the ambulance to ride with him to the hospital. She heard someone ask Ruby, "Are you coming, ma'am?"

Sheena quickly answered for her. "No, she's not coming. You can close the door, sir." She refocused on Jason. "Please, let's go."

Ruby watched the ambulance as it sped away.

Chapter 38

The Emergency Room staff worked diligently on Jason, stabilizing him enough to run an MRI and CAT scan so they could get results of the damage done to his body and where. The tests indicated that the bullet had grazed his spine, but fortunately, had not touched his spinal cord.

The doctors operated on Jason and removed the bullet from his chest cavity. It had lodged itself beneath the lungs and heart, piercing the diaphragm, making it difficult for him to breathe. The bullet was lodged within millimeters of the heart muscle. The operation was very tedious; one mistake of the surgeons' hands would have been fatal. The force of the bullet cracked three ribs, which had to be repaired also.

After the operation was over, the doctors conferred with Sheena and the rest of his family members that had arrived at the hospital.

"Your husband came through the operation fine, Mrs. Grey, but he is not out of danger," the doctor stated. "There is still a possibility that his lungs might collapse, depending on how well the diaphragm heals. The diaphragm is the muscular wall that separates the thoracic and abdominal cavities. It aids in the process of breathing."

"I think I understand what you are saying, Doctor, but could you be a little more specific?" Sheena asked him.

"Sure. The diaphragm contracts and descends with each inhalation; thus the downward motion enlarges the area in the thoracic cavity, which reduces the internal air pressure, allowing air to flow into the lungs. Therefore, when the lungs are full, the diaphragm relaxes and elevates, making the area in the thoracic cavity smaller, increasing the air pressure in the thorax. This motion allows air to be expelled out of the lungs to equalize the pressure, which is known as expiration or exhalation."

He demonstrated the workings of the diaphragm to the family.

"So, you see, if his lungs are not working properly, he will not get sufficient air to the bloodstream, which in effect, will be detrimental to his survival."

"What can be done to prevent this from happening?"

"We've eliminated the foreign body, which was the bullet, from the area. When the bullet hit the diaphragm, it caused atelectasis, or incomplete expansion of the air sacs, a collapsed functionless, airless part of the lung. The bullet wound permitted a blockage of air, fluid and blood to accumulate in the pleural cavity. By removing the foreign body, or the bullet, therapy will be given to ensure that his lungs continue to function properly."

"What type of therapy?"

"Keeping a close watch on the diaphragm to make sure it's contracting and expanding properly. This will be accomplished by the procedure of auscultation, listening to the sounds within the body by using a stethoscope to diagnose the conditions of the lungs."

"I understand, but how will that help his diaphragm heal?"

"To assist the diaphragm in healing, he will be hooked to a lung machine to alleviate some of the pressure off of the diaphragm. Thus, the machine will relieve the diaphragm muscle from struggling to contract and expand, and therefore, it can heal itself."

"I see. What about infection?"

"As with any wound or operation, the risk of infection is very precarious. We will also keep a close watch to make sure that he does not develop pneumonia resulting from an acute inflammation of alveoli, which fills with pus. Also we will administer antibiotics to decrease any edema or swelling, or fluid in the air sacs or lungs.

Sheena nodded and the doctor continued. "We don't want him to develop a pulmonary embolism." Sheena looked at him blankly so he explained further. "Pulmonary embolisms are clots or material from distal veins floating through the bloodstream that may lodge in the vessels of the lungs. To prevent this, he will be given anticoagulants. So, you see, although your husband tolerated the operation well, he still has a tough road ahead of him."

Sheena shook her head in disbelief. "I can't believe this is happening. What is your prognosis, Doctor?"

"With around-the-clock observation and care, he will heal completely. Fortunately, your husband is a healthy man with no manifestations of other illnesses, such as heart trouble, high blood pressure, or diabetes that could complicate the situation, so he should heal remarkably well. And another point that works in his favor is that he has a strong will to live. You and the rest of the family can help speed his healing process by making sure that he's stress free and relating only positive issues in his presence."

Sheena hugged the doctor. "Thank you, Doctor, you've been kind. I believe you and your staff are doing all that you can to make my husband better."

"We do our best, Mrs. Grey." He lowered his tone as if not wanting others, outside of the family, to hear his next words. "I have to give the glory to God, though. If it wasn't for Him, I couldn't do anything. He gives me the ability to perform; it's nothing that I've done on my own."

"Amen," Sheena agreed. "I am going to pray that God continues to bless you and your family, Dr. Johnson. It's a blessing to know that God reigns over doctors too."

"He does reign over doctors and anyone else who will humble themselves and allow Him to." His beeper went off. "If you'll excuse me, I have another emergency to attend to. If you have any other questions, please feel free to call me anytime. I'll be the attending physician, so I will be on call until he's released from the hospital."

"Thank you again, Dr. Johnson. May I go in to see him now?" Sheena asked.

"You can go in to see him for a few minutes. He's still in critical condition and will be admitted to I.C.U. A schedule will be set up for the rest of the immediate family to visit."

He jogged back down the corridor to the Emergency Department. Sheena stared in a trance after the doctor until he disappeared through the double doors.

"Sheena . . . Sheena," she heard Catherine calling. Sheena shook herself out of the stupor she was in and turned around to face her.

Catherine, Jason's sisters, brother and sister-in-law were gathered in a huddle, waiting for Sheena to respond.

"I think you need to come over here and sit down for a minute before you go in to see Jason, you look weak, baby, like you're going to give out," Catherine said.

"I'll be fine, Momma Catherine," Sheena heard herself say. This was the first time she had called her mother-in-law that term of endearment. "I think I need a drink of water though." She walked to the water fountain and sipped some water. "Momma Catherine, will you call my parents and tell them the news? I . . ." Sheena suddenly started crying. "Where are my children? Oh, Lord, I forgot all about the children. I don't even know where my children are."

"Calm down, baby," Catherine said as she hugged Sheena. "Cathy brought the children here. They're with her in the chapel."

"Oh, thank God. In all this confusion, I couldn't think, all I could do was pray for my husband, that he would make it through." She hugged Catherine.

Catherine was still shocked that Sheena didn't refer to her as Ms. Grey. She pulled a Kleenex from her purse and wiped Sheena's tears away. "He's going to be fine, baby. I'm sure he'll be glad to know that you're right by his side. Go on, now, go in there and be with your husband."

Sheena hurried into the room to be with Jason. She caught a glimpse of Ruby and a man with his arm around her waist standing at the far end of the waiting room. She had an urge to tell her to leave because she had no right to be there, but quickly decided against that. She didn't have the time or energy to waste on Ruby. Her priority was to attend to Jason and let him know that she was there for him. When she entered the room, she could hear Jason mumbling something.

"I'm here, Jason," she told him as she smoothed his eyebrows with her finger. "I'm not going anywhere."

Chapter 39

Jonathan recognized Ruby from the time he had visited Jason in college. He walked over to her an introduced himself.

"Hi, I'm Jason's brother, Jonathan. I'm not sure if you remember me or not, but I remember you. You *are* Ruby, right?"

Ruby was surprised that Jonathan made an effort to greet her. During their encounter years ago, he had made it crystal clear to her that he didn't like her and blatantly told her she was not suitable for his little brother.

Ruby extended her hand to him. "I remember you, Jonathan. This is my husband, Thurman. He was kind enough to drive me to the hospital."

"Your *husband*?" Jonathan shook Thurman's hand, but had a confused look on his face. *Is this cat stupid or what?* "It's nice to meet you, man." Jonathan phrased the remark like a question more so than a statement.

As if Thurman had read Jonathan's mind, he said, "It's nice to meet you too, brother. I guess you're wondering what I'm doing here."

"The thought did cross my mind. I didn't know you were in town, Jason told me that you lived in Florida." Jonathan looked at Ruby skeptically.

"Yeah, I do, but I arrived in town Monday afternoon. I know what the situation *was* with Ruby and Jason. I'm only here in the capacity to support her on behalf of my daughter." Thurman wasn't sure if Jason had told his family about Cassandra or not, but he wanted to make his position clear; that *he* was Cassandra's father.

Jason had told Jonathan about Ruby's husband and Cassandra that Wednesday night before Thanksgiving Day while they watched the football game. Jonathan raised his eyebrows at Thurman. "*Your* daughter?"

"Yeah man, *my* daughter. I've been aware since before her birth that she is your brother's *biological* daughter, but she's my daughter in all other aspects."

Jonathan looked back at his family members, who were watching them. He lowered his voice. "It wasn't a good idea for you all to come here."

"I tried to tell my wife that, but she was determined to come to see if Cassandra's father would be all right."

"She could have called," Jonathan replied as they talked about Ruby in the third person.

"I told her that, but she knows that the hospital won't give out any information over the phone. I can vouch for that, because I'm a Registered Nurse, so I know this to be true. Since she insisted on coming, I told her that I would drive her here for Cassandra's sake."

"Is Cassandra here?"

"No. She's in town, but we didn't want her to know anything about this until we found out about his condition."

"So she knows that Jason is her father?"

"She knows. Ruby and Jason were making arrangements for her to meet him tomorrow, that's why they met at the restaurant. But like I said, I didn't think it was wise to tell Cassandra until we found out more information about his condition."

"I agree. There's no need to put her through any unnecessary pain."

"I make it my business to protect my little girl from pain if that's possible."

"You seem to be a good father, man. I would like to get to meet my niece if that's all right with you."

"I guess it will be all right. It's up to Ruby." Thurman looked at Ruby and then at Jonathan and said, "My wife told me that your family dislikes her, and I suppose I can understand that, but this is my wife and I won't allow you all to disrespect her. You may think that I'm a fool for protecting her, but I've known Ruby ever since we were six years old, so I know her background and situation well and I understand a lot more than you know."

"I respect you for saying that." Jonathan faced Ruby. He softened his tone to her. "Ruby, I know our first meeting wasn't too pleasant, but I'll do my best to be respectful to you for Cassandra's sake."

"Humph," Ruby said sarcastically.

"This is an awkward situation, but we'll have to be adult about this and try to work things out on Cassandra's behalf."

"It is awkward," Thurman agreed, "but I love my little girl and I think it's only fair that she gets to meet her family. But don't think that I'm a fool because I allowed my wife to come see about Jason, she knows the deal." He looked sternly at Ruby.

"You don't have to worry about Jason and me, Thurman," Ruby assured her husband. "We agreed to end our relationship before you came to town. The only reason we were communicating was to finalize his first visitation with Cassandra." She looked up at him. "I love *you* Thurman." Thurman looked at Ruby and nodded his head as if to say he understood.

"Whenever it's convenient for you guys to let me see Cassandra will be fine with me. I just have one favor to ask you," Jonathan stated.

"What's that?" Thurman asked.

"Please don't come back to the hospital. The doctor asked us to keep Jason stress free so that he can heal properly. And if you guys are showing up here, I know it's only going to cause trouble. I don't want Sheena to see Ruby here. If she's upset, then she's not going to have a positive attitude when she sees Jason. Plus, it will affect the rest of the family negatively too."

Thurman nodded his head in agreement. "I understand. I didn't want to come today. I don't wish your brother any harm, man, but coming up here to see about my wife's baby's daddy and ex-lover hasn't been a stroll in the park for me either. It doesn't do anything to soothe my pride."

"I know what you mean." Jonathan cut his eyes at Ruby. "I'm sure you see where we're coming from, don't you?"

"I do now. I'm sorry if I made things difficult for everybody. I was concerned about Jason's life though."

"I'm sure you were. The doctor said he's still

in critical condition, but if the care instructions are followed, he should come through it just fine. It will take some time, but his prognosis is optimistic." Jonathan hesitated before he spoke again. "Excuse me for a minute." He walked to the nurse's station to borrow a pen and piece of paper. He wrote down his number, walked back to them and handed it to Thurman. "Here's my cell phone number. You can call me and I'll keep you posted on how he's doing."

"All right, man. We'll keep in touch." He put his arm around Ruby's waist and ushered her toward the door.

Chapter 40

Sheena stayed by Jason's side for the next few days, only leaving him to shower, change clothes, and go to the hospital's restaurant to get a meal. Her parents had arrived in town the day after the shooting and were staying at Sheena and Jason's house. Although the children were upset about their father, they were happy to have their grandparents take care of them while their mother was away at the hospital.

Cathy and Reana moved in with Catherine so that they could help Catherine take care of Jacob. Jacob was recovering rapidly and insisted on being chauffeured to the hospital every day to visit Jason. Jacob convinced his brother to come out of retirement long enough to resume his old duties as the CEO of the bank until he and Jason were well enough to return to work.

They promoted the bank's loan manager, a well-qualified young woman, as the temporary acting president to reside in Jacob's position.

Jacob's daughter, Shirley, who had years of administrative experience in the banking industry, took on the responsibility of assistant to the acting president. Assured that his business was in good hands, Jacob was free to concentrate on his and his son's full recovery.

Ruby called Jonathan Thursday, the day before she moved back to Florida, so he could meet Cassandra. The meeting was awkward at first. Jonathan noted that although Cassandra looked just like Ruby, their personalities were completely opposite. Cassandra was shy, nothing like her aggressive mother. The only resemblance he saw to Jason was the deep dimples. Eventually, Cassandra warmed up to him and began to ask him questions about Jason. Whoever her father is, he thought, he should be proud to have her as a daughter.

Aretha and Terri insisted on having a conference with Jason's doctor before they returned home to make sure he was getting the proper care. For confidential reasons, the doctor wouldn't disclose Jason's condition, but urged them to discuss things with his wife since it was Sheena's prerogative to reveal his health information to his family if she so desired.

Aretha and Terri approached Sheena cautiously, aware of the stress that she was under. Sheena was sitting beside Jason's bed, holding his hand while he slept. They asked her to meet them in the ICU waiting room and Sheena reluctantly agreed.

Sheena walked into the waiting room; other than Terri and Aretha, the room was empty. She looked at each of them suspiciously, and sat on the light green plaid chair across from them.

When they inquired about Jason's condition, Sheena explained in detail the information the doctor had given her. After having talked with Sheena about Jason's condition, Aretha and Terri felt better about leaving Jason so soon after the shooting. They thanked her for sharing the information with them. Sheena nodded, forced a smile, and got up to leave.

"Wait, Sheena," Terri suddenly said, stopping Sheena in her tracks. "We need to talk to you about something else."

Sheena looked at Terri, and then at Aretha before she sat back down.

"Sheena," Terri began, "I know that we haven't been the best sisters-in-law to you, but we want you to know that we do care about you and are proud to have you in our family."

Sheena looked at the two of them incredulously. "Where is this conversation leading?"

"We just felt that we had to clear the air," Aretha told her. "So much tragedy has happened in the past month that we just wanted to make amends with you and apologize for anything that we may have said to offend you."

Sheena massaged her temples and sighed before she spoke. "I accept your apologizes. Considering that I'm a Christian, I haven't exactly been cordial to you guys either."

"We haven't been very kind to you over the years, Sheena." Terri admitted. "I'm sorry for bringing up Jason's old girlfriends' names around you. I've known all along that you were the love of Jason's life, but you didn't seem to like us from the very beginning, and I guess I had a grudge against you since before you and he got married."

"If I didn't seem to like you, it was because I overheard your conversation the first day I met you with Mrs. Grey, I mean, with Momma, when you, Aretha and she were in the dining room."

"Conversation? What conversation?" Terri asked.

Sheena stared into Terri's eyes, and then repeated the conversation to her.

Aretha gasped. "Oh, my God. You heard that?" she asked sorrowfully.

Sheena cut her eyes at Aretha. "Obviously."

"Please forgive me, Sheena." Aretha's eyes were tearful. "There are no words to compensate for the hurtful things I said about you. I'm so sorry for having fun at your expense. That was so immature of me."

"I'm sorry too, Sheena," Terri confessed. "I didn't mean it. I was pissed at Jason because he had dumped the woman I introduced him too. She was so heartbroken. I thought they were going to get married one day. Ironically, by the time I found out what *she* had done to him, she was gone."

"And what did she do to him?"

"She played him like a piano. I didn't know it at the time, but she used her looks and figure to manipulate him to get what she wanted from him; namely his money. He should have dumped her long before he did."

"Jason always liked the pretty girls, didn't he?"

"Yeah, that was a weakness before he met you."

Sheena felt offended by Terri's statement. She walked to the window and gazed outside. "You really know how to rub it in, don't you, Terri? I'm well aware that you never thought I looked good enough for your handsome brother."

"Oh, no, Sheena, I didn't mean for it to sound like that. What I'm trying to say is, that although you weren't a beauty queen like the other women he'd dated, he saw the beauty *in* you; your sweet personality, kindness, and your ability to see beyond his looks and love him for the person he is. That's what captured his heart."

Sheena turned and looked at Terri. "It's obvious that my looks sure didn't capture his heart, isn't it?"

"Sheena," Aretha interceded. "What Terri is saying is that you are beautiful because of who you are. Please don't have a complex about your looks."

"I don't have a complex about my looks. I know that God made me exactly who He wanted me to be and I am beautiful in His sight."

"Amen. So, will you forgive us for acting so immature all of these years? We love you and we want you to continue to be there for our baby brother. I know he's made some stupid mistakes, but he does love you and doesn't want to lose you," Aretha assured her.

Sheena folded her arms and looked at Aretha, then Terri. "So, this is what the conversation leads to. You two are here to plead Jason's case."

"No," Terri said. "We wanted to apologize to you. We're not here to plead Jason's case."

"I will be here for as long as Jason needs me through his recovery. I can't guarantee you that I'll be here afterward. I had almost made up my mind to try to work things out with him. I was on my way to my parents' house so I could pray and meditate in peace and hear from God to make sure I was making the right decision."

"I believe you made the right decision, Sheena," Aretha said, trying to reassure her. "My brother loves you very much and I know that he doesn't want to lose you."

"I said I had *almost* made up my mind, Aretha. That is, until I saw your brother sitting with his woman in the restaurant the day he was shot."

Terri's mouth dropped open. "I didn't know he was with somebody else. When they told us the news, they said he and you were standing on the deck together when shots rang out and he covered you to protect you from the bullets and that's how he got shot in the back."

"That's true, but they failed to tell you or didn't know that he was sitting with her at a table when I walked up on them and caught them in the act."

Aretha's eyes widened. "In the act?" she asked louder than she'd anticipated.

"Yes, they were holding hands, and when I approached her, that's when he stood up to keep me from hitting her. The next thing I remember, he pushed me on the floor and I heard someone ordering Ruby to get down. Actually, I thought Ruby had shot me until I realized Jason had been shot and it was his blood on me. "

Terri's eyes stretched open. "Ruby?" Terri rubbed her temples, meditating. She refocused on Sheena. "Sheena, do you know her last name?"

"No, I don't. She's the girl he was dating in college, that's all I know. Why? Do you know her?"

Aretha's eyes met Terri's. She put her hand over her mouth.

"Unfortunately, yes, I do." Terry admitted. "I introduced Jay to her."

Sheena rolled her eyes. "I should have known you were involved," she said disgustingly.

"No, I'm not involved, Sheena, not the way you think I am."

"Humph."

Terri was agitated with Sheena's attitude, but she overlooked her behavior. "After I graduated from North Carolina Central, I worked there for eight years as an Administrator before I followed Shirley and Aretha to Atlanta. Ruby did some work-study in my office. She seemed like a really nice young lady, so I told her I wanted her to meet my brother. She and Jay hit it off from the beginning, but had I known she was the way she is, I wouldn't have introduced her to Jason."

"Well, well, it's a small world after all. So you knew he was seeing her again then?"

"No, please believe me, Sheena; I haven't seen or heard from Ruby since the day she left school. She led me to believe that Jason had done her so wrong, but I found out later, it was she, and not Jason, who was the villain.

"Until this very moment, I had no idea she was the one he was seeing again."

"I guess he wasn't over her. You were right all along, I was a rebound to him."

"You are not a rebound to Jason. I know for a fact that he loves you, and he always has."

Aretha nodded. "She's right, Sheena. Jason has always made that clear to us."

"I don't know how they hooked up again, but I will bet my last dollar that she planned it to the letter," Terri declared.

Sheena sighed. "Maybe she did, but he played his part in it too. She didn't drug him and force him to be with her."

"You're right, but I'm going to find out what happened before I leave this weekend." Terri hugged Sheena and walked toward the door. "I'll see you tomorrow and I'll have some answers for you by then." Tapping Aretha on her arm, Terri added, "Come on, Aretha; we have some investigating to do."

Sheena stayed in the room for a few moments, mulling over the conversation she'd had with her sisters-in-law. When she walked out of the room, she waved good-bye to them as they stood in the elevator, waiting for the doors to close. She walked down the corridor and entered Jason's room.

"Sheena," she heard Jason call her name out weakly.

She swiftly walked over to his side and rubbed his hand. "I'm here, Jason; I'm not going anywhere." *Not yet*, **but** *after you recover, I am leaving; this is too much.*

Chapter 41

Upon returning home, Terri and Aretha went into their parents' bedroom to see their father. Jacob was lying on the bed sleeping and Catherine was sitting in the recliner with her feet propped up, watching a segment on *HGTV*. They didn't want to awaken Jacob, so they told their mother they would come back after he woke up. They went in the kitchen where Shirley and Cathy were cooking dinner. Aretha asked them if they needed help. Shirley told them no, so Terri and Aretha walked down the hall to the living room where Jonathan was sitting on the couch reading the newspaper. "Jonathan, may I have a word with you," Terri asked.

Jonathan put the newspaper down. "Sure, what's up, sis?"

"I just learned some disturbing news tonight."

"What? What's happening?"

"In my conversation with Sheena, she told me the name of the person Jason was seeing."

"Oh, yeah?" Jonathan said evenly, as he raised his eyebrows.

Aretha sat beside him. "You sound like you already know."

"I do."

"Then you know it was Ruby that he was seeing?" Terri inquired.

"Yep." Jonathan patted the seat on the couch. "Sit down, Terri, this is going to take a while." He moved and sat on the wing chair, facing Terri and Aretha. Jonathan's wife had gone across town to visit her parents so they were free to talk without interruptions. Jonathan filled Terri and Aretha in on everything Jason had told him.

"I can't believe it," Terri said. "Jason has a daughter with Ruby? How could she have kept this a secret from him all of these years?"

"I guess she thought it was best for all concerned."

"Is Jason certain that this is his child? You know how flaky Ruby was."

"He seems to be convinced that she's his. They met at the restaurant the day he was shot to make arrangements for him to see the girl. Jason told me that Ruby had planned to make an appointment for a DNA test, but of course she didn't get a chance to. After two weeks of lying on that bed, Jason became strong enough to communicate to me that he wanted the test done while he was in the hospital. So, I arranged it; Ruby and Cassandra went to a lab in Florida. We had the letter sent here because he didn't want to take a chance on Sheena coming across it in their mail. It only took a week. The test results came in the mail yesterday. I'm waiting until the right moment to give them to Jason."

"Lord, have mercy," Aretha whispered. "So, Sheena doesn't have any idea about this child in question?"

"No. Jason told me that if the results confirmed that he was the father, he planned to wait until after Sheena returned from visiting her parents that weekend before he told her. He figured that way, she could make her final decision when she got to her appointment next Wednesday with her divorce attorney. Now that all of this has happened, I don't know when or how he's going to find the right time to tell her. Of course, if the results are negative, there won't be a need to tell Sheena."

"So, you don't know what the results are?" Aretha asked him.

"No, I'm just holding the letter for Jason, until he's in a position to read them privately. If he's the father, he'll share the results with Sheena when the time is right."

Terri walked over to the window and watched the rain as it pounded the earth. "Sheena sounded so negative about staying with Jason when we talked to her tonight. When this bomb blows up, it might push her to the edge."

Jonathan rubbed his hands together. "I know. Poor Sheena, she has enough to deal with right now. We need to pray for her and our brother. The only way that this situation can be resolved rationally with a good outcome is with God's intervention, mercy, and favor."

"I know that's right," Aretha declared.

Catherine had come down the hall and was standing in the double glass stained door in the foyer, watching the rain. Jonathan asked his mother to come into the living room.

"What's going on?" Catherine inquired as she entered.

"We were discussing Jason and Sheena's dilemma and we think we should pray for them," Jonathan replied.

"I agree with you all," Catherine said wearily. "I have been praying for weeks for the two of them, especially after I found out about that child. I sure wish I could have met the little girl. If she was a Grey, I would have seen it in her."

Jonathan stood up and stretched. "I met her."

"When?" Catherine asked him." Aretha and Terri sat straight up, waiting for him to answer also.

"I got a chance to meet her that Thursday, a few days after Jason was shot, before Ruby moved back to Florida."

"Does she resemble Jason?" Terri asked anxiously. Catherine and Aretha fastened their eyes on Jonathan.

"She has dimples like him, other than that, she's the spitting image of Ruby.

"Humph. That's not much to go on," Catherine stated, "I guess time will tell. I wish Jason could have had a DNA test done."

"He did, Momma. I arranged it while he was in the hospital. I've communicated with Ruby to let her know how Jason was progressing—"

"Why would you communicate that information to her?" Catherine asked.

"Because she's the mother of his child, Momma."

"Alleged child," Terri stated.

"Whatever, Terri. Anyway, she and Cassandra had the test done in Florida. I have the results here." Catherine opened her mouth to speak. "Before you ask, Momma. I don't know. When the time is right, Jason will open the letter."

Catherine pondered their conversation. "Wow. Now that this has happened, we really need to get on one accord and pray for them." She looked around the room at everybody. "Jonathan, go get your other two sisters so they can pray with us."

Jonathan got up and went to the kitchen to get them. They had finished cooking and were in the formal dining room, setting the table. He told them to join them in the living room for prayer and Shirley followed Jonathan in the room. Cathy made a detour to her bedroom, but quickly joined them as well.

"I brought the Bible guys," Cathy announced when she entered the room. "There's no point in praying if we haven't read God's Word to back it up."

"That's true," Catherine agreed. "Cathy, we are going to ask you to lead us in prayer because you are the prayer warrior of the family."

"Okay. I believe we all are prayer warriors, but I'll be glad to lead the prayer." Opening her Bible, she began to read Matthew 18:19, 20. "Again I say unto you, That if two of you shall agree on earth as touching any thing that they shall ask, it shall be done for them of my Father which is in heaven. For where two or three are gathered together in my name, there am I in the midst of them."

In the likeness of a bona fide Bible teacher, Cathy looked at each of them and said, "Now let's consult the Concordance about scriptures of forgiveness, and after that we can pray and ask God's mercy and favor on behalf of Jason, Sheena, and their family's well being. Let's pray that Jesus will make a way for them to work out all of their problems and heal that family. While we're praying, we might as well pray for each other too."

After the conclusion of the prayer, everybody noticed that Jacob had used his walker, without assistance, to come down the hallway and was standing at the entrance of the arched door.

"Amen," he proclaimed. "Amen and thank you Jesus."

Terri and Aretha stopped by the hospital the next day to see Jason and Sheena before they left town to go home. They visited with Jason only a short while before the nurse came in and administered his pain medicine and shortly thereafter, Jason dozed off. Sheena went into the lobby, just outside of the nursing station and sat down to chat with them.

"I'm glad we had our talk yesterday," Sheena announced. "It felt good to get that baggage out in the open. I must admit that I had bitter feelings toward you two, but I prayed last night after you all left and I believe God has forgiven me of my bitterness." She hugged Aretha and Terri. "I hope that we can have a better relationship from now on."

Terri sighed. "I hope so too, because life is too short to hold bitterness in your heart. I had to pray strife out of my life too. I talked to Jonathan last night about you-know-who, and he said he would talk to you when the time is right."

"That's fine, Terri. I don't want to discuss that right now anyway. My priority is taking care of my husband. I . . . we will deal with that later."

"Good. Things will work out for you guys, Sheena; you'll see. I have faith in God that everything is going to be fine."

Aretha chimed in. "So do I. We prayed for you guys last night and I believe God heard our cry."

Sheena nodded her head, but had a distant look in her eyes.

They walked back into Jason's room to say good-bye to him. Aretha kissed Jason on the forehead and then turned around and hugged Sheena again. "I hate to say good-bye, but I know how my husband and kids are. If I stay away too long, the house is going to be in total shambles," she laughed.

Sheena smiled. "It's good to be needed, isn't it?"

"Yes, if you can call it that. My family is pitiful, girl. Well, I'll keep in touch everyday, and don't just take care of my brother, take care of yourself too, Sheena. I love you."

"I love you too, Sheena," Terri told her. "Get well soon," she whispered to Jason as she kissed him on the cheek. "I love you." He cracked his eyes open for a few seconds and went back to sleep.

"I love you guys too," Sheena told them. "I'll keep you informed about Jason's progress. Drive safely." As they left, Sheena could hear Aretha and Terri talking loudly as they walked to the elevator. She smiled when she heard one of the nurses shush them.

Sheena adjusted Jason's pillow and sat back down to read. She put her book down and thought about how ironic it was that she and her in-laws were finally on good terms, but it was too bad that they reconciled just as they were about to become ex-in-laws.

Chapter 42

Jason had been in the hospital for three weeks. He seemed to be out of imminent danger and was healing remarkably well. Sheena had called Jonathan to see if he could sit with Jason that day. She wanted to spend some time with her mother, who had stayed the entire time, taking care of the children.

Jonathan readily agreed. He saw this as the perfect opportunity to give the letter to Jason. He thought that if Jason needed to talk, they could do so freely.

As Jonathan sat on a chair bedside the bed, he ripped the letter that held the DNA results open and handed it to Jason to read. Jonathan watched him, trying to analyze the results by the expression on Jason's face.

"Well, this confirms it, man," Jason announced to Jonathan. "The test came back 99.98% positive that Cassandra is my daughter."

Jonathan wasn't surprised. "She looks like her mother with the exception of inheriting your dimples."

"That's good. Ruby showed me a picture of her, she does look just like her mother."

"Thank God she has your easy going personality though," Jonathan replied.

Jason smiled and nodded his head as he thought about Ruby's fiery temper. "When I get well enough, I'm going to make arrangements to start paying child support payments for her. The hard part will be telling Sheena about her existence."

"What are you going to do if she doesn't accept her?"

Jason threw his hands up in the air and said, "There's nothing I can do, but respect her decision. If she wants to leave I don't have the right to try and stop her." He exhaled loudly. "But if she stays, we will have to work some type of arrangements out to include my daughter into our lives."

"That's going to be a tough trial, man. Even if Sheena does forgive you for having an affair with Ruby, it's not like she can get over the fact that you have a daughter with her."

Jason shook his head. "It's a no-win situation, man. I may lose my wife because I was unfaithful to her with my ex-girlfriend who I have a daughter with. No matter how you look at it, Sheena will always suspect that I'm involved with Ruby because I'm spending time with Cassandra. She may even resent her and be jealous of her too. I don't know, man. I want all of my children in my life, but I don't want to have to raise them from a distance."

"If you include her in everything you do regarding Cassandra, she won't be jealous or resentful of the child. It will take time, but Sheena will grow to love her eventually."

"I hope so, but there are going to be times when I need to spend alone time with Cassandra, just to make up for lost time and let her know she's special to me."

"That's true," Jonathan agreed. They were both silent for a few minutes. Jonathan broke the silence. "Don't worry, man, your wife will come around, sooner or later." Jason nodded. The rest of the day, they spent time talking and watching the *ESPN Sports Channel*.

The next day, the doctor came in the room with Jason's release papers and strict written orders for outpatient care. Although only three weeks had passed since the shooting, Jason's recovery was remarkable. His diaphragm had healed to the point where it was working on its own without the help of the lung machine. Jonathan was still on leave from the military, so he persuaded Sheena to let him pick Jason up from the hospital.

When they arrived at his home, Jeremiah and Joseph met him at the car, and helped Jonathan with the wheelchair to get Jason in the house.

"Come on, Daddy!" Joseph exclaimed, "Momma said Jeremiah and I have to be the men of the house until you get well."

"Lean on us, Daddy. We'll take care of you the way you take care of us," Jeremiah stated.

When they entered the foyer, Jason was amazed at the welcome home decorations that Sheena and the children had on display.

"Daddy! My Daddy's home!" Jessica shouted. She jumped in his lap in the wheelchair and jarred his ribs. Jason winced from the pain.

Sheena saw the look on his face and immediately rushed to Jason's side. "Jessica, baby, Daddy isn't well yet. He is still sore, so you have to handle him with care, okay?"

"Oh, I'm sorry, Daddy," Jessica apologized as she gently kissed him on the cheek. "I missed you so much. I prayed and asked God not to ever let you get hurt again. I want my daddy and momma to be here forever!"

"I'll do my best to stay around for a long time, sweetie."

Jason looked up at Sheena. "Thank you for being here for me, Sheena. I love you."

Sheena smiled at Jason. "Where else would I be?" She kissed him on the forehead and rolled him into the den where his mother, father, and other family members were waiting for him. Always one to be concerned about appearances, Sheena smiled mechanically as she entered the room. *I'm fulfilling my obligation; don't get too comfortable Jason.*

Chapter 43

After hours of celebrating his release from the hospital, Jason's family left to go home so he could rest. Sheena and Lois cleaned the house of the leftover party items. Sheena prepared the library for Jason's makeshift bedroom, because he was too weak to walk upstairs. She carried magazines, a small TV and set up his laptop so that Jason could occupy himself while she worked.

"I am going to have to arrange for a nurse to come in and take care of him while I'm at work," she confessed to Lois. "He claims he will be all right here by himself, but I know it's just his pride talking."

"I'm sure that's all it is. Have you called any of the agencies yet?"

"No, I haven't had time, but as soon as I get his room situated, I'll call them."

Lois was thoughtful for a moment, and then she clapped her hands together lightly. "I have an idea, Sheena."

Sheena squinted at her mother. "What is it?"

"Why don't you ask your neighbor, Ms. Erma, to sit with him? Didn't you say she is a retired nurse?"

"Yes, but—"

"I'm sure she'll be glad to do it. Taking care of Jason will give her something to do."

Sheena stared at Lois. "Momma, you can't be serious."

"I'm serious as a heart attack. What harm will it do?"

"Ms. Erma has the biggest mouth in the neighborhood. I don't want her coming in my house, snooping through my things and telling all of my business."

"I doubt if she'll do that. From a distance, she seems like a nice lady."

"She is nice, but Ms. Erma loves to gossip."

"She's just lonely. She could probably use some real friends in her life. And besides, what else does she have to gossip about? I don't think anything worse can happen than Jason's woman coming here fighting him or him getting shot."

"She'll think of something to say. Sometimes her lips remind me of a machine gun spraying bullets here, there and everywhere."

Lois laughed. "Now you're exaggerating."

"Before her husband died three years ago they were model neighbors. They babysat the children a few times for us when we went out to dinner or while Jason and I entertained his colleagues from out of town. Jason and her husband talked on a daily basis."

"What changed after her husband died? Did her behavior get worse or something?"

"Not really, but after her husband died, she stayed cooped up in the house all the time. Jason used to go over there and check on her every morning before he went to work and he would call her every night to see if she needed anything."

"That was nice of him. I guess that's why she's so fond of you all."

"She's fond of Jason. I don't think she cares that much for me."

"I'm sure she likes you, but you're not as outgoing as Jason is, so she probably doesn't know how to approach you, considering how prim and proper you are."

"Momma, you need to stop. I am *not* prim and proper," Sheena laughed. She smiled as she watched Lois prance around the room, mocking her. "You are a mess Momma." Sheena swatted her mother softly on her butt with a magazine.

The doorbell chimed. Sheena walked to the door and peeped through the door's sidelight. "Momma, guess who's at the door." Lois looked at her and raised her eyebrows. "It's Ms. Erma; can you believe it? We must have talked her up." Sheena opened the door.

"Hi, Sheena," Erma greeted her with a pleasant smile on her face.

Sheena hadn't seen her since their last encounter. "Hello, Ms. Erma, won't you please come in?"

"I came over to see Jason. I heard he was released from the hospital today. I know my timing is bad sometimes, so if it is not a good time, I can come back when it's convenient for you."

"Your timing is perfect, Ms. Erma. Come on in."

Erma walked into the foyer, observing everything with her fast moving eyes. "Is your husband awake? Does he feel up to having company?"

"He's doing well. He'll be glad to see you. He's sitting up in the library." She led Erma into the den where Lois was sitting. "Ms. Erma, I want to introduce you to my mother, Lois Andrews. Momma, this is my neighbor, Ms. Erma Lloyd."

Lois stood and extended her hand to Erma. "It's so nice to meet you, Ms. Erma."

"It's good to meet you too, Lois. Sheena and Jason seem like my children. They look after me, so I try to always look out for them. They're such a lovely couple."

Grinning widely, Lois said, "Thank you, Ms. Erma. It's good to know they are so cared for."

Erma walked into the library and chatted with Jason a while. When she returned, she informed Sheena that she had assisted Jason into bed.

"Ms. Erma, I appreciate you helping my husband, but I don't want you to strain yourself."

"Child, I am not going to strain myself. I am a registered nurse, I've been doing this type of work for forty years, I know how to handle patients."

"I'm sure you do, but I couldn't live with myself if you injured yourself trying to lift Jason."

Smiling, Ms. Erma said, "Girl, I didn't lift Jason, I just taught him what to do so he will know how to get in and out of that bed by himself."

Sheena blushed. "Oh, okay," she said timidly.

"Jason said he overheard you and Lois talking about hiring a nurse."

"Yes, ma'am. He's going to need someone to stay with him while I work," Sheena confirmed."

"If it's all right with you, I'll be glad to take care of him for you."

"Are you sure, Ms. Erma?" Sheena asked doubtfully. Frowning, she added, "That's a big responsibility."

"I'm sure. Jason has already agreed to me being his nurse. He said it's up to you." Erma posed her statement to sound like a question, and spread her hands out toward Sheena. "It's a simple job. All I have to do is make sure he takes his medication on time, change his dressings and make sure he eats the right food and gets plenty of rest. Later on when he's stronger, I can arrange for a physical therapist to come here so he can start doing his strength training."

"It will be fine with me. You sound like you'll have everything under control. Just quote your fee and I'll write you a check every week." Sheena glanced at Lois. "Believe it or not, Momma had suggested we hire you as his nurse before you rang the doorbell."

Erma chuckled. "Isn't that just like the Lord? He knows what's best for His children."

"He sure does," Lois agreed.

Sheena excused herself to go check on Jason. He was fast asleep. When she returned, Erma and Lois were talking like old friends.

"I'll be happy to come over here and stay with Jason while Sheena works. Since I retired, I hardly know what to do with myself," Ms. Erma was telling Lois.

"I can imagine. It must be lonesome staying in that big house by yourself, isn't it?" Lois replied.

"It sure is. I volunteer at the hospital, two days a week, for four hours, but other than that, I'm at home. I try to stay busy by reading my Bible and going to church. Occasionally, I'll take trips with the other seniors at church, but sometimes I still get lonely. We went to Myrtle Beach two weeks ago. I like it down there during the off seasons. We're scheduled to go to the Biltmore Estate in Asheville to spend Christmas Eve and Christmas Day there, but I don't know if I'll go though. My daughter and her family want to come home for Christmas, so I guess I'll stay home and prepare dinner for them."

"The Biltmore Estate is nice. We're from Asheville, you know."

"Yes, Sheena told me she loves the mountains that surround her hometown; the Blue Ridge Mountains and the nearby Great Smokey Mountains. Listening to her inspired me to take a trip up there."

Sheena nodded her head, quietly listening to the two women talk.

"It's okay, I take it for granted, I guess," Lois admitted. "Like Charlotte is to you, it's just home to me."

"I wasn't born in Charlotte, I'm from a little town in North Carolina called Pinetops. It's a small town with two stoplights, one grocery store, a post office, one fast food restaurant and a few other stores. It's a nice little peaceful town though. It's where I was born and raised. Charlotte was my husband's home. I've been living here for forty-five years now, ever since I moved up here to go to college. That's where I met my husband. I like it here, so I just adopted Charlotte as my home."

Whew, she can really talk! Lois thought. "What town were you raised in again?"

"*Pinetops*, North Carolina. It's about eighteen miles, give or take, south of a city called Rocky Mount."

"Now, I've heard of Rocky Mount. My husband and I passed Rocky Mount on I-95 a few years ago when we were vacationing. We went to visit one of his old Marine buddies in Jacksonville. Once we got to their house, he and his wife took us to Wrightsville Beach near Wilmington where we stayed for three days, it was nice. Since we are from the mountains, it's just something about the ocean that we love."

"Yes, I love the ocean too. North Carolina has some beautiful scenery from the ocean to the mountains," Sheena inputted.

Lois maneuvered the conversation in a different direction. "Have you ever considered selling that big house and moving to a smaller one?" she asked Erma.

"I thought about it for a while, but you know, if I sold my house to move into a smaller one, I'd still be alone, and I love my neighborhood. I have nice neighbors, so I came to the conclusion that I may as well stay here. Besides, I'm seventy-eight years old. I'm too old to be moving."

Sheena smiled as she reclined her chair. "You are a very determined lady, Ms. Erma. I enjoy listening to you talk."

"Well, thank you, baby, but I'd better leave now. I'm gonna be a wise woman and do like the Word tells us to do in Proverbs 26:17: *Withdraw thy foot from thy neighbor's house; lest he be weary of thee, and so hate thee.*" Smiling, she said, "Besides, I need to go home and get my beauty rest."

Sheena laughed. "Ms. Erma, you are something else."

"Child, when you get to be my age, you need to get your proper rest."

"Thank you for volunteering to take care of my husband, Ms. Erma. I know he'll be in good hands with you."

"No, thank you for letting me take care of him. I look forward to having something to do when I wake up in the mornings."

Sheena smiled and nodded. "I understand."

"Well, I don't want to hold you up, Sheena. Call me when you want me to start, and we can work the details out then."

"I'd appreciate it if you can start tomorrow morning at seven-thirty. Just have a price quote in mind, and I'll make sure you're paid every Friday afternoon."

"That'll be fine. Monday it is then." She turned to Lois. "I hope to see you again before you leave, Lois."

Lois stood up and hugged her. "That would be nice, Ms. Erma, but I'll be leaving today. I look forward to visiting with you the next time I'm here, though."

"I would like that, Lois." Erma headed for the front door. Sheena walked her to the door and hugged her. She closed the door, walked back to the den and sat back down.

Lois sat in the chair, smiling. "I told you it wouldn't hurt to ask her, didn't I? You didn't even have to ask, because the Lord worked it out so she felt led to volunteer. God is good, Sheena."

"All the time, Momma."

"I *thought* she was probably lonely. When people are lonely, they tend to act strangely sometimes because they need somebody in their life to care about 'em."

"I guess you're right, Momma. I never thought about her like that. I just thought she was a nosy old lady."

"You never know what people are going through if you don't take the time to listen to 'em. Speaking of what people are going through, I need to finish packing my bags. Gerald has already called me twice today and told me he'll be here to pick me up at four o'clock. I'm sure he's almost here by now."

"He misses you."

"I miss him too. I only have an hour left to spend with y'all. Gerald Andrews is a punctual man, bless his heart. He gets so irritated with me when I make him late for anything."

"Thanks for being here for me, Momma. You have given me a lot of strength."

"You're welcome, baby. But I didn't give you strength, that came from the Lord. Everything seems to be working out for you, Sheena."

"Momma, everything hasn't worked out."

"What do you mean? The Lord spared your husband's life. I think that's a blessing, don't you?"

"Yes, I thank God for that. But I still want some answers from Jason about why he was sitting at that restaurant with Ruby that day, considering the fact he promised me it was over between them."

"I'm sure he has a good explanation, but give him time to heal before you start questioning him, baby." Lois watched Sheena as her attitude suddenly changed.

"Oh, I'll give him time to get better, but he's going to explain this mess to me, even if I have to sit in front of him and shine a bright light in his face and interrogate his butt. I want some answers and they better be good!"

Chapter 44

Sheena woke up early the next morning and went downstairs to check on Jason. He was sitting up in the bed.

"How are you doing this morning?" she asked.

"I can't complain, I had some pain last night, but I lived through it." "Did you take your medicine last night? I left it and a cup of water on the table within your reach."

"I reached for it, but I knocked it off the table trying to get it. If you could give it to me now, I'd appreciate it."

Sheena picked up the cup and threw it in the trash and grabbed a towel to wipe up the water. The pills had rolled under his bed. "Hold on, Jason. I'll go in the kitchen and pour you a cup of orange juice to take with your medicine."

Jason groaned from pain. "Thank you, baby." She rushed to the kitchen and came back in a flash. "Here, I made you a piece of toast so you can have something to hold your medicine down.

I'm going to cook you some breakfast too. You need to regain your strength."

Jason couldn't gain his strength fast enough for Sheena. She figured, the quicker he gained his strength, the quicker she could grill him.

Sheena started frying the bacon and then ran upstairs to wake the children up so they could get ready for school. While they were getting dressed, she finished breakfast and went back upstairs to check on their progress and sent them downstairs to eat. She looked at the clock. It was already 7:15 A.M.

"You guys stop playing and finish eating your breakfast! Ms. Erma will be over here in fifteen minutes and I haven't even had time to shower and get dressed for school." She carried Jason his breakfast on a tray. "Are you feeling better since you took your medicine?" she asked.

"Yes, the pain is beginning to subside some. Sheena, you didn't have to make me breakfast. Ms. Erma can do that when she comes over."

"I didn't mind. I had to feed the children anyway, but tomorrow, we're having cereal. I don't know how you manage this every morning." She exhaled deeply. "I need to go and get ready for school. Are you sure you're going to be okay?"

"I'll be fine, go get dressed." The children ran into the room as he finished his sentence.

"Momma, we'll sit here with Daddy while you get dressed," Joseph announced.

"Did you guys finish your breakfast?" Sheena asked them.

"Yes, Momma." Jeremiah answered.

"Do you have all of your school supplies packed and ready to go?"

"Yes, ma'am. We have everything," Joseph sighed.

"Okay, I'm going upstairs to get ready." Sheena rushed upstairs. She had no idea that her life was going to be as hectic as it was now.

When she returned, Erma was in the kitchen listening to Pastor Shirley Caesar's latest CD, *Shirley Caesar & Friends,* as she washed the breakfast dishes.

"Good morning, Sheena. I thought I'd do these dishes for you while the children talked to Jason." Erma smiled.

Sheena was territorial when it came to her house and she wasn't exactly comfortable with seeing another woman in her kitchen. She knew it was for a good cause, though. "Good morning. You don't have to do the dishes, Ms. Erma. I was going to put them in the dishwasher before I left."

"I don't mind, child, it keeps me busy. You don't have time to do anything anyway, look at the time. You have usually pulled out of the driveway by now."

Sheena glanced at her watch. It was eight o'clock. "You're right, Ms. Erma. I'm ten minutes late. Come on, guys, let's go!" Sheena was amazed at the fact that Ms. Erma kept tabs on her down to the minute.

The children ran to follow Sheena, who was already in the garage. She backed up and headed out of their neighborhood, exceeding her normal speed in order to get to school before eight-thirty. As she watched the children enter the classroom, it dawned on her that she didn't say good-bye to Jason. She usually bid him a blessed day each morning.

"Life has really changed in the past three weeks," she told her colleague as they stood in their doors and talked across the hall to each other. "I miss those times. Jason was aggravating at times, but he did his part to help me around the house."

"You are blessed, Sheena. I wish I had a husband.

"Being married is better than being single, I know. I've been there and done that, girl. I'll choose a husband any day over being single."

"Yes, I suppose you're right." Sheena looked wistfully down the hallway. She couldn't tell her colleague that after what had happened between Jason and her, life would never be the same.

Chapter 45

The soft chimes of the grandfather clock that stood in the hallway awakened Jason. He looked at the clock on the wall. It was 1:00 P.M. He could see Ms. Erma sitting in the den watching television. When she heard him stir, she came in the room.

"Good afternoon, sleepyhead. That medicine knocked you out like a light didn't it?" Ms. Erma chimed.

"It sure did. I've slept the morning away." Jason yawned.

"Good. That's what you need is rest. Are you hungry?"

"Not really."

"Nonsense. I'll go warm you a bowl of chicken noodle soup and make you a sandwich. After you've eaten and let the food digest, I'll change those bandages."

Jason knew there was no need to protest, because she was determined to do her job. "What ever you say, Ms. Erma."

"After that, you need to sit up for a while. We don't want you to get bed sores now, do we?"

"No, ma'am. I don't need any more pain."

Ms. Erma made his meal and returned. She stopped in her tracks when she noticed Jason sitting on the bed staring into space. His face was distorted with a frown. "What are you so deep in thought about, Jason?"

"Oh, nothing in particular."

"Okay then, eat your food and I'll give you your medicine when I come back."

She came back a half hour later, gave him his medicine, changed his dressing and helped him up.

"Ms. Erma, I really appreciate you being here for me. I wasn't looking forward to having someone taking care of me."

"I'm happy to be of service. It meant so much to me after my husband died when you came over and checked on me every day. That's what neighbors are supposed to do; look out for one another."

"You're right."

Ms. Erma had come over every morning promptly at seven-thirty and left promptly at four o'clock when Sheena and the children returned from school. It was now the last day of school before Christmas vacation.

After Jason's morning nap and Ms. Erma had performed her daily routine, Jason sat in the chair reading a book while she watched her favorite soap opera. Jason couldn't concentrate. He felt like he needed to confide in somebody. Although Sheena considered her to be the neighborhood gossip, Jason believed she could be trusted not to scandalize their business.

"Ms. Erma."

She came into the library. "Yes, what is it, son?"

"You know the other day when you asked me what was on my mind and I said nothing in particular?"

"I remember."

"Well, I need to talk to somebody. I usually talk to my mother, but she has her hands full taking care of my dad."

"I'll be glad to listen to what you have to say." She paused. "But I don't want you to tell me your business unless you are absolutely sure about it."

"I'm sure. I believe I can trust you. You seem like a Christian lady to me."

"I do my best to be a Christian, but I'm not perfect. I make mistakes everyday because I'm human."

"I understand." Jason lowered his head from her stare.

"What's on your mind?" she asked gently, with a concerned look on her face.

"I know you're curious about what happened outside here about a month ago."

"Yes, I am curious. I haven't seen anything like that in all my seventy-eight years. Who in the world was that crazy woman?"

Jason hesitated before he said anything. "She was someone I was having an affair with; someone from my past."

Erma was quiet for a few seconds. "Jason, I am not judging you, but what on earth possessed you to cheat on your wife? And with somebody with no class like that woman."

"I would say that it was something that just happened, but we all know that's a sorry excuse for doing something."

"You're right about that. I know we all make bad decisions at times, but you said she was from your past; didn't you know how scandalous she was?"

"I gave her the benefit of the doubt. I thought she had changed, but I was wrong. We ran into each other one day; however, I didn't know she was living in Charlotte. We started talking and one thing led to another."

"It seems so. But what did you do to make the woman so mad that she came to your house and fought you?"

"It's a long story; maybe I'll tell you one day, but it's too much to discuss right now." He glanced at the clock. It was 3:35 P.M. "Sheena will be home soon and it's going to take longer than the time we have to brief you. I *can* tell you that it's over between us and she has moved back to Florida with her husband."

"Jason, the woman is *married* too?"

"Yes, ma'am, but I didn't know that at the time. Anyway, I want to talk to you about Sheena."

"Sheena? I don't think that's a good idea. I like both of you all and I really don't want to be in the midst of y'all's marriage, despite what your wife may think . . ."

Jason looked at Erma in amazement.

Erma continued. "In spite of what she may think, I'm not an old gossip. I try to mind my own business. If you see me walking from house to house, it's because I've been invited. I baby-sit occasionally for a lot of the neighbors, and in turn, they'll invite me over to have dinner with them, or ask me to come over and watch a movie with them. Your wife is on the shy side, so that's why I've never given her too much trouble."

"I haven't gotten that impression of you, Ms. Erma, that's why I took up time with you. If I felt otherwise, I wouldn't have had anything to do with you."

"Uh-huh. Everybody has an opinion. I know that your wife is quiet and reserved, but some of the neighbors think that she is stuck up. They all say that you are friendly, but they don't know how to approach her because all she ever does is wave and hurry in the house. I just tell them like I'm telling you, you can't judge people."

"Oh, I don't want to talk about my wife in a negative sense. I'm just concerned about what she is going to do."

"About you cheating on her?"

"Yes. I can't blame her if she left, but I don't want her to."

"Well, she's still here with you, Jason. That should speak volumes."

"It does, but I believe she's only here because of my condition."

"What makes you believe that?"

"Because before I got shot we hadn't resolved the issue yet. She had gone to see a lawyer about a divorce, but her lawyer advised her to wait until after the holiday so she could think about it thoroughly before she made a rash decision."

"That was good advice. Haste can make waste."

"Yes, that's true. The morning after Thanksgiving Day, she decided to go home to her mother's house so she could clear her mind and pray about our marriage to see if it was worth salvaging."

"That made sense."

"But the ironic thing is she saw the lady—her name is Ruby—and me, sitting in a restaurant together. I don't know what Sheena was doing on that side of town that morning. I thought she had gone to pick the children up from my mother's house and was on her way to Asheville. That's what she told me anyway." Jason's mouth was beginning to dry so he stopped talking to drink some water. "So, I met Ruby because we had to discuss some important business . . ." He noticed Erma staring at him in awe.

Erma's face scrunched up. "After what happened with the woman coming to your house and Sheena threatening to divorce you, you still chose to run around with that heifer?" she asked Jason indignantly.

Jason was shocked at Erma's harsh tone and the uncharacteristic language she used to describe Ruby. "Like I said, Ms. Erma, it's a long story. I can't divulge all my information, but no, I wasn't meeting her to be with her. We had some loose ends to tie up."

"You should have tied those loose ends up the day that conniving hussy showed up at your house if you wanted to keep your wife."

"I tried to end it with her, but it wasn't that simple."

"What in the world was she holding over your head? Was she blackmailing you or something?"

Jason looked at the clock. It was 3:50 P.M. He couldn't tell Erma about Cassandra. He hadn't even told Sheena about her yet. "In a sense, she was blackmailing me, but I don't have time to discuss that now. But I can tell you that I made a huge mistake by getting involved with her again. If I could turn back the hands of time, I would; but I can't."

"Well, son, what are your plans?"

"My plan is to reconcile with my wife and try to keep her from leaving me."

"Like I said before, she's still here, that speaks volumes."

"It does, but Sheena is the type of woman to worry about appearances. She's not going to leave me while I'm still bed-ridden. She's always concerned about what people might think."

"She needs to get over that. Folks are gonna think what they want to think!"

"I've tried to relay that point to her for years. She's such a private person. I believe she will be here until I'm well. I know she still loves me, but I think she is still planning to divorce me."

"Why do you think that, son?"

"I can see it in her eyes. My betrayal and who I betrayed her with is too much for her to handle."

"She knew about Ruby before?"

"Yes, she knows we dated in college."

"Uh-huh. I'm willing to bet that's why Ruby showed up at your house that day. Knowing you, you probably told her you weren't gonna leave your wife, so she was determined to make sure Sheena left you. Once she accomplished her goal, she was gonna swarm around like a buzzard and pick your bones dry."

Jason laughed at Erma's theory. "She was determined to win me back, that's for sure."

"Don't flatter yourself, Jason. The only thing that scavenger wanted was what you could give her. After she sucked you dry, she would have moved on to her next victim." Erma shook her head. "It's a crying shame. It's just scandalous, the things these trifling women will do to get what they want; it doesn't matter if the man has a family. Shoot, that's fair game to some of these tramps."

Jason cleared his throat.

"I didn't mean to ramble on, but it's the truth. And you men better take heed and seek God for some wisdom so you won't fall for everything."

"I agree. I know I played a big part in this game too, and because of my weakness, I think our marriage is beyond repair."

"There's nothing too hard for God to do."

"That's what my mother and sister have told me. But under the circumstances, I don't see how it can be repaired."

"That's because you are looking at the problem and not the problem solver." Erma grabbed the Bible that Sheena had left on Jason's reading table and started flipping through the pages. "Listen to this, son. God's Word asks in Genesis 18:14, *Is any thing too hard for the Lord?* And in Jeremiah 32:17 a prayer was proclaimed that, *Ah Lord God! Behold, thou hast made the heaven and the earth by thy great power and stretched out arm, and there is nothing too hard for thee*: This Word still applies today." Erma noticed the blank stare on Jason's face. "You need to read this Bible, Jason. Everything you need is in here. First of all, you need to repent and ask God to forgive you, pray and seek His face and then you'll see Him working miracles right before your eyes, in your personal life, your marriage and anything else you need. Hallelujah."

The sound of Sheena unlocking the kitchen door brought Erma's message to an abrupt halt. Erma looked at the clock. It was four o'clock on the dot. As soon as the door opened, the children came racing into the library.

"Hi, Ms. Erma," they shouted in unison.

"Hey, babies. Did y'all have a good day at school?" she asked.

"Yes, ma'am," they replied.

She turned to Jason and at a volume barely louder than a whisper, she said, "I probably won't see you until after the new year because my daughter and her family are going to be staying with me. The children are due to arrive here tomorrow night. The Lord willing, I'll be back when school reopens. I expect to see a changed man when I return. Trust in the Lord, Jason. He will work everything out. I love you, son. Take care."

"I love you too, Ms. Erma. Take care now."

Sheena and Ms. Erma exchanged goodbyes. Sheena hugged her and thanked her for her help. She gave Ms. Erma a box wrapped in Christmas paper with an envelope on top. "Here's an early Christmas present for you, Ms. Erma. I hope you enjoy it."

"Sheena, you shouldn't have. I really appreciate this. You all have a Merry Christmas and a Happy New Year."

"You too, Ms. Erma. I'll see you when school reopens, won't I?"

"Of course. Seven-thirty A.M. sharp."

Erma kissed each of the children on their foreheads, waved to Jason and walked out of the library with the children following her on their way to the kitchen to get a snack. Sheena walked Erma to the front door and watched her walk across the street to her home. She closed the door and walked back into the library. Jason greeted her with a huge smile.

"How was your day?" Sheena asked him.

"Good, it's getting better and better."

She noticed the Bible in his lap. "What's going on?"

"Ms. Erma gave me a Bible lesson. It was all right."

"That's great."

He noticed the skeptical look in her eyes as though she couldn't decide if he was genuine or not. "What's wrong?"

Sheena ruffled her fingers through her short immaculately cut hair. "I can't tell if you are sincere about the Word of God, or if you're just trying to impress me like you use to do. I can't trust you anymore, Jason." Before he got a chance to respond, Sheena waved him away and walked out.

Chapter 46

Catherine and Jacob came over that evening to visit Jason. They stayed for an hour, and when they were about to leave, the children begged to go home with them.

"Let's let them stay with us, Catherine," Jacob told her.

"Do you feel like being bothered with the children? You know how our babies get when they get to our house. You spoil them rotten," Catherine replied.

"They'll be fine. That's what grandparents are for, spoiling the grandkids."

Jason looked at his father in disbelief. He must be getting soft in his old age, he thought. The Jacob he grew up with was stern and unyielding. "Are you sure that's okay, Daddy?"

"I'm sure. Besides, that will give you and Sheena some time to be alone." He patted Sheena on the hand.

"Thanks, Daddy Grey. Let me run upstairs and pack an overnight bag for the kids."

After they left, Sheena and Jason watched TV for a while. Sheena dozed off in the middle of one show and slept for about an hour. During that time, Jason prayed silently, and afterward, decided that when Sheena awakened, it would be a good time to tell her about Cassandra. He didn't want to prolong the inevitable any longer.

She opened her eyes and focused on Jason starring at her with a worried look on his face. "What's wrong, Jason? Are you in pain?" She looked at her watch. "It won't be time for your medicine for another hour."

"Sheena, baby, I'm not in any physical pain right now, but. . . ."

She sat up and straightened her clothes out. "What's wrong then?"

"I need to talk to you, but this isn't going to be easy."

"It's late, Jason. We can talk tomorrow. Your mother said she's going to take the children Christmas shopping, so it'll probably be sometime late tomorrow afternoon when she brings them back."

Jason considered what she said. "I guess you are tired, aren't you? You've been working so hard lately, teaching those children, taking care of me and running the household."

"Yes, and I am exhausted. I was relieved when your dad agreed to let the children go home with them. I never thought I'd say this, but I'm glad to get a break from school!"

"I appreciate you being a good wife, Sheena."

Sheena's eyes were distant and hollow. She simply looked away and nodded her head. Jason saw that as a sign to back off. He sensed that she wasn't in the right mental state for a serious conversation. He refocused his attention on the TV.

Sheena stood up. "I'm going to take a long warm bubble bath, maybe that'll help me relax. I'll come back down after I've finished. Maybe I'll be better company to you."

While she was upstairs, Jason opened the Bible and read the scriptures that Erma had quoted to him.

When Sheena came back downstairs, she had extra covers with her. "Do you need anything else after you take your medicine? Do you want a snack or some juice?"

"No, I'm fine." Jason slowly rose up and got in his bed. "I don't need any extra covers, baby. I'm okay."

"They're not for you." Sheena walked to the loveseat and began spreading the covers across it.

"Sheena, you shouldn't try to sleep on that small love-seat. That thing is so uncomfortable.

Believe me, I know. When you wake up in the morning, you are going to have aches and pains in places that you didn't realize existed on your body."

Sheena laughed. "You're too funny, Jason."

"It's good to see you laugh again, Sheena," Jason told her with a sigh of relief in his voice.

"Well, you've always had a great sense of humor. That's one of the qualities you possessed that attracted me to you; you made me laugh."

"You had the ability to bring the comedy side out in me. It came naturally when I was around you because you were always so easy to talk to."

"Humph." Sheena cleared her throat and her countenance became serious again.

Jason looked at the covers she clutched in her arms. "I'll be fine down here, Sheena. Go back upstairs and sleep in your bed so you'll be comfortable."

Sheena smiled slightly. *My bed?* She had become lonely sleeping in bed by herself. Some nights, she would let Jessica sleep with her, to fill the void she felt. With the children gone, the silence upstairs seemed to be deafening. After her bath, she had every intention of folding the covers down on her bed and getting a good night's sleep.

She needed to check on Jason first, so instead, she decided to sleep in the room with him. But, as much as she hated to admit it, she missed the comfort of Jason's warm body.

Sheena looked at Jason wistfully. "I'm sleeping with you tonight. I'll be careful so I won't hurt you."

"I wouldn't feel it if you did. I'm just happy to have you at my side."

Sheena carefully climbed in bed with Jason and snuggled as close to him as she possibly could without hurting him.

"We'll talk in the morning, Jason. Let's just get a good night's rest."

Chapter 47

Sheena awoke from a fitful sleep. "Lord, what is this dream about?" she whispered.

Jason pulled her close to him. "What's wrong, Sheena?"

"Did I hurt you?" She rolled over gently to check his back. "Are you okay?"

"I'm fine, no, you didn't hurt me. I guess you were dreaming again though."

"I was."

She studied him for a moment before she closed her eyes again.

"Goodnight."

"Goodnight, baby."

Jason noticed the clock. It was 4:15 A.M. He sniffed the pleasant light fragrance of Sheena's hair. He closed his eyes to savor the few peaceful hours he had left to share with her. He was certain that after he told her about Cassandra tomorrow, this moment would only be a distant memory. Jason drifted off to sleep, but awakened hours later. The sun screamed its bright morning sunrays through the plantation blinds. His wife hadn't drawn the drapes like she usually did at night.

Sheena came into the room with a tray of food. "Good morning, sleepy head. I made you breakfast."

Jason rose up slowly and smiled. He looked at the country sliced ham, yellow grits, toasted English muffins, omelets, and orange juice. "It looks good." He sniffed the food. "Mmm, smells good too."

Sheena set the tray up on his bed. She gave him a warm bath cloth to wash his face and hands. "After you eat and get your bath, we can talk."

Jason nodded his head in agreement. "I loved having you next to me last night. I have missed you so much."

"I've missed you too, but we still have a lot to resolve, Jason."

"I know, but with the help of the Lord, we can work it out, baby."

Sheena's eyes pierced through his. "We'll see."

Jason had a strange feeling that she already knew somehow what he wanted to discuss with her.

After Sheena cleaned the breakfast dishes, she helped Jason with his bath and gave him his medicine. It made him drowsy, so he was sound asleep again minutes later. She took the opportunity to clean the house thoroughly. After she finished, she checked on Jason.

"Oh, I see you are awake and sitting up."

"Yes, I couldn't lie in the bed any longer, so I got up and tried to do some exercise so I won't be so stiff."

"Exercise?"

"Yes, I walk from the bed to the living room every day. Ms. Erma started me on that routine."

"Are you sure you're not overexerting yourself?"

"No, not at all. It's making me stronger. I take my time using baby steps like she taught me to."

"Okay, as long as you know what you're doing."

"I do."

"Are you ready to eat something?"

"I have a craving for some junk food. Pizza would be nice."

"Okay, pizza it is. I'll order it."

"Are you about ready for that talk?" He sensed the procrastination in her voice.

"I need to go take a shower first. I feel dirty and sweaty from cleaning the house. It should take the pizza about 30 minutes to get here. I should be back down before then."

"Sure. I'll be sitting right here on my throne when you return," he joked.

Sheena half smiled and left. Her timing was perfect. She finished her wash-up and came back downstairs just as the doorbell rang. Sheena paid for the pizza and set Jason's makeshift table with paper plates, cups and napkins. She held her piece in a plate on her lap. They ate silently as they watched a comedy show on *UPN*.

Jason used a napkin to wipe his mouth. "That was good."

"Yeah; it was."

"Sheena I need to get this talk over with. It's important."

Sheena didn't say anything. She cleaned up the trash and carried the leftover pizza to the kitchen. When she reentered the room, she was carrying a dust rag, furniture polish and the vacuum cleaner. "This room needs to be thoroughly cleaned. My Lord, look at all this dust."

Jason knew she was stalling for time. "Sheena, stop. We need to talk, now."

She dropped the rag on the table and exhaled deeply. Sheena dreaded hearing what she knew was bad news. "Okay, Jason, I'm listening."

"First of all, I want to say that I love you more than I have loved anyone. I've always loved you and I always will."

"Okay, you've established that; so give me the bad news."

Jason drank several swallows of water before he began. "Do you remember when I told you that I couldn't just end it with Ruby?"

"Yes."

"Well, the reason I couldn't make a clean break with her . . ." *This is hard.* Sheena stared at him expectedly. "I couldn't end it because we have a child together."

Sheena stared at him in disbelief. "W—What?" she stammered.

Jason inhaled and exhaled slowly. "I said we have a child together."

For a moment, Sheena didn't say anything. It was as though she was in shock. "A child?" She dropped her head and held it in her hands.

"Yes," Jason said, almost in a whisper.

"When? How? I thought you said you only saw her a few months ago?"

"That's the truth. I got involved with her four months ago."

"That can't be true, you're lying."

"It's true, Sheena."

"You said you were only with her four months ago," she repeated. "So what, is she pregnant now? But wait a minute, you said you have a *child* together. How can that be, Jason?"

"No, she's not pregnant. We do have a child though," Jason said, clearer and louder, with more depth in his tone.

"Stop lying!" Sheena hit her fist on the table. Her small light brown eyes stretched open. "For once in your life, tell the truth!"

"I'm telling the truth, Sheena. The child is eleven years old."

Sheena walked over to him and stood within inches of his face. "You mean to tell me that you kept this a secret from me all these years?"

"No, I didn't know myself until a few months ago. She blurted the news to me when I tried to end it with her a month after we started seeing each other."

"Do you really expect me to believe that lie?"

"I'm telling you the truth. She kept it from me until recently. She was pregnant when she moved back home twelve years ago."

"How do know it's yours?"

"Because I had a DNA test done while I was in the hospital."

"How?"

"Jonathan helped me. He made arrangements for the lab technician to take a swab sample of the insides of my mouth. Ruby and Cassandra went to a lab in Florida—"

"I can't believe this. You have a child by another woman? And her, of all people."

"I couldn't believe it either. It's as though my past has come back to haunt me."

"This is crazy!" Sheena paced around in the room, and then whirled back around and stood close to Jason's face. She put her hand on her hip. "How could you do this to me? I have spent my whole marriage to you living a lie."

"Honestly, Sheena, I didn't know. She kept it from me and she and her husband raised the child as his."

"You're lying! You knew all along. That's why you had so many trips to Florida. You were keeping another family!"

"Sheena, I promise you, I didn't know until Ruby told me four months ago. I hadn't laid eyes on her until then. My trips to Florida were strictly, business. I didn't try to contact her. You have to believe me."

"How do you expect me to believe anything you say anymore? You are a liar. Nothing you say sounds truthful anymore."

"It's the truth. I didn't know I had another daughter until Ruby came to town."

"So you think you have another daughter? How do you know for a fact that she is yours? You said that Ruby's been married for eleven years. It's probably his baby and she just wants to scam money from you."

"I told you that I know because I had the test done. The results are 99.98% positive that she is my daughter."

Sheena didn't want to believe it was true. "They could have paid someone at the lab to manipulate the test."

"Sheena . . . baby, I'm sorry, but she is my daughter. If I had known twelve years ago, we wouldn't be going through this. If I had known, I would have taken care of my responsibilities. Things would be entirely different between us. I could have let you decide whether you still wanted to be with me, knowing I had a baby about to be born. As it was, I didn't know anything about Ruby being pregnant when you and I started dating."

"What makes you think that I would have had anything to do with you, knowing that you had a baby on the way?"

"Honestly, I probably would have broken up with you because I would have felt responsible for my child. Having a baby would have changed everything."

"Before we started dating I asked you repeatedly, Jason, if you have any children. And you looked me in my eyes and told me a bald-faced lie!"

"I didn't lie to you. I did not have any children as far as I knew. I have been lied to too, Sheena. I didn't know I had fathered a child. I'm not the type of person to disown my responsibilities. I did not know."

"Where's the proof?" Sheena demanded. "I want to see it for myself."

"Look under that accounting book, the third one on the top shelf."

"How did it get here?"

"I asked Jonathan to put it there for me. I didn't want you to find the letter before I could tell you myself."

She found the letter and read it. "Well, I guess this is all the proof I need." Crying, she threw the letter at him. "My marriage to you has been one big disappointment after another. You used me as a rebound to get over your girlfriend until she came back into your life, then you had an affair with her and now . . . surprise, surprise . . . you all have an eleven-year-old daughter together! Isn't that special?"

"Sheena, I didn't want to hurt you with more bad news. If there was something I could do to change this situation, I would. Unfortunately, I didn't then, nor do I now have any control over this situation. I'm sorry, really I am." Jason slowly got up out of his chair to comfort Sheena. Seeing his wife cry was painful. His eyes were tearful.

Sheena waved him away. "She's won. I can't compete with her."

Jason felt his strength leaving him, so he sat back down. "Won what? This wasn't a competition between the two of you."

"My one consolation was that I had given you three children. I thought that at least that was a bond we shared that the two of you didn't share. But she has given you everything that I have, she gave birth to your oldest child. I guess I'm second best all around. You may as well call her and make arrangements for the two of you to get back together." She flopped down in the love seat and cried heart-breaking tears. "It's over between us, Jason. Nothing you say or do can make me change my mind."

"Sheena, I don't want her. I love you and I have prayed for weeks, now, for God to direct me on how to tell you about this so we can work things out and stay married in spite of the fact that I have a child that I knew nothing about."

Sheena walked over to where he was sitting. She slapped him so hard that he winced from the pain. "Are you crazy? There's no way we can stay together now. You have another family. Even if it crossed my mind to reconcile with you, this changes everything. A child isn't something that you can wipe away like dust and forget about it, because just like dust, they'll show up again sooner or later."

Sheena wiped her tears away with the back of her hands. "She's going to be a part of your life for the rest of your life. The child and her mother too! I thought we had a chance since Ruby moved back to Florida with her husband, *if* that is even true, but now she's going to be a part of your life forever. I can't handle that. Ruby will be a constant irritation and a thorn in my side as long as I'm with you."

"Sheena, I'm sorry. I can't undo this, but I do want to salvage our marriage. Ruby only has to be in our lives to a certain extent. We will have to communicate with her because of Cassandra, but other than that she has her own life with her husband."

"Cassandra, huh?" As long as they had referred to her as *the child*, she didn't seem real to Sheena. But hearing Cassandra's name made her a reality. "Do you honestly believe what you just said? Ruby wants to be with you; she's proved that by her actions. She will do whatever she has to do to get you and that illegitimate child of hers is her leverage to you."

Jason was looking down at the floor while Sheena talked, but his head snapped back up when Sheena referred to his daughter as illegitimate. Sheena saw a flicker of anger in Jason's eyes.

"Don't call my daughter out of her name!" Jason told her gruffly.

Sheena realized she had gone too far, and that obviously, Jason cared for the child. But at the same time, she felt hurt and insulted that he would defend a daughter that he didn't know. And to add insult to injury, it was Ruby's child and Jason expected her to accept the child and roll with the punches. Sheena didn't apologize. "Jason, I still think that Ruby wants you."

Jason took a deep breath and exhaled slowly. "That's not true, Sheena. She loves her husband."

"That's not what I saw that day at the restaurant. The two of you looked like a couple in love to me."

"When you walked up on us, she was encouraging me about my relationship with you."

"Get real! She looked like she had charmed you like a snake to do her will."

"That's not what was going on. We agreed to stop seeing each other earlier in the week and the reason we met that day was to discuss me meeting Cassandra. She also suggested that we have a DNA test done before they went back to Florida."

"A likely story."

Jason became frustrated with Sheena dismissing everything he said, but he knew he couldn't afford to keep offending her. "It's the truth."

"So, did you get to meet your daughter?"

"No; I was supposed to meet her the next day."

"Well, did you meet her the next day?"

"No, because I got shot, remember?"

Sheena paced the floor. "So have you met her yet?"

"No, I've been in the hospital and you were there with me. It wouldn't have been respectful if they came parading to my room in front of you with a daughter you knew nothing about. And bringing her here was out of the question."

"You got that right! That was out of the question. She's not coming here."

"To answer your question, no, I haven't had the opportunity to meet her yet."

"When did you plan on telling me about her? Or should I ask were you going to tell me about her if you hadn't have gotten shot?"

"Before all of this happened," he pointed to himself, "if the test proved that she was mine, I planned to tell you after you came back from visiting your parents that weekend. That way, you could have made an informed decision before you filed any papers."

"If the results were positive, you would have told me. What if they were negative?"

"No, I wouldn't have told you. What would have been the point?"

"I really don't know. I don't know anything anymore. I don't even know you like I thought I did."

"I have been honest with you about everything. I have no more secrets. Everything is out in the open now."

Sheena mused. "I saw her and I guess it was her husband in the waiting room that day. I wanted to go tell her to leave, but your life was at a critical point, so *she* wasn't my first priority at the time." Sheena looked at Jason. "Is he slow or something? I don't know of any man who would come to see about his wife's lover."

"He's not slow. He knew that she wanted to check on her child's father. Jonathan told me that they talked that day and he asked them not to come back. Ruby's husband readily agreed, because, according to Jonathan, he didn't want to be there in the first place. Who can blame him?"

"What did Jonathan and he talk about?"

"About Cassandra. He was there on her behalf only. He has raised the child ever since she was born. She's his child in every way but biological. From what Jonathan tells me, he's very protective of her."

"Did he agree to let you see her?"

"Yes, Ruby said that Thurman left it up to her, and of course, Cassandra."

"Of course she said, 'By all means, let my baby meet her daddy, the man that I love,'" Sheena said sarcastically.

"No, not at all. She is satisfied with the husband she has. She loves him."

"If she loves him so much, why was she after you?"

"They were having serious problems to the point where they separated, and I guess during their separation she thought about me because of our daughter, who knows?"

"So, where are they now?"

"He moved her back to Florida, and according to Jonathan, they have reconciled and are quite happy together."

"Humph. How does he know she's telling the truth?"

"We don't know that for a fact, but whether they are happy together or not is not my concern. My concern is praying and believing that the Lord will have mercy and forgive me for all the wrong I've committed against Him and you."

"God is gracious, Jason, of course He'll forgive you. I'm not sure if I can though."

"All I'm asking is for you to try."

Sheena's mind raced. "So who else knows about your daughter, besides Jonathan and of course, Mary? Have they seen her?"

"Jonathan met her before they moved back to Florida. He said she looks just like her mother, with the exception of having dimples like me."

"She must be a pretty child. Ruby is exceptionally beautiful. Compared to her, I guess I'm not much to look at, am I?"

"She's a pretty lady, but looks don't mean anything when you don't have any morals. Why are you so self-conscious about your looks? You look fine to me. I like the way you look."

"Don't patronize me Jason. I know what I look like."

"I know what you look like too. You're beautiful."

"Yeah, right. Anyway, does anyone else in the family know about her?"

"Momma and all the rest of the family know."

"Don't I feel just like a fool? The wife *is* always the last to know, huh?"

"Jonathan told them because he said Terri and Aretha approached him about Ruby, apparently, after talking to you."

"Now I understand why Terri and Aretha were so nice to me before they left."

"What do you mean?"

"They apologized to me for the way they had treated me in the past and seemed like they were sincere. I even apologized to them for my behavior toward them."

"I'm sure they were sincere. It's time to let the past go."

Sheena meditated on what Jason had said. She relaxed her face. "Yes, I guess life is too short to continue holding grudges against people; especially family."

Jason relaxed a little after seeing Sheena's facial expression soften up. "Amen to that."

Sheena's facial muscles tensed back up. "Jason, do you realize how much has changed in our lives? Things aren't ever going to be the same for us—ever!"

"I know things won't be the same, but with God's grace they will get better."

"How? You have a child outside of our marriage."

"I understand that, and there's nothing I can do about it, but I have to take care of her now that I know she's in the world."

"Fine, you can take care of her, but don't expect me to be around. How would you feel if I popped up with a child that wasn't yours ten years into our marriage?"

"That's a good question. I can't answer that, but I would hope that you would have been honest enough to tell me about it before we were married."

"You didn't tell me about yours. That's a double standard."

"No, Sheena, how can it be a double standard? I never knew about the child. That was out of my control. I had no idea that I had even produced another human being. Ruby cheated me out of that right. I can't carry a child. In your case, you would have carried the child and chosen to hide it from me. *That's* the difference."

"Now you know how I feel. It's as though you had a child and kept it from me."

"It's not the same." Jason concluded that either Sheena didn't get it, or she didn't want to believe him. "How could I keep her from you when I didn't know about her myself?"

Sheena was quiet for a minute. "How do you feel about Ruby keeping this a secret from you all this time?"

"I was outraged. It made me feel like a fool."

"A fool? Why?"

"Because I had flesh and blood walking around on this earth that I didn't even know existed. I've lost eleven years of her life and I'll never be able to make it up to her. I feel like a deadbeat parent."

"I guess I can understand why you would feel that way. If I had had a child and given it up for adoption, I would be crazy with worry wondering how he or she was doing and how they were being treated."

"I know. Ruby told me that Thurman has always treated Cassandra like she's his own. He's never mistreated her and that he loves her like his own."

"That's good. Does the child know Thurman's not her father?"

"Yes, she found out by accident."

"How?"

"She and Thurman were having a heated argument one night about Cassandra. But they were not aware that Cassandra had awakened and was standing in the doorway."

"Were they debating her paternity or something?"

"No, he's always known that Cassandra was my child."

"How could he be so sure?"

"Because after she moved back home, she saw him at the hospital where he worked and she was already five months pregnant."

"Oh. So, he married her after the baby was born?"

"No; while she was pregnant."

"That was noble of him."

"Yes, it was. Ruby said they did their best to let Cassandra know she was loved and Thurman still loved her as his daughter, but they ended up taking her to counseling."

Sheena sighed. "That's so sad."

"According to Ruby, ultimately, they ended up separating after Cassandra asked them if she could move in with Ruby's parents because of their arguing all the time.

When Ruby saw our picture on the cover of the magazine, she got the twisted idea that she could start over again with me because we had a daughter together. I guess she thought that would bring us together. In conclusion, here's where the story stands."

"So, it didn't matter to her that you already had a family?"

"Evidently, it didn't. She's always been a de-termined woman. She has grown up in a tough environment, so I guess her survival instincts drove her to go after whatever she wanted, no matter who she had to trample down to get it."

"That may be so, but you still played your part in helping her."

"I don't deny that, Sheena. I finally came to my senses and tried to end it with her, but that's when she shocked me with the news of us having a child together."

"Do you regret having a child with her, or are you happy about it?"

"I'm not jumping for joy, because as far as I knew, I only had three children. I was proud to be a full-time father to my children. I never expected to be a father with a child outside of my home."

"You are now. Besides, any time a person chooses to cheat on their husband or wife, they risk that chance. Even if you two didn't have Cassandra, you could have made Ruby pregnant, or given me some awful fatal disease."

"You're right."

"So what are you going to do about this outside child of yours?"

"I have to do the right thing and provide for her. I want to be a part of her life too. If I had known about her, I never would have laid back and let some other man take my place."

"If you had known, would you have married Ruby?"

Jason considered the question carefully. "I probably would have."

"Really? Why would you marry someone that you say you never loved?"

"I had strong feelings for her, I cared about her. If I had known she was carrying my child, I would have married her for the child's sake."

"Why? That's a thing of the past now, marrying a woman because you impregnated her. Statistics show that most of those marriages end up in divorce. You could have easily taken care of the child without being married to her mother."

"I know that, but I wouldn't have let my daughter grow up in the atmosphere that Ruby is from. I would have married her to give my baby a secure place to grow up in."

"Were her living conditions that bad?"

"Yes, Sheena. She grew up in a tough neighborhood and she survived in it, but I wouldn't want my child to have to live like that. Besides, Dad always nailed it into our heads that if we brought a child in the world, then we'd better take care of it."

"I suppose you and I would have never been together if you had known, huh?"

Jason exhaled wearily. "I don't know, Sheena. I can't foretell what the past would have held. We had already started dating before she left and went back home. Although, our dates consisted of only long distance phone conversations, who knows? This is just another case of *what ifs*. I do know that I fell in love with you shortly after I met you. And I know that I would have taken care of my responsibilities either way."

"I don't think I would have married you, Jason, knowing that you had a baby on the way."

"I understand. I wouldn't have asked you to marry me either. I had too much respect for you to bring confusion like that to your life. You deserved better. Besides, according to Ruby, she almost had an abortion, so there wouldn't have been a baby anyway. So who knows how things *would* have been?"

Sheena was silent for a few minutes. Jason waited for her to speak. "Well, this wasn't any ordinary conversation. You really blew my mind this time, Jason. It makes me wonder what's next, what other secrets are you carrying."

"There aren't any more secrets. I'm an open book now, Sheena. I dreaded having to tell you news like this, but it was unavoidable. This is what I wanted to talk to you about, I wanted to tell you weeks ago, but now was the opportunity for me to tell you. You accused me of being preoccupied several times—now you know why."

"The Bible says the truth will make you free. So I guess you are free."

"What does that mean?"

"It means that you are free to raise your daughter," she sniffled and wiped her swollen red eyes, "because I am finished with this fiasco called a marriage."

Chapter 48

A few seconds later, Sheena hurried upstairs. Jason hobbled to the kitchen to get a glass of orange juice to take with his medicine. He walked to the bottom of the kitchen stairs, looked up and raised his leg to reach the first step. A sharp pain ran up and down his spine. He quickly decided against climbing the stairs. He managed to hobble back to his bed and ease into it.

Sheena freshened her face as best she could, applying a fresh coat of makeup. She changed into a red sweat suit, a color she rarely wore, and went back downstairs. She walked back into the library.

Jason forced his eyes open wider and rose up unsteadily because the medicine was taking its effect. "That color becomes your complexion; you should wear it more often," he complimented his wife.

"Humph."

"You going somewhere?" Jason asked her groggily.

"I'm going out for a while. I need some fresh air."

Afraid that she was leaving him, he asked her, "What time will you be back?"

Sheena could hear the apprehension in his voice. "I don't have any idea; I'll be back when I'm in the mood to come home."

"Is that your way of saying that you are leaving me?"

"No, Jason, if I were leaving you, I would tell you so. When I decide to go, you'll be the first one to know."

Jason nodded. "I thought maybe you had another one of your spontaneous moments."

"I don't have spontaneous moments. I left in the middle of the night before because of you."

"You're right."

"You know that was out of character for me, but then again, considering what you've put me through lately, I'm subject to do anything."

Jason didn't respond. Sheena glared at him, putting her hand on her hip. "I'll see you when I see you. Do you need anything? Isn't it time to take your medicine?"

"I've already taken it."

"When? I didn't leave anything in here for you to drink. Did you swallow the pills dry?"

"No, I limped to the kitchen and poured myself some orange juice."

"You should have called me. You're trying to do too much."

"Actually, I tried to see if I could climb the stairs."

"What? What are you trying to do; set yourself back?"

"No, one lift of my leg brought me back to reality. The pain in my back was bad enough to bring me back to my senses."

"Why were you trying to come upstairs?"

"You left out in such a huff, I thought you were going up there to pack your things to leave me."

"Jason, I just need to get some fresh air. You gave me a lot to think about today. I have to try to process this information, so I'm going to the park and walk off some of this stress."

"Oh." He gave her a skeptical look.

"Jason, don't pressure me about what I'm going to do. I am so confused, I don't know whether I'm coming or going. The changes you have taken me through these last few months have made my life a living nightmare."

"At the risk of sounding like a broken record, I apologize," he slurred. "If I had it to do all over again, I wouldn't have made the bad decisions that I made. Again, I ask you to forgive me."

"Don't . . ." She shook her head.

"What?"

"I can't bear to hear another apology from you right now. They're beginning to sound meaningless."

"I don't know what to say."

"At the moment, I'd prefer you didn't say anything."

"Sure."

"Let's try to take one day at a time. Our first priority is to get you healed. Once that has been accomplished, I'll decide what to do about you and your problem."

"The way you sounded when you walked out, I thought you were finished with us."

"I am." Sheena observed the disappointment in Jason's countenance. "I don't hate you, Jason, but I can't deal with the drama you bring into my life anymore. I don't know what's going to happen from one day to the next with you. The security and trust that I should have in you has been destroyed. The closeness is not there anymore. When you slept with Ruby, you alienated the bond between us, shattering the spiritual unity that we shared."

"Sheena . . . you say you don't hate me, so is there a possibility that you still love me?"

Sheena exhaled deeply. "To be honest, I still love you, Jason, but sometimes love isn't enough. I can't talk about *us* now; I have to concentrate on *my* emotional survival and well being." Jason opened his mouth to speak. Sheena turned away from him, walked out and slammed the library door closed.

Chapter 49

Catherine rang the doorbell several times. "What in the world is taking Sheena so long to answer the door?" She went back to her car and sat down, searching in her purse for her cell phone. The boys had run to the huge backyard to play with their new football, while Jessica played on her swing set.

"Jeremiah! Joseph!"

Joseph ran back around to the front of the house, ahead of Jeremiah to see what Catherine wanted. "Yeah, Grandma?" Joseph answered.

"What do you mean, yeah, Grandma? You know better than to talk to me like that."

"I'm sorry. Yes, ma'am?"

"That's better." She patted him on the head. "I can't get your Momma to come to the door. I rang the doorbell several times and knocked until my fist is sore. Is she in the backyard? I know how she loves working in her flower garden."

"No, she's not back there, Grandma."

"Umph, that's odd. Where in the world could she be? I called the home phone and I've called her cell phone, but she didn't answer either one."

Jeremiah had run back to the backyard to get Jessica.

"She's probably upstairs cleaning up. That's what she usually does on Saturday," Joseph said. "Sometimes she plays her music real loud when she's cleaning. She said it puts her in a mood to clean. That's probably why she didn't hear you."

"I don't think Jason is able to answer the door, because he can barely walk from his chair to his bed." Catherine patted her temple, trying to decide what to do. "Do you know if your parents keep an extra key hidden anywhere?"

"I know the code to the garage, and the key is hidden in there. Momma and Daddy told us how to get in the house in case we needed to if they weren't around."

"Well, I think that time has come, baby. Open the garage so we can get in, I'm worried about your parents."

Joseph put the code in to open the garage. He waited until the garage door closed behind them before he got the key from its hidden place, just like Jason had taught him. "Okay, Grandma. We're in."

"I sure hope nothing has happened to them."

Catherine rushed into the house. "Sheena! Where are you? I rang the doorbell. I stayed out there so long I had to get Joseph to let me in the house."

Jeremiah and Jessica ran upstairs to look for Sheena. Catherine headed to the library to check on Jason; she opened the door. He was sound asleep. He's knocked out from those painkillers so he probably didn't hear the doorbell anyway, she mused.

"She's not up stairs anywhere, Grandma," Jeremiah informed her.

"Where in the world could she be?" Catherine questioned.

"She probably went to the grocery store," Jessica stated hopefully with fearful tears in her eyes.

"I'm sure that's where she is." Catherine consoled her. She could tell from the fear in Jessica's eyes, that she thought her mother had left her again. She turned to Joseph. "Wasn't her car in the garage?"

"I think so." Joseph ran to the kitchen and flung the door open. He ran back into the library where Catherine was. "She's not gone to the store," Joseph announced. "Both of their cars are here. Daddy's truck is out back. Momma can't drive that anyway. It's a stick shift."

"Where's my mommy?" Jessica wailed.

Jason woke up when he heard Jessica crying. His red eyes focused on his mother's worried face. He sat up slowly. "What's wrong, pumpkin?"

"I can't find Mommy!" Jessica wiggled out of Catherine's embrace and jumped on the bed with Jason. "She left us again, Daddy!"

Wincing from the pain of his daughter's tight embrace he said, "She went for a walk, sweetie. She didn't leave us."

"Where'd she go?"

"She said she was going to the park." His eyes switched to the digital clock on the radio. "She should be back any minute, pumpkin." Sheena had been gone for hours, which gave Jason an uneasy feeling. "Is her truck still in the garage?"

"Yes, her truck is still outside and so is your car," Catherine answered. She then asked him cautiously, "How long has she been gone?"

"For awhile, but she'll be back soon." He looked worriedly at Catherine.

"I'm sure. Well, I'll sit here with you until she gets back. I'm disappointed that she left you here by yourself.

"Anything could have happened with you lying flat on your back helpless. I don't know what to say about that wife of yours. Humph!"

Jason noticed the sad expression on the children's faces. "I'm fine, Momma. It's okay."

"Do you need anything?"

"Just a little privacy to use the bathroom."

"Oh, okay. Come on kids, let's go and see what we can make your daddy for dinner." Once the kids were out of the room, she asked him, "What's wrong Jason? I can see it all over your face." She scanned the disarray in the room. "What in the world?" She bent over to pick the paper up. "Why did she leave with this paper lying all over the floor, rags and this cleaning material strewn all over the place? This is ridiculous. Your wife is getting slack. It's filthy in here. She knows you're sick. What if some of your colleagues had come to visit you?"

"Calm down, Momma. Don't worry about that stuff. You're exaggerating anyway; it's not filthy in here."

She stopped straightening up the room and faced Jason. "She needs to do better than this."

"Momma, don't criticize my wife." Catherine scrunched up her face. "She knows."

"She knows what?"

Jason lowered his voice. "I confided in her about Cassandra. Those are the test results in your hand."

"Oh." Catherine read the letter. "Oh, my," she gasped. "How did she take it?"

"Not too well."

"Lord, have mercy. I was afraid that you were going to say that."

"I couldn't expect her to leap for joy about it. I know if the shoe had been on the other foot, I probably would have gone berserk."

"Yes, I know you're right, son. So . . ."

"Don't ask, Momma. I have no clue about what she's going to do."

"Well, all we can do is pray, son."

"That's all I've been doing, Momma, every waking moment I have."

"That's good. It's in God's hands now, Jason. We just have to keep praying."

"Grandma!" Jessica called. "We're waiting on you. Are you ready?"

"I'll be right there, baby."

"I need to take care of that business, Momma." Catherine frowned, confused. Jason pointed toward the bathroom. "I need to go *now*."

"Right, let me go attend to the children."

"Okay, Momma." Jason looked at the clock again and wondered where Sheena was. It had been four hours since she left.

Sheena walked four miles. Twice around the lake equaled one mile. Exhausted, she sat on a park bench for an hour, watching children feed the ducks and admiring couples as they strolled slowly by her.

"Hi, Sheena."

She looked around. "Hi, Ms. Erma. What are you doing here?"

"Taking a walk. I come out here three times a week and walk a mile each time. I'm trying to stay in shape so my old bones won't be so brittle. Besides, walking is good for your heart, plus it helps control your blood pressure and cholesterol."

"You're right. I need to come out here more. It's so beautiful and peaceful here."

"It sure is. I believe this is the first time that I've seen you out here."

"Jason and I used to take walks out here before we got too busy with our lives. With him working so many hours every day and me working as well as taking care of the household and the children, we've neglected to take the time to walk anymore. It's been about two years, I think, since I've been here."

"I enjoy my walks. I don't walk fast, but I take leisurely strolls."

"I enjoyed my walk today too. I walked four miles."

"That's wonderful." Erma pointed at the bench. "Do you mind if I sit down?"

"Of course not, Ms. Erma." Sheena sighed. "I feel better. I need to start exercising."

"Walking can do wonders for the body and psyche."

Sheena stared at the ground. Not wanting to pry, Erma changed the subject.

"My grandchildren are flying in this evening. They are due to arrive at eight-thirty."

"That's great, Ms. Erma. Are your daughter and her husband coming home for Christmas?"

"Yes, but they won't be able to come until Christmas Eve, because Henry has clients scheduled until the twenty-third. He's dedicated to his profession."

"That's good. Are you excited to have your grandchildren spend time with you?"

"I am. They love Charlotte. I like for them to visit me, because they're on my turf when they're here. They know that Grandma doesn't play. When I tell them no, that's what I mean. My daughter and her husband are too soft with them."

"There must be something special about Grandmas, children behave themselves so well around them."

"There is something special about us. We believe in exercising the switch on their behinds."

Sheena laughed. "You sound like my momma."

"We are from the old school, girl. I know your mother is younger than me, but she learned from the old school too."

"My dad and Jason's father are both wimps when it comes to discipline. They let the grand-kids have their way," Sheena admitted to Erma.

"My husband was too. I suppose because they were the strong force raising their children, they get soft in their old age."

"I suppose."

They sat on the bench in silence. After a few minutes of uncomfortable silence, Erma spoke up. "Well, I guess I should start toward home. It'll be dark soon."

"I should leave too. I'll walk with you if you don't mind."

"Why should I mind?" Erma groaned as she stood up. "Chile, these old bones aren't as strong as they used to be. "Come on, sugar, let's go home."

As they slowly walked, they made small talk. The closer they got to the neighborhood, the more Sheena dreaded going home. She noticed Jason's mother's car parked in their driveway.

"Well, here we are," Sheena stated as they approached her house.

"Yep. Thank you for walking with me, Sheena. I enjoyed your company."

"You're welcome. I enjoyed your company too."

Erma headed for her driveway, but Sheena's voice broke her stride. "Ms. Erma?"

"Yes?" Erma studied the melancholy expression on Sheena's face. "What is it, baby?"

Sheena hesitated and Erma waited patiently for her to speak. "Ms. Erma, would I be imposing on you if I come home with you and visited for a few minutes?"

Erma's mouth dropped open from the shock of Sheena's inquiry. They had been neighbors for ten years, but Sheena had never set foot in her house. "Of course not. Please come in."

While Erma unlocked the door, Sheena glanced toward her house. *I hope the children don't see me, because I can't deal with them right now.*

"Come on in, baby. It's not as clean as I would like it to be, but considering my age, I do the best I can."

Sheena stepped into the foyer behind Erma. Her eyes looked up toward the high ceiling with its grand chandelier. She scanned the antique pictures that were placed around the wall and up along the wrought iron and oak staircase. She followed Erma into the living room. The hardwood oak floors were adorned with beautiful Persian rugs. "It's immaculate, Ms. Erma. Your house is beautiful!"

"Thank you, but the glory belongs to God. Everything in here is as old as dirt."

"I love this antique living room set. These end tables are beautiful too. These things are very valuable. Some people would love to own furniture like this. I have a friend that goes around to different markets searching for antiques, but the pieces she buys don't compare to yours."

"Humph. I've had some of this stuff ever since my husband and I got married. We struggled and bought one piece at a time." Erma pointed to the formal dining room. "That set belonged to my mother."

Sheena took a closer look at the antique dining table and its matching China closet. "It's beautiful." She followed Erma into her family room.

"Make yourself at home. The bathroom is over there if you need to use it. I'll be back in a few minutes."

Sheena walked around the room looking at Erma's family photos. Erma's family reminded Sheena of her own. Erma returned with chamomile tea and finger sandwiches. "Ms. Erma, you shouldn't have gone to any trouble for me."

"I didn't. You are my guest and I always offer guests something to drink and eat, it's called hospitality," she smiled. "Would you like honey or sugar in your tea?"

"I'll take honey. Thanks."

Erma used her remote to turn on her CD player. "My grandchildren bought me this for Christmas last year. It operates the TV too." Sheena was surprised to see a 50" flat screen TV on the wall. "They informed me that I should start using the latest technology. I told them all this technology is why children are so spoiled."

Sheena nodded. They ate in silence as they listened to a variety of gospel melodies.

"Thank you so much for spending your valuable time with me, Ms. Erma."

"Any time that you want to visit me, you are more than welcome to come over."

Sheena stared at the floor. "Ms. Erma, I know that you can see that something is wrong with me, but you've been kind enough not to pry."

"I sensed you were upset, but I didn't want to get into your business."

"Well, you would have had to be blind to not see my swollen red eyes."

Erma smiled and nodded. "After seventy-eight years, a person learns to be wise. I knew if you wanted to talk about it, you would do so without me prying. Besides, I learned my lesson from the last time I tried to get in your business."

"I apologize for the way I acted, Ms. Erma. Please forgive me."

"I apologize for barging in on you the way I did."

"There's no need to apologize, I realize now that you were only concerned for my safety."

Erma smiled and patted Sheena's hand. "That's right," she said softly.

"Jason gave me more bad news today." Erma was silent. "Did he tell you about it?"

"No, he didn't. He admitted that there were still some things that he needed to confide to you and he was worried that you wouldn't be able to handle it or forgive him, but he didn't discuss the details of it."

Sheena looked beyond Erma's head at the antique family photo. "He told me that he has a child with the woman you saw over here fighting him. I couldn't believe it, but it's true. I saw the test results." A single tear rolled down her face.

"Oh, my Lord. I'm so sorry, Sheena. I had no idea it was something that devastating." Erma handed her a Kleenex.

"I wasn't shocked though."

"You weren't?"

"No. He tried to tell me last night, but my mind couldn't absorb any more disappointments, so I told him to wait until today. I had a feeling it was something about a child, because I had dreamed about this pretty little girl last night. I'd had the dream once before when I was at my momma's house, the day before Ruby showed up at my house."

"Lord, have mercy. I bet that's why she went to your house and fought him too. She probably wanted him to tell you about the child and he wouldn't."

"Maybe. I just don't know. I'm at my wit's end, Ms. Erma. I don't think I can stay with him after this news. I wanted to reconcile with him, but too much has happened. The last thing I expected him to do was disrespect me by bringing another woman's child into our marriage. I'm devastated."

"I can imagine. How old is the baby?"

"She's not a baby. She's eleven years old."

"Huh? Jason kept that a secret from you all this time?"

Sheena enlightened Erma with all the sordid details.

After listening quietly, Erma replied, "Sheena, I may sound insensitive to your feelings, but considering what you just told me, Jason has been misled too. I don't expect you to rejoice over this child, but she couldn't help the fact that she was born, or the fact that her mother chose to cheat her out of knowing her real father."

"That's true, but I still need time to deal with this situation. I can't make a rational decision concerning him and his daughter right now."

"I understand, baby. I'll keep you all in prayer and you keep praying too, okay? We don't know how God is going to work this out, but I do know that there's nothing too hard for God to do."

"Thank you for listening. I guess I'd better go home now. They are probably wondering what happened to me."

"Okay, baby. God bless you." She walked Sheena to the door. "Just remember Psalm 32:7. It says, *Thou art my hiding place; thou shalt preserve me from trouble; thou shalt compass me about with songs of deliverance.*"

"Thank you for that scripture. I'll read it when I get home. If I don't see you during the holidays, you have a blessed Christmas and a wonderful New Year."

"You do the same. Just remember to pray before you make any decisions about you and your husband. Take care now." Erma held the door open for Sheena to leave. She watched her until she walked down the last step of her porch and then she closed her door.

Sheena sauntered across the street to her house. She eased the key in the lock. As though Jessica had supersonic hearing, she ran to the door and flung it opened. "Momma, I thought you would never come back! I missed you, Mommy. Where have you been?"

"I went to the park and walked, baby. After that, I went to visit a friend."

"Well, I'm just happy that you're home!" She squeezed Sheena tightly. "Mommy?"

"Yes, honey?" She picked Jessica up and held her tightly.

"Don't leave us like that again, please."

"I didn't leave you, sweetie; but from now on, I'll tell you guys where I'm going so you won't be worried. Okay?"

"Okay. But next time, can you take us with you? That will be better."

Sheena observed that Jessica had developed a separation complex toward her. "I'll do my best to be here for you every possible moment, sweetie."

The twins greeted her and hugged her tightly, observing her disheveled appearance, but not saying anything. She kissed them both on their foreheads. "Are you guys okay?"

"We're fine, Momma," Joseph spoke up. "Daddy kept walking to the window to see if you were coming home. I think he was in pain though. Grandma made dinner for us. Are you okay?" Joseph searched her face.

"I'm okay now, baby."

"Well, hello, Sheena," Catherine interrupted. "I'm relieved to see that you made it back home safely."

Jeremiah ran to tell Jason that Sheena was home. Joseph stood in the doorway watching Sheena.

"I'm here, safe and sound, Ms. Grey." Sheena noticed Joseph watching her every move. "Joseph, honey will you check to see if there is any mail in the box?"

"Okay, Momma," he replied.

"I understand you have another granddaughter, Mrs. Grey. Congratulations."

Catherine noticed Sheena's obvious change in behavior toward her. She had reverted to calling her Mrs. Grey again. "I don't know what you want me to say, Sheena. I was just as surprised as you are about the child."

"How long have you known about her?"

"Jason told me about her a few weeks ago when Jacob was in the hospital."

"It appears that I am the last person that he shared his secret with. Is there anything else that your son has hidden from me that you know about, Mrs. Grey?"

Sheena's unruly behavior toward her made Catherine uncomfortable. "Sheena, I don't keep secrets for Jason and I certainly don't understand your attitude toward me."

"You purposely kept his daughter's existence a secret from me, didn't you?"

"It wasn't my place to tell you that."

"Have you been cloaking for him the whole time we've been married? What's next? Tell me, what else is going on in his life that I'm oblivious to?"

"Have I done something to offend you, Sheena? Why are you angry with *me*?"

"Here's the mail, Momma," Joseph interrupted. He glanced from Sheena's distorted face to Catherine's obviously upset demeanor. "What's wrong, Momma?"

Sheena took a deep breath just as Jason appeared in the doorway. "Everything's okay, Joseph," she lied. "Grandma and I were having a discussion."

Joseph looked at her skeptically. Jason hobbled into the kitchen. "J, you and JJ take your sister upstairs to watch TV."

Joseph hesitated.

"Go on, son. It'll be okay," Jason assured him with a forced smile.

"Yes, sir."

Sheena brushed past Jason and went in the den to sit down.

"I think I'd better leave, Jason," Catherine suggested. "I don't understand why your wife is angry at me. It seems like the harder I try to get along with her, the more difficult she behaves toward me." Catherine was close to tears. "I don't understand her . . ."

"It's okay, Momma. Don't let her make you upset. You haven't done anything wrong. She's just going through a difficult time right now because of me."

"I suppose you're right. I need to go home and check on Jacob anyway." She patted him on the arm. "Take care, son."

"I apologize for her behavior Momma. I'll talk to her."

"Don't worry about it, I'll be fine. I think you should give her time to cool off before you say anything else to her. I suppose I can understand why she's so angry. If those cards were dealt to you, you'd feel the same way she does."

"You're right, but she's targeting her anger at you and you don't have any control in this situation. She needs to apologize to you for her behavior."

"I'll be all right, Jason. We've overcome our differences before, and with the help of the Lord, we will overcome this too. I just want you to take care of yourself and get well. I'll call and check on you tomorrow."

"Okay. Drive carefully now." Jason hobbled back to the library, took his medicine and eased into bed.

Sheena heard Catherine's car door slam. She hurried outside. Catherine looked back toward the house before she drove off and saw Sheena flagging her down. She stopped and pulled back into the driveway.

Sheena had had a moment to survey her outrageous behavior toward Catherine. The two of them had been getting along well until now. Even though she wanted to blame Catherine for the pain she felt, she knew her mother-in-law had no more control over the situation than she did. "Mrs. Grey . . . Momma, please forgive me for mistreating you. I shouldn't have taken my anger out on you. I know that you don't have any control over this issue. I'm sorry for being disrespectful toward you."

"It's okay, Sheena. I understand."

"Thank you for understanding, but I shouldn't have talked to you the way I did. I hope you can forgive me."

"It's okay, baby. I forgive you. Try to get some rest, okay?"

"I will. Thank you for making dinner and taking care of Jason and the children."

"You're welcome. I'll be here anytime that you all need my help."

"Thanks again." She watched Catherine drive away before walking back into the house and looking toward the library. "He's going to need someone to take care of him from now on," Sheena mumbled under her breath, "because I'm taking my children and moving to Asheville."

Chapter 50

Sheena peeped in on Jason and saw that he was half asleep, so she went upstairs and brought the children back downstairs. She popped popcorn for them and they watched a movie. Jessica curled up in her arms and went to sleep. The twins sat on each side of her, analyzing her every move.

Jeremiah spoke first. "Momma, why were you so mad with Grandma? What did she do to you?"

"She didn't do anything to me, JJ. I was upset about something, and I selfishly blamed your grandmother for my problems, but I apologized to her," Sheena explained.

"Oh." "But why are you mad all the time, Momma?" Joseph persisted. "J, it's nothing for you to be concerned about. I'm fine, okay?"

"Are you and Daddy gonna get a divorce?"

"What gave you that idea?"

"I'm not a baby. You act like you hate Daddy sometimes, and today when you and Grandma were talking, you acted like you hated her too."

"Baby, I don't hate your Daddy and I certainly don't hate your grandmother."

"What's wrong with you then?"

Sheena exhaled loudly. "Sweetheart, sometimes grownups get upset with each other and they don't behave well toward one another. I'm sorry I've been acting mean lately. I'll try and be nicer from now on. I didn't mean to upset you guys with my behavior."

"So does that mean that you guys are gonna stay together?"

Sheena didn't want to lie to her children, but she felt that they needed to be comforted. "We are not getting a divorce, Joseph."

"Good! I don't want my parents to get a divorce like Thomas's parents did. He has to live with his mom all the time and now he hardly sees his dad because he moved away."

"Oh, that's so sad."

"It is," Jeremiah chimed in. "I hope that you and Daddy stay together forever."

"Me too!" Joseph said as he gave Jeremiah a high five.

"Your father and I are going to do our best to give you kids a stable home, okay, guys? Now stop worrying and enjoy your movie and popcorn."

Satisfied with Sheena's response to their questions, they sprawled across the floor at Sheena's feet, ate the popcorn and watched the movie until they fell asleep.

Sheena dozed off for a couple of hours. When she woke up, she got the children up and put them to bed. She came back down and checked on Jason. He was awake.

"Hi. How are you feeling?" she asked him.

"I'm okay. How about you?"

"I'm okay. Jason, we need to talk."

"I know. We do."

"I had the opportunity to do a lot of thinking today while I walked at the park." She hesitated, waiting for him to speak. He stayed silent. "I still care about you, but I need a break from you. I don't want to be irresponsible and leave you while you are recuperating, but I can't handle being around you any longer."

"What are you saying?"

"I need to go away for a while. I am going to take the children and go to my parents' house for the holidays."

"I was under the impression that we would spend the holidays together."

"It would be the feasible thing to do for the children's sake, but I am stressed to my capacity. I was hurting enough as it was, Jason, but today, when you told me that you had another child, I felt so betrayed. It feels like you have poured salt into my open wound."

"If I had the power to undo the mistakes I made of having an affair with her, I would turn back the hands of time and never betray you or hurt you like I have. But unfortunately, I don't have that power and all I can do is beg you to forgive me."

"It would be nice if you could undo what you did, but you can't. I believe you are sorry for hurting me, and maybe with time, I would be able to forgive you. I wouldn't ever forget it, though. And the truth is, you can't undo the fact that you have another child."

"I'm sorry, but that's out of my control. I pray that we can deal with this together and with God's help we can make our marriage work, baby. I love you and I don't want to lose you."

"I want to believe you, Jason, but I need time to sort things out. The children have noticed the change in my behavior. Joseph wanted to know why I am angry all the time. He expressed that he thought I hated you and your mother."

"Joseph is a sensitive kid, isn't he?"

"Yes, he is a sharp little boy."

"He reminds me of myself when I was that age. Because of my father's mistreatment of my mother, I watched her behavior like a hawk. If something was wrong with her, I could detect it even when she tried to hide it."

"I'm beginning to understand the emotional detachment you have toward your father now,"

Sheena said. "If you're not careful, Jason, your sons are going to respond to you likewise."

"I understand my situation better now too. It's kind of like a generational curse, isn't it?"

"That's exactly what it is. I've been trying to tell you that all along."

"You're a wise woman, Sheena. I can't risk having my sons or daughter hating me. I sure have made a mess for my family. I never intended for my children to live in a stressful environment the way I did growing up. What you told me a few weeks ago is true."

"What did I say?" Sheena had a clueless expression on her face.

"That I was my father's son." Sheena frowned. "You said I don't hit you, but the blatant disrespect toward you has the same effect on our children's lives as my dad's beating on my mom had on me."

"Yes, they are under a lot of pressure. I didn't realize it until tonight when they started questioning me about my anger. They can sense the tension between us. And Jessica has become very insecure about me leaving her."

"Humph. Like it or not, we need to try to be civil toward each other when they're around. I hate the thought of my children suffering because of me."

Sheena nodded in agreement. "I don't want to see them suffer any more either. Joseph wanted to know if we were getting a divorce."

"What did you tell him?"

"I told him no."

"Is that how you feel, or were you reassuring him to ease his mind?"

"I don't know. At times, I believe a divorce is best, but when I look at their faces, I don't want to break up their home."

"I don't want to break up their home either."

Sheena was silent for a long time.

"What's on your mind?"

"Jason, I'm not mentally able to make a decision about us right now. I have this rage inside of me and it scares me. There are still times when I want to cause you bodily harm for what you did to me." Jason stared at her. "I know it's wrong; that's why I need to separate from you."

Jason straightened up as best he could. "You want to separate?" he asked Sheena anxiously.

Sheena shrugged her shoulders. "For a while." She gazed into his eyes.

Jason threw his hands up in the air. "How long is a while?"

"At least through the Christmas and New Year's. I know the children will be disappointed because we won't be here for Christmas, but I need to do this, Jason. I hope you can understand. It's for my sanity and their peace of mind."

"Are you going to tell them that we are separating?"

"No. I'll tell them that we are going to spend the holidays with my parents and leave it at that."

"Our children are smart, Sheena. Do you think they will believe that?"

"I don't know, but at this point, what they need is a mother that can act normally instead of a mother that goes off the deep end at a moment's notice."

"I understand where you're coming from. I just hope that your respite at your mother's house doesn't become permanent."

"I don't know; time will tell. All I'm sure about right now is that I need a vacation from this atmosphere."

"Well, it sounds like you've made up your mind. As bad as it pains me to see you go, I know I need to give you some space."

"Jason, I just need to remove myself from this environment and pray and seek God, because my mind is guiding me toward getting a divorce, but I need time to be still and listen to what God has to say. Okay?"

"That's fair. So, when are you leaving?"

"Tomorrow after church. I need to go, badly. Do you realize that I haven't been to church in over two months?" Not knowing what to say, Jason didn't respond. Sheena glared at him. "I feel like a heathen. I've separated myself from my church, the pastor and his wife, and the members that I enjoyed fellowshipping with, because of the mess you brought into my life!"

Jason was confused by her sudden burst of anger. He scratched his head, glanced at her and looked away, focusing on the television.

"I've alienated myself from just about everybody, because I feel so ashamed that some of my church members in the neighborhood saw you and your girlfriend out in *my* front yard fighting!" Sheena said angrily.

Jason repositioned himself in the chair. He wanted to tell her that it was Ruby who was fighting him, but he knew that was irrelevant.

"I remember that night in bed, when you told me that I didn't have to be at church every time the doors swung open. And little stupid me wanted to please my husband, so I slacked up going, and for *what*? I should have been running to the church, instead of running away from it. I suppose you're happy now, aren't you?" Jason cut his eyes at her and looked away. "I guess you thought you had me going, but I'm putting a stop to that foolishness, as of tomorrow. From now on, I'm taking my focus off of my problem," Sheena pointed at Jason, "and I'm going to delight myself in the Lord, the problem solver."

Jason sat quietly and listened to her vent. From his viewpoint, this was a time to listen, not a time to defend himself.

Sheena expelled a deep breath, feeling a little calmer. She focused on the television for a few minutes, and then looked back at Jason. "I'm going to leave the children with you while I'm at church, if that's all right with you," she said, more like an order than a question.

Jason threw his hands up in the surrender mode. "That's fine. That'll give me some time to spend with them before you leave."

Sheena's countenance softened. "That's the idea."

Minutes passed by before they spoke again. Sheena broke the silence. "I'm going to get ready for bed. Do you need anything before I go upstairs?"

"Yes, I do need something."

"What do you need? A snack, some juice? It's not time for your medicine yet."

Jason looked at her innocently. "No, I don't need any of those things. I just need you."

His statement and the sincerity of his voice touched Sheena's heart. Tears welled up in her eyes. She looked away from him. "I—I'll see you in the morning. Good-night."

Chapter 51

Jason awoke in the middle of the night to find Sheena lying next to him. She stirred and opened her eyes, startled to see him watching her. "You okay, Sheena?"

"I'm fine. Did I disturb your sleep?"

"No, not at all. I usually wake up about this same time every night. I'm pleased to find you lying next to me."

"I probably shouldn't have come down here, but I couldn't sleep, so I thought I'd at least come to check on you to see if you were doing all right. Once I got down here, I didn't want to go back upstairs so I just eased into bed with you."

"It sure would be nice if you could sleep with me every night. I miss you."

Sheena sighed. "It would be nice if things were the way they used to be, but they're not, so that's the name of that tune."

"Things can't be like they used to be, but if we work on it, they can be better."

Sheena turned her back to him. "How? There's a matter of you having another child. Not to mention that her mother is going to make my life miserable."

"Ruby's not going to do anything to disrespect you, Sheena."

"How do you know that? She's been a pain in the butt before. What makes you think she's not going to assert herself in our lives now? Especially since she has Cassandra to rub in my face."

Jason breathed heavily. "I know because she's changed."

Sheena turned around to face him. "How? Just how has she changed, Jason?"

"We talked for a long time on the phone about it. Remember the day you came by my office? I told you we decided to stop seeing each other and she admitted that she had done some soul searching. She told me that after her father witnessed to her, she repented of her wrong doing and she confessed salvation."

"Sure she did. She just told you what she thought you wanted to hear," Sheena said harshly.

"Sheena, all I can do is accept her word and believe her. I'm not God. I can't judge her, but she sounded sincere."

"The devil can sound sincere."

"Yes, you're right. But when I saw her that day at the restaurant, her demeanor had changed and I saw a huge difference in her behavior. People don't change overnight, unless the Holy Spirit has anointed them with His glory."

Sheena sat up in bed and stared at Jason. "What makes you such an authority on the Holy Spirit so suddenly?"

"I'm not an authority on the Holy Spirit. No one is. Not even you, Sheena."

"What's that supposed to mean?"

"It means, *judge* not, that ye be not judged. Isn't that what Jesus tells us in Matthew 7:1?"

Sheena was flabbergasted.

"Is that what it says, Sheena?"

"Yes, that's exactly what it says."

"So if we are going to be doers of the Word and not just hearers, like it says in James 1:22, we have to take heed to His Word then, don't we?"

Sheena was impressed that he had been studying the Bible. "Yes we do, but . . . I just don't trust her. I don't believe that she is saved all of a sudden."

"It's not our job to believe whether she is or isn't saved." He hunched her lightly. "Right?"

"Yes, you're right. Since when did you become such a Bible scholar?"

"Since I've had all of this free time on my hands. I guess sometimes when a person is obnoxious like you say I was, God will allow tragedy to happen to them so they can repent of their foolish ways."

"So are you saying that you are saved now?"

"I hope I am, Sheena. Ms. Erma has been witnessing to me every day while she takes care of me. We had Bible study a couple of days. She's an awesome lady. She had me to read and confess your favorite scripture, Romans 10:9.

Sheena nodded her head. "I'm glad that you gave your life to Christ, Jason, but I hope that you didn't just get saved on my account, because if you did, you're doing it for the wrong reason. I didn't die for you, Jesus did."

"I didn't do it on your account. When I was lying on that bed in the hospital fighting for my life, I knew I had to call on Jesus because I wasn't going to make it any other way. I know He had mercy on me and spared my life. I need Jesus more than I ever could have imagined."

Sheena inched closer to him. "I do too. We all do." "Thank you, baby." "What are you thanking me for?"

"For being here for me. I don't deserve you, but I thank God for you every day. After what I've done to you, you didn't have to stick around and take care of me, but you did. That means a lot to me, you are a virtuous woman."

"I've been here for you all along. You just didn't appreciate me. You don't know how many times I've contemplated getting revenge on you. I thought I hated you at one point."

"I know. I could see it in your face. I don't want to ever do anything to hurt you again. I hope that you can forgive me for trampling on your heart and betraying your trust."

"I'm trying, Jason, but forgiving and forgetting is hard to do. I'm a Christian, but I'm not perfect. I need God to mend my broken heart. It feels like it's been shattered into a million pieces."

"I understand." He gently stroked her hair.

"Jason?" He looked at her and raised his eyebrows expectedly. "I still can't get over the fact that you have another daughter. I know that she couldn't help being born, but I don't think I can accept her into my life, into our family's life." Jason didn't reply. "It's just that I resent the idea of you having another child by someone else. Especially the fact that Ruby's her mother."

"I'm sorry that you feel that way, but there's nothing that I can do about that, baby," he replied. Sheena's eyes reflected the hurt she carried. "I don't know what to say without sounding insensitive to your feelings. What do you want me to do? Deny my own flesh and blood?"

"No, I don't expect you to do that. I would lose respect for you as a man if you did that."

"So what's going to happen between us? You sound as though you are asking me to choose between you and my daughter."

"I'm not asking you to do that. If the situation were reversed, I wouldn't deny my child for you. I'm just saying that I can't accept her into *my* life."

"I don't want to lose you, Sheena. I love you and I hope that we can work on our marriage so that we can stay together, but I'm obligated to support my daughter. I'm praying that one day I'll be able to spend time with her without losing you and my other children."

"Jason, you said your *other* children as though Joseph, Jeremiah, and Jessica are the outside children."

Jason exhaled loudly. "Sheena, you know I didn't mean it like that. You're twisting my words. I mean that I want us to be able to get along without any animosity between me and you, or you and Cassandra; that's all."

"That's too much to ask of me. After all, she's your daughter by another woman. I just feel resentful toward the child. I don't want her in our . . . well, in *my* life. And what about Ruby?"

"What about her?"

"In your fantasy world, is she going to be a part of this family too?"

"Come on, Sheena, you're being ridiculous. You know we will have to communicate when it comes to Cassandra, but she has a life with her own husband."

"How do you know she's happy with him? How do you know that as soon as her daughter starts spending time with you that she won't try and get back with you?"

"I know she won't because she's happy with her husband, and even if she's not, I don't have any intention of being with her."

"The road to hell is paved with good intentions, Jason."

"I'm being honest with you. That's all I can do. I don't want her. I respect her as my child's mother, but that's it. The best thing I can do is pray and do my part to be a good husband to you, *if* you'll allow me to be."

"I don't know what to do. A part of me wants to make our marriage work, but a part of me wants to end our marriage too. I don't want to hurt the little girl's feelings, but I don't know if I can treat her right. She's your child, but to me, she's an unwanted intruder."

Jason sighed. "It's not her fault that she was born, Sheena."

"Precisely. But the fact that she looks so much like her mother will only remind me of you and Ruby being together."

"Again, that's not the child's fault. I understand where you're coming from, but I don't know how I can convince you that having a daughter with Ruby does not make me want to be with her."

"It's just that . . ."

"What? It's just that what, baby? Finish your statement."

"Maybe I wouldn't be so insecure about her if you hadn't had an affair with her recently. In my mind, it's as though the two of you rekindled your relationship and now, the relationship has been forever sealed with Cassandra."

"Sheena, I regret having been gullible enough to get involved with her again, but as God is my witness, I don't love her. I love you. Nothing has been sealed with us, other than we have a child together and we have to be respectful of each other because of her."

Sheena searched his face for the truth. He seemed to be sincere. "I want to believe you, but I just need time. That's why I want to get away for a few days and consider everything you've said, as well as pray and fast for deliverance from this pain."

"When you mentioned leaving before, I didn't think it was a good idea. I thought it would be best if we stayed together and talked things out, but considering the things we've talked about so far, I think it's a good idea. I don't want you to go, but maybe it's for the best. At least you will have some space from me and you can pray about our future."

"I do need some space, Jason. I'm pleased that you understand."

"I just hope that once you've had time to pray, the Lord will work it out so we can stay together."

"We'll see. I'm sleepy now. We've been talking for two hours. Aren't you tired?" Sheena asked him.

"Yeah, I am." When Sheena slid out of bed, he asked, "Where are you going? I thought you were going to stay with me for the rest of the night."

"I'm thirsty. You want something to drink?"

"A glass of that white grape juice would be nice."

"Okay, I'll be right back."

Sheena went to get the juice. She came back within two minutes with two champagne glasses, and a bottle of sparkling white grape juice. They drank their juice and Sheena placed the glasses down on the table and crawled back into bed.

"I feel a little better now that I've told you how I feel. I'm not proud of what I told you, but at least I had a chance to vent."

"I'm glad you were honest."

Sheena laid her arm across Jason's shoulder and was sound asleep and snoring lightly in a matter of minutes.

Jason prayed. "Please have mercy on us and show us the way to reconcile our marriage. I thank you in advance, Lord, for touching my wife's heart so that she'll be able to accept my daughter into her heart. In Jesus' name I pray. Amen."

Chapter 52

Sheena and Jason were still asleep when the children came into the room. "Momma, wake up." Jeremiah said as he shook her.

Startled, Sheena opened her eyes. "What is it, Jeremiah?"

"Grandma wants to speak to you." He handed her the cordless phone. Sheena squinted from the bright overhead light that was shining in her eyes. "What time is it?"

Jeremiah looked at the clock. "It's eight-thirty."

"Hello?" It was her mother. "Hi, Momma." Sheena listened to what Lois had to say. She responded with, "That's great, that's good," and an "Oh, no!" Then she told Lois that she was driving to Asheville that afternoon."

Jason sat up. "Is everything all right with your folks?"

Sheena eased out of the bed. "Yes. Momma wanted to know how we were doing. I hadn't talked to her since Wednesday." Sheena chuckled. "She was still excited because Daddy and she went out last night to a jazz club to celebrate his retirement from the factory where he worked for forty years."

Jason smiled. "That's nice. Your father has talked about retiring for years, I'm glad he finally retired. After forty years, he deserves a rest."

The children had turned the television on to the *Disney Channel* and were watching cartoons.

Sheena put her robe on. "Well, I slept too late to go to the eight o'clock service. I'm going to make you guys a huge Sunday breakfast this morning. How about that?" She noticed the children looking at her and Jason with a satisfied smile on their faces.

Joseph was grinning from ear to ear. "That sounds good, Momma," he said, giving Jeremiah a high five.

"I know, right?" Jeremiah concurred.

"Mommy, you do love Daddy, don't you? Daddy loves you too, right? Did you kiss Daddy goodnight last night, Mommy?" Jessica asked with a wide-eyed expression on her face.

Sheena picked her up and kissed her. "Baby girl, you ask so many questions sometimes."

Jason slowly stood up and walked to the bathroom. "She's just like her mother. She's got to know." Standing in the doorway of the bathroom he said, "The answers to all of your questions, Jessica, are yes, yes, and yes."

"I told you guys." Jessica pointed to Jeremiah and Joseph. "I was right again!"

"Jessica, we know! Why do you have to be such a brat about everything?" Joseph bemoaned.

"Okay, Joseph, that's enough. Don't call your sister names," Sheena warned.

"Yes, ma'am. Momma can I go upstairs and play video games in your room?"

"*May* I, and the answer is no. Those games are restricted to your room only. I don't want you all playing in our bedroom."

Jason entered the room in time to hear Sheena refer to the room as *our room*.

"Your mother's right, J. You and your brother have plenty of space to play in."

"You and Jeremiah can go and clean your room up and then if you want to watch TV in our room you can, but I don't want that play station hooked up to my TV," Sheena said.

"Yes, ma'am." The twins raced upstairs. Jessica sat in the middle of Jason's bed, playing with her dolls.

"I'm going to take a shower before I cook breakfast," Sheena announced to Jason. He nodded his head. Sheena turned to Jessica. "Sweetie, you stay down here and keep your Daddy company, okay?"

"Okay, Mommy. You're coming right back, right?" She asked sadly, close to tears.

Sheena looked at Jason and then back at her daughter. "I'm not going anywhere, sweetie. I'm only going to take a shower."

"Okay, Mommy. Just don't leave us."

Jason intervened. "Pumpkin, your mother can't be with you every second of the day. She has to take time to do some things for herself too."

"I know, Daddy. I just don't want her to leave us again without telling us where she's going."

Sheena raised her eyebrows at Jason. "You see what I mean?" she asked. Jason nodded. Planting a reassuring kiss on Jessica's forehead, Sheena said, "I'll be back shortly, sweetie," and then left the room.

Jason's cell phone rang. "Jessica can you hand me my phone?"

"Sure, Daddy." Jessica jumped off the bed, grabbed the phone and handed it to Jason.

"Hello?"

"Hi," a sweet familiar voice on the other end said.

Jason's forehead creased. He didn't respond.

"Hello? Are you still there?"

"I'm still here. You shouldn't be calling me."

"I just wanted to check on you to see how you were progressing?"

"I'm doing well. I really can't talk right now."

"I understand. Is Sheena there?"

"She's here. Is something wrong?" he whispered into the phone. "Is Cassandra okay?"

"She's doing fine. Have you told your wife about her yet?"

"Yes, I told her yesterday and she's not a happy camper."

"I understand. Well, I guess it's too soon to ask you if you want to speak to your daughter, isn't it?"

"It's not that I don't want to speak to her, it's just not a good time."

"I see. Maybe I can call back at a later date."

"Yes, try me one day next week. Okay?" He watched the door to make sure Sheena wasn't coming back. "So how are things with you and your husband?"

"Thurman and I are doing great. We've been going to church counseling and we are working on our marriage. He's working on forgiving me, but it's hard on him. Betrayal is a hard thing to forgive."

"I can vouch for that."

"So do you think Sheena's gonna be able to forgive you?"

"It's hard to tell. I had a glimmer of hope until I told her about Cassandra yesterday. She's having a hard time accepting the fact that . . . hold on for a second." He waved his hand at Jessica, to get her attention. It worked.

"Jessica, baby, will you take these napkins and put them in the trash can in the kitchen for Daddy?"

"Okay." She picked up the napkins and skipped off toward the kitchen.

Jason waited to make sure she was gone. "Okay, I'm back."

"What were you saying?" Ruby asked.

"Oh. I was saying that Sheena is having a really hard time accepting the fact that I have a child that's not hers. She's really hurt by the fact that it's *your* child too."

"I'm sorry, Jason. Knowing the things that I know now, maybe I shouldn't have told you about her. I've made so many foolish mistakes in my past."

"Well, there's no need to cry over spilled milk. What's done is done. Even though I may lose my marriage, I'm glad I know the truth."

"Yeah, I had no right to keep her away from you, but I did what I thought was best for everyone concerned."

"Ruby, I really can't stay on this phone any longer. If Sheena knew I was talking to you, she'd go ballistic. She's upstairs, but she'll be back any moment."

"I understand. I didn't call to cause any more trouble. Thurman doesn't know I made this call either. I just called to see how you were doing because your daughter asked about you today."

Jason smiled. "Oh, yeah? What did she say?" he asked excitedly.

"She wanted to know if you were getting better. She surprised me because she hadn't mentioned you since we moved back, not since the test. We were watching TV and out of the blue she just asked me, 'Is my daddy getting any better?' Thurman hasn't been sick, so I realized right away that she was talking about you."

"That was sweet of her. Where is she now?"

"She's at her grandparents' house. I told her I'd call and check on you."

"Tell her I said hello and that I look forward to meeting her as soon as I'm well enough to travel."

"All right. I'll continue to pray that you and your wife can reconcile."

"Me too, same to you. Bye." His phone rang immediately again. Without looking at the window, he answered on the first ring. *She must have forgotten something.* "Hello?"

"Hello. I just wanted to check on you to make sure you were doing all right this morning."

"I'm doing fine, Momma."

"That's good. Have you had breakfast?"

"Not yet. Sheena's upstairs taking a shower and she's going to cook breakfast when she comes down."

"Mmm. I hope she got some rest last night. She looked exhausted."

"Yes, she is, mentally and physically."

"She flagged me down after I got in my car last night and apologized to me."

"Oh, did she? That's good, because I was going to speak to her today about her rude behavior toward you."

"She didn't mean it. I understand that she's under a lot of pressure."

"Yes, she's going through. We both are. Keep us in your prayers, Momma."

"Of course, you don't have to ask me to do that. Okay, I don't want to hold you up. I just wanted to make sure you were doing all right. I'll check with you later."

"All right, I'll talk to you later. Bye." Like a lot of other older people, Catherine hung up without saying good-bye.

"Who was that on the phone?" Sheena asked suspiciously. She had come into the room without Jason's knowledge.

Jason was grateful he wasn't talking to Ruby. "Momma. She called to check on me."

"She probably was worried about you after last night, wasn't she?"

"Probably."

"I'm sorry I was so short with her last night, but I apologized to her before she left."

"She told me you did. I'm glad you apologized, because I didn't appreciate the way you spoke to her. I know my mother isn't perfect, but she was just trying to help."

"I know. I feel bad about that because I've never heard you speak that way to either one of my parents. When I was home last month, Momma spoke about how respectful you've always been to her and Daddy."

"I try my best to respect them but your ma—" He stopped himself.

"You can finish your sentence, Jason. I know Momma has given you a hard way to go sometimes. You've done well not to lose your temper with her."

Jason nodded his head and laughed. "I plead the fifth."

Sheena laughed. "Let me get started on breakfast."

He admired Sheena in her casual wear. "You look nice in jeans. You should wear them more often."

"Thanks." She smiled at him and walked toward the door.

"It's going to be lonesome without you around the house for the holidays."

Sheena stopped and turned around but she didn't look at him. "I have to go, Jason. I have to clear my head."

Chapter 53

After Sheena cooked breakfast, took Jason a plate of food on a tray, and she and the children ate, she put the dishes in the dishwasher. The children went outside to play in the backyard. She looked in the phone book under the listing of Home Health Care. After she talked to a few agencies, she chose the one whose services seemed adequate. They agreed to send a nurse out the next morning.

Then she called Catherine. "Hello, Mrs. Grey . . . I mean, Momma."

"Hi, Sheena. How are you?"

"I'm doing okay. How about you?"

"I'm fine." Catherine waited for Sheena to speak.

"Momma, I wonder . . ." she cleared her throat, "if you could do me a huge favor?" Catherine hesitated.

"Sure, if I can. What is it?"

"I need to leave for a few days to visit my parents. I don't want to be irresponsible and leave Jason while he's recuperating, but I really need a break from the stress that I'm going through."

"I hate that you are under so much stress, Sheena, but do you think it's wise to leave Jason while he's still so weak?"

"No, I don't think it's wise to leave him," Catherine's accusatory tone agitated Sheena, "but I know it's in my best interest as well as the children's for me to get away for a while. I can't take too much more of the stress that your son has put me through. I don't think it's wise to let my children see me angry and frustrated all the time either."

"You're right. That's not good for them. How long do you plan to stay?"

"Through the holiday; both Christmas and New Year's."

"Uh-huh."

Sheena could hear the disapproval in Catherine's voice. "I know it looks bad, but I need to do this. I need to make some decisions about our marriage and I can't concentrate here. Jason's trying to convince me to stay, but I don't want to be pressured into anything."

"I see."

Sheena continued despite Catherine's judgmental tone. "I don't fully expect you to understand because he is your son, but I'd really appreciate it if you would come over and take care of him while I'm gone. After all, you did volunteer just last night to help in any way you could."

"I did, but I can't very well just leave my house and move in with Jason, you know. I'm still taking care of Jacob. He's not fully recovered from his illness."

"I understand that." Sheena was getting frustrated. "I've hired a nurse to come in and take care of him during the day, and I thought maybe you and Daddy Grey could stay with him at night."

"That just won't be sensible, Sheena, for me or Jacob." She heard Sheena blow into the phone. Then there was silence. "But, I'll tell you what I can do."

"Yes, ma'am?" Sheena's voice softened.

"I can ask Shirley if she minds spending the night there. That way, I can stay here and take care of my *husband*. I'll be glad to check on Jason during the day, but my vision is not that good at night. And I hate to take Jacob out in the night air."

"I understand." Sheena figured that Catherine must have expected her to stand by her man like she did, no matter what he'd done. She knew she was not that loyal. "Do you think Shirley would mind coming over and staying with him at night, then?"

"I don't know, but she's coming in the house now. I'll ask her. Hold on." Catherine briefed Shirley about Sheena's request. Shirley got on the phone.

"Hello, Sheena. Momma told me what you asked her."

"I hate to be a burden to you all, but I really need to get away for a while."

"I'll be glad to stay with him at night. As a matter of fact, if you don't mind, I'll just move in the guest room until you get back. That way, I won't have to go back and forth."

"Oh, Shirley, you are a life saver! Thank you so much. I'll be glad to pay you for your services."

"Girl, you know I'm not going to take any money from you. It's not a problem."

"Thank you so much."

"How long are you gonna be gone?"

"Until January 2nd."

"Oh, okay. I hope that you don't plan on leaving my brother for good. He loves you so much."

Sheena hesitated before she spoke. "Shirley, to be honest with you, I don't know what I'm going to do. I can't make any promises to anyone right now."

"I've been praying that you all can make amends so you guys can stay together."

"We'll see. The reason I'm going to my parents' house is so I can spend time relaxing my mind and thinking, and praying, of course."

"When do you need me to come over?"

"Tomorrow morning about nine will be fine. The nurse is scheduled to get here at seven."

"Okay, I'll see you at nine. I'm usually at the bank by that time, but I'll let Alicia know that I won't be coming in until eleven. That'll give me time to put my things in the guest bedroom before I go to work."

"Are you sure it won't be a problem if you get to work at a later time? You don't want her to report you to your father," Sheena teased.

Shirley laughed. "I'm the boss's daughter, she'll cooperate with me."

"Thanks again, Shirley. Bye."

Sheena got dressed for church. She left instructions with the children on what to do if Jason needed something, then said good-bye and headed for the eleven-thirty church service. On her way to church, she called her mother and told her that she would be leaving for Asheville at nine, tomorrow morning, instead of that afternoon.

Two hours later, Sheena drove back home. She was relieved that even though her neighbors looked at her strangely, they had enough decorum not to mention the incident that happened in her yard. She spent the rest of the afternoon cooking Sunday dinner for her family. The children entertained Jason until he drifted off to sleep. They ate their late Sunday afternoon dinner in the formal dining room. When Jason woke up, Sheena brought his meal to him on a tray.

"This food is delicious, Sheena. I'm surprised that you made a big meal like this today."

"Why? I cook Sunday dinner at least twice a month, or whenever we decide not to eat out."

"Oh, I'm not complaining. I appreciate it."

"If you're wondering if I'm still leaving, Jason, the answer is yes." Sheena studied the blank expression on his face. "Since it was so late when I woke up this morning, I decided to wait until tomorrow morning before I left," she answered antagonistically. Sheena put her hand on her hip.

He raised his hand up in a peaceful jester. "Okay, okay, I was only trying to keep my family together."

"You should have thought about trying to keep your family together while you were gallivanting around with that hussy!" Once again, anger had suddenly taken over Sheena. She stood up abruptly and left the room.

The children entered the room as Sheena rushed past them. Joseph gave his parents a puzzling look. "Is Momma all right, Daddy?"

"She'll be fine Joseph. Just give her some space."

Chapter 54

Sheena came back downstairs two hours later and found Jason and the children looking at a movie. Jessica ran to her and hugged her tightly around the waist. Jason and the twins glanced at her, but continued to watch the screen.

She scanned their faces. "Jason, I apologize for screaming at you earlier. You guys, I'm sorry for the outburst." Nobody responded. Jessica let go of her.

"I'm sorry if I made you guys uncomfortable, it's just that I think I need a vacation." "Momma, do you need a vacation from us?" Joseph asked.

Sheena shot Jason a suspicious look. "No, Joseph I don't need a vacation from you guys. I'm going through something that I can't explain to you, but it has nothing to do with you all."

"Are you mad with Daddy again?" Jessica wanted to know.

"Jessica, sweetheart I'm not mad with your . . ." she hesitated before she spoke again. "Look, sweetie. I just need some rest, that's all."

Jeremiah gazed at Sheena with a doubtful look and Sheena continued. "I'm okay, babies; I think I'm just exhausted." Sheena looked to Jason for support. He didn't budge. Sheena sat on the burgundy wing chair. "How would you guys like to go and visit Grandma and Grandpa for the holidays?"

"That'll be great, Momma," Jeremiah said enthusiastically.

"Yeah, Momma, I think that's a good idea," Joseph agreed.

"What about you, Jessica? Don't you want to spend Christmas and New Year's at your grandparents' house?"

"Are you going, Mommy?"

"Of course, baby, how do you think *you* are getting there?"

Jessica hunched her shoulders. "I thought they were going to come and pick us up."

"No, sweetheart. I'm driving my truck. Remember how disappointed you were the last time I went by myself?" Jessica shook her head. "I promised you that I wouldn't go back to Grandma's without you guys, so I'm keeping my promise."

Joseph looked at Jason. "What about Daddy? We can't leave him here alone."

Sheena cut her eyes at Jason, who gave Joseph an approving smile. She wondered if Jason had been putting ideas into Joseph's head. "Your father is not going to be alone, J. Your aunt Shirley is going to stay here with him until we get back." The smile disappeared from Jason's face. "I talked with her today and she'll be over here tomorrow morning before we leave."

"But what about Christmas?" Joseph turned to Jason. "Daddy, aren't you gonna be lonely?" Sheena stared at Jason and put her hand on her hip.

"I'll miss you guys, but your aunt, grandma and grandpa will come over here, so I'll be just fine," Jason assured them. Sheena relaxed. "Besides, your mother does need a vacation. I think she needs to spend some time with her parents and let her mother take care of her for a few days. You can understand that, can't you, J? Sometimes we grownups still need our parents to take care of us. Just like my mom comes over to help Sheena take care of me until I get better."

Joseph was thoughtful. "Yes, I understand, Daddy."

"Good," Sheena said. "Now that we all agree, you guys need to go upstairs and take your baths and get ready for bed. Come on, Jessica, I'll give you your bath. Say goodnight to your daddy."

They hugged Jason and he kissed them in return. "Goodnight, guys. I love you. Don't forget to brush your teeth and say your prayers."

"We love you too, Daddy," they said in unison.

"Are you gone to bed for the night too, Sheena?"

Sheena glanced back at Jason. "No, I'll be back after I tuck them in. Do you need anything before I go up?"

"No. I'll wait up for you, but I'm going to get in bed, though. I'm a little tired."

"Okay; suit yourself."

Sheena sat on the edge of the bed. "Jason? Are you sleeping?"

Jason turned his head toward Sheena. "No, I was just resting my eyes. You got the kids tucked away for the night?"

"Yes. They're excited about spending Christmas with my parents. They hate to leave you though. They said they wished that you could come with us, but I explained to them that you weren't well enough to travel yet."

"So, you've already arranged for Shirley to come over, huh?"

"Yes. She will be moving in here until I . . . we get back. I hired a nurse for you this morning. She'll be here tomorrow morning at seven o'clock. It'll probably be two nurses that will split twelve-hour shifts. I don't know how they will arrange it, but they'll be here from seven in the morning to seven at night. That will give Shirley time to get home from work and rest."

"I don't want some strange nurse taking care of me. I'm well enough to take care of myself."

"Jason, that's just your pride talking. You know you aren't able to take care of yourself at this stage. Ms. Erma is not available during the holidays, so that's why I asked Shirley to come over and stay with you. I asked your mother to come, but she said she couldn't do it because she has to take care of her *husband*."

Jason laughed as he thought about Sheena's rendition of his mother's words.

"What's so funny?"

"The way you said *husband*."

Sheena smiled. "Well, that's what she said. 'My *husband*.'"

"That's my momma. She loves herself some Jacob Grey."

"Humph. I could hear the disappointment in her voice because I'm not catering to your every move; but I'm not like her."

"You know Momma is from the old school and she expects her daughters and daughters-in-law to be just like her."

"I sure hate it for her."

"Seriously though, Momma does have her hands full with Daddy."

"I know. I wasn't thinking clearly. At the time I called her, I felt so overwhelmed that I didn't take into consideration that your father was still sick. I just need some peace of mind."

"I understand. If you were like a lot of women, you wouldn't have given me a second thought, especially after what you're dealing with."

Sheena slid off of the bed, and sat in the chair beside the bed. "You got that right. So you understand why I have to go? I know it'll probably look bad to people, me leaving you while you're sick—"

"You need to stop worrying about what people think. I'm not pleased with the fact that you're leaving, but after witnessing your outburst earlier, I think you really need to go. You shook the children up pretty good."

"I know. I feel terrible about that." They were silent for a few minutes. "Jason, I appreciate you explaining to the children why I need to go. For a minute there, I thought you had talked them against me."

"What gave you that idea?"

"When I came into the room and apologized, nobody said anything. I thought you had said something negative about me to them."

"I wouldn't do anything to turn our children against you, Sheena. They probably didn't say anything because I told them that you needed some space. No matter what happens between us, I'll always show you the utmost respect as their mother."

"You'll get the same respect from me. I'm probably paranoid because of what I'm going through."

"I'm sure that's what it is."

Sheena stood up. "It's getting late. I need to go to bed so I can get up early in the morning and pack our clothes." She walked toward the door.

"Sheena."

"Yes?"

Jason hesitated before he spoke, so Sheena turned around, walked to the bed and stood in front of him. Her eyes pierced his.

"I don't know what the future holds for us after tonight," he admitted. "You say that you are only leaving for a few days, but I have a feeling that this might be permanent."

Sheena eyes watered. "I don't know what the future holds for us, Jason. That's why I need to go away so I can fast and pray about it."

"Right." He rubbed her face softly. "Will you sleep with me tonight? I just want to have you close to me one more time before you leave."

Chapter 55

Sheena studied the peaceful expression on Jason's face before she slipped out of bed with him the next morning. *Lord, I don't know if I'll come back to my husband, only you can direct my path. He has caused me to suffer so much pain; I don't think I can forgive him. Jesus, please keep him covered under your blood and let your angels protect him.* She tipped out of the room and softly closed the door.

Sheena went upstairs, showered and got dressed. She was about to go downstairs when the doorbell rang. She hurried down to get the door. It was the nurse. She glanced back at the clock that was hanging on the wall in the foyer. It was six-fifty. She opened the door and the nurse introduced herself. Sheena invited her in and they sat down in the den and attended to the business at hand.

By the time Jason had awakened, Sheena and the children were in the kitchen eating breakfast. The nurse was in the den, adjacent to the kitchen, entering data into her laptop computer. He hobbled to the bathroom and afterward, he ambled toward the kitchen entrance. Jason noticed the four suitcases neatly lined up at the kitchen door. *Lord, please don't let this be the last time I see my family together. Thank you for keeping them safe and putting a hedge of protection around them as they travel and touch my wife's heart to forgive me and send her back home to me.*

Jessica ran to him and hugged him. "Hi, Daddy!"

"Good morning, pumpkin. I see you all are packed and ready to go."

"I'm so excited! I can't wait to see Grandma and Grandpa."

Joseph and Jeremiah greeted him with a hug. Jason saw the sadness in their eyes. He rubbed them on their heads as he leaned against the doorway. The doorbell rang.

"I'll get it," Sheena informed them. She smiled at Jason and said, "Good morning. Did you sleep well last night?"

"Yes," he returned her smile, "I did."

Sheena nodded and hurried to answer the door.

Jason peered in the den at the nurse, then turned around and went back to the library.

"Good morning. You are punctual, Shirley. I didn't expect you to be here at exactly 9:00."

"I told you I'd be here at nine and I wanted to keep my word." Shirley smiled.

"Come on in. We were having breakfast; would you like some?"

"No, thank you. I've already eaten. You know Momma gets up with the chickens. She has Daddy's breakfast sitting on the table every morning at seven o'clock sharp," she laughed, entering the house with her luggage in hand.

"She is a faithful wife."

"Humph. Girlfriend, she and her generation are the last breed."

"You're right."

Sheena and Shirley made small talk while the children finished breakfast. "Shirley, I'm going to take this breakfast in to Jason."

"Of course. Take your time." Shirley smiled. "I know you probably want to spend a few minutes alone with your husband before you go."

Sheena didn't reply. Shirley's statement irked her. His family is relentless, she thought. She felt like they were all experts at throwing hints to make her feel guilty about leaving Jason. She fixed him a plate of food and poured some juice into a glass and put it on the tray. She walked into Jason's room with the food tray. "I brought you some food." Sheena couldn't bring herself to look Jason in the eyes.

"Thanks." Jason stared at her. He wondered why she wouldn't look at him.

"I'm about to take off. I need to get on the road before it gets too late."

"Sheena." She still wouldn't look at him. "You're not coming back, are you?"

"Probably not, Jason. I won't be back to stay anyway. When I do come back, it'll be to pack the rest of our things. You can have everything else in the house; it will only remind me of you."

He grabbed her hand. "I know you are hurt, but please pray about us before you make a final decision to end our marriage."

Sheena shook her head yes, pecked him on the cheek and walked away.

"I love you, Sheena."

She didn't look back. Before she disappeared through the door she said, "I love you too, Jason; but sometimes love is not enough." Sheena exited the room and sent the children in the room to say good-bye to their father.

Jason's children surrounded him; he kissed each one and told them that he loved them. Jason heard the garage door open.

Shirley came in the room and announced, "Children, your mother wants you all to go get in the truck. It's time to go." They told Jason good-bye and left.

Jason struggled to get to the window. He watched the Denali back out of the driveway and onto the street. He looked until he could no longer see the back of it. Jason sat down and opened his Bible. His eyes settled on Hebrews 11:1, and he read aloud. "Now faith is the substance of things hoped for, the evidence of things not seen." He sighed. "Thank you, Jesus."

Sheena arrived in Asheville at 11:30 A.M. Lois was waiting for them at the door. Seeing her mother's face and breathing the fresh mountain air consoled Sheena's spirit. She held on to her mother tightly. "I'm home, Momma. Back where I belong."

Lois didn't like the sound of that. She pulled away from Sheena, frowning. "I'm glad to see you too, baby. You look like you could use some rest and relaxation. Go on in the house and greet your daddy; he's anxious to see you. I'll help the kids get the suitcases out of the car."

After Lois and the children dragged the suitcases in the house, she disappeared to the kitchen to make lunch for everybody.

"Momma, you don't have to cook for us. We can just as easily go to a fast food restaurant and order some to-go meals."

"Sheena Ann, don't try to tell me how to feed my grandchildren," Lois smiled. "I'm only making soup and sandwiches. I'm sure they'd much rather have that than those stale burgers."

"Okay, Momma. I don't want you to tire yourself out waiting on us."

"I'm not. They said they were hungry and you look like you need some rest; so let me take care of this. Okay?"

"Sure. Where's Daddy? I thought you said he was in the house?"

"He was five minutes ago. He's probably out there in that barn tinkering again."

Sheena peeped out the back door. Gerald was pouring salt from the house steps to the barn's door. "Hi, Daddy. What are you doing?"

He stood straight up to greet her.

"Hey there, pumpkin. I'm prepping the walkway. According to the weatherman, we're supposed to get some freezing rain tonight. How're you doing?"

"I'm doing well, considering." They sat beside each other in the swing chair.

"Well, you're home now. I'm glad you decided to spend the holidays with us. It's been a long time since we had children running around the house on Christmas morning."

"I may stay a little longer than the holidays, Daddy." Gerald looked at her surprisingly. "I'm considering moving back here. I've left Jason for good this time."

"Oh? Things didn't get any better between you two, huh?"

"No. As a matter of fact, things are worse now."

Gerald sat upright. "Did he hit you?"

"No, nothing like that. It's just that things aren't working out between us. Our marriage is beyond reconciliation."

Gerald relaxed a little. "I thought I was gonna have to pull out my double barrel shot gun and take me a trip to Charlotte."

Sheena laughed. "Daddy, you are so funny." She cut the laughter off when she heard Gerald grunt. "You were serious weren't you, Daddy?"

"Doggone right, I'm serious. I don't play that mess. Ain't nobody gonna be beating on my child," Gerald huffed.

Sheena's eyes widened. "Daddy, I don't think I've ever seen you get that angry before."

"Humph. I hope he hasn't forgotten the talk we had before y'all got married."

Sheena rested her head on Gerald's shoulder. "He's never hit me, Daddy. I remember what you told me, too, about not letting a man hit me."

"That's good."

"The kids and I may have to stay here until I can get a teaching position and find our own place, if that's all right with you and Momma."

"You know you and the kids can stay as long as you want to, pumpkin."

"Thanks Daddy."

Chapter 56

The next day, Gerald and the children went out to buy a Christmas tree. Sheena and Lois went shopping for presents for the children and they bought groceries to cook Christmas dinner. Lois drove her car so Sheena could be as relaxed as possible. Sheena reclined her seat a little and enjoyed the scenery of the snow-capped Blue Ridge Mountains.

"It's gonna be a good Christmas this year. I've missed cooking a big family dinner for Christmas," Lois admitted to Sheena.

"I've missed being here for the holidays. I wasn't looking forward to having dinner with Jason's family."

Lois smiled. "You sure look a lot better since you've been here. Yesterday, you looked like you had the weight of the world on your shoulders."

"That's how I felt. It's amazing how a change of scenery can give you a whole new perspective on your life."

"Hmmm."

"Momma, thank you for being patient with me. I know you're curious to know why I left Jason again so suddenly."

"You do seem to have your sudden spurts here lately. The last time I spoke with you, I was under the impression that you were gonna try and make your marriage work."

Sheena's eyebrows furrowed. "I was considering that, but something else happened," she lamented.

Lois cut her eyes at Sheena. "What in the world could have happened? The man is on his sickbed." She parked the car in the mall's parking lot. They walked inside through the main entrance.

"This is going to blow your mind, Momma."

"Girl, don't nothing surprise me no mo'. What happened? Did you catch him talking to that woman on the phone? I know that heifer didn't come to your house again, did she?"

"No. He hasn't talked to her since the day he got shot. Or, I'd better say, to my knowledge he hasn't."

"What happened then?"

"Jason has a child by the woman, Momma."

Lois stopped walking and stared at Sheena. She opened her mouth, but decided to be quiet and let Sheena continue.

Sheena sniffled. "I didn't want to believe him when he told me, but he had the DNA test to prove it." Sheena's voice went up an octave.

"Lord, have mercy. I wasn't expecting nothing like that," Lois said incredulously. "I guess I *can* be surprised. I can understand why you left. Him having an affair with his ex-girlfriend was bad enough, and now he's went out and got her pregnant!" Lois was outraged. "You should have left the no-good rascal. When is the baby due?"

"She was born eleven years ago."

"Come again?"

"Momma, let's sit down and have lunch." They walked into the Italian Pizza restaurant. They were seated and shortly thereafter, the waitress came and took their order. Sheena continued. "This is going to take a while." She updated Lois on all of the recent findings and ended her spiel with, "So, now you see why I can't reconcile with him?"

Lois shook her head. "That's a crying shame. Are you sure he's lying about not having knowledge of the child all these years?"

"I'm not sure of anything anymore. Whether he knew the truth or not, the fact remains that he has another child and she's not mine."

Lois was deep in thought. "Sheena, baby, if he didn't know, you can't hold that against him."

"That's the problem. I don't know if he knew or not."

"Have you prayed about it?"

"No."

"Well, you know what you need to do."

"I know. I originally had planned to come up here and do that. Seek God about my marriage, but when I woke up yesterday morning to come up here, it's as though I made my mind up to leave him for good."

Lois shook her head. "So you've already made your mind up?"

"Basically."

"Before you learned about this, did you have faith in God that He was gonna make a way for you and Jason to reconcile?"

"Yes, I thought I had the faith."

"What happened to your faith?"

"An eleven-year-old girl happened to it."

"You don't have faith in God, Sheena. You put your faith in the circumstances. That child can't help how she came into this world no more than you can help how you came here."

"I know that, Momma, but I can't bring myself to accept her. I resent him for having another child that's not mine."

"You sound just like a selfish brat."

Sheena was hurt by her mother's words. "I can't believe you don't understand how I feel." A tear rolled down her face. She wiped it away with the napkin.

"I can't pretend that I understand what you're going through, because I haven't walked a mile in your shoes. But I do know that children can't help what their parents do. Ruby is gonna pay a price for keeping that child's father from her, because the child is gonna resent her, but you can best believe they're gonna work through it. The bottom line is, she is gonna forgive her mother, and whether you want her to or not, she is probably going to have a relationship with Jason. If he's any kind of man, he won't deny his own flesh and blood. Not even if it has to cost him his marriage."

"You sound like you are taking his side. Am I not supposed to be hurt? I feel betrayed."

"I'm not taking his side, baby. Yes, you have a right to be hurt, because you have been betrayed. If you think about it, Jason has been betrayed too. But the point is, what are you gonna do about it?"

"I've done all I know how to do."

"No you haven't, baby. You haven't prayed and talked to God about it. You need wisdom to know what to do. Ask God for it and He'll surely give it to you. I don't want to quote the wrong scripture, but I believe it's John ...no it's James 1:5 and it says: If any of you lack wisdom, let him ask God. That's not all of it, but I do remember that part."

Sheena hung her head in shame. "You're right, Momma. I know I need to be wise in my decisions."

"All of us do. While you are praying, don't forget to ask God to show you how to forgive, and renew your faith in Him too."

"I have a confession to make." Sheena glanced at Lois, and then looked down.

Lois gazed at her. "What's that?" she asked her cautiously.

"I don't think I have it in my heart to accept the child in our life. I already feel resentment and jealously toward her. I'm afraid she's going to take my children's place in Jason's heart, especially Jessica's. Suppose he chooses her over us? I know that's not right, but that's how I feel."

"It's not right, but God can help you through those feelings. Number one, no one can replace your children in Jason's heart. Number two, that child is going to have a special place in his heart too. And number three, it's up to you to put him in a position to choose between you all and that little girl . . ."

"But—"

Lois gave Sheena the hand. "With the help of the Lord, it's possible for you and Jason to stay together and make a space for that child in your lives together. This doesn't have to be a take it or leave it situation." Lois finished her slice of pizza and waited patiently while Sheena ate and talked.

"I don't think that's possible. I can't imagine that."

"Seek the Lord, Sheena. This is my last piece of advice. This is going to be a decision you will have to make. You have a good heart, and those feelings are nothing but the work of the enemy. Just keep praying about it and you'll see with time those wounds are going to heal and you'll be able to love that child like she's your own."

"I don't know, Momma. I'm in so much pain from Jason's cheating on me and now he has a daughter with the woman he cheated with. It's just too much," she cried.

"Time heals all wounds, baby. I don't know if you want your marriage to work, but if you do, God is able. If you don't, God will still heal your broken heart. Just give it time. God will work it all out, you'll see."

"Thanks for listening, Momma." Sheena exhaled loudly. "Do you mind if we change the subject for a while?"

"No I don't. I was gonna suggest that we not talk about this again until you got a chance to seek God's face. For the rest of the week, I want you to rest and relax and enjoy your time with your daddy, those sweet children, and me. You are now officially on vacation, so you better act like you know." Lois pinched her cheek. "I love you."

Sheena finished her last bite of pizza, wiped her mouth and put a tip on the table. The waitress came and picked the bill and money up. She inquired if they needed anything else.

"No, thank you," Sheena replied. The waitress left. Sheena stood up. "I love you too, Momma. Let's finish shopping so we can go home."

Chapter 57

The following days went smoothly for Sheena. She was relaxed and at peace. She woke up Christmas morning with a renewed outlook on life. After the children had opened their gifts, they wanted to call Jason and wish him a Merry Christmas. After they spoke with him, he asked to speak to Sheena.

"Hello," she said in a cheery voice. She walked upstairs to her room. "Hi. Merry Christmas. You sound like you're having a good time."

"I am. This is what I needed."

"That's good."

"How's your Christmas so far?" Sheena asked him.

"It's okay. I miss you and the kids though." Sheena was silent.

Jason coughed.

"How are your nurses working out?" Sheena asked.

"They're great, very professional. Ms. Erma came over to bring the children's presents. She was surprised to learn that you weren't here."

"What did you tell her?"

"I told her the truth; that you went to spend the holidays with your parents."

"Great. I don't want everyone to know my business."

"Obviously you don't mind her being in your business. She told me she saw you at the park that day and that you went home with her for a while. Now it makes sense who the friend was you mentioned you visited that day."

"Yes, it was Ms. Erma. She's a really sweet person and a good listener too."

"She was concerned about you. She told me that you confided in her about Cassandra."

"Yes, I did. I had to talk to somebody that day. I felt like I was losing my mind."

"She told me to let you know that she would be praying for us."

"That's nice of her."

"Momma and Daddy came over early this morning, they brought presents over for the children too."

"Why did they do that? They knew we were in Asheville."

"They said they thought maybe you had changed your mind and come back for Christmas. It's been five days."

His last remark irritated Sheena. "I'm aware of how many days we've been gone. You don't need to keep tabs on me. I'm a grown woman." Jason didn't reply. "What did she and Shirley cook for dinner?"

"The usual. Turkey, ham, greens, desserts, some of everything."

"I don't like the fact that they have taken over my kitchen."

"You can't have it both ways, Sheena. Either it's your kitchen or it's not."

"I haven't moved my things yet. I know what I said, but I haven't decided whether I'm coming back or not. I just don't want them in my kitchen taking over."

"You seem to have forgotten that this is my house too. You aren't here, so I don't see anything wrong with my mother coming over to prepare me a nice meal for Christmas."

"She could have cooked the meal and brought it over there. I hope that she and Shirley put my things back where they belong," Sheena said sharply.

"You know, I didn't realize until now what a control freak you are," Jason shot back. His baritone voice reverberated through the phone.

Sheena took the phone away from her ear, momentarily. "I'm not a control freak. I just don't want people in my house going through my things."

Jason exhaled loudly into the phone. "You know what? Not only are you a control freak, but you are a selfish brat too."

"Where do you get off calling me selfish? I'm not the one who had an affair and have an outside child that I expect you to accept," Sheena said indignantly.

"I didn't expect to get into an argument with you, Sheena. I simply wanted to wish you a Merry Christmas. I should have known the mere sound of my voice would irritate you."

"I was fine until I talked to you."

"Fine, maybe we shouldn't talk for a while. Since you've been away, I've had a chance to think things over too."

"Concerning what?"

"Concerning how I've taken your love and kindness for granted all of these years. Maybe I don't deserve you. As much as I love you, I have no right to expect you to just forget and forgive me for the things that I've done to you. And as far as Cassandra is concerned, I can understand why you feel that you can't accept her into your life. If the circumstances were turned around,

I don't know if I could accept a child that you might have had eleven years ago. If I knew about it from the beginning, that would be different, I would open my arms to the child and love him or her like she was my own." He waited for Sheena to respond. She didn't. "I just wish that you would take into consideration that I *didn't* know about my daughter."

"Hearing you say your daughter as though she's right there with you makes me angry."

"Why?"

"I don't know."

"I can't comprehend that. She hasn't done anything to you, Sheena."

"I know she hasn't, but I can't stand the sound of her name. Maybe something's wrong with me."

"I just think we both need counseling. There was a time when I'd never agree to that, but I don't have the answers anymore. Other than we should pray about it. Maybe it would help if we talked to the pastor."

"You want to talk to the pastor? Now that's a switch."

"It is, isn't it? My point is, if you want to end our marriage, I'm no longer going to try convincing you not to leave me. I don't have a right to pressure you to stay."

"So you're giving up on us?"

"No. You have already done that. I'm simply saying that I don't want you to be miserable or put on a façade to stay in a marriage for the children's sake."

"Do you want to end our marriage? What's happened since I've been gone? Have you heard from your baby's momma?"

"No, I don't want to end our marriage, you know that. And this isn't about Ruby."

"You didn't answer my question. Have you heard from Ruby and Cassandra?"

"I promised you I would be honest with you from now on. Yes, she called me the day before you left."

"I knew you were still talking to her! That's why you've had a sudden change of heart about our marriage, isn't it?"

"I haven't had a sudden change of heart. If it were up to me, you'd still be here with me so we could work on our marriage. She called to check on my progress because she said Cassandra asked about my health, so she told her she would call me to find out."

"If you were going to be so honest, you would have told me this information before I left. What else did you all talk about?" Sheena was furious with jealousy. "Did you discuss how long it would be before she and her daughter could move into my house?"

"No, we talked about our marriages; hers is going well. She wished us well."

Sheena paced around in her old bedroom. "Did she call my house again?"

"No, she called my cell phone," Jason said calmly.

"That's not acceptable either. She shouldn't be calling you on your cell phone. I'll tell you what, your cell phone number is going to be changed when I get home."

Sheena kicked her shoes off with such force that they flew across the room.

"So, you're coming home?" Jason asked her in a soothing voice.

Sheena was frustrated. "Maybe. I don't know. But she needs to stop calling you. You see that's exactly what I'm talking about. She's going to be constantly interfering in our lives. How do you expect me to put up with that mess?" she said angrily. Sheena looked at the phone as though she could see Jason.

Jason sighed loudly. "I don't expect you put up with it. I assure you that the only time we will communicate is when we need to touch base about Cassandra."

"I don't want you talking to her at all."

Jason exhaled loudly. "I don't know what it's going to take to convince you that the only thing Ruby and I have in common is Cassandra. I don't want her and she doesn't want me."

"Then prove it."

"How?"

"By cutting all ties with her," Sheena demanded.

"How? By not communicating with or supporting my child?"

"If you want our marriage to work, that's what you'll do."

"Sheena, you know you are being ridiculous. I wouldn't be able to live with myself if I did that. I am saved now and the Word says: But if any provide not for his own, and specially for those of his own house, he hath denied the faith, and is worse than an infidel." Jason paused and then said, "Cassandra is not in my house, but she *is* my own and I plan on taking care of the child. Baby, I'm sorry if you can't accept that, but I have to do what's right."

Sheena sighed. *I know he's right, but I can't help how I feel. Lately, he's been quoting scriptures to me and I'm supposed to be the Christian.* "Okay, Jason. I guess we have both made our minds up, haven't we?"

"It seems that way. I pray that God will touch your heart to forgive me so we can reconcile, but I have to be a man of integrity. It's only right, and besides, isn't that what you have always asked me to be?"

"Yes it is, but—"

"Let's keep praying about this, Sheena. I know God will hear both our prayers. I don't believe that your heart has calloused to the point that you can't forgive me. Maybe one day you'll be able to accept my daughter too." Sheena was silent. "I love you, Sheena. I'm going to respect you and give you the space that you need. Good-bye."

Before Sheena could respond, Jason hung up. Bewildered, Sheena closed her bedroom door and got down on her knees and prayed. "Father, I need you," she cried.

Chapter 58

Christmas Day had been a lonely time for Sheena. She spent the remainder of the week fasting and praying for direction. On the 30th of December, she treated herself to a day at the spa, at the Grove Park Inn Spa and Resort. New Year's Eve was upon them. She and Jason hadn't spoken since Christmas Day.

Lois knocked on her partially closed door. "Good morning."

"Good morning, Momma. How are you?"

"I'm blessed. Judging from the peaceful expression on your face, I can tell that you are doing well also."

"I am. I'm doing great. Being here has worked wonders for me. I can see life in a whole new perspective now."

"You look a whole lot better than you did when you came here."

"I know. I can see the difference in myself when I look in the mirror. It's true what Proverbs 18:22 says: A merry heart doeth good like a medicine: but a broken spirit drieth the bones. God is so good. Thanks to you and Daddy, I've had the chance to rest and relax, pray, and I've even pampered myself."

"You needed some time to yourself. We women are always so busy taking care of everybody else that we don't take time to take care of ourselves."

"You're right. I appreciate you and Daddy taking care of the children while I spent the day at the spa yesterday."

"It was our pleasure. We rarely get to see them, so we enjoyed every minute with 'em. You and Jason really have done a great job raising them. They're so well-mannered. We didn't have to scold them once while you were away. Not that Gerald is gonna do that anyway. He always leaves the discipline to me."

"Daddy does spoil them rotten, doesn't he?"

"Yep, he sure does. But I can't complain, because I'm guilty of that too. It's been a long time since we had a little one running around here."

"It has been quite a few years since I was small, hasn't it?"

"Yeah, it's been some years. I can remember like it was yesterday how you used to be so excited when your cousins came over to play with you. You were such a tomboy. You never wanted to play hopscotch or jump rope with your female cousins; you always challenged the boys to see if they could out climb you on that ole tree out there or a game of basketball or something. Do you remember that?"

"Of course. Those were the days."

"I'm still amazed at how prissy you turned out to be because you were a rough little girl. Gerald was so proud of you. He bragged about you to his sisters and brothers. He loved to take you fishing. You guys would leave home early in the morning and not come back until late that afternoon, always with a big bucket of smelly fish for me to clean. You loved being with your daddy. It didn't matter what you guys were doing, as long as you were with him."

"I do have fond memories of my childhood. You and Daddy were good parents. I never felt anxious about my home life because you guys always made me feel protected and secure."

"It was the grace of God, baby girl, because we have had some rocky times together."

"I never knew it. I remember the few times when you all argued, but before the day was over, you guys would have made up and were at ease with each other."

"Yeah, Gerald and I never could stay mad at each other for long. Besides, he hardly ever raised his voice to me, which is amazing, because I had a nasty disposition before I got saved. Gerald, bless his heart, would just walk away from me when I got in my moods because he didn't want to argue with me. I didn't know it until after I got saved, but he said he would get in his car and drive to our favorite spot and just pray for me."

"You did have a temper, Momma."

"I did, but prayer changes things. I never took it out on you though, did I?"

"Miraculously, you didn't. Whenever you got in your moods, you would always apologize to me after Daddy left, and assure me everything was going to be all right. True to your word, when he came back home, you all would make up and all was well."

"After I gave my life to Christ, I no longer had those bad temper tantrums. That's why I'm a testimony to God's grace and mercy. I know that He is a loving and forgiving God."

Sheena raised her hand in agreement. "Amen. God is awesome." Sheena sighed. "Momma?"

"Yes?"

"I believe I know what I need to do concerning my marriage." Sheena had tears in her eyes.

"Are you sure?"

"I'm sure, Momma. School is about to reopen for the next semester and I need to go home and get my house in order. With or without us together, my children need to have peace of mind about their parents' relationship. The first order of business is to have a family meeting and let them know what's going on."

"Do you think that's wise? They've already been through so much."

"Yes, I think it's the right thing to do. Children are resilient."

"Have you prayed about this?"

"Yes I have, and I have peace about it."

"Okay. As long as you have peace of mind, you'll make the right decision."

Sheena hugged Lois. "Thank you so much for being patient with me and the children. I love you, Momma."

"I love you too. Do you mind telling me what you've decided to do?"

"I don't mind at all." Sheena sat down on the bed and discussed her plans with her mother like she did when she was growing up.

"So you're leaving today?" Lois asked her daughter.

"Yes. I want to spend some quality time with you and Daddy first though. I feel so guilty because the last time I was here, I left so suddenly, I didn't take the time to say good-bye properly."

"We understood after we spoke to you on the phone and you let us know what was going on. Don't worry about your daddy and me. If it's God's will, we will have lots of time to spend together."

"I still want to spend the rest of the day with you all. I'll leave at six. I'm going to order take-out food too, because I don't want you to be scrambling around in the kitchen all day trying to cook us a meal. I just want to sit here and enjoy you and Daddy's company. The children love it outside so much that I know they are going to keep themselves busy."

"They really have enjoyed themselves."

"I have too. You made it possible for me to have the vacation that I needed without having to deal with the children constantly."

"Well, I'm glad you enjoyed yourself. I'm going to have to take myself a day at the spa. You really look relaxed."

Sheena breathed deeply and exhaled. "The spa yesterday was just the icing on the cake. Being able to spend time with the Lord and talk to Him and let Him talk to me was the recipe that I needed to make my life whole."

"God is good . . . all the time."

Sheena hugged Lois and Gerald. "I love you guys. I can't thank you enough for spending time with us and helping me in my time of need."

"We loved having you here, pumpkin. Y'all come back again soon." Gerald closed the truck door for Sheena. He looked in the back where the children were. "Don't forget, guys, as soon as the weather breaks, we're going fishing." He glanced at Sheena. "That was one of our favorite pastimes wasn't it, pumpkin?"

"It sure was, Daddy." Sheena leaned out of the truck and kissed him on the cheek.

Gerald patted Sheena on the arm. She knew that was his sign for I love you. Lois watched her husband and daughter. She thanked God for the close bond between father and daughter.

"I hate to see you leave, Sheena, but you need to get started. It's eight," Lois reminded her. "I don't want you on the road too late at night."

"I know, Momma. I'll call you when we get there to let you know that I arrived safely." Sheena looked in her rearview mirror and saw her parents hug each other as they watched her drive off. *Thank you for my parents, Lord.*

Sheena pulled into the garage at ten-ten. "Wake up, guys. We're here."

After they awoke, Jeremiah, Joseph and Jessica ran into the house. Jessica jumped on Jason's bed. He was asleep. "Hi, Daddy! I missed you so much! Did you miss me?"

Jason pulled himself up as he wiped the sleep out of his eyes. "Hey, pumpkin! I sure did miss you! How's my baby girl?"

"Good. I had a good time at Grandma and Grandpa's house, but I was ready to come home to see you." Jason smiled. Joseph and Jeremiah hugged him and sat on the foot of the bed.

"I missed you guys too. What's up?"

"Not much. Are you doing okay, Daddy? " Joseph asked. Jason nodded his head.

Jeremiah slid off the bed and walked up to Jason and gave him a high five. "We missed you too, Daddy."

Jason smiled at his children. He strained to see if Sheena was coming in the room. He could hear her talking to Shirley somewhere beyond his bedroom door. Moments later, she appeared in the doorway.

"Guys, your Aunt Shirley wants to talk to you all," Sheena informed them. She then looked to Jason. "Hi."

"Hi. This is a surprise."

"I thought it would be. Are you pleasantly surprised or disappointed?"

"I'm happy to see you, baby."

Sheena shrugged. "We haven't talked since Christmas, so I wasn't sure how it would be between us," she stated softly.

"I told you that I was going to give you some space, so that's why I didn't contact you. I'm glad you're here now, though." Jason noticed that Sheena's eyes sparkled when she smiled.

"You know I always say that it's good to be home." Sheena sighed.

"Are you home for good?" Before she could answer, the children came running in the room with Shirley following behind them.

"Sheena, would you and Jason mind if I take the children to Watch Night service with me?"

"I don't mind. It's up to Sheena," Jason answered.

"Aren't you guys sleepy?" Sheena asked the children.

"No," they said simultaneously.

"Sure, Shirley, I don't see why not. They all seem to be anxious to go. They might as well start the year off right, because in the past, we didn't go like we should have. But in this New Year, hopefully, we're going to honor God by going every Sunday." She looked at Jason expectantly. "Right, honey?"

Jason smiled. He realized it had been a long time since Sheena called him "honey." "That's right. It's time for a change in the Grey household. We're going to start by going to church regularly. *All* of us," he confirmed.

"Good," Shirley exclaimed. "It would be nice if you guys saw the New Year come in together. We'll be back sometime tomorrow," she said as she winked at Jason.

Jason got out of bed and sat in the wing chair. He relaxed as best as his injury allowed him to. "Well, it's just us."

Sheena smiled. "I guess so." She pulled off her sneakers and folded her legs under her in the loveseat. They watched the remaining hour of the New Year count down on TV. Firecrackers sounded off throughout the neighborhood.

"I suppose I got the answer to my question when the kids were in here, right?"

"What question?"

"I asked if you were here for good? Your statement about going to church was your answer, wasn't it?"

Sheena searched his face. "Yes. We still have a lot of issues to work out, but yes, I'm willing to stay. I had a long talk with God and now I realize I don't want to end our marriage. However, I do insist that you do one thing sometime in the very near future."

"What's that?"

"Submit to be tested for AIDS and any other venereal disease you could have contracted while you were with Ruby."

Astonished, Jason answered, "I'm willing to do what I have to do to amend our marriage."

"Our marriage won't be amended or consummated unless you take those tests. I'm not going to risk my life for you, Jason."

"I said I would take the tests, Sheena. I don't think that I have contracted anything; if I did, it would have shown up in my blood work."

"Not necessarily. Not if they weren't testing for it."

Jason shrugged. "If that's what you want me to do, I have no problem with it."

"I don't want to offend you, Jason, but I can't take any chances with my life. I know I'm going to die from something, but I don't plan on dying from AIDS or any other sexually transmitted disease. I have three children to raise and I want to live as long as I can for them. I'm sure you thought she was clean, but I don't know whether you used protection or not and—"

"I'll do it, Sheena. I understand, I don't want to jeopardize your life either. I don't think she's been with anybody besides her husband—"

"That's my point exactly. You don't know whether she's been with someone or not. Even if she were faithful to her husband before she became involved with you, there's a possibility that *he* could have been messing around with someone." Frowning, she said, "You know the facts, Jason; did you consider the consequences before you jumped into bed with her?"

Jason looked away from her and stared at the television.

"I do want to reconcile with you, but this is only one of the issues we have to work through."

"I understand that. I'm willing to take any tests that I need to take. That includes emotional tests, going to counseling with you, or whatever."

Sheena stared into his eyes. "Do you really mean what you're saying?"

"I'm sincere."

Satisfied that he was being truthful, Sheena nodded her head in agreement. "Okay. We both have a lot of issues to resolve, but with the help of Jesus, I believe we can make our marriage work."

"Five, four, three, two," the TV announcer shouted.

"Happy New Year, baby," Jason shouted. He stood up carefully.

"Happy New Year, honey." Sheena stood up, walked to him and hugged him tenderly.

"I love you."

"I love you too, Jason."

They climbed on the bed and snuggled closely. Exhausted, Sheena fell asleep a few minutes afterward. When she awoke, it was morning. Jason was not beside her. She called his name softly. "Jason."

He was sitting in his chair. He looked up at her. "I'm here, Sheena."

She looked at her husband, the man she almost gave up on, but for God's grace. "Are you okay?" she asked him.

"I'm fine, baby. I'm just reading." He put the Bible on the table. "Are you okay?"

"I just had another dream."

Epilogue

For weeks, the relationship between Sheena and Jason was awkward. After counseling from their pastor, they managed to communicate honestly. Soon, they started going to church again—together. Sheena knew that if her marriage was to work, she couldn't reject Jason's daughter. She sought God's direction fervently and trusted that by the grace of God, she would be able to accept the child.

Her most difficult issue was with Ruby. She knew as long as Cassandra existed, she would have to deal with her mother. Jason assured Sheena that all that existed between him and Ruby was Cassandra. Nonetheless, that was Sheena's toughest trial. She knew she would probably always be insecure where Ruby was concerned, but she made up her mind to trust God to work things out.

She constantly reminded her self of Psalm 86:5: *For thou, Lord, art good, and ready to for-*

give; and plenteous in mercy unto all them that call upon thee. Therefore, she knew that if God forgives, she, as a Christian, had to learn how to forgive also.

Six months had passed since the unfortunate day of the shooting. During his recovery, Jason developed a closer relationship with God. He joined and attended church every Sunday with Sheena and the children. Their relationship was stronger than it had ever been.

Jason prepared for his first day back at work. School had ended for summer vacation. Since Sheena didn't have to work, she arose early to make breakfast for Jason while the children slept.

Sheena watched her husband as he backed out of the driveway. "Lord, I thank you for restoring our relationship. Thank you for saving him and giving me the grace and ability to forgive him. I thank you for revealing things to me in dreams. Lord, you encouraged me on New Year's Eve with the dream of my husband being saved and becoming the type of husband you desired him to be in Ephesians 5:25, which states: *Husbands, love your wives, even as Christ also loved the church and gave himself for it.* Please give me the grace to honor him like you require in Ephesians 5:22: *Wives, submit yourselves unto your own husbands, as unto the Lord."*

Ruby and Thurman worked diligently on their relationship. They purchased a three-bedroom, two-and-a-half bath home together. Ruby was elated to be in a nice home, which was what she really wanted anyway—a secure place to live. Although it was only 1,400 square foot, no comparison to the 4,000 square foot house Jason and Sheena owned, she thanked God for blessing them with a home. She and Thurman were both excited about the pending arrival of their baby, due to be born in five months.

Cassandra was due to arrive in town on a 6:30 P.M. flight. For peace of mind, Ruby's parents had flown with Cassandra. Jason was scheduled to meet her at the airport and bring her to their home to visit for a week. He had taken Jeremiah, Joseph, and Jessica along with him. Jason's mother and father went with them too.

Jason met them at Gate 7, at the Delta Airlines terminal in the Charlotte/Douglas International Airport. Although Jason had flown to Florida once to meet her, Jessica held a "Welcome, Cassandra" sign in her hand, to greet her when she walked through the gate. Jason introduced the grandparents to each other. The children hovered around Cassandra; they warmed up to each other immediately. Jason, his parents, and Ruby's parents, chatted for a while before Jason asked Cassandra if she was ready to go. She nodded. Her grandparents assured her that they would be at the hotel if she needed them. Ruby's mother checked to make sure she had her cell phone turned on, and then they walked outside and caught a shuttle bus to their hotel. Jason and his family walked to the parking deck, got in the truck and headed home.

Sheena felt anxious. She peeped out of the door's sidelight, checking to see if Jason was driving up. "Lord, in Jesus' name, please bless me with the grace to accept this child into my life and love her as though she was my own. Jesus, I need you to show me mercy so that I won't resent her. Father, help me in Jesus' name. Amen." She saw Ms. Erma outside, digging in her flowerbed. She opened the door and waved a friendly hello to the elderly woman and Erma waved back. Sheena went back inside and closed the door. Ms. Erma had turned out to be a good neighbor after all. Throughout Jason's recovery, she continued to be his in-home day nurse while Sheena worked.

At 7:45 P.M., Jason walked in the house. He had dropped his parents off at their house. Jessica held Cassandra's hand and when Jason introduced her to Sheena, Cassandra shyly greeted her.

Sheena knew immediately that this was the manifestation of the dream she had at her parents' house months ago. Cassandra was the pretty little girl that came to visit them. Sheena smiled brightly. "Hi, Cassandra." Sheena greeted her by taking both of Cassandra's hands into hers. "I'm Sheena. It's so nice to meet you. Welcome to our home. I want you to make yourself at home and be comfortable here. Okay? After all, this is going to be your second home if you want it to be."

Cassandra nodded her head and smiled timidly at Sheena. Sheena pulled her close and hugged her. She felt Cassandra's body tense and then she remembered how, in the dream, the girl seemed uncomfortable and annoyed when she touched her. *God really does deal with us in dreams. He worked a miracle for Jason and me, and I know he'll perform a miracle in this situation too.* She backed away from Cassandra, giving her some space. Sheena smiled at the girl and asked her, "Would you like for your daddy to show you your room?"

Cassandra nodded her head yes.

Jason saw the apprehension in Sheena's eyes. He kissed her lightly on the cheek. "It'll be fine, baby. Let's just trust God and everything will fall into place." He led Cassandra upstairs; Joseph, Jeremiah, and Jessica, were right on her heels. Sheena watched as Jessica ran to catch up with Cassandra and slipped her hand into her big sister's hand. Sheena smiled as she thought about the children's reaction when they told them about their older sister. "Cool," was the excited response.

Sheena's eyes focused on the words displayed on the plaque that Jason had hung on the wall in the foyer entrance: *O Praise the Lord, all ye nations: praise him all ye people. For his merciful kindness is great toward us: and the truth of the Lord endureth forever. Praise ye the Lord.* Psalm 117.

Readers' Group Guide Questions

1 Sheena had several dreams about the events about to take place in her life. Although the dreams were not an exact manifestation of the actual events, did you analyze her dreams as being stress related as Jason suggested?

2 Sheena didn't deal with Jason's infidelity until months after she suspected he was being unfaithful. How would you have handled the issue? What would you have done differently?

3 Sheena was a Christian, but keeping up appearances was very important to her. What are your thoughts on that?

4 Jason loved his father, but he also resented him because as a child, he witnessed his father abusing his mother. Sheena

warned Jason that his sons would grow up to resent him for the same reason. Do you think his behavior was a generational curse? Why or why not?

5   Sheena's mother was supportive of her daughter. She also gave her tough love when Sheena needed it. How many of you agree that their interactions mirror realistic mother-daughter relationships?

6   How would you handle it if your husband of ten years announced that he had fathered a child with his ex-girl friend? Hypothetically, would you welcome the child into your home to save your marriage?

7   What are your thoughts about Ruby? Do you believe she loved Jason or was she obsessed with what he could have given her, the way her mother suggested. Would you keep the conception of your child from his/her father because the relationship didn't work out between the two of you?

8   Sheena was not a very attractive woman, but her looks didn't matter to Jason. What are your thoughts about her in-laws? Are

most in-laws spiteful toward each other? Do you think the majority of in-laws respect/accept the person(s) that marry into their family?

9 Sheena had a lot of issues to deal with. Throughout the novel, what did you think of her character? Was she too indecisive? Do you think she wavered in her faith?

10 At what point did you feel that Sheena and Jason's marriage was irreconcilable?

11 Do you agree with the way Sheena handled her issues? Would you have done anything differently?

About the Author

Marilyn Mayo Anderson was born and raised in the small town of Pinetops, North Carolina. She has a Degree in Health Information Technology. She is also the author of the novel, *Black Pearl*. She resides in Raleigh, North Carolina.

UC HIS GLORY BOOK CLUB!

www.uchisglorybookclub.net

UC His Glory Book Club is the spirit-inspired brainchild of Joylynn Jossel, Author and Acquisitions Editor of Urban Christian, and Kendra Norman-Bellamy, Author for Urban Christian. This is an online book club that hosts authors of Urban Christian. We welcome as members all men and women who have a passion for reading Christian-based fiction.

UC His Glory Book Club pledges our commitment to provide support, positive feedback, encouragement, and a forum whereby members can openly discuss and review the literary works of Urban Christian authors.

There is no membership fee associated with UC His Glory Book Club; however, we do ask that you support the authors through purchasing, encouraging, providing book reviews, and of course, your prayers. We also ask that you respect our beliefs and follow the guidelines of the book club. We hope to receive your valuable input, opinions, and reviews that build up, rather than tear down our authors.

WHAT WE BELIEVE:

—We believe that Jesus is the Christ, Son of the Living God.

—We believe the Bible is the true, living Word of God.

—We believe all Urban Christian authors should use their God-given writing abilities to honor God and share the message of the written word God has given to each of them uniquely.

—We believe in supporting Urban Christian authors in their literary endeavors by reading, purchasing and sharing their titles with our on-line community.

—We believe that in everything we do in our literary arena should be done in a manner that will lead to God being glorified and honored.

—We look forward to the online fellowship with you. Please visit us often at *www.uchisglorybookclub.net*.

Many Blessing to You!

Shelia E. Lipsey,
President, UC His Glory Book Club

ORDER FORM
URBAN BOOKS, LLC
78 E. Industry Ct
Deer Park, NY 11729

Name: (please print):_____

Address:_____

City/State:_____

Zip:_____

QTY	TITLES	PRICE

Shipping and handling-add \$3.50 for 1ˢᵗ book, then \$1.75 for each additional book.
Please send a check payable to:
Urban Books, LLC
Please allow 4-6 weeks for delivery

ORDER FORM
URBAN BOOKS, LLC
78 E. Industry Ct
Deer Park, NY 11729

Name: (please print):_____

Address:_____

City/State:_____

Zip:_____

QTY	TITLES	PRICE
	3:57 A.M Timing Is Everything	$14.95
	A Man's Worth	$14.95
	A Woman's Worth	$14.95
	Abundant Rain	$14.95
	After The Feeling	$14.95
	Amaryllis	$14.95
	An Inconvenient Friend	$14.95

Shipping and handling-add $3.50 for 1st book, then $1.75 for each additional book.

Please send a check payable to:

Urban Books, LLC

Please allow 4-6 weeks for delivery

ORDER FORM
URBAN BOOKS, LLC
78 E. Industry Ct
Deer Park, NY 11729

Name: (please print):_____

Address:_____

City/State:_____

Zip:_____

QTY	TITLES	PRICE
	Battle of Jericho	$14.95
	Be Careful What You Pray For	$14.95
	Beautiful Ugly	$14.95
	Been There Prayed That:	$14.95
	Before Redemption	$14.95
	By the Grace of God	$14.95

Shipping and handling-add $3.50 for 1st book, then $1.75 for each additional book.
Please send a check payable to:
Urban Books, LLC
Please allow 4-6 weeks for delivery

ORDER FORM
URBAN BOOKS, LLC
78 E. Industry Ct
Deer Park, NY 11729

Name: (please print):_____

Address:_____

City/State:_____

Zip:_____

QTY	TITLES	PRICE
	Confessions Of A preachers Wife	$14.95
	Dance Into Destiny	$14.95
	Deliver Me From My Enemies	$14.95
	Desperate Decisions	$14.95
	Divorcing the Devil	$14.95

Shipping and handling-add $3.50 for 1st book, then $1.75 for each additional book.
Please send a check payable to:
Urban Books, LLC
Please allow 4-6 weeks for delivery

ORDER FORM
URBAN BOOKS, LLC
78 E. Industry Ct
Deer Park, NY 11729

Name: (please print):_____

Address:_____

City/State:_____

Zip:_____

QTY	TITLES	PRICE
	Faith	$14.95
	First Comes Love	$14.95
	Flaws and All	$14.95
	Forgiven	$14.95
	Former Rain	$14.95
	Forsaken	$14.95
	From Sinner To Saint	$14.95

Shipping and handling-add $3.50 for 1st book, then $1.75 for each additional book. Please send a check payable to:

Urban Books, LLC

Please allow 4-6 weeks for delivery

ORDER FORM
URBAN BOOKS, LLC
78 E. Industry Ct
Deer Park, NY 11729

Name: (please print):_____

Address:_____

City/State:_____

Zip:_____

QTY	TITLES	PRICE
	From The Extreme	14.95
	God Is In Love With You	14.95
	God Speaks To Me	14.95
	Grace And Mercy	14.95
	Guilty Of Love	14.95
	Happily Ever Now	14.95
	Heaven Bound	14.95

Shipping and handling-add $3.50 for 1st book, then $1.75 for each additional book. Please send a check payable to:

Urban Books, LLC

Please allow 4-6 weeks for delivery